Published 2017 by Joffe Books, London.

www.joffebooks.com

© Joy Ellis

ISBN- 978-1-912106-43-1

Dedicated to Jill Burkinshaw, her amazing band of bloggers and reviewers, and all my lovely 'Crazies,' the Joffe Books authors. We chat, we laugh, we threaten, taunt and take the rise out of each other, then laugh some more. But what we always do, is support each other. I love you guys and wish you the best of everything!

PROLOGUE

The Fens, 1991

'Do you like the dark, Matt?'

DC Matt Ballard did not hesitate, 'No, I bloody don't. Especially not in a place like this. It's treacherous!'

There was a soft chuckle in the darkness. 'I know what you mean. Not the most hospitable of spots, is it?'

Matt shivered and felt mud squeeze between his boots as he tried to find a more comfortable position. 'How much longer do we have to watch this dump, Sarge? I reckon your informant just wanted to make sure we spent a really miserable couple of hours, freezing our butts off out on this blasted marsh.'

'Patience, Matt, my boy, another half an hour and it will be dawn. My snout's never been wrong yet. If she says someone is using this ramshackle old place for a drugs drop, then they are, simple as that.'

Matt stared at the shadowy outline of the decaying cottage. 'I suppose she could be right. If you know your way around this terrain, five minutes on foot and you're at the river, catch the right tide and another ten in a boat, and you're out into the Wash.

'Exactly. Where a nice Dutch cruiser is waiting to fill your little dinghy with enough junk to make half of Fenfleet high as a kite, then bugger off back into the North Sea with a sackful of wonga ready to buy the next load,' Sergeant Bill Morris said as the thick, dark night clouds parted, and moonlight flooded down.

Matt saw the great stretch of silvery water that was the salt marsh and the decaying ruin that was the object of their surveillance. He realised just how remote and inhospitable Gibbet Fen really was. It was late spring, almost summer, but his teeth chattered with the damp and the chill of the watery marshland.

'So why don't you like the dark, Matt?'

As the moon selfishly withdrew its pale light, he was glad to talk, even if he didn't much like the topic of conversation. 'Because nothing's real. The dark changes things.' He paused, frowning. 'You sound like you actually like it?'

'Oh, I do. I love it.'

Matt might not be able to see his sergeant, but he knew he was smiling. 'Great! Why is that?'

'Because, in the dark, I'm equally as frightening as any other nasty bastard that's lurking out there.'

'You *like* frightening people? Aren't we supposed to be the good guys?'

'Oh, I love scaring the shit out of people, Mattie, but only the bad guys.' Bill chuckled softly.

'That's reassuring.' He was about to say more but heard a sharp intake of breath from his colleague.

'And speaking of bad guys,' he touched Matt's arm. 'On the track from the seabank. See, the beam of a torch?'

It took a moment to spot the tiny light moving along the rough track, but when he saw it, Matt felt a thrill pass through him. 'Result! No one else would be in this God forsaken hole, unless they were up to something they shouldn't be.'

'That'll teach you to doubt my snout, Matthew Ballard. Now, we'll let 'em get into the cottage, then radio for uniform to block the path back to the seabank, okay?'

'And then we take them, Sarge?'

'Oh, so right, my son. Then we take them.'

Thoughtfully, the moon made another short appearance, and the policemen could see two shadowy figures on the path. Matt thought they were men, but it was hard to tell. They walked confidently, obviously used to this clandestine trip. The first one led, flashing the powerful torch this way and that in order to find the safest passage along the rough lane. The other, a shorter, heavier individual followed a few steps behind and carried a bulky bag over one shoulder.

'C'mon, c'mon,' Bill said. 'Come to Daddy, you naughty children.'

Matt felt cool breath on his cheek as the sergeant whispered close to his ear.

The two figures seemed to be taking an eternity, but finally they were at the broken and dilapidated bridge that crossed the drainage ditch that surrounded the cottage. Just a moment or two more and they would have them. Matt tensed, he could hardly wait to hear the click of the ratchet as his handcuffs secured themselves to the criminals' fleshy wrists.

The hand on his shoulder suddenly tightened its grip. 'What the—'

The men had stopped. One knelt down on the frail wood, then pulled sharply back and grabbed at his friend. There was a muffled shout, then the other man moved forward, peered over the bridge and recoiled back in the same manner.

As Matt and the sergeant stood stock still and watched, the two suspected drug dealers turned on their heels and fled back up the incline. This time there was apparently no thought of danger and no care for personal safety. They slipped and slid on the wet grass but still ran as if pursued by demons.

'Radio uniform! Quick! Let's get down there and see what the devil's going on!' The sergeant broke cover and ran towards the bridge.

'All units! Attention drawn to two men, suspected drug dealers, on the Gibbet Fen marsh path, heading up towards the seabank. Apprehend and detain!' Matt shouted into his radio as he ran after his friend.

As he approached the edge of the bridge, an arm shot out and stopped him in his tracks. 'Dear God in Heaven!'

'Sarge?'

The arm slowly dropped down, allowing him access to whatever horror his sergeant had seen.

Matt felt a coldness slither between his shoulder blades as he stared over the splintery planks of rotting wood. Below him in the shallow, reed-tangled water, was the naked body of a boy. It took Matt a few moments to assimilate what he was looking at. His flashlight and the weak glow from the moon made the surreal scene seem too weird to comprehend. Maybe it was a mannequin? A tailor's dummy? Surely a youngster's body could not be so impossibly white? Could it? He stared harder. No matter how much he wanted it to be, this was no mannequin.

He looked around helplessly and saw that his sergeant had abruptly returned to consciousness and was barking orders into his radio. 'Get hold of DI Raymond immediately. We are going to need the full team out here, and forensics, oh, and a vanload of uniforms to secure the area, okay?'

Now Matt could do nothing but wait. There would be no heroic wading into the brackish dyke and dragging the lifeless boy from the water. No frantic pumping his young chest or desperately trying to refill his flaccid lungs with air. It wasn't that he wouldn't have tried, of course he would. It was the fact that the youngster was secured firmly and purposefully beneath the water level. His thin arms were tied to the heavy wooden stanchions that supported the bridge with lengths of barbed wire. In fact, he was snared in a tangled cocoon of the vicious fencing, and the wire that held his feet was weighted by heavy pieces of concrete.

Matt dropped to his knees, as close to the edge of the bridge as he dared, and stared down at the boy's face. Maybe it was because the boy was about the age of his best mate's son, Harry. Maybe it was because, like Harry, the lad was thin and lanky, with hair too long to be cool. Whatever, this one affected him differently to anything else he'd ever seen. And he'd seen plenty of bodies. Old ones, young ones, burnt ones, meat puzzles from the railway tracks, he'd coped with it all. Until now. He swallowed back a sob. 'He can't be more than eleven or twelve, can he?'

'Looks that way.' Bill's voice crackled with emotion. 'So, I guess this is number three.' He knelt awkwardly down next to Matt. 'It's been six months since the last poor kid, I really thought the murdering bastard had either topped himself or buggered off out of the area when things got too hot. Can you see if his signature mark is on the boy?'

Matt shone his torch down into the water. 'I think so, Sarge.' He swallowed bile and tried not to heave. It was hard to see between the weeds and the strands of wire. 'Yes, it's there.' On the front of the boy's naked shoulder was a symbol carved into the young flesh. Matt had seen it before on the other two victims. No one had quite deciphered its meaning, but it looked like some sort of hieroglyphic set in a triangle. 'It's him alright. He must have been lying low, just biding his time, waiting for the next opportunity.'

'The sick son of a bitch! I'd like to rip his . . .' The older man's words faded into silence, then he sighed and rubbed a broad hand across his stubbly face.

'We'll catch him, Sarge.' Matt's voice wavered as he stared at the boy's black hair flaring out from his cold white face like a beautiful dark sea anemone. 'Won't we?' He had done six years in uniform, and almost six months in CID, but his voice sounded like that of a small child who had just found his pet rabbit dead in its cage.

An arm encircled his shoulders, and as the two men stared down at the dead boy, the dawn broke over the silent and desolate landscape, casting an eerie pale light on the strange tableau. 'Oh, we'll catch him, Mattie. One way or another. We'll catch the bastard.'

CHAPTER ONE

Present day

'Sorry to drag you all away from your duties.' He surveyed the room of police officers and acknowledged their puzzled expressions with a smile. 'I thought you should be the first to know . . .' He paused, because he knew exactly how much his news would mean to his team. 'I've just heard from London. Brendan Kyle and Tricia Brown have been given life sentences.'

The room erupted with shouts and cheers. Men and women punched the air, slapped their colleagues on the back and hugged each other.

Detective Chief Inspector Matthew Ballard held up his hand and slowly the furore died down. 'Without your painstaking work and dedication, we would never have got a result like that. I know that every one of you sweated blood to see those two go down. It was a difficult and a delicate case, but your attention to detail and thoroughness has paid off. Well done! Thank you all.'

'Well, we couldn't have done it without you, boss.' The unusually bright voice of his detective inspector, Jason Hammond rang out. 'Three cheers for the guv'nor!'

Matt shook his head. 'Thanks, but it was a team effort, a bloody good team effort. Which means, if you have the time when the shift finishes, meet me in the Dragon bar. The drinks are on me.'

'Again!' shouted someone.

'Yes, we've had a pretty good run over the last few years, haven't we?' Matt ran a hand through his iron-grey crew cut. 'But it looks as though this may be my last big case as your DCI. Only six months to go, and you scruffy lot will be dancing to a new piper.'

'DCI Ballard retire? Never! It's just a ruse to keep us all on our toes.' Detective Sergeant Liz Haynes smiled at him.

'Sorry to disappoint you, but thirty-two years is enough for anyone, including me.'

'We'll believe it when they hand over the gold watch!'

'With the budget they allow us these days, I don't think I'll be that lucky!'

The congratulations went on for a few minutes more, then slowly the room began to empty.

'Sir? May I talk to you?'

Matt looked around and saw the short blond hair and friendly smile of PC Gemma Goddard standing behind him.

'Gemma.' He pulled up two chairs. 'Come and sit down for a moment. I think I need a break after all that excitement. What's the problem?' He sat back heavily.

The police woman sat down and stared at him, biting her lip and apparently unsure of what to say. This was not like the PC Goddard that had worked with him for the last five months. She was bright, forthright, a bit gobby, and apparently at her best when it was a slanging match in the mess room. If he had to be hypercritical, her only failing seemed to be that she didn't suffer fools gladly, and didn't disguise the fact.

After a while, she said, 'This is pretty weird, sir.' She pulled an envelope from her jacket pocket. 'This came in this morning's post. I opened it, I mean, it's addressed to me, but inside I found a second envelope.' She offered it to him with a shrug, 'I really can't think why anyone would do this, can you, sir?'

Matt stared at it, then almost without thinking, produced the ever-present disposable gloves from his pocket, slipped them on, and took the brown envelope from her. He handled it as if it were made of fine spun gossamer. Thankfully, she'd had the sense to leave it sealed. 'It came to your home address?'

'Yes, sir.'

'By normal Royal Mail, not pushed through the door by hand?'

'Along with all the bills and the junk mail, sir. Look, the postmark is local, it was mailed here in Fenfleet.'

He glanced at the outer envelope. 'Has anyone else handled this, Constable?'

'Only my dad. He picked up the post from the mat and put it on the breakfast table. Other than that, just me.'

'Bag it and seal it, PC Goddard. I really don't like the look of this. Why on earth use you as a go-between and not send whatever it is to me directly. It doesn't make sense.' He stared at the neatly typed envelope. *For the personal attention of Detective Chief Inspector Matthew Ballard. Please pass on immediately.*

'Maybe we should let the explosives boys have a butchers at it, sir?'

Matt felt it gently. It was certainly thick enough to contain more than just a single sheet of paper, but it was flat, not uneven or bulky. Chemicals, maybe? They had been sent a directive about how to deal with suspicious mail after an anthrax scare some time before. But for some reason he thought it was nothing physically dangerous. 'No, Constable, I get the feeling that it won't kill us.'

Gemma Goddard didn't look convinced. 'What shall I do with this, sir, when it's bagged?' She was holding the outer envelope by a corner, as if it had suddenly turned venomous.

'Put it on my desk. If there is anything in here that I don't understand, I'll get forensics to take a look.' He frowned at the packet and almost whispered to the woman, 'Why you, I wonder?' He knew there was no answer, and Gemma could only shrug helplessly.

'Sorry, sir, I really have no idea.'

Gemma Goddard went to fetch an evidence bag, leaving Matt to stare thoughtfully at the unopened letter.

After a few moments Matt carefully withdrew a folded sheet of paper from the envelope. It was blank, but it protected a single photograph.

With a small gasp, Matt brought it closer, then with a snort of disgust, threw it angrily onto his desk. 'Who the hell sent me this?' He stared disbelievingly at the picture.

'Guv? What is it? You look white as a sheet. Gemma's just told me about the letter, is that it?'

Matt looked up and saw the slim figure of Detective Inspector Jason Hammond standing in the doorway. His gaze returned to the horribly familiar scene in the photograph.

'It's Gibbet Fen.'

Jason's mouth dropped open and he hurried in, closing the door behind him. 'Surely you don't mean the Matravers' crime scene?'

'Too bloody right, I do.'

He picked up the photograph. He was shocked to notice the slight tremor in his hand as he held the piece of glossy paper. Over twenty-five years had just vanished. Again he knelt on the bridge and saw Jamie Matravers' body glimmering in the water. What had Sergeant Bill Morris said? Oh yes, "We'll catch the bastard." But he'd been wrong, hadn't he? They never did actually catch him. Twenty-five sodding years on and there was still no concrete case. All they had were the same old hunches and suspicions, nothing more. Through his whole career, it was his only real, gut-wrenching failure. Sure, he had brought felons to court only to have the judge slap their wrists and let them go, and he'd prepared complex cases that the CPS had thrown out for one damn silly technicality or another. It happened. It happened all the time. But this one was different. It was the only case that still denied him sleep and gnawed away at his sanity every time he allowed his thoughts to stray out to Gibbet Fen.

As he saw again the rickety bridge and the lonely marsh, he felt the reassuring weight of an arm around his shoulder. Sergeant Bill Morris. He'd been one of the good old boys: a great copper, a brilliant detective and a nice man to boot. But even he'd been wrong about some things. Catching the Gibbet Fen killer was one, but maybe even worse, the fact that he misjudged the dark. He had died in the darkness that he loved so much. One night, six months after he retired, he took his dog for a late walk around Fenfleet Recreation ground. Sadly he met one of the nasty bastards that he had so often talked about. This particular one was a crackhead with a knife, and the fact that it was mistaken identity was no comfort to his widow or his three kids. Bill might have laughed at the irony of it. He died because his thick shit of an attacker didn't know a Labrador from a Rottweiler. He picked on the wrong dog walker, and killed a brave and honest retired policeman out with his pet, instead of a dodgy dealer with a guard dog.

'Sir? Are you okay?' Jason always looked miserable, it was his natural state, but right now he looked downright concerned.

Matt got up and paced his small bare office. 'To be honest, Jason, the answer is an emphatic "No!"'

He wasn't sure what this was all about, but if someone was trying to rattle his cage, they had certainly succeeded. With a face as hard as winter ground, Matt picked up the photo from his desk 'It's time I took this to the superintendent.'

11

CHAPTER TWO

Superintendent David Redpath was unimpressed. 'So what? Someone's having a dig at you. For God's sake, how many villains have you upset over the last twenty-something years?' He gave Matt a disparaging look. 'I never thought I'd see you running around having a hissy fit like some schoolgirl who's discovered a big zit an hour before her first date.'

Even Matt was forced to smile, but it didn't last. 'There's more to it than that, sir. I'm sure of it.'

'So convince me.' The super flopped into his chair and pointed for Matt to sit down.

'Mainly because of that particular case, sir. It's unsolved and has haunted me for years.'

'So what better case to pick on? Lord, everybody and their granny knows that you bring it out and dust it down every time there's some sort of advance in technology.' His brow furrowed. 'You do know that rumour has it that you are only retiring so that you can spend all your time on the Gibbet Fen killings?'

Matt shifted uncomfortably in his seat. 'As you said, sir. Rumours, just rumours.'

'I do hope so, Matt. You are the best detective I've got here. I could say probably the best DCI that the Fenland Constabulary has seen for years. Don't you think it's time to let it go?' He stared across the desk at Matt, 'I'll bet you've had that damned old file open within the last month, right or wrong?'

'It was never closed, sir,' Matt replied.

'And until we have a proven killer, it never will be. It's a triple murder, man! No one here could ever be accused of forgetting it. It's just that we have to prioritise, and for one thing it's a decades' old cold case, and another, when our main suspect died . . . the killings stopped. We all care, Matt, but we need to keep it in perspective.'

His boss's eyes bored into Matt. It was almost impossible to argue in the face of such an irritatingly sensible man.

'Okay, well, would you entertain the concept of Copper's Nose? I really do have a very bad feeling about this.'

The superintendent moved his hands in a juggling action. 'Normally, and with any other officer, I would. With you and your bloody bête noir, it's only a very shaky maybe.'

Matt knew that he was in with a chance, and immediately seized the opportunity.

'Look at the picture, sir. It's a photo alright, but I think it's been printed off a computer.'

'Your point? With digital photography, that's the norm, isn't it?'

'When those killings took place very few people even knew about digital cameras.'

'So it's a recent photo.'

'It was taken years ago, and if I'm right, I believe it was taken *before* the murder.'

The super leaned forward and stared at the miserable scene.

Matt knew that look. Bingo! He had him! 'Sir, look at the tree to the left of the bridge. That cottage was demolished years ago and the whole area is now a wildlife and bird reserve, but the bridge was rebuilt and the tree is still there, but it's ten times the size.'

'That proves nothing. You can scan and print old photos, easy-peasy. Even my wife has mastered that, and she's a technophobe of the first order!'

'So who would have old photos of a murder scene?'

'Dozens of people! We would. Journalists would. Archivists, locals, and ghouls and ambulance chasers, and . . .'

'And they'd all be taken *after* the event, wouldn't they, sir?'

There was a silence. David Redpath sat back in his chair and peered at Matt, 'And why are you so damn sure this was taken prior to the place attaining notoriety?'

'We broke the railings on the bridge when we freed Jamie's body from the water. We had to get the fire service down there with some cutting gear to slice through the barbed wire. The bridge was collapsing even before Trumpton stamped all over it in their size twelves.' He picked up the picture from the desk. 'The bridge in this snapshot is undamaged, it's exactly as it was when Sergeant Morris and I arrived that night.'

Superintendent Redpath closed his eyes and sighed, 'Who in heaven's name would have a picture of a crime scene *before* the murder?'

Matt gave a sigh of relief. 'I rest my case.'

The super leaned back in his chair and swore softly, 'Okay, okay. You can get that photo and the two envelopes down to forensics. Just don't make too much of a song and dance about it.'

'Thank you, sir. And, uh, well, as we're pretty quiet at present,' Matt decided to go for broke. 'Could the team make a few low-key enquiries?'

'On what, for God's sake? I still think it's just some clever arsehole sticking two fingers up at you. You know exactly what I mean, "Ballard's coming up for retirement, let's remind him about the one that got away!"'

Matt shrugged. This was not the moment to push it. 'You're probably right, sir. I hope so.' He stood up and carefully picked up the photo, 'And thanks for this. I'll get it down to the lab. I'll keep you posted if they find anything.' He glanced back as he closed the door and saw his boss staring at him thoughtfully.

* * *

In the outer office, Jason clicked through a file on a local car thief. No matter how hard he tried to concentrate, his mind kept going back to that sinister picture that his boss had received.

'Want a coffee, sir?'

He looked up to see PC Goddard grinning at him. 'Thanks, Gemma. Black, very strong, no sugar, please.'

'Wow! Brave man! You do realise I'm talking about Fenland Constabulary coffee, not finely roasted Arabica beans, don't you?'

'Whatever. Right now, I'd drink paint stripper if it had enough caffeine in it. Somehow young Mr Barry "Call me Baz" Barstow just isn't holding my attention.'

Gemma leaned over his shoulder and stared at the image on the screen. As she did, Jason detected a hint of the light flowery perfume that his eldest daughter wore.

'He's an ugly little bugger, isn't he? Possibly more rat than human? No wonder your mind keeps wandering.' She stepped away, then turned and perched on the edge of his desk. 'Did the boss tell you about the letter I received this morning?'

'Yes.'

'It really bothered him, didn't it?'

'Of course, it did. You of all people should know just how badly he wanted that case solved before he jacked in the job. The Gibbet Fen murder is why you're here, instead of pushing paper clips around the front office.'

'Sorry?' Gemma looked puzzled.

Jason gave her a long-suffering smile. 'Didn't you think it a teensy bit funny when the DCI offered you a temporary desk job in CID, after you hurt your ankle in that football match riot?'

She frowned. 'Not really. The injury stopped me going out on foot patrol, but the rest of me was okay. I thought I was just being put to best use, that's all.' The frown deepened. 'Okay, spill the beans, have I been duped?'

Jason broke into a rare smile. 'Not really. You've been a great help actually. It's just that the chief doesn't like his team detectives spending too much time on that old cold case. If the super catches them, he's in hot water, so you were a gift, a total blessing in disguise. And, if you don't believe me, tell me what's been your main occupation in the last few months?'

Gemma gave him a withering look. 'Checking what new DNA techniques are available to us. Reading updates in forensics, oh yes, and bringing the Gibbet Fen case information up to date: checking on the status of all the original witnesses and suspects, who's dead, who's still alive, etc., etc. Yeah, yeah, I'm starting to get the picture.'

Jason smiled at her knowingly, 'But you've enjoyed it, haven't you?'

'Of course, I have. It certainly beats sorting out the old lags and binge drinkers on a Friday night.'

'And it's given you a good insight into how CID works, which at such an early stage in your career is more than most ever get to see.' He looked at her thoughtfully, 'I can't see a smart girl like you wanting to pound the beat forever.'

Gemma shrugged. 'I joined up because I wanted to make a difference, I don't really care how I achieve that goal, as long as I do.'

'Well, I can give you one really good tip to do that.'

She leaned forward expectantly.

'Never promise an inspector a coffee and then keep him waiting.'

Gemma almost jumped off the edge of the desk. 'Thanks a bunch, guv. One strong mug of paint stripper coming up.'

* * *

About a five minute walk from Fenfleet police station, a man wearing heavy, thick-soled trainers and a hooded tracksuit, jogged purposefully along the river walk. After about five minutes he paused in his run, squatted on the grass beside the river and did a series of leg stretches. After a while he took several deep breaths, and resumed his road training, stopping only once on the two mile run home, to slip a carefully typed envelope into one of the many town post boxes.

CHAPTER THREE

It had been hard getting to sleep, but somewhere around two in the morning, he must have finally dropped off. Now, as the pale dawn allowed a silver trickle of early-morning light through his bedroom window, Matt opened a bleary eye, and searched for the LED display on his alarm clock. Six fifteen. With a groan, he pushed back the duvet and slowly swung his feet over the edge of the bed, yawning noisily as he did so. It didn't matter, there was no one next to him to disturb. Liz rarely stayed the night. In fact, she didn't often come out to his place at all. He wasn't sure why. There was always a different excuse, like it was too far out on the marsh, or her staying was 'not appropriate,' or the rutted road knocked the tracking out on her prissy little sporty car. Maybe it was really the state of the place. He glanced around. It wasn't dirty, it wasn't even untidy, it was just old and lacked TLC. When he retired, he'd do it up. Really get to grips with it. Make it a project. He looked from the old sash windows to the solid wooden latch doors, then down to the dull sheen of the original floorboards. The old family home deserved better, and as soon as he retired he would make sure he did it justice.

He stood up, pushed his feet into a battered pair of slippers, and made his way along the wide hallway to the bathroom.

The face that looked back at him from the mirror still didn't look old enough to belong to man who was about to retire. His thick, wavy hair had begun to change colour way back in his early thirties, and now he wore it short and bristly. He forced a grin. Life had dealt him some shitty knocks in the past, but in time he had learned how to cover them up. At least physically they didn't show. With luck, he might even keep his hair into his dotage, along with a small something of the 'bad-boy' cheekiness that had enabled him to get his fair share of the girls as a young man. When Liz had seen a snapshot of him in his twenties sitting on his old motorbike, she swore he had substituted it with a still from *The Great Escape*.

His expression hardened, then his full fifty years showed themselves. The memory of the photo of his smiling self had morphed into the desolate landscape that was Gibbet Fen.

He turned on the shower and stripped off the shorts and T-shirt that he slept in. As he stepped into the powerful stream of hot water, all the worries of the day before returned. He couldn't shake the nagging concern that there was more to this than some old enemy rubbing salt into the wound.

He took his time, soaping himself over and over again, then letting the water pound onto his stiff, aching shoulders. Suddenly he flipped the temperature control to cold, and gave a loud grunt of shock. He needed to get moving and that was one sure fire way to get his arse into gear.

As he wrapped a large towel around himself and rubbed vigorously at his hair, the phone rang.

With wet feet slapping on the boards, he hurried back to the bedroom. 'DCI Ballard.'

'Sorry, boss, but before you remind me, I do know it's only six thirty.'

'It's alright, Jason. Apart from the fact that I'm standing here stark bloody naked, dripping wet, and freezing my bollocks off.'

'Oh, well, uh, sorry about that, but I think you'd better hear this.'

Matt didn't like his inspector's tone. It had its usual despondent quality, but there was a nasty hint of apprehension behind it. 'Go on.'

'When I got home last night, Michelle had taken the youngest girls to their friends for a sleep-over, she'd then gone on to visit her mother so she was really late in and . . .'

'For Christ's sake, Jace, get on with it! I'm causing wet rot here!'

There was an irritated snort from the receiver. 'Yes, well the thing is, Michelle forgot to tell me there was a letter for me in the morning post.'

Matt shivered.

'I haven't opened it, sir, but I'm dead certain it's the same as the one PC Goddard received. Same brown envelope and identical typed address.'

For a moment Matt was silent. If it was another photo, it confirmed his fears, but fears of what, he wondered. 'Can you bring it over here, Jason. Before work.'

'Certainly, sir, I'm already showered and dressed, but can I have breakfast first?'

'No. I want to see that envelope. *Then* we'll have breakfast.'

* * *

The photo was of a car. A dark Ford Cortina Crusader. As before, it was a computer-printed black-and-white picture, and showed the vehicle parked on the side of a long straight drove. The rest of the frame showed huge stretches of farmland and a sky full of clouds.

Jason broke the silence. 'Isn't that the same model of car the killer used to incinerate his second victim, sir?'

Matt found it hard to speak. When he did, it was little more than a whisper. 'Worse than that. It *is* the same car.'

'What?' Jason's voice rarely changed its grave timbre, but it had gone up several octaves. 'But it was torched! Totally gutted,' He swallowed then added, 'Along with the body in the boot.'

'Christopher Ray Fellowes, you mean.' He knew he sounded angry as he stared at the photograph, but there was nothing he could do about it. He *was* angry. 'Christopher, aged eleven when he died. One of two children, sporty, fit, showed great promise as a long jumper. Said to be a future Olympic hope for English athletics. So, do me a favour, and don't just call him "the body in the boot."'

'Sorry, boss. I wasn't meaning to be disrespectful. I'm just shocked, that's all.'

Matt threw an apologetic glance at his friend. 'Yeah, me too, on both counts, sorry and shocked.'

'Would I be a complete plank if I asked why you are absolutely certain it's the same vehicle?' Jason raised an eyebrow.

'Look.' Matt moved the picture closer to Jason, 'The killer's car was, as you said, burnt out, but the forensic report said that the driver's wing mirror was damaged prior to being torched.' He pointed to the smashed wing mirror in the picture, 'and if I had any doubts, take a look at the number plate. It's emblazoned in my brain, Y345 UEG, clear as daylight.'

Jason bit his lip and stared at Matt. 'So what do you think all this means, sir?'

'I'd rather not be the one to put thoughts into words, Jace. Let's take this into the super and see if he has the balls to admit to what's going on, shall we?'

'After breakfast, sir?'

'Jesus, Jason, you could look miserable for England! Come on! Once we've seen Superintendent Redpath, I'll take you to the greasy spoon of your choice and buy you the biggest fry-up you can fit inside that scrawny frame of yours. Deal?'

With a sigh, Jason stood up and nodded gloomily. 'Have to be, I suppose.'

* * *

The superintendent's office was something of a respite from the cheap office desks and uncomfortable chairs of the CID room. David Redpath's desk was made of a dark wood, veneer maybe, but he kept it polished and uncluttered. Even the chairs had padded seats, unheard of in the rest of the station.

Matt placed the latest photo on the polished surface and sat back down, next to Jason.

The super opened a drawer, took out a magnifying glass and scrutinised the picture of the Ford car for several minutes. Neither of the other two men said a word. Finally, the super sat back and stared at them.

'What is your position at present? Case wise?'

Matt paused. 'Eh, well, the Stockbridge case is pretty well tied up, and I saw William Cross's brief yesterday. They are planning on changing his plea to guilty, so that more or less wraps that up. What have you got pending, Jason?'

'Nothing much. Small stuff, really. I've been helping DI Short sort out a few loose ends.'

The super nodded, his expression serious. 'Then I'm going to suggest you get your team together and take a fresh look at the Gibbet Fen killings.' He directed his gaze at Matt, 'And listen hard, I still think this is an elaborate hoax, something to get at you personally, okay? But I can't ignore the fact that there is a small chance that it may be something far more serious.'

Matt wanted more, wanted to hear the super say the words that he was thinking. 'Like what, sir?'

'As if you damn well hadn't already reached this conclusion on your own.' The super stared at him stonily. 'Well, if you want it spelled out, it's this: at the very far end of the spectrum, the most extreme explanation, Matt, is that the killer is still alive and *he* sent you those photos. You are the last serving officer here at Fenfleet who had any dealings with that case. Work the rest out for yourself.' He leaned forward across the desk. 'And for God's sake keep this low-key. I don't think the chief constable would like it too much if he knew I'd committed a damn great chunk of our budget to a cold case, and on the strength of only two black-and-white photos, right?'

Matt swallowed hard. 'Understood. And thank you, sir. I really appreciate this.'

'Oh, do bugger off, DCI Ballard! Leave me to start juggling the bloody finances for this little fiasco. And please, for all our sakes, sort it out, fast!'

CHAPTER FOUR

Matt decided to keep his team small and discrete. He chose DI Jason Hammond, Detective Sergeant Liz Haynes, DC Bryn Owen and PC Gemma Goddard. If her medical said she was hundred per cent fit, Gemma was due to return to uniform later that week, but he thought he would have little trouble extending her stay until the case was sorted. After everything she had done over the last few months, she would be invaluable to the enquiry.

Jason rounded them up, brought them into Matt's office and briefed them on the basics. After allowing them some time to assimilate what they had been told, Matt sent out for some coffees and then set about explaining what he wanted from them.

He perched on the edge of his desk and looked down at the four familiar faces. 'First, I guess you all know I've been interested in this case for many years.' He expected a murmur of assent, and wasn't disappointed, although he slightly resented the muttered 'Obsessed, more like!' from Jason. Matt gave them an apologetic smile. 'I believe it started because of my old sergeant, Bill Morris. He never, up to the day he died, believed that our main suspect, Paul Underhill, was the killer. He told me to keep an open mind and never let the case get forgotten.' He shrugged. 'Over the years, I've been haunted by the thought, what if he was right? What if the killer is still out there?' He sat down. 'Now, this won't be easy, after all, you've all heard me bleating on about it for years, but I want you guys to forget about my theories and try to look at this case with fresh eyes. Take it from the top. Use every new system available to us, and see what you come up with, okay?'

There was a ripple of agreement.

'I've already sent down to the evidence store, sir. All the boxes will be brought up here this afternoon.' Jason said.

'Good. And the car? The burnt out Cortina?'

'I've notified the secure unit at Braytoft, sir. I've told the exhibit officer that we'll want it out of wraps for further investigation.'

'Excellent, Inspector. And hopefully the lab should have some results back today about the first photograph. Now, I'm going to suggest that you spend the rest of today completing, or getting someone else to take over everything that you are working on at present. I want you all on this case full time, right?'

The team nodded, then Gemma raised a hand. 'Something bothers me, sir.'

Matt tilted his head on one side. 'And that is?'

'There were three killings, on or near Gibbet Fen, sir, but whoever is contacting you only sent two photos. I mean, I know you only received the second one today, but according to the postmarks they were posted at the same time, so why just two?'

'Good point. I've been wondering the same thing, and I don't have an answer.' He shrugged. 'Royal Mail hitch? Gone missing? Or all part of the plan, whatever that is?'

'Like keeping you guessing?' said Liz.

'Maybe. Whatever, I don't want you to leave for work before the post arrives tomorrow morning.'

'Who? Me?' asked Liz with a startled look.

'Why not? Gemma was first, then Jason. You or Bryn are the next logical recipients.' He gave her a long, hard stare, 'So no late-night clubbing, or whatever you guys get up to, and not getting home to check your mail, okay?'

Liz lowered her eyes and quietly said, 'Me, sir? As if.'

Matt fought back a smile. 'Right. We'll meet back here at four o'clock, when I'll give you a brief outline of what happened back in the nineties, then we'll sort out individual tasks. Oh, and the superintendent has asked us to keep it low profile for the present, so we'll not be using the main murder room. We'll continue to use my office here as a base for meetings, and you'll have to use your own desks and computers. Jason, can you organise a whiteboard and a projector? Hardly high-tech, I know, but with a dozen evidence boxes and five of us in here, it'll give "cosy" a new meaning.'

'Oh, bring it on,' Liz Haynes grinned, pushed a dark auburn curtain of long, straight hair back over shoulder and said. 'I'm sure we all love cosy!'

* * *

By three thirty, Matt's office bore little resemblance to its former tidy self. He looked around. It wasn't particularly satisfactory, but it would do. Jason had managed to forage everything they needed, now as long as there was room for the five of them to get in and still breathe, it was all systems go.

The team arrived promptly at four. Matt sensed an air of contained excitement about them. They'd had several weeks of mundane cases, but this was different, it was a proper mystery, and it was clear they all wanted a piece of it.

'Well, I think we'll be fine as long as no one farts,' Bryn said.

'Thank you for that sage and illuminating piece of information, Bryn.' Liz was perched on a pile of heavy sealed cardboard boxes. 'I'll hold you personally responsible if there is even the faintest whiff of something unpleasant.'

Matt was grateful for the banter between his team. Going over the old case was going to be painful for him. Somewhere in his mind there was a small, locked compartment with Jamie Matravers' name on it. He still saw the dead boy in his nightmares, and they were frequent, even after all this time.

'Right, well, I know that you are all familiar with the outline of the case but I'd like to fill you in on what it was actually like here at the time.' He took a deep breath and plunged into the past. 'Over a period of nine months, from July 1990 to April 1991, three boys were murdered. Their names were Danny Carter, Christopher Ray Fellowes and Jamie Matravers.' Matt paused. 'And you probably know that it was me who found Jamie.' This time there was no humour as the members of his small team nodded silently. He took a deep breath and continued, 'The only thing they had in common was their age, which was eleven. They came from different backgrounds, went to different schools, had different interests, different doctors, dentists, hairdressers, they even looked different. After extensive investigation however, we made one tentative connection. Each boy had been to St Mary's Hospital at some time in the year prior to their being murdered.'

He shrugged. 'As I said, it was a very vague connection considering an awful lot of other eleven-year-old boys probably went there too, but it was a link.'

'And that's what led to Paul Underhill becoming the main suspect?' Bryn asked.

'Yes. Underhill was a psychiatric out-patient there. He'd been attending the clinic for five years, off and on, and had been admitted there on a couple of occasions.' Matt sat down, put his elbows on his desk, leaned forwards and stared at his colleagues. 'I want you all to read the case history about that, but as you do, remember this, three children were killed in the most horrific manner. Most of the men and women working the case had kids of their own. It was hard to be totally objective when fear and anger were running riot in Fenfleet. And *everyone*, not just the public and the media, but even our own top brass were putting us under the most extreme pressure, demanding we find the killer before another child died. Believe me, it was a bad time. This was the early nineties, new technology was coming along, but it wasn't readily available to us, and what there was took a very long time to get results.'

Liz raised her hand. 'So Underhill died and the killings stopped. What actually happened to him?'

Matt leaned back. 'Hit-and-run. A dark night, a lonely, unlit fen lane. He was knocked into a dyke and lay there for almost a week before he was found by a waterways worker clearing the ditches with a JCB.'

'Deliberate?' Gemma raised her eyebrows.

'Who knows? The driver was never traced.'

Bryn frowned. 'So if the murders then stopped, surely it was Underhill?'

'Most people believed that, but Sergeant Morris never bought into it. He reckoned the real murderer just stopped killing, knowing that if everything went quiet, we would assume it was Underhill and scale the case down. Which, of course, was exactly what happened.'

'And you've found nothing new in your more recent investigations, sir?' Gemma asked.

'I've found a hundred things, but sadly not the name of a new suspect.' Matt stood up and passed out folders to each of his team. 'This may help you. It's something I've been preparing over the last few months, a sort of overview of the case from day one. I thought it would help whoever stepped into my shoes after I left. It has only facts, no suppositions or theories. It contains witness statements, forensic reports and a mass of other relevant data. Naturally you can access everything in full detail from the computer database, but I'm hoping this will make your job easier.'

The officers leafed through the document.

'Phew! This is pretty thorough, sir. It must have taken forever to collate.' Bryn looked impressed.

'Yes. Sadly it just proves that I don't get out much these days.' Matt grimaced. It wouldn't do to tell them that the file had been intended entirely for his own use. Something to help fill the days and nights after he left the force. DIY was all well and good, but there were only so many rooms you could re-paint or wallpaper. 'So, get yourselves home now, use that for your bedtime reading tonight, and we'll start fresh in the morning.'

The team made their way out.

'Sergeant Haynes. One minute before you go, please?' Matt said.

Liz stepped back into the room and pushed the door to. 'Sir?'

Matt made sure the others were out of earshot, then said softly, 'There's a cold bottle of Chablis in my fridge at home. It's definitely too good to drink alone.'

'Dear me! I thought I was supposed to be tucked up in bed with a murder report and not leave home until postie has delivered my mail?' She flashed him a supposedly innocent smile.

'I can read you the bedtime story, *and* get you home in time for the postman.'

'Tempting, Mattie, but perhaps not tonight.'

He felt a rush of irritation and something like fear. He really did not want to spend another night alone. 'Come on, Liz. It's important. These photos have really got under my skin. I need a distraction.'

'Oh, so that's what I am! Wonderful!'

He moved a little closer. 'That's not what I meant, Liz, and you know it.'

'I'm really not sure it's a good idea, Mattie.'

He could smell her perfume and almost feel the softness of her hair and the warmth of her skin. 'Is it the house? Because if it is, we could go to the hotel.'

'Adie's place again?'

He shrugged. 'Well, it's out of town, and it's safe. Adie would roll naked in red ants before he was indiscreet.' He gave her a lop-sided smile, 'And it's clean.'

The faintest hint of amusement crossed her lips. 'What more could a girl ask for?'

'You'll come?'

She passed her tongue slowly across her lips and said, 'I usually do, don't I?'

He grinned. 'Usually? Always, I sincerely hope!'

'You'd better ring Adie, then, make sure he has a room.'

'No need.'

'You've not been assuming things again, have you?'

He threw her a disparaging look. 'No! And I wouldn't dream of it.'

'Oh yes, I forgot. There's always a room for you, isn't there?'

'Adie Clarkson and I go way back.'

'Mm. Funny that.' Liz tilted her head provocatively, making it desperately difficult for him not to reach out and touch her.

'He really doesn't seem the type that a detective chief inspector would associate with.'

'Long story. And as I said, we go back a long way.'

'Wanna tell me about it?'

'No.'

'Never?'

'Maybe one day, but not today. See you there at seven?'

'Only as long as you order one of his juicy fillet steaks and a bottle of something very expensive.'

He brushed past her, ostensibly to open the door, and whispered, 'Whatever you want. It's yours.'

'Excellent. I'll tell you exactly what I want at seven, okay?'

CHAPTER FIVE

As Matt and Liz made their way up the back stairs of Adie's hotel, Ted sat quietly in front of the computer and stared at the image on the screen. Ted wasn't his real name. He had adopted it in honour of one of his childhood heroes, and although he had no inclination to follow in the man's footsteps, he felt that they did share a few characteristics, and he just liked the idea of being called Ted. It was, at least, a lot better than the name he had been given at birth.

His latex-gloved fingers sped over the keyboard. He adjusted the picture, enhanced it, then sat back and nodded. That was just right. Exactly as he wanted it. His heart thumped against his ribcage. Ted took a deep breath. It was hard to believe that after all this time, things were actually happening. Years of planning and scheming, now he was actually doing something concrete. He wondered what had kept him going. Hate? Revenge? He stared at the screen and shook his head slightly. No, it wasn't that. It was more a sense of justice being done. The truth finally coming to light.

He pressed a button and the printer whirred into life. After a moment or two he carefully picked up the photograph and smiled with satisfaction. Perfect.

Ted pushed his chair back and walked over to another desk where he found a plain sheet of white paper and a large brown, pre-addressed envelope. He knew that it was far too early to post it. The timing for this second part of the game had to be minutely accurate. But it was ready, that was the main thing. It was too damned important to rush it. He smiled again, this time a full-blooded grin. If nothing else, no one in the land could accuse him of impatience. How many people would wait over twenty years to make things right?

With one last searching stare at the picture, he slid it between the folded white sheet of A4 paper and slipped it into the envelope.

Ted went back to the computer and closed it down. No point leaving it on. After all, it was never used except in connection with the project. He looked at it scornfully. What a piece of junk! Nothing like his own little wizard, but there, that was the idea, wasn't it? Keep everything neat and tidy. No one would ever trace it. He'd paid cash, bought it second-hand from a mate of a mate, then put it back to its factory settings. It was a bog-standard, obsolete PC, and apart from the project, there was nothing on it; not a single piece of personalised wallpaper, not even Spider Solitaire! And definitely no connection to the Internet.

The monitor light turned from green to amber, and he leaned forward and switched it off. As he pushed back his chair, his contentment faded. He stood still and listened. From somewhere else in the house he heard a faint mewling sound, half cry, half sob. Damn! The boy shouldn't be awake yet. He'd given him enough stuff to keep him down until at least dawn. With a curse, he went to deal with the problem.

* * *

At the same time as the needle slid into pale flesh and the sobbing slowly subsided, Matt awoke to find himself covered in sweat and shaking from head to toe.

'Mattie! For God's sake! Your screams will wake the whole hotel!'

He felt arms around him, rocking him back and forth. 'I'm sorry. I'm so sorry, it was another bloody nightmare,' he told her.

'I should think it was! Even my orgasms couldn't compare with that racket!'

Her voice sounded amused, but in the soft light of the bedside lamp, he saw that her eyes held deep concern.

She poured him a glass of water and passed it to him. 'That was a bad one, wasn't it?'

He drank gratefully. 'Could be said.'

'I thought they were getting better, you haven't had one for months.'

'I've had a few recently, but nothing as horrible as this.'

'It's those bloody pictures, isn't it? Stirring up the memories of that dead boy again.'

He stretched and sat up, wiping the sweat from his brow with the edge of the duvet cover. The idea of sleep had abruptly left him. 'That and other things.'

'Want to talk?'

He leaned back against the thick padded headboard and sighed, 'Why not? Is there any wine left in that bottle?'

Liz leaned across to her bedside table. 'Strangely, yes. Well, enough for one each.' She poured the wine into their two glasses and moved back close to him.

He took the drink and stared into the glass. It was strange, being emotionally intimate with Liz. Their relationship, if you could call it that, had been to this point, purely physical. A powerful attraction that had proved most satisfactory to both of them. Maybe 'attraction' was something of an understatement. The chemistry had been so strong that he had slept with Liz the day after she arrived in Fenfleet following her transfer from Hampshire. That was a year ago, and none of that first passion had worn off.

'I know about Jamie, but what did you mean when you said, "other things"?'

Matt took a deep swallow, almost emptying the glass. 'Don't take this the wrong way, Liz. I'm talking ancient history here. The fact is, there have only been two women in my life, and I'm meaning women who I wanted to come home to, walk the dog with, and put a ring on their finger. One ran away and the other died.'

Liz sipped her drink, but said nothing.

Matt drained his glass. 'Believe it or not, when I was in uniform, back in the late 80s, I met a girl and fell in love. Her name was Laura, and I was totally besotted with her. We were going to get engaged, but, well, I guess my job started to take off . . .'

'Get in the way, more like.'

Matt nodded. 'Maybe. From day one on the force I loved being a copper, but I loved Laura too. The problem was, we never talked enough. We both had high pressure jobs and well, we tiptoed around each other, trying to second guess what the other one wanted, but never had the sense to actually ask.'

Liz smiled sadly. 'So what happened to Laura?'

'She disappeared. Left her parent's home, took only an overnight bag, cleared out her bank account and vanished into thin air. I tried everything to find her, but . . .'

'Sounds like she didn't want to be found, Matt. If she stripped her account, that indicates premeditation, like planning the start of a new life, doesn't it?'

'I guess so. It was weird though. The night she left, I was going to propose. I had the ring and everything. Got it all sorted in my head, how we'd manage, what we'd do, rehearsed what I'd say, but when I got there, she'd gone. I never saw her again.'

'And she'd given you no reason to suspect that she was unhappy?'

'None.'

Liz frowned. 'What about her friends and family?'

'As shocked as I was.'

'Did they blame you in any way?'

'To begin with it was quite the opposite, they really felt for me. Can't you just picture it? The love-struck suitor standing on the doorstep with a bunch of wilting flowers and a cheap ring in a fake velvet box?' For a moment he could almost feel the smooth velour in his hand. 'Later, it was different. It was the not knowing. It ate into us all. Destroyed her parents and split her family into two warring camps. Then they closed ranks and all turned against me.'

'Easier to blame the outsider, I suppose.'

Matt rolled over on to one elbow and stared at Liz. 'This is really bizarre! I never talk about my life!'

She kissed him lightly on the forehead. 'You know you're safe talking to me. I like you. I respect you as a damned good detective, but more than that, well, there's no ties, no complications, just great sex. Oh yes, and you've just learned that I can also be a very good listener.'

They slid back down into the bed and lay facing each other.

'So Laura broke your heart, now tell me about the one who died?'

This was uncharted territory for Matt. After everything that had happened in his personal life, he had become a loner, a right Mattie-No-Mates, as Jason loved to call him. Talking, in his world, was done in the interview room, or from the dock, not lying beside a beautiful woman in a hotel room. To his surprise, he heard himself say, 'My wife, Maggie.'

'You were married!' Her voice shot up several octaves.

'For one whole year. After Laura, I couldn't believe that I'd ever be happy again, But I was. Maggie was a truly lovely person, inside and out, and I fell in love all over again. Then we found she had cancer.' As he spoke, he knew that the pain was still there, as sharp and raw as ever. 'Maggie died. I took it very badly. End of story.'

Liz ran a finger gently down his breast bone. 'Which explains why you've settled for a no-strings arrangement. Too scared to let another woman in, in case you lose her as well. My poor Mattie.'

Matt gazed into her deep brown eyes and nodded. 'Perhaps.' He'd certainly not planned on this outpouring, but as he looked at her, he was forced to admit to a feeling of relief wash over him. Maybe he could never have talked like this to another living person. Liz had been right. He felt safe with her. In that moment, he knew he hadn't made a mistake by opening up to her.

'Wanna swap secrets?' He smiled at her. 'Come on. We've spent a whole year up to our armpits in carnal knowledge, and we've never once opened up about ourselves. So, now I've bared my soul, it's your turn.'

'With what we've been up to, there hasn't been *time* to talk.' Her smile faded. 'And there's nothing to tell. There's only one big skeleton in my cupboard and you know all about that.'

'Do I? All I know is that your husband is away more than he is at home, and . . .' He eased closer to her. 'A woman as wickedly sexy as you, should *never* be left wanting.' He traced lazy circles with his fingertip around one of her nipples, and smiled as it hardened under his touch. 'What I don't know, is why you hate coming to my home.'

Liz shook her head, making her lustrous auburn hair slide gracefully from side to side. 'Home? It's not a home, Matt, it's a time warp! No, worse than that, it's a bloody museum!'

Matt wasn't sure whether he felt amused or hurt, and his confusion must have showed.

Liz threw back her head and laughed softly. 'Okay, okay, so you grew up there. What's changed since your parents' time?'

'Uh, nothing really. Except the heating and rewiring, and naturally I've painted it.'

'Different colours?'

'No, actually I just sort of freshened everything up.'

'Exactly. And I bet if your grandparents reincarnated tonight, they'd feel totally at home.'

Matt pulled a face.

'When you married, what did Maggie think of the farmhouse?'

Matt stared around the bland hotel room. 'We had great plans for it. Well, Maggie had plans. I would have just gone along with her. She did cheer it up a bit, plants, flowers, that kind of stuff, but then . . .' His voice faded.

'It was too late?' Liz took his hand in hers as he nodded silently. 'So why not do the whole place up? Change it, modernise it, revamp it. Blow away the ghosts and invite some fresh air in.'

'I thought maybe when I retired I'd do something like that.'

'Don't wait. Get on with it. Then when you meet someone special, she won't feel like I did: like I'd just crept into a mausoleum for the night! Hell, Matt, it still *feels* like another woman's domain, another woman's bed. And it's damned creepy as there's nothing around to substantiate that feeling. You've got no photos of her, no feminine toiletries, no stray clothes left in the wardrobe.' She gave a theatrical shiver. 'And as there's not a sniff of anything devious about you on the mess-room grapevine, it's bloody unsettling.'

'Oh dear. And I thought it just oozed old world, rustic charm.'

'Sorry, but it doesn't. Although I have to say that the things that you've told me tonight do explain one little mystery.' She grinned at him mischievously. 'One thing that I'd often wondered about.'

Matt frowned. 'And what is that exactly?'

'Just how you managed to become such a sensitive and exciting lover.'

It was Matt's turn to grin. 'Glad you noticed.'

'I mean it. Really I do. My marriage, being as it is, has left a lot to be desired in the bedroom department. But you, well, you're something else altogether. And to be quite candid, it's a very pleasant surprise, knowing what most blokes are like.'

'You mean, "Wham-bam-thank-you-ma'am?"'

'From what I've seen in the past, even the "thank you" is too much to ask from some of them.' She lifted his hand to her lips and gently kissed his fingers. 'So which one taught you? Laura or Maggie?'

He shivered as he felt her tongue touch his fingertips. 'Maggie.' He drew in a deep breath. 'I was a mess after Laura disappeared. Thought maybe I'd let her down as a partner. So, when I met Maggie, I guess I went about it all wrong.'

'Ah, a testosterone-fest! Trying to prove your alpha male sexual prowess at every opportunity?'

'Something like that. Being a total prat, more like. Luckily for me, Maggie had the sense and the patience to take me in hand, so to speak. Made me understand that there's more to lovemaking than a swift grope and some thrusting.'

'Well, she did a sterling job, and you must have been a very good pupil.'

'When she got ill,' Matt bit his lip, 'when she realised that she was going to die, she said she wanted me to find someone else, and when I did, to treat them like they were the most special and precious woman in the world. She believed that very few women have the kind of satisfying sex life that they deserve.'

'Don't tell me that surprised you?'

'I'm a bloke! It shocked me rigid!'

Liz laughed softly, then lifted her hand, placed it around his neck and pulled him gently towards her. 'Speaking of rigid, I think I've had enough of talking. Maybe you could show me a little more of what you picked up in your more advanced lessons?'

He responded by kissing her, and in seconds her body was pushed tightly against his, moving rhythmically against him. A shudder of excitement burnt through him. Whatever else they had talked about tonight, she had been dead right about the great sex.

An hour later, Liz slept while Matt lay awake watching her. He tentatively ran a hand over her tanned shoulder and she murmured something in her sleep. He thought it might be her husband's name. He hoped it was. Things were perfect as they were, he wanted nothing to upset the status quo.

Matt closed his eyes. The talking seemed to have helped, although he knew that the reasons for his nightmares were far more complicated than he could have ever explained, it was good to know why she hated to stay over at the farmhouse with him.

He drifted off to sleep with the scent of her perfume soothing him. He would have felt completely relaxed had it not been for the nagging concern about the next morning's post.

* * *

In a three-storey townhouse that overlooked Fenfleet Park, Superintendent David Redpath was still awake. He had tried the usual double malt but it had had no effect. At around three o'clock, he got up and wandered into his study. He booted his computer and logged on to the family tree project that had recently filled his meagre amount of spare time. Up until now he'd found it addictive, but tonight it held no attraction.

He browsed it for a minute or two, then closed it down and flipped over to his image gallery.

David poured himself another drink and sat staring as the stored images flashed onto the screen, then faded away and made room for the next picture. The whisky warmed his throat as he watched a photo of his eldest girl's wedding morph into an action shot of his pet Labrador leaping to catch a Frisbee. Then he wondered what kind of computer programme had produced those awful photos of the murder scenes. He swilled back his drink and wondered what the hell else was going to turn up. He'd seen some pretty dreadful things in his time on the force, and he knew the stinking, depraved depths that some people's minds could reach. He wondered what little gem this case would unearth.

He pushed back his chair and began to pace the office. He'd told everyone at the station that he thought it was someone with a grudge against the DCI, but he didn't really believe that. Matt wasn't the only one with Copper's Nose. His gut was telling him that someone very nasty was walking the streets of Fenfleet, and whoever it was, he had the feeling that they had only just begun to get their teeth into Matt Ballard.

He drew his dressing gown tighter around him. That man had suffered enough over the years, he did not deserve this as a leaving present. Damn! Matt was his best officer. In his time, the man had been to hell and back, one way or another, and he still remained one of a dying breed of dedicated, well-respected policemen who really cared about people. Why the hell couldn't he convince the fool to stay on? As an officer of his rank, Matt could stay on for ten more years, if he wanted. He must have read the obituaries in the *Fen Beat* monthly. It was a sad fact that a massive percentage of coppers died in their first two years of retirement. After such a high tension, high risk, high adrenalin job, the men and women who just hung up their handcuffs and did a spot of gardening and walked the dog, more often than not pegged it before ever seeing their old age.

He stopped pacing, his face wrinkled into a frown. *Of course, that's it! Matt has no intention of stopping!* He was going private. A personal crusade to find out whether Sergeant Morris was right or not. David snorted. The rumour was true, and by God, the man had some pretty powerful friends in high places, and some low ones for that matter. If he wanted help or information, he'd get it.

He walked over to the window and looked down into the dark, shadowy, tree-lined park. He shivered, not because of the cold, but because the thought had just struck him that maybe Matt's plans to catch the cold case killer were about to be upset. From where he was standing, it looked rather more as though the murderer was looking for Matt.

CHAPTER SIX

'Sergeant Haynes not in yet, sir?' Bryn asked.

'Guess her post hasn't arrived.' Jason looked edgy. 'I assume you didn't get anything, Bryn?'

'No, sir. I asked my flatmate to ring me as soon as it arrived. My post consisted of two credit card statements, one pizza delivery advert, two offers for loans and a discount magazine for surgical appliances.'

'That's useful. Well, as the boss didn't get anything, and Gemma and I have already received one, it looks as though we're going to be hanging by our eyelashes until we hear from Liz.' Jason pushed his hands deep into his pocket and began to jingle some loose change.

'Tried worry beads, guv? My girlfriend swears by them when she's stressed.'

'I'm not stressed,' grumbled Jason.

Bryn smiled innocently. 'Oh, I never assumed you were, sir. I meant my girlfriend, not you.'

Jason grunted something unintelligible and continued to jingle the coins.

'Uh-oh.' Bryn looked up. 'That's the DCI's phone ringing.'

Matt looked serious as he approached them. 'That was Sergeant Haynes. There was nothing in her mail. She's on her way in now. When she gets here we'll discuss what this may mean and how we'll proceed.' He turned on his heel and left the two detectives looking glumly at each other.

'I never thought I'd be upset by *not* receiving bad news.' Bryn chewed on his lip.

'Mm. I know what you mean. I think this bastard's playing mind games with us. Getting us all heated up, waiting for the third murder scene photo, and bingo, nothing.'

'If he is, he's succeeding. My nerves are jangling more than those bloody coins in your pocket, guv! Want a coffee?'

'Is the Pope Catholic?'

Bryn grinned, 'On its way, sir.'

* * *

Matt's office was once again filled to bursting with boxes and police officers.

'Well, it's not what we expected, but we have to give the post a chance, I suppose. Not everything arrives on time. We'll give Royal Mail one more day and assume that it will arrive tomorrow.'

'So do I get another lie-in tomorrow, sir?'

Liz's insinuation was not lost on Matt. 'Exactly as this morning, Sergeant.'

'Oh lovely.'

Matt concealed a grin, sat down and endeavoured not to look at her. 'Right. Now I suggest we proceed in this manner. Jason, Liz and Gemma, I want the three of you to concentrate on the deaths of the three boys. Jason, you take Jamie Matravers. Liz, would you take the Christopher Ray Fellowes murder, and Gemma, investigate the killing of Danny Carter. Do this on your own, look at them as completely individual cases, then we'll get together, compare our findings and hopefully make some interesting crossover comparisons, okay? Bryn, you are the boffin, I want you to concentrate on the present situation, i.e. the photos, the envelopes, and if there is any way to find out where the letters were posted. If we can, then CCTV may come into play. Are you all happy with that?'

Before the team could reply, Gemma's mobile phone began playing a tinny rendition of some awful pop song.

'Sorry, sir. I thought it was switched off.' She grabbed it from her pocket and glanced at the display before moving to cancel the call. Her face clouded slightly. 'Sir? May I take this? My mother is not very well at present and it's my father calling.'

'Go ahead, Constable, but be quick.'

Matt was about to continue talking to the others when he saw Gemma's expression change. Holding the phone away from her, she said softly, 'Dad says I've had another letter. Same as before.'

'Has he touched it?' barked Matt.

'After the last one, I'd already warned him not to, sir.' She passed the question on to her father, then said, 'No, it's still on the floor where it landed.'

'Jason. Go with PC Goddard to collect that letter. Take all precautions with it.' Matt watched as the two officers hurriedly left the office.

Liz sat back down and gave a theatrical sigh. 'Oh well, there goes my lie-in.'

For once Matt was thinking of other things. Clearly the new letter would have a photo pertaining to the murder of Danny Carter, and young Danny's passing had been far from peaceful. Thankfully, Matt had not been on night shift when he was found, or maybe his nightmares would have started eight months earlier. The boy had been found by a friend of Matt's, a uniformed bobby called PC Andy Lowe. A distant member of Andy's family had owned a small farmhouse out on Snape Fen. When the old man died and left no will, there was a family feud that resulted in a long and complicated probate. Half hoping that he might inherit a part of the old place, Andy had taken regular trips out there to keep an eye on it, check for vandalism or, worst case scenario, for squatters. Andy was something of a hard nut, but finding Danny Carter's mutilated body in his great uncle's storehouse hit him hard.

Matt slowly slid open a drawer and removed a file with the name 'Danny Carter' written on it. This report was strictly off the record. Part of his unofficial enquiry. He carefully removed some typed sheets of paper and laid them on his desk. Maybe it was time to share this little piece of history with his team.

Bryn interrupted his thoughts. 'So, any guesses what the next photo will be of, boss?'

He had plenty of ideas, all unpleasant. 'Danny was the first boy to die. I suppose it will be an old picture of the location of the murder.'

'It was some old ruin out on Snape Fen, wasn't it?' asked Liz.

'Thorntree Farm, to be exact.'

'Is it still there?'

Matt nodded, 'Yes, although no one would recognise it. None of the locals would touch the place after what happened, so it was sold off to a developer who ripped it to shreds and built a small complex of holiday homes there.'

'At Snape Fen? Who'd want to take a holiday there?' Bryn pulled a face. 'There's nothing there but muddy fields, salt marsh and sky!'

Liz shrugged. 'You never know. It might be perfect for someone who doesn't like crowds.'

'One heron, two oystercatchers and a pink-footed goose constitutes a crowd out there. Smashing fun for your hols, I *don't* think.' Bryn stood up and stretched. 'Anyone fancy a drink while we're waiting for the others to get back?'

Matt and Liz asked for coffees and the younger man left.

'What's that?' Liz pointed to the folder.

'An account of the finding of Danny's body.' Matt stared at her. 'Not one you'll find in the case records either.'

'Why?'

'PC Andy Lowe, the officer who found the boy, suffered a breakdown afterwards. He was older than me, but a good mate. I spent quite a bit of time with him, trying to help.' He paused, recalling the nights when Andy was out of his head on booze, just trying to make the memories go away. 'He was referred to a psychologist who suggested he have a course of hypnosis, to make him relive it.'

'Oh God! The old "face your demons" package. And did it work?'

'He never went. He found his own way of dealing with it. One night he invited me around to his flat. He locked the door, unplugged the phone, produced a litre of Scotch and two glasses, and sat opposite me at the kitchen table. He talked until dawn, went over every disgusting detail, every sick making feeling and every horror he witnessed.' Matt shook his head in something like disbelief. 'Two days later he reported back for work again. He got a transfer to another constabulary up north, somewhere where the mess room gossip was not about the murders and got on with his life. Maybe he never made inspector, but he saw out enough years to get him to his pension.'

'And this file?' Liz looked slightly suspicious.

'I taped everything he said, then I transcribed it onto my computer. That's the hard copy.'

Liz let out a low whistle. 'Remind me to check your pockets next time we spend time together.'

He gave a small laugh. 'Don't worry, you're quite safe. It was just that I had a sick feeling about that case from the very outset. Somehow I always knew that one day it would come back to haunt me.'

Liz leaned forward to pick up the file but he stopped her, laying his hand over hers. 'Not yet. Let's see the photo first, then I'll let you all have an insight into what the killer was capable of.'

* * *

Before they could finish their coffee, Jason and Gemma were bursting through the office door. 'It's exactly the same, guv. Think we're safe opening it? This guy is such a trickster I wouldn't put it past him to booby trap one.' Jason carefully placed the evidence bag containing the envelope on Matt's desk.

It was the same size and thickness as before. Matt was sure it was just a photograph, but he couldn't risk his team's safety. 'Okay, outside, all of you and make sure no one is in the corridor for a moment or two. Go, go.' As they trooped out, he realised that part of this charade was purely for his own benefit, to let him be the first to see the picture. To allow his feelings and emotions to surface without the others around him.

With gloved fingers, he withdrew the black-and-white photograph, then almost dropped it in shock. He had been right about the location. It was Thorntree Farm, and it was certainly taken many years ago. What he hadn't bargained for was the smiling face of Danny Carter beaming at him. The photo showed the boy sitting on an upturned barrel just outside the door to the storeroom where he was to spend his final hours.

Matt's mouth felt as dry as chaff as he stared at the image. Suddenly it was hard to swallow. He carefully placed the picture on his desk and hurried out into the corridor.

'Okay to come in, sir?' Bryn was waiting at the far end of the hall.

Matt brushed past him. 'One minute, right. Give me one minute.' He crossed the hall and went down the stairs to the foyer and the water cooler. As he drank back the paper cup of water, he saw that his hands were shaking uncontrollably, which was not exactly something he wanted a station full of wooden tops to witness. He swallowed another cup of cold water and shook himself. This last photo had nothing to do with a crime scene, it was all about the abduction of a child. No one could have taken that shot other than the man who'd tortured and killed Danny Carter. He wiped his damp lips and took a deep breath. He would show it to the team then take it to the super. Damn the budget, and damn the chief constable, it was time to bring this case out from the shadows and throw everything they had at it.

As far as Matt was concerned, a killer, maybe *the* killer was back, and that meant every eleven-year-old boy in the fens was in danger.

CHAPTER SEVEN

Two hours later, the investigation team had been allowed out of their closet. The murder room was his, and already large blow-ups of the three photographs were on one wall, and the floor to ceiling whiteboards showed both family pictures and the scene-of-crime photographs of the boys, Danny Carter, Christopher Ray Fellowes and Jamie Matravers. Matt's team remained the same, but he now had several uniformed officers with him, and the promise of backup, as and when he needed it.

'Those forensic shots in no way convey the horror of what the killer did to them.' Matt stood beside one of the gruesome pictures and looked at each of his team in turn. 'I think it's time to come clean with you guys about my involvement in this case. You,' he indicated Jason, 'say I'm obsessed. Well, you're right. I am. I have been for twenty years. And yes, I was intending to follow this case up after I retired. I have amassed a whole cartload of information about this case, and I will gladly share it, if it brings this madman to justice.'

He turned and picked up the folder that had so interested Liz. 'This is one policeman's personal record of what the Gibbet Fen killer could do. I was going to read it to you.' He paused, then threw it back on the desk. 'But instead I'm going to play you the original tape recording, not all of it, the actual conversation went on for many hours. I've selected the section that I believe you should hear. Listen to the voice of PC Andy Lowe, and remember, if the man who did this is still out there and we don't catch him, this could be you one day. That is the sort of monster that we are dealing with.'

Matt leaned across and switched on the player. There was a crackle, then the tinny clink of bottle on glass and the sound of a chair being moved. The voice that began the conversation sounded strained. The accent was clearly a local one.

'You still up for this, Mattie? You can bugger off if you like, and no hard feelings?'

Matt's voice joined in. It was much younger, but distinctly his. 'No way, mate. If this is what you want, I'm here for as long as it takes.'

'Okay, well, as you already know, I kept an eye on the old place. The evening in question,' There was a long break and a deep sigh before the man continued, '. . . we were really quiet and I'd just checked out a call to Snape Village, so I went up to the farm and had a good nose around. Normally I'd only check the house itself, but for some goddamned reason I thought I'd check the outbuildings too. There were two of them. The first was a sort of stone shed, stank to high heaven. It had obviously been his vegetable store, and rotten potatoes were still stacked in large brown paper sacks, or what was left of them after the rats had chewed through them. There was other stuff too, all mouldy and stinking. I remember covering my nose, and almost running back out into the daylight. I wanted to puke at that smell.'

There was the sound of another long drink being taken and then the glass was placed heavily on the table.

'Well, then I eyed up the other building and I thought, I hope the old bastard hadn't owned a cow that no one knew about. That'd be really nice, now wouldn't it? This is good whisky, Mattie. Don't

lag behind, we're getting to the bit where we're going to need the bleedin' Dutch courage, believe me.'

In the present, in the long silence that followed, Matt could see the amber liquid sloshing into the glasses and could smell the mellow, malty Glenlivet. He could also smell Andy's fear and see him biting angrily on his thumb nail as he prepared himself to continue.

'You alright, boss?' Jason asked.

'Yeah, it's just a bit heavy, that's all. Listen, he's speaking again.'

Everyone was silent, the pain of their fellow officer drifting around the room like a living thing.

'It was a stronger, larger place, brick built with a pantile roof and an arched stone doorframe. It had two big old doors, weathered but still sturdy, and I couldn't get the buggering things to open. I didn't remember there being any keys to the outbuildings, so they couldn't have been locked. I reckoned they must have just jammed shut with lack of use, until I noticed the traces of oil on the hinges. I felt totally confused, Matt. I remember touching it with my finger to prove it was what I thought it was. Uncle Lionel wouldn't have known what an oilcan was, let alone know how to use one. It felt all wrong, mate, you know that gutty feeling that says, this ain't right, watch your back! Well, I finally decided to put my shoulder to it. I can hear it now, it gave one almighty groan and then it swung open. I thought, Oh well, it can't smell worse than his veggie store, so I went in. It was dark. The light from the doorway didn't reach to the far end of the building and my torch was back in the car. I could just make out some sort of fixtures, wooden stalls, or something, and I thought, Oh God, perhaps he owned that cow after all! I walked inside, and it hit me. You know it, Mattie, once smelt never forgotten, huh? I don't know why I didn't call for backup straightaway. I should have. I really should have.' There was something like a sob in his voice. *'I froze, Mattie, just froze. Didn't know what I was looking at. Maybe my mind didn't want to know, whatever, the old brain didn't quite compute with what my eyes were*

looking at. Jesus, Mattie, if I'd believed things were bad when I looked in the veggie store, I was sadly mistaken. Bad was where I was standing right then.'

'You okay, mate?' The young Matt's voice was full of compassion for his friend.

'Yeah. Gotta do this. Just this once, Matt, then that's it, finito! Never again.' There was a sniff and an intake of breath and he struggled on, 'I thought, it had to be a joke, a really sick joke. Or maybe someone was using the place as a venue for some trashy home video stuff? For some scary, thrill-kill shit? I remember edging backwards and pulling at the other door. I needed all the light I could get to give me the courage to get closer to, to whatever it was that was in those shadows. I wedged it open and, oh hell, Mattie, I still don't know how I managed to walk to the back of that fucking barn.'

He swallowed more Scotch and coughed. 'I thought it was a dummy. Maybe someone had dumped some sort of special effects model there. After all, the place had been empty for a while. Then I thought, since when do dummies smell like rotting meat, you arsehole!' He laughed bitterly, 'I think that was the point when my brain gave up trying to make damn stupid excuses. I was looking at the mutilated corpse of a boy. He was suspended upside down. His legs were bent at the knees and draped and tied over the back of the wooden animal stall. His arms hung from the shoulders, the hands palm out with his thin fingers pointing downwards, just an inch or so above the floor. And he seemed to be wearing some kind of long, dark brownish-red scarf around his neck.' The police officer took a deep shuddery breath. 'But it wasn't a scarf, Matt. It was the blood from the gaping wound that had once been his throat. It had flooded down both sides of his face, and drained into a gully that ran the length of the stable.' There was another sob, this time a full-blown heartrending cry. 'Some bastard had taken a little kid and done that to him! Some sick bastard had bled him like an animal being sacrificed!'

The sound of sobbing intensified and almost filled the room with its anguish, then it was abruptly stopped, as

Matt flipped the switch on the recorder. 'There is a lot more, but I think we've heard enough.'

No one spoke. Police Constable Andy Lowe's voice was still in their heads.

'I'll let you all have copies of the transcript of the entire conversation.' Matt felt drained having just relived such a horrible moment from his past. 'And in case anyone is wondering, Andy gave me his full permission to use this in any way that I wanted, if it meant catching the murderer. His only stipulation was that I never involved him personally. When he said he'd talk about it just once, he meant it.' Matt silently wondered if Andy still felt the same. There was a chance that if more evidence came to light he would be questioned again. Whatever, for Andy's sake, he'd do his best to make sure that never happened.

'Surely he made an official statement at the time, sir?' asked Bryn.

'Yes, but it was pretty sketchy and he wasn't pushed too hard to elaborate. Even at that time, it was recognised that he was badly affected by what he'd found. Plus, the crime scene wasn't compromised, everyone who saw it afterwards, saw the same as PC Lowe.'

'Except everyone else was prepared for it. That poor sod thought he was just checking on his prospective inheritance,' added Liz.

'Exactly.' Matt leaned against the wall and stared at them. 'I know what you just heard tells you no more than all this will.' He pointed to the photos and information boards. 'But these images,' he shrugged and shook his head, 'we see them all the time. They become like pictures in a book or scenes from a horror movie. I believe we become immune to them, lose the reality, the true nature of the evil that killers like this inflict on innocents.' He pushed his hands deep into his pocket. 'That's why I thought I'd let you hear first-hand what it's like to find something like that.'

Gemma raised a hand and said, 'But *you* found one of the children too?'

Matt looked at her. 'Oh yes. And you'll hear about that at some point. It's just that with the passing of time, I find I can talk about it in a more controlled and clinical fashion. Andy told it in the "now," the real story, warts and all.' He hoped the lie sounded convincing.

'Was the boy actually killed there, sir? Or moved there after death?' asked Jason.

'Pathology says that he was killed in situ, and the new photo more or less confirms it. Although the boy had been stripped of his clothes, they were found in a neat pile close to the body. Those clothes are identical to the ones that the boy is wearing in the picture.'

They all looked at the huge enlargement on the wall. An eleven-year-old lad, skinny for his years, dirty blond hair and a toothy smile. He wore a pair of faded denim jeans and a well-worn, royal blue polo shirt with a small logo on the breast pocket. On his feet were a pair of trainers, not mega-expensive ones. It was hard to connect the smiling youngster with the macabre tableau that followed.

Jason shifted uncomfortably in his chair. 'He knew his killer, didn't he? You don't smile like that for a stranger.'

Matt nodded. 'I agree.'

'Wasn't it a bit risky? I mean picking that particular property. If he'd done a bit of homework, the killer would have known that a copper had an interest in it.'

'To be honest, Jason, I think that's the very reason he did pick that house. He wanted to make quite sure that we'd find the dead boy. It was his first kill. He was proud of it. He didn't want it going unnoticed for weeks.'

'Sorry to interrupt, sir.' A uniformed officer entered the room carrying an envelope. 'DC Owen is expecting these. These have just arrived from forensics.'

'That'll be about the photographs, sir,' said Bryn, handing the package to him.

As the man left, Matt ripped open the envelope and quickly scanned the reports. *Sod it! Exactly as expected.* He cursed under his breath.

'All three pictures were produced on the most bog-standard all-in-one Print Scan Copy machine available. Paper used was the same sort of thing, premium inkjet photo quality, sold in supermarkets, stationers and every computer store in the country.' He glared at the report, almost willing it to tell him something useful. 'Apparently the machine used is not a modern one, so he's either had it for ages or picked it up dirt cheap when someone was upgrading their system, and even the paper is not new, so no point in checking outlets. Everything is pristine. No prints or contaminants noted.'

Gemma looked worried. 'So what happens now, boss? He's sent you a picture relating to each of the three murders. What's he going to do next?'

Matt bit his lip. He really wished that he had an answer for her, but he didn't. 'I'm afraid we are rather in his hands regarding that, unless we come up with something fast. So, get back to work. Strip those reports to bits and find me something that says Paul Underhill wasn't the killer, or that someone else should have been in the frame. And, Bryn, after seeing this report, put your investigation regarding the photos on the back burner. You'll be wasting your time. Help Gemma with the Danny Carter murder instead, alright?'

As his team filed back to their desks, he thought about Gemma's question and the concern etched on her face. She was quite right, there had only been three murders, so what the hell was he going to do next?

* * *

By nine that night, the whole team felt dizzy from either watching computer screens or scanning reams of paper printouts and reports. No one had found anything that was even vaguely interesting or new. At nine thirty,

Matt sent them home, telling them to grab what rest they could and get back in for eight the next morning. As he tidied his desk, he saw Liz pulling on her coat. She looked exhausted, but he knew from past experience that there was one thing she would always have the energy for. He tapped on his office window and beckoned to her. With a knowing smile, she turned, called out 'Goodnight' to the retreating shapes of Gemma and Bryn, and strolled casually towards his door.

'If you say the word "distraction," I'll not be responsible for my actions.'

Matt grinned. 'Actually, I was simply going to mention that bottle of Chablis that's still in my fridge. Maybe it'd help us unwind.'

'Well, now I know a little of the history of you and your creepy old family home, maybe I should try to get used to it.' Her face became serious. 'Actually, I need to speak to you about something, so that wine sounds like a very good idea. I'll have to go home and grab some clothes for the morning, though.'

'No problem. I'll throw some pasta and a salad together, if that's okay?'

'Perfect.' She began to walk from the office, then turned around. 'I was meaning to ask, what were you really doing earlier, playing that tape to the team?'

Matt shrugged. 'Sorry? I'm not with you on that?'

'You know exactly what I mean.'

'I wanted them to *feel* it.'

'What, to feel like you did when you found Jamie? To see what you see every time you close your eyes? Every time you wake up screaming at two in the morning?'

Matt slumped down into his chair. 'I know how it must seem to you, Liz, but I hear them talking. The young rookie officers, they are so blasé, so bloody gung ho. They don't have a clue what it's really like to come face to face with something like that.'

'Stop right there. You sound like Methuselah.' She gave him a look that contained both reproach and compassion, 'We live in a violent society, Matt, you know that better than any. The youngsters get it stuffed down their throats day and night, and that's just watching the news on TV! Give them a break, if they are called on to deal with something horrible, then I'm sure they'll cope in whatever way they need to.' The smile became all compassion. 'If the truth be known, you just don't want any of our kids to finish up like Andy Lowe, or maybe like Matt Ballard, do you?'

He didn't answer. There was nothing to say.

'I thought that was the case, but you can't wrap us in cotton wool, Matt. We all know the risks. You look after yourself, and your team will still be right behind you. Now, chill out, and I'll see you later.' Liz walked from the office, calling out a loud, 'Night, boss. See you tomorrow.'

* * *

Later that night, as Liz carefully parked her MG TF in Matt's barn, a dark figure moved silently along the edge of the dyke that ran beside the marsh lane. Ted was clothed in black jeans and a thick black waterproof jacket, his features obscured by a peaked cap and the hood from the jacket. He pulled up his sleeve and pressed a tiny button on his watch. A pale light told him it was ten thirty. He made a mental note of that, then carefully made his way up the bank and onto the narrow lane. It was odd for the woman to stay, and that was obviously what she had in mind. It was far too late to be paying a casual visit, and he knew they certainly wouldn't be talking shop. He almost giggled. In fact, he knew exactly what the two police officers would be doing in a very short time from now. He gave a lecherous smile in the darkness. They'd be doing exactly the same as they did at that seedy hotel that they used. He felt a pressure building in the close-fitting jeans. He wondered what they'd do if they knew how many times he'd watched them. He clutched himself. This was not the time or the place. And he had far too much to do to play the peeping tom tonight. He licked his lips, much as he'd love to.

As he walked across the dark and lonely fen, he felt a strange feeling of empowerment. He knew such a lot about Ballard, certainly more than any of his police colleagues. And not just about his sex life, although for someone of the policeman's years, he was quite impressive. Ballard knew how to treat a woman, there was no question there. He had watched the woman detective wriggle and squeal often enough. The dirty bitch couldn't get enough of him.

Ted increased his stride, partly wanting to get home and attend to his house guest, and partly to exercise his body, to calm the physical reaction he was getting after thinking about that naked woman writhing beneath her lover. Yes, he knew everything there was to know about DCI Matthew Ballard, and it was that knowledge that made him feel powerful and in control. Ted sighed. For once in his life, that was exactly where he was. And he liked it. He liked it very much indeed.

* * *

Matt chopped lettuce, cucumber, tomatoes and yellow peppers, threw them into a large wooden salad bowl and drizzled some vinaigrette over them. 'Pour the wine, Liz. The glasses are in the cupboard over the fridge.' He tossed the salad together. 'Pasta's nearly ready.' He left the salad and turned back to the old-fashioned range where pasta boiled and a delicious-smelling tomato, miso and lemongrass sauce was gently heating.

'Matt, you're a policeman. They don't make their own sauces. Policemen keep the ready meal industry alive, remember?'

'Sorry to disappoint you, Sergeant.' He hung his head in mock shame. 'So, I'd better not tell you that I also cook fresh meals for the freezer.' He grinned. 'Go on, take a look.'

Liz pulled open the door of the big larder freezer and gave a yelp of surprise. 'Good Lord! Is this some kind of fetish? You've got more frozen dinners than Iceland!'

'I love every kind of cooking. It's a sort of therapy, it calms me down.'

Liz laughed. 'Well, I suppose making a delicate soufflé is about as far as you can get from grilling villains, but I still manage to chill out with a glass of plonk and a takeaway.'

Matt laid two places at the kitchen table. 'Sorry, the dining room hasn't been used for quite a while.' He thought it better not to say that it was actually last used for his wife's wake. 'I always eat here, I find it cosier. Is that okay?'

'I'd eat in the coal shed if I were hungry. Please, no standing on ceremony for me.'

'Right. Well, grab a chair and enjoy.' He placed the food on the table and sat down opposite her. 'So, what did you want to talk to me about?'

She sipped her wine and looked at him over the top of the glass. 'Gary is coming home on Thursday.'

He raised his eyebrows. 'Really? I thought his tour of duty was keeping him out there for months yet?'

'It is. He's escorting the bodies of two of his battalion back home for burial.'

'Oh.' Matt wasn't sure what to say.

Liz gave him a wry smile. 'It's okay. He'll only be here for a few days. It's true those poor boys were caught by ISIS terrorists, but the escort duty is a bit of a cover-up for why he's really coming back.' She sampled the pasta, 'This is really lovely! Beats Tesco's, doesn't it?'

'It bloody better! That's got organic tomatoes, fresh grown basil and . . . !'

'I'm joking, Mattie, don't blow a gasket. As I was saying, Gary has to report to his commanding officer over here. He has some information about some sort of in-house problem. He told me before he left that he may be home on some pretext or other. Whatever he's got his finger on, it's too hot to use telecommunications. He needs to deliver the report in person.' She gently forked up more food. 'And that means he will be pretty busy.'

'I don't expect to see you if your husband's home, Liz. You know that.' Matt knew the rules.

'Matt, there are other people that he'll need to see, not just me and his mum. Believe me, if we want to meet, there will be plenty of time. I just wanted you to know before I tell the others at work. Remember, my usual Oscar-winning performance as the excited little *hausfrau* thrilled at the master's return?'

'Don't be like that. You know you love him.'

She helped herself to more salad, 'Why don't I eat this leafy stuff at home? Oh, yes, of course, I love him.' She looked up at Matt provocatively from beneath lowered lids. 'But you also know this is no ordinary marriage.'

Matt shrugged and lifted his glass of wine in a toast. 'Then here's to *extra*ordinary marriages.'

She touched her glass lightly against his. 'Absolutely.'

CHAPTER EIGHT

Bryn and Gemma stared at the monitor screen.

'The more I look at all this data, the more I believe it had to be Underhill.' Bryn pushed back his chair and scratched his head, 'But unless he's found a way of sending photos from beyond the grave . . . ?'

Gemma rested her chin in her hands and leaned on the desk. 'I have an idea.'

'We use a clairvoyant? We buy a Ouija board?'

She balled up a sheet of paper and threw it at him. 'Be sensible, you great pillock. No, I really do have an idea, and as far as I can see, no one has used it as a line of enquiry, yet.'

Bryn leaned closer, his eyes wide. 'Then tell me everything! Gaze into your crystal ball and tell me what you see!'

Gemma scowled at him. 'For Christ's sake! This is a triple murder enquiry — you need to get serious!'

He raised his hands in submission. 'Okay! Okay! It's just my way of dealing with it. So, tell me, Miss Marple, what have you thought of, that two decades of detecting has missed?'

'Was the body in the ditch *really* Underhill? Who identified him?'

Bryn frowned but remained silent, then he opened a large file and began to leaf through the paperwork inside.

After five minutes, he stared at her blankly. 'I'm damned if know. I can't find anything about the identification process.'

'Nor can I, and I've been searching for hours.'

Bryn puffed out his cheeks. 'Thing is, we can lose information about a case that happened last week. We haven't got a cat in hell's chance of locating something that's missing from a twenty-six-year-old case.'

'Then if we can't find it, we use the oral history route. Word of mouth, and I suggest we start with the boss. He might well remember. He may even have seen the body himself.'

Bryn nodded. 'Good idea.' Then he glanced towards Matt Ballard's office door. 'Have you seen him this morning?'

'Not yet. DI Hammond and Sergeant Haynes are deep in conversation in the murder room, but I've not seen the boss.' She gave Bryn a long look, 'Do you think I should I tell Jason about my idea, or wait for the guv'nor?'

'Definitely wait. He's the only one with first-hand knowledge of this case. He may know straightaway, then it's either drinks all round, or back to the drawing board. He'll be in soon, he's probably up-dating the super.'

'Yeah, guess you're right.' Gemma turned back to the screen and resumed her hunt.

* * *

Matt was no longer with the superintendent. He was driving back across the fen towards his home. Several minutes after giving the super his morning report, he had received a call from Mrs Cable, his cleaning lady. A few days before, he had left her a note asking her to contact him when his post arrived. Obviously believing it to be an

62

ongoing task she had unexpectedly rung him, and from her rather florid description of all of his mail, he deduced that he had been the recipient of another letter.

Why, for God's sake? His mouth felt dry and his palms felt sweaty on the steering wheel as he turned onto the lane to his farmhouse. What now? Three murders. Three photos. There *was* nothing else, so what was he going to see when he opened the envelope?

Mrs Cable was standing over the post, her arms crossed and wearing a look that defied the offending envelope to try to make a dash for freedom. For a moment Matt wondered if she had been a custody sergeant in a previous life, then his thoughts turned unwillingly back to the letter.

'I hope you didn't mind me ringing like that, Mr Matthew. It was just that that one there,' she jabbed a podgy finger down towards the brown envelope, 'looked just like what you described.'

He placed an arm around her shoulder. 'You are quite right, Mrs C. You've done really well, but I'd like you to go home now.'

'Oh Mr Matthew, I can't! I still got the upstairs to do!'

'It can wait till another day. Now you get away.' He took out his wallet and gave her a ten pound note. 'That's just a little thank you, for being so observant and for ringing me, okay?'

He waited until he saw her and her old bicycle wobble up the lane, then bent down and carefully lifted up the envelope. Through the thin gloves it felt exactly the same as the others. He carefully ran his finger under the seal and drew out the familiar white paper. He unfolded it and stared uncomprehendingly at the photograph. It was a black-and-white landscape view. But where of? He looked closer. In the foreground, there was a small moss-covered brick structure with some rusting ironwork and a gate attached to it. The whole thing spanned a reed-filled culvert or ditch. He bit his lip thoughtfully, the countryside here was littered with things like that, sluices, flood gates, anything to control the water flow across the reclaimed land, but there was something vaguely familiar about it, but sure as hell, he couldn't place it. *Shit! This means nothing!* He stood up and pulled out his mobile.

'Jason? Listen, there's another picture. In my mail, this time.' He waited until his inspector had finished exclaiming, then said, 'I'm bringing it in now. I need every available officer to come and look at it. It's a fen location, but as far as I can recall, it not related to any of the three murders. We have to know where it is, understand?'

He hung up, pushed the phone roughly into his pocket and after carefully bagging the picture, locked his front door and made for the car. He had no time to lose. The other three photos had been crime scenes. Why should this one be any different?

* * *

One after the other, the gathered officers made their suggestions.

'Maybe a culvert under the lane that runs dyke-side down to Mares Fen Lane?'

'No way, that lane surface is too smooth. Mares Fen is potholed to buggery.'

'How do we know it's a modern photo, anyway?'

'Don't be a plank! Look at the quality of the shot. That's digital clarity, unless he has a Kodak Brownie with 8.1 Mega Pixel resolution!'

'I think it's near Greenlands Farm, out near Morton Lees.'

'No, the treeline is wrong. Morton Lees only has trees around the village itself, the rest is open farmland.'

Matt ran a hand through his hair in frustration and stared at the room full of police officers. 'Okay, okay! This is bloody useless. We'll never identify the spot like this.'

Liz stared thoughtfully at the picture. 'Why not ask Sierra Alpha Four Zero to take a look?'

'The helicopter crew?'

'Yes, they might see something topographically that we'd miss.' She shrugged, 'Worth a try?'

'Ring them now, and if they're local, take a copy of this to the helipad. As you say, it's certainly worth a try.'

It was almost noon before they agreed on a possible location. With coordinates from the helicopter pilot, Jason headed up a unit of three cars and sped away to a remote spot near the estuary of the River Westland. At 12.45 hours he rang in saying that it was a false lead.

'It's similar to the place in the photo, but not quite right, sir. In fact, thinking about it, it's very similar to a spot I used to go fishing when I was a kid.' Jason's voice suddenly intensified, he almost shouted down the phone. 'Boss! Get down to Allen's Gowt! There's a spot about half a mile north of the river, I used to leave my bike there and walk the rest of the way. I'm sure that's it! It's almost identical to this place.'

'Yes! I know where you mean! That's why it's so damned familiar. We used to do school nature rambles there.' Matt's heart began to race. 'Thanks, Jace. Good work! We'll meet you there, ASAP.' He glanced at his watch. The letter had arrived at nine thirty. He could only suspect that whoever sent the picture knew that fact. They had taken a further three hours to pinpoint the location, if it *were* the right location, of course. Add another twenty minutes to get there. He felt slightly sick. He could only imagine what a madman could have done in that time frame. 'Team! With me! Now!'

CHAPTER NINE

Matt's car was first to arrive. He parked, off road, about two hundred yards from the sluice, and signalled for the following vehicles to do the same. He had no idea what they would find, but whatever it was, he didn't want a possible crime scene contaminated by a stampede of police boots.

He gathered his team and they moved slowly towards the sluice gate. His feet and legs felt unnaturally heavy. He really did not want to look down into that water again, just in case a long-dead Jamie Matravers was lying there in a wicked web spun from barbed wire.

Liz and Jason moved ahead of him. He knew, as the boss, he should be leading. He had a responsibility to his people, but they pushed forward, and he let them. Although this time he was prepared for the worst, he just didn't want to be there.

'Nothing, sir.' Liz moved to the other side of the gate. 'Not so easy to see down here though. This ditch hasn't been cleared this season. It's a mass of black grass and reeds.'

'Someone better get down there, and be very, very careful.'

Bryn moved forward, a long stick in his hand. 'I'll do it.'

No one argued. He slid carefully down the bank and balanced on a narrow shelf of dried mud, just a few inches above the brackish water. He moved the stick back and forwards through the reeds, parting them and looking to see what may hide there.

'It's clear, sir. Nothing in the water or close to the sluice gate.'

'We have got the right place, haven't we, sir?' asked Gemma, holding out a hand to assist Bryn back up the bank.

'No doubt about that. This is it.' Matt took a copy of the photo from his jacket pocket. 'Not only is it the same spot, it's been taken very recently, in the last day or so, I'd guess.' He looked around. Weeds, reeds, grass and a field left fallow for one planting season. Nature didn't allow her precious produce to remain the same for long, even a week could make a huge difference in the growth of plants. These were identical to the picture. He could even identify one particular tall, skeleton-like stem of giant hog weed next to a broken panel of fencing. He stared at the picture, and froze.

The fence. In the picture, it was hanging drunkenly from one semi-rotten post. His gaze moved back to the scene in front of him. The fence lay on the ground, one end slightly raised up. He swallowed. What lay beneath the raised end?

'Quiet everyone! Stay where you are.' There was no getting away from this one. This was down to him. Without further thought, he moved between the still figures of his team and approached the fence. Initially he could see nothing, but as he moved around to the portion that was slightly elevated, he was brought to a sudden halt. He dropped to his knees. Just visible, half hidden by the long grass, he could see part of the back of a pale, motionless hand. A small hand, with bitten fingernails and a patch of dried blood on one knuckle.

It took Matt several moments to speak. Then he said, 'There's a child here. I believe it's a boy and I think he's dead. I need help to get to him, but this is now a crime scene, so if you approach, be careful!'

Jason called out, 'Bryn! Just you and me. Everyone else stay put, got it?'

There was a murmur of assent, and in seconds Matt's two officers arrived at his side.

'How do we tackle this, sir?' Jason asked.

'Very gently, I want you two to lift the fence. Not far, just enough so that I can slide underneath and check his vital signs. If you're ready, now!'

Bryn and Jason took a side each, and with great difficulty, eased the old wood from the ground.

'Oh dear God!' Matt scrambled backwards away from the child. He lay in the damp grass, took a deep breath, then almost whispered, 'Put it down! Put it back down.' He stood up unsteadily. 'I'm sorry. I'm afraid we're too late. We're going to need forensics out here, fast.'

'Sir?' Jason was looking at him, deep furrows of concern etching his face. 'He's dead?'

'Oh yes. He's dead alright. The bastard has nailed him to the fucking fence.' He shuddered. 'As you lifted the panel, I could see what looked like long nails sticking up through his wrists. Lord! He's just a kid.'

Jason closed his eyes. 'Oh hell. I thought it was too heavy for a piece of fencing.'

Matt looked hard at Jason. 'I did see one thing though, on his shoulder, there's some sort of mark, like a tattoo or something.'

'You mean, like the others?'

'I couldn't tell for sure. I only had a fleeting glance, but my money says yes.'

Matt felt a hand on his arm.

'Are you okay?' Liz had broken ranks. 'You're white as a sheet.'

He was touched by her concern. His voice dropped so that only Liz and Jason would hear. 'It's starting again. He's back.'

* * *

An hour and a half later, the blue-and-white cordoning was lifted, and Professor Rory Wilkinson, the Home Office pathologist, approached Matt with one of his usual black-humoured greetings.

'Much as I *love* your company, dear Detective Chief Inspector, I do object to driving halfway across the county from Greenborough, because some weirdo has clearly decided that I might fancy a change from the usual boring heart attacks and age-related deaths.' He glowered at Matt. 'When you find this creep, tell him I do *not* appreciate his twisted sense of humour! Window dressing!' He almost snorted the words, 'All this frippery! Just for show!'

'Explain, if you would?' Matt was confused.

Rory stared at him from beneath the hood of his protective suit. 'Sorry, Matt, but this sort of thing makes me so angry! People who treat death as a sick game. This poor little kid wasn't killed here. He wasn't crucified. And that very poor attempt at a bit of artwork on his shoulder was done post-mortem, not before. Hence he wasn't tortured, and an educated guess, from his facial expression and the ruptured blood vessels in his eyes, I'd says he suffocated or was choked. Tests will confirm.'

'Right.' A part of him felt enormous relief that although the boy was dead, the dreadful things that had happened to his young body had at least been done after his death. 'I suppose I shouldn't ask this, but can you give this case priority, Professor?'

'Of course it takes priority! What do you think I'm going to do, Matt? Shove him in the fridge and leave him while I do a spot of knitting! I will attend to it immediately, and considering the state of the mind of the person who did this, I'd suggest you act with equal speed and efficiency. I don't want too many more like this, thank you very much.'

Rory was about as ruffled as Matt had ever seen him, but then the pathologist was a man who respected the people who passed through his mortuary, and the desecration of a young body was hard to take, no matter who you were.

'I'll notify you of my preliminary findings immediately I've finished the post-mortem.' He abruptly pulled up his face mask and turned back. 'This young man needs me, and I plan on giving him my full attention, not freezing my nuts off chatting to you. Bye.'

'Thank you, Professor,' said Matt, realising he was talking to a retreating white suit. He couldn't quite make out the muffled reply, and was thankful for small mercies. Jason and Liz were standing a short way away, looking across at him with mild amusement. They'd seen this all before, and never failed to take the piss out of him for it. Somehow, it made his recent discovery easier to deal with, brought back a bit of normality. Gallows humour was not a bad thing in their job, every copper knew that it helped you cope. And he badly needed to cope. Whatever happened, he knew he must not let this situation get to him, not like it had before. He threw them a hopeless grin and beckoned them to return to their vehicles.

'Don't say a word! It's not my fault that I have no idea how to handle that man!

'Really! Well, I'd never have guessed, would you, DI Hammond?'

'Not in a million years.' Jason's hang dog expression remained in place. 'I always find the professor a real breath of fresh air when it comes to death.'

'Then, dear boy, you can be the one who goes down to the mortuary tonight to check on how the post-mortem is going.'

'Lovely. Can't wait.'

Matt opened his car door. 'Okay, round up the others, it's time to get back to the station. The SOCOs have plenty to keep them happy right now, and they sure don't need us getting in the way. Now that uniform have secured the area and got that protective awning up over the immediate scene, I guess we're redundant. See you back in the murder room.'

Matt's expression was grim as he drove off ahead of them. On mentioning the murder room, he had suddenly realised that by later that evening, there would be a new face added to the photo gallery of dead boys, and somehow he needed to ensure that there would be no more.

* * *

Ted opened the bottle of vodka and poured himself a stiff drink. Not to steady his nerves, not to calm himself, he simply thought he deserved a little something by way of celebration. Everything had gone as smooth as silk. His timing had been spot on, the Old Bill had reacted exactly as planned, and hell, he'd even managed to sort out the guest room.

He walked slowly around the house, glass in hand, and rechecked everything. Yup, the pigs could stroll in here with a whole unit of forensic investigators, and they'd find zilch. He sipped his vodka and gave a little laugh. He certainly knew how to clean up, and if he had any doubts about his own skill, well, the SOCOs weren't the only ones who knew how to use Luminol.

In the office he paused, then sat down at the old computer. As he was on something of a roll, he may as well prepare the next picture. This one was something of a gamble. A definite change of direction. He chuckled softly to himself as he booted up the machine. Yes, if nothing else, this should throw a damn great spanner in the works for DCI Ballard.

CHAPTER TEN

Jason, wearing a green gown and face mask, stood at the end of the stainless steel table and stared at the remains of the boy. For some reason, this part of the job had never bothered him. Having three children himself, he was always waiting for the time when one particular nasty death would sneak up on him and get his heart in a stranglehold. Like it had Matt. Or Andy Lowe. As he stared at the naked child he knew that this wasn't going to be the one. Even sliced neatly across the chest, from shoulder blade to shoulder blade, and slit down the abdomen to the pubis, the boy looked more normal, more human, than when he'd been nailed to a fence. Jason had seen the forensic photos, and they were not for the faint-hearted.

'Definitely choked, Inspector. I have recovered several fibres from his mouth.' Rory Wilkinson carefully removed the stomach, pancreas and intestines en bloc, and placed them on the scales. 'I've sent them off for analysis, but to be honest, I'm certain a man's sock was stuffed into his mouth and taped there. There are traces of adhesive on the far extremities of his jaw.'

'And everything else that was done to him, was done post-mortem?'

The professor gave a small shake of the head. 'Mostly. I mean, certainly all that silly stuff with the nails and the symbol carved on him, but . . .' There was a long silence.

'But he'd been abused?'

'Yes, poor little tyke. I'm just about to deal with that area now, so I can tell you more in a moment or two, but I have to say, this wasn't just a recent thing. This boy has been abused for years.'

Jason frowned. 'Do you think he may have been held captive, then?'

Rory shook his head vigorously. 'No, no. Look at him. He's thin, almost emaciated, but not through starvation, just a very poor diet. His skin is bad, his hair dry and brittle, he has blisters, that I think were caused by ill-fitting, hand-me-down shoes. There are no deep-seated bruises or contusions from being tied or restrained over a long period of time . . . no, I'm sure this boy's family were on the breadline. And maybe he ran away from it.'

The pathologist, unusually quiet and taciturn, continued his examination.

Jason felt despondency creep over him. 'Then the killer has been pretty clever in his choice of victim. The chances of a regularly abused boy being reported as missing are somewhere around nil.'

Rory looked up. 'And I can confirm this was the case, poor child.' He sighed. 'Still, there is the chance that if our murderer also used or abused him prior to death, we might just find some DNA.'

'You say there were no ligature marks on him, so how do you think he was held captive?'

'Most likely drugged, Inspector. Toxicology will soon show the presence of anything of that nature in his urine.'

'Or maybe he knew his captor. Maybe he went to whoever killed him quite willingly.' Jason thought of young Danny Carter's smile, just before he was killed.

'That's possible, too.'

'One more thing, Professor, then I'll let you get on uninterrupted. Were you around here at the time of the Gibbet Fen Killings?'

'Oh no, dear heart! It feels as if I've been with this constabulary *forever,* but I was still studying in London at that time.' He adjusted his glasses and thought for a moment, 'The pathologist back then would have been Charles Wilson, I think.'

Jason nodded. 'Yes, I've seen his name on some of the reports. I just wondered if maybe you were here, too?'

'Sorry, Inspector, I'm clearly not as old as I look! But, if I ever get over the hurt of your comments, I'll be in touch with anything more of interest.'

* * *

At seven that evening, Superintendent Redpath called Matt to his office. Without asking, he poured two scotches and handed one to Matt.

'Are you alright, my friend? That was a nasty shout to have to deal with.' Then he added, 'Especially for you.'

Matt sipped his whisky gratefully. 'I'm fine, sir. Honestly. Yeah, it was a grim find, but, I'm okay with it.'

'Good. Glad to hear it. Now, from your preliminary findings, what do you think? Is it the same murderer?'

Matt tugged on his ear. 'Tough one to call, sir. I'd prefer to leave my judgement until we get all the forensic reports back.'

'What about an educated guess?'

'Well, as you know, at the time of the original killings, we decided to keep that signature symbol from the press. It was never common knowledge. But whoever killed this new boy knew it. He reproduced it perfectly. And the photographs, sir, the ones that predate the deaths, I just don't know.' He took a long slow swallow, allowing the whisky to burn his throat. 'I really want to say, "Yes, it's him." But somehow, I can't get my head around it.'

'Can any of us?' The super looked intently at Matt. 'And while we're talking about concealing things, Inspector. What about that other little secret? The one that only you and Charles Wilson knew about? Can I assume you haven't told your team about that?'

Anger flooded through Matt. How the hell had the super found out about that? Charles was dead, and he'd certainly never told another living soul.

'Sorry to land that on you, Matt, but with this new murder, I think it's time to bring everything we know out into the open, don't you? Especially something as serious as the misappropriation of evidence.'

Matt rubbed his temples, stared at the polished surface of the desk and wondered just what the super really knew. 'How did you know about that?'

'I have a letter in my possession. It was sent to me by the pathologist, Charles Wilson, just a few months before he died. He was retiring at the time and he thought that maybe someone else should know what you two found. Just in case anything happened to you and the information was lost.' He gave Matt a strange look, it was almost kindly. 'You see, he had a good idea that this case would come back to haunt us one day, and in his heart, he agreed with your old sergeant. He didn't believe that Paul Underhill was the killer, either.'

Matt leaned back in his chair and wondered how he should deal with this untimely revelation. Knowing the super as he did, he decided to grovel. 'Look, I'm really sorry, sir. I should have told you myself, and much sooner than this, but the first thing I have to tell you is that Charles and I had very serious reasons for doing what we did, and we never tampered with the evidence, sir. It's quite safe.'

'So tell me about your reasons.'

'I'm sure Charles described them most thoroughly, didn't he?' Matt knew he sounded bitter, but he was fighting a losing battle with his emotions. He felt a deep reproach that this piece of undisclosed information about the Gibbet Fen murderer had been discovered, and now the super would be making it bloody common knowledge.

'Come on, Matt. Don't go all precious on me. Those gold charms are evidence, and they sure don't belong to you, even if you have got them locked away somewhere. You do know that I could hang you out to dry, if I wanted to?'

'I didn't take them, sir. They are in the police security evidence store, filed under the name Charles Wilson.' He drained his glass, and mentally threw up his hands in surrender. What was the point? 'We didn't make the connection immediately. Danny Carter wore a small crucifix on a thin chain around his neck. Christopher Ray Fellowes had a small cross and a gold St Christopher on a key ring. Jamie Matravers had a cross as a single earring. It wasn't until much later, in fact it was quite by accident, that I discovered that they were identical. We suspected they were a gift from the killer.' In his mind, he could see himself and the pathologist sitting in the morgue debating what to do. 'We decided to keep quiet for a while, because we knew that someone closely connected with the case was being indiscreet.'

The super sat forwards and glared at him. 'How so?'

'Someone was leaking information, inadvertently or deliberately, we never knew which. Whatever, sensitive details were finding their way into the public domain. That's why Charles and I kept the crucifixes to ourselves. If the time had come, we would have produced them as evidence, but it never did.'

'And Underhill? You must have checked his place for more crosses?'

'We did, and we stripped his paperwork looking for receipts or some sort of proof of purchase, but we found nothing. He had nothing in his home that was in any way religious, not even a Bible.'

'And this new murder? What are we calling the dead boy?'

'They are calling him Gabriel, sir. PC Goddard commented that he had the face of an angel.'

'He had no cross on him?'

'He was naked, sir, and we've found nothing so far. I just want to be sure that one doesn't turn up, either from inside his body, or left in his clothes, if we can locate them.'

The super lifted the Scotch bottle and proffered it to Matt.

'No thanks, sir. Gotta drive home.' He cursed silently. He could have gladly drained the bottle. 'If it's alright with you, can we keep the crosses just between us for a while?'

'I see no problem with that, Matt, as you say, if we need them as evidence, then we produce them, right?'

'Absolutely. And sir, if you asked me again for an educated guess, in retrospect and having seen this latest victim, I'd say, no, it's a copycat killer.'

'Why?'

'The Gibbet Fen killer was unspeakably brutal. All the boys were tortured and all suffered horrible deaths. Think about Jamie, he was alive when he went into that water in that goddamned razor-wire cocoon.' The memory almost rendered him speechless but somehow he struggled on. 'Gabriel's death, on the other hand, was made to look horrendous, but compared to the viciousness of the old crimes, it doesn't come close.'

'Twenty-six years on, maybe our killer's not as inventive as he was?' The super, obviously not driving himself home, sloshed more Scotch into his glass. 'Or maybe he *wants* you to think it's a copycat, have you thought of that?'

'Don't worry, sir, my mind is in overdrive right now. Frankly, I don't think there's a single scenario that I haven't considered.' He paused, the resentment about the gold crosses had abated and he was left with a strange sort of relief. 'And I'm sorry I never mentioned the crucifixes. You do know that I would only ever have used them in an appropriate manner, don't you?'

'Why do you think we are just sitting here enjoying a whisky, and I'm not reading you the bloody riot act?'

'Thank you, sir.'

He left the office and made his way back to what he thought would be a deserted murder room. Instead, he found Bryn and Gemma waiting for him. 'I thought you two would have been long gone. We are going to have to work late enough when we finally get something to go on.'

Bryn nodded, 'True enough, sir. The DI and Sergeant Haynes have left, but Gemma has had an idea, something she'd like to run past you?'

Maybe it was the result of his unexpected discussion with the super, but Matt felt a sick tiredness wash over him, and with it an unnatural irritation at his two colleagues. 'Couldn't it wait till the morning? I'm bloody knackered.'

Their expressions said it all, and with a sigh, he threw himself down onto an empty chair and looked up at them. 'Sorry, sorry. I shouldn't take a fucking awful day out on you two. So, what is it?'

Bryn sat opposite him. 'The old case, sir. Do you know who identified the body of Underhill?'

Matt felt a chill pass through him. 'I'm not sure.' He paused trying to sort out his thoughts. 'His brother, I think. Why do you ask?'

'Gemma has the idea that it wasn't Underhill at all, and he's still alive and kicking, or should I say, killing?'

Matthew felt a numbness steal over him, then he stared almost blankly at the young PC. 'Surely you've checked the reports? They would confirm it.'

'They're missing, sir. '

'What?'

'Yeah, that's the problem, boss.' Bryn frowned, 'We hoped that you'd be able to fill in the gaps, you being here at the time, and all that.'

'Actually, I wasn't here when Underhill was identified.' He frowned, trying to push unwanted memories back into the box in his brain where they usually festered silently. 'I think I was on leave,' he added lamely.

Gemma's eyes almost glittered with excitement. 'Then there's a damn good chance my hunch is correct.'

Matt rubbed his sore eyes. 'No, no, Gemma. Look, I'm sorry to disappoint you, but it *was* Underhill. When I got back the whole station was full of it. They would never have made a mistake like that. He was the prime suspect. Everyone knew him.'

'Maybe, but how many people actually saw his dead body? Apparently he was in a ditch for a week! You know the state his corpse would have been in, boss!' The eyes had not lost their enthusiastic glow. 'What if Underhill did it? Find someone roughly the same height and build, dress him in some of his own clothes, shove some sort of identity in his pockets, and hey! Underhill runs him over in some deserted spot, makes sure he finishes up where he won't get noticed immediately, and then he stops killing. What are we to think? Number one suspect dies, and no more deaths. The real Underhill is off the hook.'

'Makes sense,' said Bryn, trying to stifle a yawn.

'Sorry, but I really don't buy it. That would have been a class A, gold-plated cock-up. It just couldn't have happened.' Matt searched his memory. Where the hell had those reports gone? He was certain that over all the years he had spent trawling through the case, he would have noticed if something had been amiss? Especially something of that importance.

Bryn stood up and stretched, 'Well, with all due respect, sir, I'm not so sure myself. We're talking about almost three decades ago. Just how careful would they have been back then? They had some genuine ID on the body. Even recently I've known people identify bodies by the clothes or a piece of jewellery. I suppose not everyone likes staring into dead loved ones' eyes.'

Matt stiffened. Dead eyes stared at him from a familiar white face. He forced the image away and said, 'Time to call it a day. We'll sleep on it. I'll talk to you both tomorrow.'

As they left, he heard an angry Gemma mutter something under her breath. The only word he caught was 'dinosaur.'

CHAPTER ELEVEN

There was a note from Mrs Cable on the kitchen table. She had returned that afternoon and finished her cleaning. She'd left him a bag of fresh picked winter vegetables from her husband's garden, and a large slice of homemade carrot cake, carefully wrapped in cling film. Matt welcomed the warmth that the old woman's fleeting presence brought to the farmhouse. Without Mrs Cable's messages telling him important things, like the need to buy more bleach, and her small but thoughtful gifts, Cannon Farm would be a very lonely place indeed.

Out of habit, he poured himself a large Scotch then opened the fridge and stared at the contents. After a moment's deliberation he took out a pork chop, a red pepper, several slices of bacon, an onion and a handful of button mushrooms. He knew that the freezer was stacked with meals that he had already prepared, but he needed to do something. Cutting, slicing, dicing, frying, simmering — now that was therapy.

Tonight however, it didn't seem to work, and he felt a terrible loneliness descend over him. The finding of Gabriel's body had brought a whole, horrible chunk of his past crashing back around him. Not just Jamie Matravers, and not only Laura and Maggie. It seemed that there were almost two years of his life that were dark and distorted, a place full of twisted memories that refused to disappear. They had always returned in his nightmares, now Gabriel's death had allowed them access to his waking hours as well. He chopped an onion almost brutally, and resented the fact that the only way he could find some sort of solace these days was in the oblivion of sex.

As the chef's knife slashed through a handful of fresh herbs, he cursed Liz's husband for the extraordinary bad timing of his unexpected return from Iraq. He needed Liz right now, and although he knew he should feel ashamed of himself, he didn't. At that moment the craving was so great that he wasn't ashamed about anything. Not that he was having a sexual affair with the soldier's wife, or even the fact that the officer was bringing back dead heroes for burial.

Matt laid the knife down, stared at the chopped herbs, and wondered what sort of hard, selfish bastard he had become.

When the meal was finally cooked, he ate a little, threw the remainder in the bin and returned to his whisky. Too many problems were swirling through his mind. Like where the devil were those missing reports on the identification of Underhill? Of course it had been bloody Underhill in the sodding ditch, and okay, even if he were to agree with PC Goddard that it was a deliberate killing, Matt knew without a doubt that the hit-and-run driver was not the Gibbet Fen killer. Everyone had thought that it was someone who truly believed that Paul Underhill was guilty, and had taken it upon himself to stop the child murders. In doing so, he had also made quite sure that no legal eagle had the chance to get the bastard off on a technicality. And if Underhill were guilty, then well done! Here's to you!

He suddenly felt uncomfortable. A small sound had invaded his thoughts. A mouse in the attic? A creaking

82

stair? The old house talked to him sometimes. He looked around, but saw nothing and decided he was becoming paranoid. . He dearly wished that he could hear the sound of tyres crunching across the gravel drive to the barn behind the house. He wanted to hear a car door slam and feet make their way hurriedly to his door. What he really wanted was to feel Liz's naked body crushed against his own. That, and to forget everything else that was crowding in on him, except for the way she made him feel.

He got up, his almost empty glass still firmly in his hand, and walked to the window where he looked out across the darkened fenland. He had never underestimated the astonishing circumstances that surrounded his affair with Liz. For both of them, the situation was near perfect. As long as they were discreet, and they took great pains to be just that, he was free, and all too willing to provide what was missing from her marriage, and she happily accommodated his voracious appetite.

He took a sip from his glass and grimaced. The police force was full of illicit sexual liaisons. It had always been like that, and nothing was likely to change, it was the sort of job that provided a thousand plausible excuses for not being where you were supposed to be. "Sorry, darling, I'm stuck out at a traffic accident, I've no idea what time I'll get away." "Can't get home, sweetheart, I'm doing observations. It'll probably be all night." Etc. etc., etc. He had never had the slightest inclination to keep up with who was shagging whom. In fact, if the mess-room gossips were to be believed, he doubted it was within his capabilities. Whatever, he was pretty sure no one had the good luck that they did. One unattached male, and a woman with a husband who spent most of his time working hundreds of miles away. And Liz was clever. She made sure that her station reputation was purely as a harmless flirt, Frankly, she was damned good-looking and the blokes loved the attention she gave them, but somehow they all seemed to believe that she was a happily married woman, totally committed to her army officer husband.

Matt grinned to himself. And he was simply thought of as a workaholic. End of. If they only knew what Detective Sergeant Haynes really got up to! And with that boring old fart of a DCI to boot! He felt a surge of undisguised pleasure.

He flopped back down in his chair and thumped the now empty glass back on the table. Except that really didn't help him much tonight; tonight he was hurting.

Liz would no doubt be shopping, cleaning or doing whatever she needed to, to get the house ready for Gary's return the next day. Or would she? Matt fished in his pocket and pulled out his phone. After a moment of hesitation, he pressed the letter L.

'Mattie! I was just thinking about you! I'm in Tesco, looking for some of that green leafy stuff, what's it called?'

Her laughing voice sent the ghosts scurrying back into the shadows.

'Sorry to tell you, but you've just failed the *Master Chef* test! It's called lettuce! But, Liz, I was wondering . . .'

'Of course you were. But it'll have to be Adie's place. I have got all these boring groceries to get home yet, and I still have a house to get in order. It's the best I can offer, so how does ten thirty sound?'

Matt looked at the whisky bottle. Risky. Very risky. He wouldn't have a leg to stand on if he got stopped by traffic. These days they liked nothing more than to nab one of their own, and the more brass the better. He looked around the quiet room. The shadows in the corners called to him. Echoes from the past desperate to make themselves known. 'Perfect. See you then.'

* * *

For some reason, their lovemaking seemed to have moved up to another level. Matt flopped down beside her, gasping for breath.

Liz eased herself up onto one elbow and looked down at him. '*That*, I have to tell you, was incredible!' The breast, that gently brushed his own chest as she did so, looked like soft white silk in the subdued lamp light.

He swallowed, then smiled at her. 'Do I get a gold star?'

'You get the freedom of the city for a performance like that!'

'Really? You mean I can access all areas? Come and go as I please?' He grinned and pulled her down onto him.

'God! Man! Surely you don't want more?'

He raised an eyebrow, then planted a quick kiss full on her lips before whispering in her ear. 'Do you need a moment to revive yourself? Don't tell me you can't stand the pace? Because,' he flicked his tongue backwards and forwards across her earlobe, 'I've had this wonderful idea! And seeing how flexible you are tonight, perhaps you'd like me to . . .' He nuzzled in close to her ear and whispered the last few words.

She groaned aloud. 'You have to be joking!'

He whispered a few more words of encouragement, and in quite a short time, all things considered, he managed to prove to her that he was deadly serious.

* * *

At around two in the morning, Ted carefully climbed down from the attic space of the deserted schoolhouse. It had taken several months to select the perfect spot. The one that gave a clear view into the window of the second floor room at the Waggoner's Rest Hotel. They were always careful to pull the main curtains in the bedroom, but for some reason they never considered the side window in the dressing room, or to be more exact, the peculiar angle of the full-length mirror that covered half the wall. He was thrilled that he had picked this particular night to try out his new toy; a very special camera. The thought that he had managed to capture on film, the show that he had just witnessed, made him shudder. If those sizzling shots were half as good as he believed they would be, they could be used not only for blackmail, but to bring some heat to his own lonely nights.

He edged down the dangerously tilting staircase, then silently slipped across the dust and debris covered hall, and out into the night. One thing for certain, *he* didn't know any women who would put out like that. A heat raged through him every time he thought about the gyrating rhythm of the woman's hips as she rode that lucky bastard of a detective. In the damp, dark place that was the derelict school storeroom, he had almost felt the squeezing and releasing, the stroking and the caressing, and he wanted some for himself.

Luckily the night was cold as he moved across the potholed, concrete playground and it helped to cool his ardour somewhat. Like a wraith, he drifted between the bushes and overgrown shrubbery, to the wire that surrounded the site. With a sigh of longing, he ducked down beneath it and walked out into the fields beyond. It had never been part of the plan, but maybe, just maybe, he could alter the game a little, and find a way to feel that warm flesh for real.

* * *

Jason sat quietly on the edge of his youngest daughter's bed and gently stroked her hair. He wondered how much longer he should sit there. The bad dream was over and the child now slept, but something made him wait until he felt quite sure that the new dreams were happy ones. As he marvelled at the softness of the girl's hair, he allowed his thoughts to wander to the murder case, and perhaps more to his DCI's long-term obsession with it. It was weird. Matt Ballard was something of an enigma. A bloody good detective, there was no doubting that, but as a man . . . Jason pulled a face and stared about the shadowy room. What did he really know about

Ballard? Surely no one could be as completely work-orientated as he appeared? He knew he lived alone out on Tanner's Fen. He knew that he had no brothers or sisters. He also knew his father was dead, and his mother was in some kind of home. Matt had intimated to Jason that there was a long-running and irreconcilable family rift and he saw her only occasionally, on purely obligatory visits. What else? Oh yeah, he loved cooking. And that was where the facts ended and supposition began. Jason didn't like gossip, but he knew there were unsubstantiated rumours about the DCI's past. One concerned some sort of illness, a breakdown or something, but that was way back when he was just a DC. The grapevine said it was most likely due to finding the Matravers boy. Jason shuddered. That kind of thing had been known to push even the toughest copper over the edge, and it sure wasn't the kind of thing that you brought up in polite conversation with your boss. And there was another rumour about a lost love. Well, most people had one or two of those at some point in their lives, it didn't always turn you into a recluse, did it?

He smoothed the child's duvet and told himself that he should leave her to sleep, but he didn't want to go. In a few days' time they would be working every hour God gave, and he had no idea when he'd get another chance to spend some quality time with his kids. And this was quality. Peaceful and calming. A very long way from dealing with the dross of Fenfleet. He moved closer to the child and placed a light kiss on her forehead. He could hardly believe that right now, there was a killer out there. Maybe someone so close that he had walked past him on the streets, maybe someone he already knew, but whatever, someone with a horrible, evil, dark side, and a predilection for vulnerable kids. He swallowed hard and gazed at his daughter, her blonde hair spilling across her pillow. Lord help him, he loved his children so much, he would kill to protect them.

As he moved silently to the door, he considered this idea of killing to protect. He knew that it wasn't just a figure of speech, which in the eyes of the law made him no better than the killer himself.

With a stifled snort, he pulled the door to on the sleeping child. Well, he might be one of the law's loyal and faithful protectors, but if anyone threatened his kids, or his wife, he'd tear them limb from limb, and have the blessing of every good parent on the planet as he did so.

He walked slowly down the stairs and back to where Louise and their eldest daughter were giggling together over some inane reality programme on the TV. The happy sound made his heart beat faster.

CHAPTER TWELVE

Matt immediately saw the report on his desk. The note attached was from Rory Wilkinson, and was a brief overview of the forensic findings inside.

There was little that he didn't know already. The child they'd called Gabriel had suffered for most of his short life, one way or another. He was malnourished and poorly developed. The post-mortem had revealed at least twenty old injuries, all connected to abuse over a considerable period of time. The cause of death was classified as homicidal choking as a result of an obstruction in the airway. A rare occurrence, apparently, but not unheard of. Rory had added a comment to say it was possible, although not probable, that he died accidentally. A sock had been balled up, shoved in his mouth and a gag then taped over it. Perhaps an attempt to keep the boy silent that had gone badly wrong. He'd choked and died. Toxicology would consider considerably longer, but early indications showed that he had been sedated or heavily drugged. Time of death was estimated at approximately eight hours before the discovery of the body. He had certainly been dead when he was taken to the marsh to be used as some sort of gory prop in the killer's sick production. At this point Rory added a few colourful suggestions as to what Matt might like to do to the killer when he caught him, and signed off with a cheery offer to assist, day or night, if he needed help with the aforementioned castration.

'Matt, we need to talk.' The superintendent stood in the doorway, his voice was cloaked with concern.

'Come in, sir. I was just reading the preliminary path report.'

'Mm, I've seen it, and I've just had a call from Rory Wilkinson himself.' The big man pulled up a chair and sat back staring at Matt. 'He believes Gabriel was a town kid, more precisely, a city boy. He has sent off samples to a forensic botanist, a palynologist who specialises in pollen found in human remains. That should provide us with some sort of location or link as to where the boy is from.' He kicked at a worn spot in the carpet. 'Thing is, Matt, I believe he was snatched purely because he will be so hard to trace, not because of who he is. And the reason I think he's been killed,' he paused for effect, 'is connected to you.'

Matt felt sick.

'Frankly there is little doubt that someone is desperate for your attention. We just need to know why.'

'And *who* would be quite helpful too, sir,' said Matt bitterly.

'That goes without saying. Now, I've pulled up a list of villains who have a particular reason to hate you. Sadly, they run into double figures, but I've involved DI Packer, her team are tracing them and checking them out.'

Matt leaned forward with his elbows on the desk and his face in his hands. 'Who would kill an innocent boy, just to get me to sit up and take notice? Jesus Christ! I was bloody well doing that from the moment I saw that first photograph.'

'I know. Maybe he's just making quite sure that we know he means business.'

'But what does he want? And do we really think it's the original killer come back from the dead?'

David Redpath looked thoughtful, then said, 'If we don't get anywhere with Gabriel, we're just going to have to wait until the murderer tells us what he's after.'

'Oh yes! And allow God knows how many other children to die while we all wait.'

'Matt, this isn't your fault. You may be his target, but this is the work of a dangerously sick person.'

'Sorry, sir, but I've obviously done something to seriously piss this madman off. The question is what?"

'And does it *really* have a connection to the Gibbet Fen killings, or is that just a cover, a smokescreen to send us off on a wild goose chase?' The super leaned back. 'This may be a waste of time, but I've also asked DI Packer to get me a list of every man and woman that worked the original case with you. It's a longshot, but someone might remember something useful.'

Matt shrugged. 'I should think that most of them are either well into retirement or dead.'

'Perhaps, but it won't hurt to speak to them, the living ones, that is. And, Matt, I don't really want to ask this, but I'm forced to, considering the severity of the situation.'

Matt looked into the super's dark eyes and wondered what was coming.

'Do you have anyone that you're . . .' he looked mildly embarrassed. 'Uh, that you're particularly close to? You see they may be in danger, too.'

'What? How do you mean?' Matt's thoughts had thrown up only one name: Liz Haynes.

'For God's sake, Matt, you know exactly what I mean! And I was also thinking of your mother.'

A hardness crept into his heart. Matt let out a long, low sigh. 'There's not much left of my mother to threaten, sir. These days she only exists, she doesn't live.'

'She's still in the nursing home?'

'Yes, sir.'

'The killer may not know the extent of her illness. I think we should notify the home, and we should also provide some low-key protection for her.'

'If you think so. I'll get hold of them and explain.'

'Go in person. She's your only family, isn't she?'

Matt nodded. He didn't relish seeing her again.

'Any close mates? Lady friends? Anyone special, I mean?'

'No, sir.' He wondered if that were strictly true. 'You know me. Married to the job.' He wasn't sure if he was imagining it, but he thought that the super had thrown him a very odd look. 'Honestly, sir. My colleagues are closer to me than anyone.' Now, that *was* true, even though one was far closer than the others.

'Well, they should be able to look after themselves and each other, so we'll concentrate on your mother, okay?'

'I'll go now. I'll pass everything over to DI Hammond until I get back.'

'Where is Sergeant Haynes this morning? I haven't seen her.'

'I've allowed her the morning off. Her husband is on a brief and unexpected leave from Iraq. He's flying in,' he glanced at his watch, 'more or less, right now. I know we're up to our eyes here, but under the circumstances, I hope that was in order?'

Redpath nodded and stood up. 'Of course, of course. Ah, the morning post.' He held out a hand and accepted a thick wad of mail from the smiling civilian with the post trolley. 'Nothing nasty, I hope.'

Matt quickly sifted through the pile, then froze. 'I don't know about that, sir.' He pulled on a glove and extracted a familiar envelope. 'I think we have another one.'

'Careful, Matt! This could be the day that he chooses to hurt you! Remember that psycho who sent anthrax through the post a while back?'

'He's not ready for that.' Matt's mouth felt dry, but he was convinced it was just going to be another photo. 'I think he has a lot more taunting to do before we get to that stage.' He looked up. 'If you want to wait outside, sir? Maybe make sure no one else is in the corridor?'

The super glowered at him. 'I'll certainly check the corridor, but if you're going to open that, you do it with me here, understand?'

A moment later, Matt removed the folded sheet of white paper, and slid the photo from its protection. He turned it over and stared at it.

'Very pretty, I'm sure. But what the hell is that supposed to tell us?'

Redpath's voice seemed to come from a very long way away. Matt continued to stare at the landscape photograph, until he realised that he was hardly breathing.

'Matt? What's this all about?'

He found speech difficult and desperately wanted to be alone, to try and make some sense of what he was looking at. But that wasn't going to happen. The super looked like he was about to shake him.

'Matt! For heaven's sake, what the hell is that photo of?'

He slumped back into his chair, took a deep breath and forced himself to speak. 'After I found Jamie Matravers, and after my wife died, I was a mess.'

'Yes, yes. I've read your file, I know about that, but what . . . ?'

'I needed help, and finally I went to the police convalescent home for a while.' He shivered at the memory of sitting in the counselling circle, the Ring of Damaged Minds, as he'd named it, and trying to talk about things. 'I made a good recovery, but afterwards I knew that I'd reached some sort of turning point in my life, so I took a couple of week annual leave and went off on my own to do some serious soul-searching.' He was making a cataclysmic personal crisis sound like something out of a trashy magazine. 'I wasn't sure if I wanted to continue in the force, sir. I needed some time away to evaluate my life.' He stared at the photo, remembered the heat from the dusty road, smelt the crushed wild thyme beneath his feet and the eucalyptus on the air, saw the olive grove that stretched up to where it met the dense packed pine forest on the hills. He remembered the cool azure water of the Aegean Sea lapping around his bare ankles.

'You went to this place in the photo?' The super sounded genuinely surprised.

He nodded mutely. 'I walked that path every day, through the grove and up to that chapel.' He pointed to a small white square with a bell arch on its roof, nestled into the side of the hill. 'I'd recognise it anywhere, sir. It's the Greek island of Karissa.'

'Is this photo yours? Did you take this picture?'

'No, sir. I didn't even take a camera with me, and back then there were no cameras on your phone. And anyway, it wasn't that kind of holiday.'

'And who knew you'd gone there?'

If he'd had the slightest hope that this wasn't deeply personal, then it evaporated at that moment. 'No one, sir. Absolutely no one.'

David Redpath walked around the desk and stared down at the picture, an image so evocative of a path through a Greek olive grove, that Matt knew his boss was almost tasting ouzo.

A big hand gripped his shoulder for a second before releasing it. 'Sorry, Matt, but you're obviously wrong on that score. *Someone* certainly knows where you were back in the early nineties.'

* * *

As Matt tried to come to terms with the fact that his world was shattering, Ted, sweat glistening on his pale skin, was working out with a set of dumbbells. The next part of the game was more physical, and he relished the challenge. The mind stuff was great, but he'd done years of that, now he needed something earthy, something gritty, something real. Not that disposing of his reluctant guest hadn't been, of course. He replaced the coloured weights back in their box and glanced at his watch. Thirty minutes to go. Time for a shower, a change of clothes, and to do this job well, he'd need a complete change of mindset.

* * *

Jason shoved his hand into his pocket and produced a fiver. 'Make mine two jam doughnuts, a Belgian bun, oh, and a sausage roll for later.'

Gemma held out her hand for the note and raised her eyebrows. 'On a diet, guv?'

'Bugger off before they run out of fresh doughnuts.'

Gemma laughed and made towards the door. 'Do you think the boss would like anything?'

'Frankly I wouldn't want to go in to ask, Constable. Him and the super have been shut up in his office for nearly an hour. I dread to think what they're talking about.'

'Little doubt about that, sir. I saw a forensic report get taken in earlier. Bound to be Gabriel.' She shrugged, 'Maybe I'll buy him a chocolate éclair, to cheer him up.'

Gemma pulled on her thick navy police sweater and made her way to the foyer.

Because of her ankle injury she'd managed to evade the boring chore of doing the bun run, but now it was considered good exercise, and as the most junior of the officers on the team it had become a regular morning trip.

Valentino's patisserie was down a narrow cobbled street that led to the river. There was a shortcut through the churchyard of St Benedict's, and then out onto the towpath.

A thin rain began to fall as she approached the church. She strode purposefully up the path between the old, moss-covered gravestones. High above her in the tall tower, a bell began to ring. A tall figure stepped from the shelter of the rear porch, grabbed her arm, wrenched it up behind her back, and pushed her to the ground. The wind was forced from her lungs as she hit the worn concrete of the path. Instinctively, she rolled over and flung out an arm, trying to catch the man's legs. Her hand grasped nothing but air, as he skilfully stepped away from her and swung a vicious kick into her ribs. A searing pain burnt through her, but in desperation she scrambled forward, clutching at a slippery ancient stone cross to help her get to her feet. But then she felt the full force of a foot in the small of her back and she pitched onto her face. She tasted blood on her lips.

'One more move, bitch, and you'll never use your legs again.'

The voice was cold and harsh. This was not someone to mess with, unless you really liked long-term hospital stays. Gemma immediately stopped fighting and sank down beneath the weight of the boot.

'Sensible woman.'

Her leather bag was wrenched from her shoulder. She yelped with pain.

'Shut up!' The man increased the pressure on the back of her ribcage and she fought for breath. She heard him open the bag and there was the sound of him rustling around in it.

'Hey! You! Let her go!' someone shouted.

Instantly the bone-crushing pain stopped and he was gone. Gemma flipped over and saw the dark shape of a man vault over the low wall of the churchyard. Another much younger man chased after him. In seconds, her assailant had outrun his pursuer and disappeared along the towpath, leaving the teenager panting and clutching at his side.

Gemma grabbed at her radio and took a breath, wincing with pain. The bastard! She hoped he hadn't broken her ribs. She flipped the channel open and coughed, spitting blood onto her hand. She wasn't sure whether it was through anger or injury, but she could hardly speak. She managed to whisper, 'Priority. Assistance required. St Benedict's church. Assailant made off towards river.' She coughed again. 'Only description, male, wearing dark clothing.'

* * *

In the A&E Department of St Anne's Hospital, Matthew and Jason waited outside the cubicle.

'This poor kid has taken more knocks in the last few months than Tyson Fury,' Jason said quietly.

'You can say that again.' Matt frowned. 'I wonder what the hell provoked this attack?'

The flowered curtain was pulled back and the doctor emerged. 'You can go in now, Chief Inspector. Looks like she was lucky this time. No broken bones, but a lot of nasty bruising. She'll be very sore for some time. We are just going to arrange some pain relief and let the shock subside, then all being well, we'll discharge her.'

Gemma looked at them with an expression of pain, frustration and anger. 'Sorry, boss, I screwed up. I should have stopped him but, I was miles away. I've walked that route a hundred times, I never dreamed . . .'

'For heaven's sake, it could happen to anyone. Are you up to talking about it?'

The policewoman nodded miserably. 'Not that my description is going to be much help, the bastard made sure I never got a good look at him, no matter how hard I tried.'

'Impression, then? Height, build, age, you know the sort of thing.'

'Not a kid, most definitely. He was too strong, too,' she paused, 'too ruthless. Not desperate like a crackhead, but more calculated, controlled. He seemed taller than me, and he was wearing black tracksuit trousers and, I think, a black zippered jacket.' She lightly touched her ribs and winced. 'And I'm pretty sure he wore gloves.'

'Did he speak to you?'

'Yes. Cold, emotionless voice. Volunteered to permanently disable me. I believed him.'

'Accent?'

'Local.'

'Anything else stand out? Anything odd?'

Gemma thought for a moment then said, 'Yes. He smelt good. You know, fresh, like he'd just showered.'

Jason's jaw dropped. 'How many scumbags do you know who have a nice bath and scrub their armpits before mugging someone?'

'Not too many. Anything else?'

'He was pretty fit. I don't know how old he was, but he went over that wall like an Olympic hurdler.'

Matt sat down on the end of Gemma's bed. 'So, did he take anything?'

For a moment the policewoman looked blank. 'I guess he just nicked my bag.'

Jason looked under the trolley, 'No, he didn't, it's here. Did he open it?'

Gemma's face clouded, 'Yes, I think so. But he grabbed it from me, look.' She moved her gown down across her shoulder and revealed an angry red welt where the strap had forced the material of her uniform into her skin. 'I thought he'd taken it with him. I mean, unless he was just a cop-hater, surely that's what he wanted?' She looked confused, 'I suppose he dropped it and the ambulance crew picked it up.'

'Check it, Jason, see if he took anything. Then get it to forensics, although if he wore gloves . . .' He left the sentence unfinished.

The DI carefully took the bag. Matt stared at Gemma. She was pale and bruised. Her bottom lip was split and swollen and there were signs of a large discolouration across her cheekbone. He hated to think what her chest and rib cage looked like. For a moment he was consumed by a deep feeling of compassion for the girl. Something about her vulnerability, laying on the hospital trolley, no uniform to hide behind and no asp at the ready, she looked so different from the usual stroppy and outspoken woman they worked with. 'Would you like us to phone anyone for you?

'No thanks, sir, I don't want to worry Mum and Dad.' She lightly touched her cheekbone with a fingertip, then winced, 'Although I'd better give my boyfriend a ring, let him know what's happened. If he hears second-hand, he'll freak out.'

'I'll do it, if you like?'

'Sorry, boss,' Jason interrupted. The voice was ten degrees below its usual gloomy level. 'It was no mugging, and he wasn't stealing anything. He was delivering something.'

He held out an envelope addressed to DCI Matthew Ballard.

* * *

'Lexie! Stop staring. He'll see you!' Amy Hammond tugged on her friend's sleeve and tried to pull her away.

'I want him to see me. He's really lush, isn't he?' Lexie smoothed her uniform skirt and looked unashamedly at the boy who was unloading a delivery of soft drinks to the café.

'You are such a tart! Your mum would kill you if she saw you. Now, *please* hurry up, the bus will be here any minute. Miss Cairns will put us on detention if we're late again.'

'That old bag! She's really got it in for us, hasn't she?' Lexie looked sadly at the boy as he climbed back in the van without even glancing at her. 'Cross-eyed old witch.'

Amy tried not to smile. 'She's not that bad really, and we were . . .' she faltered, and stared up at the man who had appeared immediately in front of her.

'Amy? Please, don't be alarmed.' He looked around swiftly then pulled a wallet from his inside pocket. 'Here's my ID. I'm a police officer and I work with your dad.'

Amy's mouth had gone dry. Dad had said never to accept anything on face value and never go with a stranger, no matter what they told her.

The man smiled at her. 'And don't panic, I tell my daughter exactly the same as your father tells you, I promise.'

She looked at the silver, blue and red emblem. The warrant card was for real, she was sure of that. She'd seen her father's often enough. Still, no way was she going anywhere with this weirdo. She edged closer to Lexie and slipped her arm through her friend's. 'What do you want?'

The man looked around again. 'Has your father explained what surveillance is?'

Amy almost snorted in disgust. 'Of course.'

'Well, I've got a problem. I need to get something to your dad, and I daren't blow my cover. That's all I want, just for you to pass something on, okay?'

'Ever heard of a mobile phone?' Lexie said disdainfully.

'I would, but it's not a message. It's this.' He held out a brown envelope to Amy. 'That's all.'

Amy was wavering. He looked pretty harmless. And he wasn't asking them to get into a car or anything dumb like that. 'What's your name?'

'Edward. He'll know what it's about, I promise you.'

Amy glanced up and over his shoulder she could see the bus slowly moving towards them. She really didn't want to miss it.

'Look why don't you ring your dad and check it with him? I know you have the cell phone he bought you, the one you use to ring him or your mum if you're late or anything.'

He paused and grinned at her. He didn't look like a perv, and he had a very reassuring smile as he said, 'Same goes for your sisters, Samantha and Faith. They have one too, your dad said it's a safety thing.'

The bus edged closer. The prospect of detention clouded her judgement. He had to be a friend of her dad, after all how else would he know so much about her family. Amy held out her hand. 'Okay. But what do I tell him?'

'No message. Just ring him as soon as you can. It's a very important case, he'll know all about it.'

CHAPTER THIRTEEN

Jason tried to stop his hands shaking as he climbed back into the car. 'Sorry, sir, but going after you is one thing, going after my children is a different fucking ballgame altogether.' He dropped his phone on the floor and scrabbled around trying to find it. 'Jesus! I've got to get hold of Louise. I've got to get them all out of here!'

Matt had never seen his inspector so animated.

'He knew their names! He knew my children's names! All of them!' He found his phone and jabbed at the keypad. 'The bastard even knew the exact bus that Amy takes every Wednesday. Oh dear God, Louise! Answer the bloody phone!'

Matt eased the car into top gear. 'Easy, Jason. Come on. You know that Amy's safe with your parents. You've contacted both Samantha and Faith at school. They are being looked after until we pick them up. You said yourself that Louise was treating herself to a pampering session with her friend. She's probably chilling out under a seaweed blanket or something.' It scared Matt as to just how calm his voice could sound when inside he was panicking along with Jason.

'I know, I know.' Jason drew in a long, deep intake of breath. 'Oh God, I'm sorry. I didn't mean it when I said that he could go after you. It's just realising that someone is actually watching your family, and not just anyone — a fucking murdering psycho watching your family! And in the guise of a copper too!' He sat back, swallowing hard. 'I'm not sure if I can go on with this case, Matt.'

'Don't try to make decisions right now. Let's just gather up your kids and get them somewhere safe. Then we'll find Louise and decide where to go from there, okay?' A selfish fear flooded through him. He couldn't lose Jason from the team. Not now.

'Yeah, yeah, I know you're right. It's just the thought of him being that close to my little girl, it makes me want to vomit.'

Relief replaced the fear. 'I'm with you there, Jace, but you have to hand it to your Amy. Cool as a cucumber, and she's given us one hell of a good description of him, hasn't she?'

Jason began to relax. 'As good as any eleven-year-old, I guess. I'm not too sure about the bit that went, "He was really old, Dad. Like you."'

'Okay, so the age may be a bit iffy, but between Amy and her friend Lexie, they certainly got the clothes taped.'

'They're kids, they notice the really important things in life.'

'Like black-and-red Air Max 360 sports shoes at £119 a pair?'

'Exactly.'

Matt dropped a gear, overtook a slow-moving tractor, then accelerated hard. He was glad he was driving. Concentrating on the road dulled the memories that kept stabbing at his mind. The call about Jason's daughter had come in just as they were opening the new envelope pushed into Gemma's bag. The envelope that contained another moment of his life. A second photograph from Greece.

As the car flew past vast fields of green crops, and Jason tried again to contact his wife, Matt saw the picture in his mind. More felt it than saw it. It wasn't just a view, although the misty hills and trees did form a panoramic backdrop to the shady courtyard in front of the chapel. It was taken from some distance, a study of two men. One young, European, maybe in his twenties, and one considerably older, undoubtedly Greek, wearing a straw hat that partially obscured his face. They sat on a low white painted wall and were deep in conversation. It was a picture of Matt and the man who had become his mentor on that idyllic island. A man he'd never met before and never seen since, but someone who'd changed Matt's life. Someone whose wisdom and clarity had helped to bring that young Matt Ballard back from a very dark place indeed. He remembered the reassuring tones of the man's voice, and felt his own anguish. The place, the chapel, the island itself, had been special, very special. A secret place where he still went in his head when things got tricky. Somewhere he'd never told anyone else about.

He eased off the accelerator. They were almost at Faith's school, and he needed to pull himself together. But that photograph had hurt him. The island, the peace and tranquillity, the healing process, had been violated — corrupted. Someone had been there, watching him. Watching his pain. Now, as he pulled between the school gates, he felt a little of that old agony returning, and along with it, a slow-growing tendril of hate forming.

'Over there, sir. Park right outside the entrance, then we can get Faith straight into the car.'

As Matt pulled on the handbrake, Jason was already out of the car and running. He watched him throw open the big doors and dash inside. Matt wondered just what it must be like to have children, and have them threatened.

He shut the car door, following his colleague into the building. He thought about the kind of game the killer was playing with them. Amy's envelope had contained the same folded sheet of white paper, and nothing else. No photo. No message. Nothing. Maybe the simple act of placing the item in the child's hand was enough. It had certainly got to Jason.

* * *

'Yes, sir. We have all three children and Louise Hammond has been contacted,' Matt said.

The crackly voice on the other end of the line barked an order.

'Okay, sir. On our way.'

Jason sat in the back. A man desperate for three arms, but forced to hold the two smaller girls in one, all-enveloping, bear hug. 'Was that the super?'

'He wants us all in for a briefing. Uniform are collecting Louise. Special arrangements have been made for your family.'

A small war broke out on the back seat as he tried to explain. But it seemed that they couldn't leave Fluffy Cat. They wanted their stuff. Clothes! Shoes! Make-up!

Matt eased the car out into the main road, feeling a deep respect for Jason. In a matter of minutes, the exhausted detective had calmed, reasoned with and cajoled his dissenting offspring into near silence.

'Impressive. Ever considered a post with the UN?'

'Well, it couldn't be more harrowing than the one I've got right now, could it?'

Matt glanced into the rear mirror and saw Jason's dark, sunken eyes and furrowed brow. The killer's move had been a smart one. Until today, DI Hammond had been completely and professionally focused on the enquiry. Now he was consumed by fear for his family's safety. What better way to disrupt the investigation?

He felt a tingle of fear. Was this the plan? Take away his army, one by one? Gemma had already been attacked and hurt, and now his number one man's emotions had been turned to high-voltage porridge. So who would be next? Bryn? Liz? Without making it too obvious to his passengers, Matt pushed his foot gently down on the accelerator.

CHAPTER FOURTEEN

Two down, one to go. Ted was flying. It would have been easy to get carried away with his success, but he was controlled enough to know that this was not the moment to congratulate himself. Sure, the scenario with Miss Fuzz had been pretty successful, and he could only imagine what DI Hammond was going through right now. He smiled bitterly, and hoped whatever it was, it was truly terrible.

Now, onto stage three. He checked his watch, then counted backwards, calculating pace, running time and distance. With a deep breath, he zipped up the tracksuit top, looked out across the long marsh path, and began his run.

It took fifteen minutes at a steady pace to reach the lane to the lake. As he expected it was empty. To his right, the endless salt marsh stretched out and disappeared into a grey misty horizon. To his left, one or two scattered dwellings were visible across the fields. A lonely place, but a few people still lived here. Ted gave another swift glance to his watch, then sat down carefully on a low wall that edged a reed-choked dyke, and removed one of his trainers. 'Fifteen, fourteen, thirteen . . .'

'You alright, mister?'

Oh perfect, perfect timing, young man! Ted looked up and blinked at the boy. 'Sorry. Didn't see you there. Yeah, I'm fine.' He rubbed at his foot and winced. 'Stone in my shoe, damned great blister. Must have made me miss my stride. I've twisted my ankle a bit. Still, nothing to worry about.' He grinned up at the boy, and saw a scruffy child with a messy haircut and a face that sported more spots than areas of clear skin.

'They 360s?' The boy was staring at his trainers.

'Yep, but I wouldn't rate them. Not if this blister is anything to go by.'

'I'm gonna get a pair of those one day.'

'Why? Do you like getting blisters?'

'Don't care. Shoes like those say something about you.'

Maybe, but not what you think, child. 'Right now all they are saying is bin me!'

Ted looked at them as if they were rubbish, then looked back at the boy. 'Tell you what, I've got an idea. Are you strong enough to support me?'

The boy frowned. 'How do you mean?'

Ted pulled a face. 'I reckon this ankle is worse than I thought. My van is about a hundred yards along the lane, near that disused barn.' He pointed ahead of them. 'If I can lean on you, just as far as the van, the trainers are yours, free gratis. What do you say? Are you tough enough?'

A look of pure disbelief crossed the boy's face. It didn't seem to matter whether they were his size or not — he didn't even ask. Possession was everything. 'No sweat.' He stuck out a hand and allowed Ted to haul himself up to lean on the scrawny shoulder. 'You rich or something? That tracksuit top is Lacoste.'

'Not rich, just got good taste, and the deal is for the trainers, not my whole wardrobe, okay?'

'Oh, it's a deal, mister.' He braced himself to take the weight and together they moved off down the path.

'Just finished school?' asked Ted.

'Nah, I do a few errands every Wednesday. One of the old ducks who lives out here can't get about much. I drops her shopping off for her.'

Oh I know, my boy, I know. 'So won't she be waiting for you?'

'Already done it. I'm on my way home now.'

I know that too, but something tells me that you are going to be late, very late.

'Sorry to hold you up, the van's just there.'

'No sweat. No one's home till late, not that they'd miss me if they weren't.'

Perfect. With a theatrical sigh, Ted leaned against the side of the vehicle. 'Phew! I reckon you've earned these.' He eased the shoes from his feet and handed them to the boy. It was like handing over gold, incense and myrrh. The small hands that reached out almost shook with pleasure.

'Just hold on while I find my driving shoes, will you? Can't drive home in bare feet, can I?'

The boy muttered a reply but never took his eyes from the Nike Air Max logo.

Ted opened the back door and reached inside. 'Damn! Sorry, mate. Can you just get these out for me? This ankle's really giving me gyp.'

The boy looked in the back door, located the pair of loafers lying just out of reach, and leaned forward.

Ted moved with him, only faster. He plunged a thumb into a spot just below the boy's skull, and pressed hard. The boy went limp and pitched forward onto the metal floor of the van.

He had plenty of time before the boy woke up, but Ted was thorough. He clambered into the old van and secured the small arms and legs with rope, then placed a length of duct tape over the boy's mouth. He wasn't too worried if the child suffocated on the journey home, but he preferred to choose the moment. Because this time it was Ted calling the shots, and he liked it that way.

It took over twenty-five minutes to reach his temporary home, but that was fine, it was never worth dirtying your own doorstep. Ted parked carefully, with the back door only inches from the entrance to the utility room. He slipped from the driver's seat and looked around. The air smelt salty and fresh. He listened. The only sound he heard was birdsong and the whisper of a breeze moving through the rushes. Far away, he picked out the grumbling sound of a tractor, but the way the wind carried sound out here, it might have been five miles away for all he knew. He took one more glance across the vast expanse of farmland to the river, took a key from his pocket and unlocked the utility room door.

The boy was surprisingly heavy. Something of a shock, after the last one. Ted gave a little laugh. That one had been like a sack of feathers. This one was more like a sack of potatoes. He dragged him from the van and dropped him onto the quarry tiled floor. Still unconscious, the boy was dead weight, but at least that meant he wouldn't be putting up a fight. Ted grabbed one of the child's wrists and hauled him out into a narrow passage that led to the annexe.

'Your bed awaits, young man. I do hope you'll be comfortable for your short stay here.' He kicked open the door and revealed the bare room. Bare, except for a low metal-framed bed and a small wooden chest. Leaving the boy on the floor, he walked the few steps to the window and carefully checked that the blinds were secured. That done, he unlocked the chest and took out a syringe and a single ampoule. He checked the dosage, then pushed up the boy's sleeve. He needed the child to stay unconscious. He had some serious work to do, and a carefully planned schedule to adhere to. After emptying the drug into the child's arm, he grasped the boy around the waist and pulled him onto the bed. He placed a thin pillow under the floppy head, then secured a series of thick leather restraints to both his arms and his legs. Just before he left, he placed the red-and-black trainers, one either side of the boy's pillow. 'Greed is a bad thing, young man, and although I know it's far too late for you to start learning lessons about life, it's something maybe you should think about while you still have the time.'

He placed the empty syringe and the broken ampoule back in the cupboard, closed the door and locked it. He checked the restraints and the duct tape, then pleased that all was as it should be, closed the door and made his way back to the van.

The property had a big garage cum workshop, one of the many reasons that he'd chosen to lease this particular place. He reversed the van in and turned off the engine. He sat in the gloom for a moment and took several deep breaths. Timing. He looked at his watch. Fine. Right, down to business. He jumped out, went to the back and took out the jack.

It took him thirty minutes to change all the tyres, including the spare. The ones that he replaced them with were the originals, the ones he had used for the abduction were an odd foreign make, easily identified. He grinned as he threw them into the back of the van. He had arranged the perfect place to dump them. All he needed were a few props. He went to the back of the garage and selected an umbrella, a collapsible chair and a large green nylon bag of fishing gear. Perfect. He placed them in the van with the tyres and wiped his hands on a cloth. He now had choices. Go now and get it over with, or wait for the evening. He stretched. No time like the present.

A fifteen minute drive along one of the fen's many long, straight, hellishly boring droves, brought him to a small private fishing lake surrounded by scrubby bushes and wind-stunted trees. His permit was in his pocket if old man Butler was around, although he rarely was.

He bumped his way along the track that circled the lake, looking for anyone else around. Luck was with him again. Other than one teenager sitting on a ramshackle wooden jetty, headphones in ears and a blank expression, the place was deserted. Which meant that his carefully pre-selected spot would be free. He eased the vehicle into a gap between two elder bushes and got out. Behind him was a rusting chain-link fence that separated him from old man Butler's main money-spinner. A small scrapyard.

Whistling happily, he opened the back doors and took out his fishing tackle. He set up the chair and landing net, giving the only other person on the lake a friendly wave. The lad raised a gloved hand unenthusiastically and went back to his music and gazing into the depths. Ted nodded to himself. Excellent. Now he had to be quick, and quiet.

On his previous visit, he had released a large square of the old wire from its fixings, pulled it up, then folded it back again to appear untouched. He moved silently to the back of the van and ripped back the wire. One by one he fed the tyres through the gap and into the junkyard beyond. Lastly he slipped through after them, and rolled them over to the back of a small mountain of rubber tyres. Weeds grew through the untidy and precarious pile, and it was plain that they had sat here undisturbed for a very long time. He swiftly covered them with some older, mouldering hunks of rubber, then slipped back through the fence. Before he secured it again, he took some more equipment to his lakeside spot, baited up his line and cast it out into the water. Leaving the rod on a stand, he went back and closed the hole in the fence. The whole job had taken less than ten minutes.

He sank down onto his chair and gazed across the still waters of the lake. He breathed out, long and slow. One hour here. One hour of complete relaxation. Then back to work.

If anyone had noticed him, they might have envied him. He sat quietly staring into the cold water, a small contented smile on his face. At peace with the world. And he might have been, had his mind not been in such a dark and dangerous place. A place no one would ever want to go.

CHAPTER FIFTEEN

Matt's return to the station had been a gruelling exercise in self-control. The last thing he wanted to do was convey his immediate fears to the others, but his relief at finding both Liz and Bryn working at their desks, required all his acting skills. He had then briefed the super on everything that had happened, and his senior officer had immediately put official wheels into motion.

After an emotional goodbye, Jason's family had been spirited away. Matt had watched with admiration as his second-in-command took a deep breath, drew himself up, and strode back into the murder room.

Gemma had shown up as well, bruised and obviously in pain, she had blankly refused time off and pitched straight back in.

Now Matt allowed himself to breathe again. He sank down into his chair, gratefully accepted the coffee that Liz handed him, and found that miraculously, he was more or less back to full strength.

'So what have we got, boss?' Bryn's impatience was barely in control.

'A description, courtesy of young Amy Hammond and her friend, Lexie, backed up by the witness who chased off Gemma's attacker. They are certainly the same man, only this time he was impersonating a police officer, and referred to himself as Edward.'

'He's stretching himself a bit, isn't he? How long between giving Gemma here a good kicking to locating Amy?' Liz was writing figures on a pad. 'An hour, maybe an hour and a half?'

'He's organised, that's for sure.' Matt looked at his notes and continued. 'So, what we have is, white male, approx five ten, well-built and athletic, greying hair, a tash and a close-cut beard. Age, we can't even hazard a guess. Amy thinks he's like her dad, Gemma thinks around forty-ish, and the witness who gave chase wasn't sure at all.'

'Grey hair? Surely he's older?' asked Jason.

'Really fit? Maybe younger?' said Bryn.

'*I* was grey at thirty,' Matt threw in, and shrugged, trying not to look at Liz. 'And I'm still pretty fit.'

He felt Gemma's eyes bore into him. 'So it's just possible it's Paul Underhill? You were almost the same age, weren't you?'

He took a deep breath. 'I believe we were. But . . .'

'Then I think we should find out, once and for all. We have enough of his things still in the evidence boxes, we can certainly get DNA samples from something, then we should arrange to dig him up and—'

Matt held up his hand, 'Whoa! Gemma, hold it right there. Have you any idea of the complexities involved in an exhumation?'

Jason looked at him with interest. 'Frankly, boss, she may have a point.'

'Oh, come on, you guys. Why him? Why now?'

'Why not?' asked Bryn.

This was going all wrong. 'Let's think about this logically. The photos that he's sent us, the later ones, they are all pertaining to *me*.' He paused, this was not somewhere he wanted to go. He really wasn't ready to share everything yet. 'They refer to things in my past life.

But why me? I wasn't in charge. I hardly even knew Underhill. Well, not enough for him to come after me alone.'

Liz looked at him thoughtfully. 'Maybe it's not you as a person. You are the last serving officer, so who else can he vent his spleen on? Maybe you represent the whole enquiry.'

'Yes, you may have got just close enough to stop him doing what he enjoyed best.'

'But why leave it all this time?' Matt felt exasperated with them.

Jason raised his eyebrows. 'What is it they say? Revenge is a dish best served cold?'

'Yeah, but not fucking freezing. It's been decades!'

'Have you considered that he may have been banged up doing time for something else? Plenty of time on his hands to plot and plan. Festering in a cell would be a good place for that, I'd say.' Gemma sat up straight, then clutched at her ribs and groaned. 'Whoever he is, I'd like to meet him again, on my terms.'

There was a silence, then Jason said, 'That could answer a lot. Maybe we should check on who has recently been released from a long prison sentence?'

Matt took a deep breath. He needed to move them on. Fighting them was getting him nowhere, and the thought of someone hatching a complex plot while banged up was a distinct possibility. 'Yes, you're right. That is definitely a line to follow. And,' he looked at Gemma, 'if you want to consider that our present day stalker may be Underhill, why not run a computer comparison check with the witness descriptions and the photo from Underhill's file? I know it's not going to be perfect, but the techies' computer graphics ageing process could, at least, give you a maybe. If there's a close match,' he raised his eyebrows, 'then I might consider that exhumation request.' He drew in a deep breath. 'The truth is, my recollection of Underhill's face is hazy. You can see from his file that he wasn't a man who had distinctive features, and as I said before, although I was acutely aware of the carnage he caused, I had very little to do with him personally. Plus, he was interviewed but never arrested as he had an alibi for each of the murders. Hence only one rather poor mugshot.'

Gemma made to speak, but Matt held up his hand to silence her. 'Right now, my biggest worry is you guys.' He looked at each of them in turn. 'It certainly won't have escaped your notice that three of us have been targeted in one way or another. If he's trying to attack the whole unit, then it doesn't take Einstein to work out that that leaves Liz and Bryn, and considering what has just happened to Jason, those closest to them.'

'Just let the fucker try,' Bryn said.

'Well, that's the problem, isn't it? We have to assume that he may, and for all your posturing, Bryn, you'll never make front row for the Scarlets.' With a half-smile he added, 'And as Liz won't either, we have to try to protect you as best we can. All of you.' Matt felt a sudden tiredness. Responsibility was weighing heavy on his shoulders and he dearly wished he could magic them all away to a safe place, a safe place miles away from the fens.

He looked up. Liz was staring at him, her expression unusually grave.

'I hope you're not going to suggest we drop this case, sir? Threats or no threats, I for one am in this to the bitter end.'

'Me, too, boss.' Jason's pale face took on a determined look. 'He's parted me from my family, and I want them back! Now I know they're safe, I'm going to spend every damn waking hour trying to catch this bastard.'

Gemma nodded vigorously and rubbed her ribcage. 'And I have a grudge to settle.'

'Don't leave me out! I may not make the front row, but I can run as fast as any bloody winger! I'm in, sir. All the way.'

Matt nodded and looked down at his desk, partly to cover his emotions, and partly with sheer relief that they were all still with him. 'Right. Then we need some rules. *No one* moves around on their own or goes off without someone else knowing their exact whereabouts. We check in regularly, and I suggest we set up a series of code words should any of us get into trouble.'

The team nodded in agreement.

'And I suggest we consider your family and home situations carefully. We don't want to be the cause of any innocents getting hurt. So, who has concerns in this area, Gemma? Bryn?'

They spent the next fifteen minutes going through the arrangements for keeping their families and loved ones safe, and at the end Matt decided they could do no more. The only one he really worried about was Liz. She was fine while her husband was at home, but afterwards? He expressed his concerns. 'I'd say come and use my guest room, but as I'm apparently the main target, you'd probably be in more danger with me than on your own.'

'I've got a spare room.' Jason looked across to Liz. 'If you don't mind sharing it with a computer and a few dozen kid's toys?'

'Only if there's a My Little Pony?'

'Sure to be.'

'Then I'll definitely talk to Gary tonight. Thanks for that.' Liz looked back to Matt, 'Now, what about you, guv? Where you live is creepy enough, even without a psychotic killer wandering around. *And* as you seem to be the prime target, perhaps you should join Jason's home for waifs and strays?'

'Oh, why don't we all just camp in the office? Save on petrol,' muttered Jason. 'But she has got a point, boss. Even a hard nut like you shouldn't be alone out on the marsh.'

Matt listened to their half-hearted jokes, but felt the undeniable tension in the room. They were putting up a front for the sake of each other, but beneath the veneer, he knew that they were all frightened.

'Okay, I'll think about it. But right now, let's tie up a few more points, then I suggest you all go sort yourselves and your families out.' *Family! Oh shit! Mother.* He'd rung, but not managed to go in person like he'd promised. *She'll be fine. I'll get there when I can.* He picked up a short list from his desk. 'CCTV? Anything from the churchyard where Gemma was attacked?'

'Nothing, sir. The back of the church doesn't have any coverage.'

'And the street where Jason's girl catches the bus?'

'Uniform are asking the local shops if they can help us.' Bryn frowned. 'The town camera CCTV lens had been conveniently spray-painted, so we've got nothing there. Shall I go and see if they've found anything helpful yet?'

'Yes. And ask them to see if any other cameras picked up who did the spray-painting. Bit too much of a coincidence, wouldn't you say?'

The others murmured their agreement as Bryn left the room.

'Sir?' Gemma lifted her hand. 'Do you think it's really necessary about the safe house? Surely the killer won't have another go at me? He's used me as his mail-delivery girl, don't you think he may have finished with me?'

'Probably, but I can't risk it. This man is playing a complicated game with us, and right now we have no idea what he's going to do next.'

'Then if he's that clever, he'll find me anyway. Apart from taking me off the case and sending me away, which before you suggest it, is *not* an option, he can just follow me when I leave the station, can't he?'

'That's true, sir,' said Jason. 'And as there's safety in numbers, why don't I add Gemma to my guest list along with Liz? After all, the girl's rooms are empty.' He said the last words bitterly.

'What about your boyfriend? Roy, was it?' asked Matt.

'Thinking about that, I don't think he's in danger, do you?' Gemma smiled, 'I said he's no fighter, but he's not a shrinking violet either. Plus his home is in the Caster Fields Private Estate, you can't even drive into the grounds without a pass card.'

'Ooh, very posh!' Liz looked impressed. 'They have better security there than the nick! What is he, for God's sake? A lottery winner or an investment banker?'

Gemma gave a small laugh. 'Nothing so impressive, I'm afraid. He's in advertising.' Her voice dropped. 'Oh yeah, and his family owns the company.'

'Then perhaps, with a fancy pad like that, you should go and stay with him, instead?'

'No.' She left no room for discussion. 'It's really not my kind of place, so I'd rather share My Little Pony with you, Liz, if it's all the same.'

'Lovely! We can hold a gymkhana!'

'Okay, okay, fun over!' Matt looked at Jason, 'If you're sure about that offer, I guess it's probably the best and safest idea. If you think you can put up with these two big kids?'

'It sounds like it'll be home from home,' Jason said, glancing up as Bryn returned. 'And from that expression, it looks like Bryn has got something, sir.'

Bryn hurried in and closed the door. He placed a tape on the desk in front of Matt and said. 'From the bookies, two door along from the bus stop, sir. One ace shot!'

A few moments later they were all looking at a slightly grainy shot of a man earnestly talking to someone who was just out of the picture.

'That's him! I'm sure of it!' Gemma clasped her ribs. 'Same build, same black trousers, probably the same zipper jacket.'

Matt stared at the man. Was this the killer? Was this the man who knew so much about him? He swallowed hard and looked closer. He looked around forty-five or fifty, but no matter how hard he searched the face, he could find nothing familiar. Was it Underhill? He had no idea but as far as he could see, it was a total stranger. 'I want this picture enhanced and printed off. I want to see a close-up.'

Gemma grabbed the tape from the machine. 'I'm onto it now, sir. Fantastic! This will be absolutely perfect once we get a print! I'll get IT to run a computer comparison with Paul Underhill!'

Before Matt could reply, Gemma had gone.

CHAPTER SIXTEEN

The clock in his car showed 9.55p.m. He had done everything he could to protect his team, but as Matt drove across the misty expanse of farmland towards home, he felt ill at ease.

He parked his car and made his way up the path to the front door. The house looked as desolate as he felt, and there was certainly no chance of any company tonight. He slipped the key into the lock, and actually felt a pang of guilt. God, he could be an arsehole sometimes. Liz was safe, and where she belonged. He should feel only thankful for that fact, not selfishly put out by it.

He flicked on the hall light and the warmth of the central heating hit him. Hell, he liked it comfortable, but not like a bloody Kew Gardens hothouse. He walked across to the thermostat and stared at it. The needle was set to maximum. He turned it down and walked into the kitchen.

No point in getting twitchy, old Mrs Cable must have simply knocked it when she dusted.

As usual, there was a note on the table. Today's request was for polish, 'Proper polish this time, Mr Matthew, wax in a tin, not that spray stuff you like to buy, it goes all smeary and don't give a nice shine.' Matt smiled. He saw the familiar cake tin next to the note. He licked his lips, opening the lid to reveal a neat pile of homemade Bakewell tarts. Grabbing one, he nibbled round the edge, then just as he had as a child, bit the red glacé cherry in the centre, before polishing off the rest of the cake.

Even therapy-cooking was out tonight and he felt too tired to heat up one of his freezer meals. A Scotch and the Bakewells were going to be about all he could manage.

Before he poured his drink, he did a quick check of the ground floor of the house. No good organising code words and safety calls, then forgetting to make sure that your daily had locked the back door! Not that she'd ever done that before, bless her.

Finally, with a Bakewell in one hand and the glass of whisky in the other, he went upstairs. Exhausted or not, he needed a shower.

Ten minutes later, he was propped up in bed and sipping the Scotch. Stifling a yawn, he picked up the phone and rang Jason's number.

'Any problems?'

'No, sir. Gemma's tucked up in my Amy's room with a hot cocoa and some painkillers. She managed to get her parents away without too much of a fight. I think seeing her bruises put the fear of God in them. And I've just spoken to Bryn, all's well with him, so I was just about to call Liz.'

'Shall I do that?'

'It's alright. I need to talk to her about when she's going to be moving in here.'

Matt didn't push the point. Speaking to Liz while laying naked in bed might not be one of his brightest moves.

'Okay, well, check in when you wake. Hope you get some rest and try not to worry too much about your family. Good night, Jason.'

He hung up, finished his drink and switched off the light. Tonight there were no voices calling to him from the dark corners of the room. No ghosts trying to draw him into their wispy embraces. There was just one face that lingered behind his closed eyelids, and it was that of a stranger, a man he didn't know. As he drifted into the first stages of sleep, the stranger smiled, and Matt drew the duvet closer around him and shivered.

* * *

Eyes wide open, he lay in the dark room and listened. Something had woken Matt up.

He glanced at the digital display on his clock. Three fifteen. He pushed back the bedclothes, and felt sweat on his body. The room was stuffy and hot, almost unbearable. Matt stiffened. Unless Mrs Cable had taken up all-night dusting, she wasn't to blame this time. And if she wasn't . . . ?

He quietly got out of bed and moved across the room to the chair where his clothes were folded. He slipped on his trousers and a T-shirt. That would have to do for now. Close to the bed, he had placed a heavy iron poker. He had never dreamed that he would ever need to pick it up, but right now, its weight felt good in his hand. With a deep breath, he slipped through the doorway and out onto the landing.

Nothing moved. No footfalls or muted voices. There were no lights on. No torchlight beams sweeping the hall. He crept to the top of the stairs and strained his ears to listen for the slightest sound. He heard the ticking of the mantle clock in the lounge, and nothing else. Could there be some sort of malfunction with the heating regulator? Matt approached the stairs. He knew they creaked, and if anyone was down there, he didn't want to lose the element of surprise. He put one foot close to the wall, then the next foot close to the banister rail side. It took a while, but he managed to avoid all the central areas of the old, noisy treads.

At the bottom, he stood and listened again. Hearing nothing, he lunged at the light switch, flipped it on and shouted, 'Come out! Come out right now, or you're in serious trouble!'

His voice sounded ridiculous. But there was no one else to hear it. Still gripping the poker, he moved swiftly through all the rooms and checked the doors and windows. Nothing had been touched. No intruder.

With a sigh of relief, he began to relax. This was stupid! Really stupid! With a noisy grunt, he went back into the hall to check the thermostat. Once again the needle pointed to high. Matt was no mechanic, but he did know that dials didn't turn themselves. But if he hadn't done it, and the house was shut up tighter than a duck's backside, it had to be some sort of fault.

He flipped the knob backwards and forwards. It didn't feel loose. He settled it once again on low, and stared at it. Was this really worth almost having a heart attack over?

Probably not, but he hated unanswered questions.

Barefoot, he padded through to the kitchen, ran himself a glass of cold water and drank it back noisily. Tomorrow, he'd get a heating engineer in. He had enough real problems to cope with right now, he could do without dysfunctional boilers frightening the shit out of him at three in the morning. He put the glass in the drainer and turned to leave, when something jarred his heightened senses.

Matt froze. Something was not right. But what? Very slowly he looked around the familiar room, then he saw it. Mrs Cable's cake tin.

It still sat in the centre of the pine table, but the lid was half off. Shivers coursed between Matt's shoulder blades and once again his whole body tensed. He inched towards the table and looked at the old tin. He edged around it, trying to see inside, but the gap was too small. He reached out, then stopped. Matt knew he had carefully replaced the lid, just as surely as he knew that Mrs Cable had never touched the heating controls. But the tin was partially open.

With a sharp intake of breath, he almost ran to the other side of the kitchen and grabbed a large cook's knife from the block. He then tore off a length of cling film from the catering roll that stood next to the knives, and hurriedly returned to the table. There could be prints, so holding the film in his fingers, he lifted the lid.

A cry escaped him before he could stop it. *Oh no! Oh please! This isn't happening!*

* * *

'You have absolutely no doubt that this is your wife's ring?'

Although the heating had been fired up to maximum, Matt felt icy cold. Matt shivered as he felt the superintendent's hard grey eyes bore into him, and before answering, he watched the stare return to the innocent-looking tin of homemade cakes. Especially the centre one. Its decorative cherry had been removed from the sweet white icing and replaced by a gold wedding ring.

'No doubt at all, sir.'

'One ring looks much like another, Matt. You could be mistaken.'

'Maggie lost weight . . .' His voice faltered. 'It was when she got really ill. She had it made smaller, but the jeweller made a balls-up with the detail around the edge. I noticed it straight away. It's hers, sir.'

The super took a deep breath. 'And when did you last see this ring, Matt?'

He pulled his sweater closer around him. 'On Maggie's finger. Just before they sealed the coffin.'

CHAPTER SEVENTEEN

The air felt chilly and damp. Matt shivered and zipped up his old Barbour jacket. The sun had not shown itself over the horizon, but the sky was slowly changing from forty shades of grey, to muted pinks, blues and peaches. A late frost still clung to the grass, and Matt could see his single line of footsteps across the shaggy and uncut lawn. He might need a new mower this year. The old one had been his father's, but now it was more antique than utilitarian.

He gazed across the deep, dark furrows of the ploughed fields behind the house, and wondered how he could stand there and consider something as mundane a lawnmower. It actually wasn't too difficult to work out. Anything was better than considering what had just happened.

Two SOCOs were painstakingly checking his house and garden for any trace of his unwanted visitor. He leaned on the rough wood of the fence that divided his property from his neighbour's farm, and sincerely doubted that his clever night stalker would have left any trace evidence. In fact he would have put money on the fact forensics would find nothing of him. Not a print, not a track, not a hair or a hint of anything to point to the identity of the intruder, but there might be evidence to indicate the presence of his lover. He gnawed at his bottom lip. He had almost shit a brick when he first thought about that little gem. Thank God, Mrs Cable had changed the bed linen, and her cleaning techniques might be old-fashioned, but they were thorough. The headboard would have been wiped and polished, door handles rubbed with a clean duster, and after her vigorous scrubbing, the bathroom always sparkled as if it were awaiting a Health and Safety check. He sighed, he could only hope and pray that forensics found nothing other than a few stray hairs, which as most of his team had been out to his home at one time or another, could be explained. Certain other evidence, if discovered, could not.

Matt gazed out across the landscape that he'd known all his life. Today, for the first time that he could remember, Tanner's Fen seemed sinister. In the early-morning light, it was hard to make out where the river met the North Sea and where the sky began. They all seemed to merge into the shimmering silver-grey horizon.

He took a big gulp of cold salty air, but even that seemed tainted. *Whoever is doing this, must really loathe me.* Everything he loved, or had once loved, was being blighted, contaminated by someone's hatred. He felt exposed, and more vulnerable than he would have ever believed.

'Matt.' The superintendent was striding down the mossy path towards him.

He held out a mug of steaming coffee. Matt accepted it gratefully. He felt chilled to the marrow.

'They've almost finished.'

'You don't have to tell me, sir. They've found absolutely nothing.'

The super shrugged. 'No indication of forced entry and nothing suspicious, although they have collected a vanload of samples.'

Oh great! 'All of which will belong to myself or those close to me. Everything he's done so far has been calculated and meticulously planned. He's very clever and ultra-careful.' Matt kicked viciously at an upturned flower pot, sending it crashing across the stone path. He felt dangerously close to breaking point. 'God, if this man's intention is to drive me mad, then he's doing a bloody good job! How did he get that ring, sir? How?'

His senior officer stared out over the fields. 'I don't know, Matthew. Like I don't know how he got those photographs, or why he chose to kill young Gabriel.' His face hardened, 'But we have to find out, don't we?' He turned abruptly. 'And I can't do it without you.' Matt felt a heavy hand on his shoulder. 'Now, listen to me. This is how it is. Normally I'd take you straight off this case, but you are the link between us and the killer, and I'm fully aware that you know more about the old murders than anyone else alive. So you *have* to pull yourself together and work with me. You need to.'

Matt said nothing. Part of him felt dead, incapable of movement or logical thought. Then, just as he believed that his mind was about to become as empty and inaccessible as the grey and inhospitable marshland in front of them, he imagined the face of an old friend: Sergeant Bill Morris. *"I always said we'd get the bastard, Mattie, and it looks like it's down to you now."* For a second he saw the face as clearly as he saw that of Superintendent David Redpath. *"One last favour, Mattie? Get him for me."* The features suddenly faded, like his own warm breath in the winter morning, and Matt heard the words drift across the fields to where the sun was finally rising in the form of a vivid flame-orange ball. *"Get him for me."* Matt blinked.

'What?' The super stared at him, his expression slowly deepening into real concern. 'Matt? Are you alright?'

Matt looked down. Coffee had spilled over the ground from the cup which he held limply in his hand. He jerked it back up and shook his head violently as if to clear it.

'Sorry, sir. I thought, just for a minute . . .' With a steadier hand, he carefully placed the mug on the fence post, then turned and looked the super full in the face. 'I'm okay, sir. Honestly. I'm fine, and you're right, of course we have to get him.'

The hand gripped his shoulder tightly. 'Good man. Now, we need to get back to the station and decide how to proceed. Are you up for that?'

Matt nodded. 'I must get dressed. Then I need to ring the team, to make sure they didn't get any unwanted visitors last night.'

'Already done, Matt. Everyone is safe and accounted for. They'll be waiting for us in the murder room when we get there.'

From the back door of his home, he saw the two white-suited SOCOs waving and pointing towards their van.

'Looks like they're off. Hope they haven't made too much mess.'

They walked back to the farmhouse. 'I don't think the old place will ever feel right again, sir.' He took a deep breath. 'When all this is over, I'm going to gut it. A good friend has already suggested that it needs a makeover, if that's what you call it, and that was before the intruder.'

'Good idea. It's a lovely old property, Matt.' The super looked up at the grey stone walls and tall chimneys. 'But you know you have to move out for a while, don't you?'

It was for the best, he knew that, but right now he couldn't bring himself to say yes.

* * *

Ted woke early to find the pale light of dawn creeping into the room that he was using as his bedroom. He turned over and looked at the clock. Just before seven. Not that it mattered. It had been such a hectic day yesterday followed by a very late night, that he had promised himself a lie-in. He pulled the duvet up under his chin, then turned and punched his pillows into shape before settling back into them. Today would be far less demanding, although there were still several things to do.

He stretched his legs and closed his eyes. He could afford another half hour at least. He needed his sleep to keep himself fit and alert. That was the mistake so many people made. You couldn't work as hard as he did without plenty of rest and good food. When he got up, he would have breakfast, work out for a while, then check the day's schedule.

As if he needed to. It was tattooed on his brain.

He turned on his side and yawned. The programme was progressing very nicely, and there was no reason why it shouldn't continue that way. Even his change to the original plan should slide into place perfectly. As long as he kept his cool. He smiled when he thought about the pleasure that his small deviation would bring him, then the smile faded into an irritated frown. He couldn't deny that this alteration was important to him. It was something he wanted really badly, but he couldn't let it cause a problem and ruin the end game, not after all this time and meticulous planning. It would be nice, very nice, but he wasn't going to jeopardise the final act just for a bit of carnal delight.

He took a very deep breath and the smile returned. For now he would just have to dream about it.

* * *

The morning meeting had taken much longer than usual. There had been a lot to say.

As the superintendent walked back to his office, he wondered about Matt's present state of mind. There was just so much a man could take, and back there on Tanner's

Fen, for one nasty moment, he had thought that Matt was going to lose it.

Apparently, he wasn't the only one concerned.

'Sir? Could I talk to you?' Jason said, looking almost as rattled as David felt. Then he remembered the officer's family had already been threatened by the killer.

'Come in.' David opened the door, stepped inside and indicated for Jason to close it behind him. The relative peace of the room closed around them like a warm security blanket. He sank down in his chair and let out a long, low breath. 'Have a seat, Inspector. This case is becoming something of a nightmare, isn't it?'

Jason nodded and looked around at the dozen or so framed photographs that hung on his wall.

'It all seemed so different when I joined the force.' David glanced at the smiling faces in the pictures. 'It was pretty simple really. The good guys versus the bad guys. Everyone knew exactly where they stood.'

'Surely it wasn't all *Dixon of Dock Green*, though, sir?'

'Of course not. Even Dixon got shot, didn't he?' David smiled. 'But there seemed to be some kind of order, and more respect on all sides.'

'I guess you were able to get on and do your job without things like budgets, human rights and political correctness getting rammed down your throat every waking hour.'

David wondered if he could actually pinpoint the moment when he had stopped being a proper policeman, and become the resources and financial manager that he seemed to have evolved into. This time when he looked up, the pictures offered no help, only a sort of regret about the passing of time, and David forced his thoughts back to the matter in hand.

'What can I do for you, Jason?'

'It's Matt, sir. Sorry, I mean I'm worried about the DCI. At a time like this, he shouldn't be stuck out on that fen, all alone in that old house.'

'I agree, and I've asked him to relocate temporarily.' He threw up his hands in frustration. 'He didn't actually refuse to go, but up to now he's showing no immediate signs of budging.'

'Can't you insist, sir. The team and I believe he's in real danger.'

'And he feels the same about all of you. I think he has the twisted belief that if the killer concentrates on him, then he will leave you guys alone.'

'That's rubbish, sir!'

'Well, I can see where he's coming from, but it's actually not helping at all, and whereas I applaud his loyalty to his team, I don't want him jeopardising himself, or cutting himself off from us and the investigation.' David picked up a thick file from the desk. A file of notes that he had made for the meeting. 'This is confusing stuff, Jason. Someone really has Matt by the balls and is squeezing the life out of him.' He looked at the heading, *Wedding Ring*. 'This last incident is horrible. It's shaken him to the core.'

Jason pulled a face. It held a hint of something like hurt. 'None of us even knew he'd been married, sir. After all the years I've known him, it came as a bit of a shock, I can tell you.'

'Matt's a very private man, Jason. I'm sure he had his reasons for keeping his past under wraps.'

'So it seems. Reading between the lines it looks like he was knocked sideways by the combination of his wife's death and finding the dead boy.'

'Do you know what synergy is?'

'Sounds like the face cream my wife uses.'

David gave a small smile. 'Not exactly. It's when two things come together, and the effect caused is far greater than the sum of the two original parts.'

'Like two plus two equals five?'

'Sort of. I think that's what may have happened to Matt. Maybe, now that all this has blown up, you should talk to him.'

'I will. I just thought perhaps I should let him come to us. When he's ready.'

'If I were you, I wouldn't wait. You need to know the facts, or you're playing a game with a half deck of cards.' David looked Jason in the eyes. 'It's not some personal affront to you, you know. Until this point in time he's never been able to speak of his past, now he'll have to. And he'll need your help, as a colleague and a friend. Matt thinks very highly of you, Jason.'

'Okay, sir. Thank you.' Jason managed to look a little less injured. 'So, what's happening with the ring?'

'It's with forensics at present. They'll be able to define its origins, and at least tell us what type of gold it is, its age and whether it's English. Right now, we have to assume that it's a fake. The alternative, and a theory that worryingly Matt seems to be favouring, is pretty grisly.'

'And that is, sir?'

'Maggie Ballard was buried in Fenfleet Cemetery, and Matt had been insistent that her wedding band be left on her finger.' David exhaled, 'Now, I'm not so naïve as to believe that all last wishes and requests are dealt with honestly, but if the ring had been removed prior to burial, it would have been smartly disposed of some twenty years ago.'

'Dead right. It would be long gone. How could it turn up now?'

'It makes no sense.' He ran a hand though his thinning hair. 'But then little does. Even the thought of entering a policeman's house while he's at home is really chancy. Whoever is stalking Matthew is one hell of a cool character.'

'And very dangerous.'

David agreed, then turned to a new section of his file. 'Any luck with checking the list of officers and colleagues who worked the old case?'

'Mostly dead, sir. Two transferred to other areas. Two or three retired to far-flung places. A couple in warden-controlled homes, and one in a psychiatric hospital. Only three men are still what I'd call 'active.' One runs a small security firm; one has taken a part-time job as a nature warden at a bird reserve further down the coast; and one is a driver for an importing business based near Boston.'

David scanned the list of names, but none were actually known to him. 'Has Matt seen this?'

'Yes, sir. No one stood out as a possible troublemaker, and I've spoken to each man individually. Not one held any form of grudge against Matt, and apart from asking to be remembered to him, they all seemed to have moved on with their new lives outside the force.'

'Well, I've checked this list.' David pointed to a much longer one. 'Offenders. Men and women that Matt has put away. None of *them* sent their best wishes, but so far, no one seems to have either the freedom, the wherewithal or the inclination to take up murder and deception as a way to pay the chief inspector back for their incarceration.'

'Which leaves one nasty supposition, doesn't it, sir? The killer *is* the original Gibbet Fen killer, a cold-blooded child murderer, and he's still out there.'

David felt his heart thud in his chest. This was not a new hypothesis, in fact it echoed his own thinking precisely. 'Mm, maybe he wasn't killed on that lonely marsh road after all. I just pray we're wrong and that he hasn't finally come back for a very special victim. A man he seems determined to torment and torture before he finishes with him. We *have* to stop him, Jason, and quickly.' His words were resolute, but inside, he really wasn't sure how they were going to achieve that result.

* * *

'Come with me, Liz?' Matt asked.

'Surely you aren't serious about this?'

Matt's face was very serious. 'I *have* to make sure.'

Liz sighed and removed her jacket from the back of her chair. 'Okay, but we must tell the team what we're doing.'

'No. We'll be back in half an hour, and we're perfectly safe if we go together.'

'This is madness,' Liz said. 'The lab will have an answer in no time. Why can't you just wait a bit?'

'Sorry. I shouldn't have asked you.' Matt bit his lip. 'Forget it.'

'You'll wait?'

'No. I'm just not asking you to come with me.' He moved towards the door.

'You absolute sod,' she muttered, but she followed him out. 'Well, I'm damn well driving. Keys.' She held out her hand and glared at him.

Trying not to show his relief, he meekly handed them over and they made their way silently out to the car.

* * *

The cemetery was on the outskirts of the town. On one side of the road there was a large car park for the crematorium, on the other, a smaller area for visitors to the graveyard.

It was like other cemeteries. Neat, tidy, well cared for, peaceful, and Matt hated it.

'Do you come here a lot?' Liz asked.

'No.'

'Christmas? Birthday? Anniversary?' Liz looked along the rows of crosses, marble headstones and angelic statues.

Matt found it hard to answer. He felt jittery and just wanted to get to his wife's grave. 'I come when I feel the need. And that is rarely, if I'm honest.'

Liz didn't reply and he felt a pang of guilt. Maybe he should visit more often. Like he should visit his shell of a mother more often. He began to walk faster, trying to leave the unwanted thoughts behind. 'The grave is over there, just past that big holly tree.'

'What, the grave with all the flowers?' Liz sounded mildly puzzled, '*You* may not visit too often, but her family obviously does.'

Matt's mouth felt dry. 'Maggie was Canadian. She has no family here.' He began to run towards her grave. 'Oh my God! Look at it!'

Matt dropped to his knees in front of the marble stone. The whole area had been dug over and tightly planted with dozens of bright flowering pansies. The vase that stood in front of the inscription was filled with white lilies, Maggie's favourite. The flowers that he had laid on her coffin, twenty years ago.

A sob wrenched its way from his throat. *What has he done?* He leant forward and touched the freshly turned soil. *Oh please, don't let him have got to her.* Without thinking he began to dig, to scrabble with bare hands, tearing at the ground like a dog scrabbling for a bone.

'Matt! Stop this! Right now!'

He felt her arms around him, pulling him away from the damp earth.

'Can't you see what he's doing? This is pure theatre! He's messing with your mind.' She placed her hands either side of his face and forced him to look at her. 'Mattie! He hasn't violated this grave, but he wants you to believe he has. If you do, then he's winning. He's using every single one of your weaknesses to get at you, and while you are like this, you aren't doing your job. You are useless. Which means he's in control, not you. Do you really want that?'

Matt stared down at his dirty scratched hands, the uprooted plants and the scattered petals. He felt as if this man had taken every little piece of his life, stripped him bare, and laid it out for everyone to see. 'I don't know what to do.' He knew he sounded pathetic, but that was how he felt.

Liz knelt beside him on the grassy edge to the grave and held him close. He could smell her perfume and, just for a moment, he felt safe. Loved. *Why did my mother never do this?* No answer came to mind.

Without leaving her embrace, he looked around, wondering if they were being watched. He felt almost embarrassed, then he considered that what they were doing would have looked quite natural to a passer-by. People did kneel at gravesides. Whether it was to weed or pray, or comfort the bereaved, it didn't matter.

'I'm so sorry, Liz. I mean, really sorry.' He moved back and sat on the neatly mown grass. 'Everything has been so intense, you know, one thing after another, bang, bang, bang.' He punched a clenched fist into his palm for each word. 'As soon as I get myself together, he's there again with some new torment. I just . . .' Matt threw out his dirty hands in exasperation. 'I don't think I can take much more of this.'

Liz sat down beside him and put a hand on his arm. He was glad of the contact. Right now, she seemed to be his only anchor to sanity.

'Listen, Mattie. You *have* to hang in there. No one else must see you like this, or you know what will happen, don't you?'

'The super will take me off the case. And maybe he should.'

'The super will have you declared mentally unstable, Matt. You won't just be off this case. Think about it.'

He did. His shoulders sank forward and he let his head sink into his hands. 'Then what do we do? Where do we go from here?'

'For starters, we go find Detective Chief Inspector Matthew Ballard. We need some solid detective work done here and he's the best man that I know for that.' She touched his face lightly. 'I know you're in a very bad place right now, Mattie, but you have to find the strength from somewhere. You know that it's your past that holds the key to all this. It's the reason that this lunatic wants you finishing your career as a gibbering wreck instead of a capable, successful and well-respected police officer.' She looked at him sadly. 'We have to get the team together, lay the whole messy package in front of them, and take it from there. They are a loyal bunch, Matt. They really care about you, so tell it like it is, okay? No secrets, no lies, nothing but the truth.'

He straightened up. He heard his dead sergeant's voice. *Get him for me.*

'You're right. I owe it to everyone to get myself together.'

'Bugger everyone else. You owe it to yourself, Matt.'

He stared at the mess all around them. It seemed to reflect his whole life right now. For a moment he gazed at a bright yellow and purple flower. Pansies for thoughts, Maggie had said. She had planted tubs and containers everywhere, all full of the vivid flowers. A sudden anger ripped through him. No one . . . no one had the right to take his beloved memories and use them in such a disgusting way. *Yeah, Liz is absolutely right. I really do have to get a grip on all this. Because catching this psychopath is most definitely down to me.*

With a new determination, he straightened his slumped shoulders and looked at the woman sitting next to him. 'Right, well, I guess I can't leave Maggie's grave in this state, can I?' He leaned forward and began to push the piles of dirt back around the plants.

'Welcome back, chief.' Liz smiled at him, then leaned across and picked up the broken stems of lilies. 'Perhaps we should check the CCTV camera, I saw one as we drove into the car park. Then we should speak to whoever looks after this place. There's bound to be groundsman or a caretaker and this bit of gardening would have taken quite a ti . . .' Her voice trailed off. 'Matt? What's that?' She was pointing to where he was unsuccessfully trying to rub mud from the grave vase.

Oh no, no more, please. A piece of white plastic was protruding from the soil just in front of the vase. He carefully cleared the soil away from it. It was a thick plastic envelope with a zip seal.

'Hold on. Don't touch it.' Liz leaned forward, pulling a protective glove from her pocket. 'I'll get it.'

Matt watched as she unearthed the folder. He didn't have to ask her what it was. He could see the envelope through the semi-opaque plastic.

'Oh, fuck! Shit! Bugger! Balls! What the hell is he doing now?'

Liz's uncharacteristic and almost comical tirade helped to keep him stable. She had been right about having to find a way to hold it together, and he was going to take a hold on his emotions and damn well deal with this. After all, he should be used to it by now. It was just another envelope, one of many.

'I wonder which particular skeleton he's dug out this time?'

'Just how many have you got?' Liz raised her eyebrows and gave a short staccato laugh.

'Too many, apparently.' He held out his hand for the folder, but Liz held it back.

'Whatever this is, we have to deal with it rationally, agreed?'

'Agreed.'

'Good. So shall we get it back to the station? To avoid contamination?'

Matt pulled on a glove. 'The only thing we'll be avoiding is looking inside that envelope. Give it here.'

'In the car, Matt.' She began to walk back towards the car park. 'Not out here. And I suggest we ring Jason and get him to chase up the CCTV right away.'

Matt nodded. He pulled out his phone and rang the nick. By the time Liz was unlocking the door to his Landcruiser, Jason had already got the wheels in motion and a squad car was on its way to check with the cemetery caretaker.

'Can't procrastinate any longer, Sergeant Haynes. Time to open the envelope.'

She passed it to him reluctantly. 'Go ahead. Just don't ask me to get out of the car and hide behind a tombstone.'

Matt slid the photograph from the usual sheet of pristine white paper, and stared at it silently.

'Who is that?' Liz's voice was little more than a whisper.

Matt tried to answer, but his brain failed to compute.

'Mattie? Who is it?'

'Laura.'

'Your old girlfriend? The one who disappeared?'

He nodded mutely and stared at the picture. Laura. Memories flooded back. They had been at a motorcycle rally. It had been sunny and warm. She had turned up at his place in shorts. He'd freaked out and made her wear a pair of his protective leather trousers. She had sulked all day. A friend had taken the picture. Young Matt was smiling, Laura wasn't. It seemed like yesterday.

He gently touched the glossy surface with a gloved fingertip. There she was, sitting on the pillion of his old bike, pouting for England, but he wasn't there. He had been ripped from the picture.

CHAPTER EIGHTEEN

He'd had a pleasant start to the day. It would have been even more enjoyable if not for his new guest, but, there, you couldn't have it all ways.

Ted had hoped to keep the boy conscious, after all, they were in the middle of nowhere. Even the mail had to be collected from the post office, and with the nearest neighbour miles away, he felt pretty safe. However, the child had proved to be extraordinarily vocal, which was irritating when you needed to concentrate, so he was forced to administer a small, but very effective, sedative.

Ted ran a bath. His recent exertions had made him feel less than fresh. The thing he hated most was feeling dirty. As he scrubbed at his body with a soft brush and some sea mineral bath crème, he wondered if he was getting OCD. He smiled and turned the handheld shower to hot. As it cascaded over his face he shuddered with pleasure. Hey-ho! What was one more little idiosyncrasy when you were as screwed up as he was.

Ted lay back in the steaming water and laughed out loud.

* * *

Superintendent David Redpath had allowed Matt the use of the conference room for the special meeting that he'd called. The murder room had seemed inappropriate as he particularly didn't want the talk to take the form of a lecture. He certainly didn't want to stand before his team and spill his guts like some old-style abstinence meeting. It was ironic, but he had chosen the same format that he'd suffered so many years before. The Circle. He still shuddered when he recalled his Ring of Damaged Minds, but he had to agree, it was still the best way to engage with your colleagues. Everyone equally important.

No lies, no secrets, just the truth. Liz had said those words sincerely, but she had no idea exactly what she was asking of him, or how difficult this was going to be.

Matt looked around the empty room. Dark mahogany bookcases, a severe portrait of the Queen and heavy patterned curtains gave the room a chilly formality. It was rarely used and Matt sniffed the canned air. It smelt of polish and dust. Maybe he'd made a mistake choosing it.

He sat down to wait for his team, he decided it was the best he could do. No lies, no secrets, just the truth. He interlocked his fingers and leaned forward, leaning his chin into his hands. No lies? He could do that. The truth? Yes, he was a truthful man. But secrets? Now that was the bummer, wasn't it?

'Guv?' Bryn stuck his head around the door. 'Sorry to barge in, but before the others get here, I've got something from the lab for you.' He placed an enlarged copy of the last picture on the table in front of Matt. 'They've found something.'

Confronted by the blow-up of the beautiful serious face of Laura, Matt couldn't prevent an involuntary gasp, then he looked at where Bryn was holding his index finger. In the right-hand corner of the photo was a tiny string of numbers.

'It's a telephone number, sir.'

Matt stiffened. Had the killer changed tack and finally given them something to go on?

'The lab have checked it out, sir. It was obviously not on the original image. It was added digitally.'

'So it's been put there specifically for us to find?'

'Definitely.'

'And has anyone rung it?'

'Yes, sir.' He passed Matt another sheet of paper with an address on it: 16 Baltimore Street. Sunderland. 'It's a tattoo parlour.'

Instantly, the image of the strange mark on the dead boys sprang to Matt's mind. 'Has anyone spoken to them yet?'

'Only to ascertain that the number was kosher, and to get an address.'

'Okay,' Matt stood up. 'We might have to postpone this meeting. I want someone to go there and talk to them, immediately. In fact, maybe it should be me that goes.'

'Respectfully, boss, might that not be just what the killer wants? It would be safer to let the Northumbrian boys send a few uniforms around to ask the questions.'

Matt flopped back down onto his chair. 'Yeah, yeah, you're right. And we really need to get this meeting done and dusted as soon as possible. Look, ring them and ask for their help. Send a copy of the mark found on each of the three victims of the Gibbet Fen killer, and see what they come up with. I also want to know who owns that place and everything there is to know about it.'

'Yes, boss. I'll be back as soon as I've contacted them.'

As Bryn left, the rest of the team arrived.

'He's in a hurry, isn't he, sir?' Gemma said.

'We've been thrown a scrap from the table of the killer. Sit down and I'll fill you in.'

Jason pulled out a chair. 'The super's on his way down, sir, if you want to wait for him?' He looked at the six chairs around the table. 'It's just us and the superintendent, then?'

'Yes. You guys are the closest to me, and as it has become relevant to the case, it's time that I told you something about my past.' *Oh I'm really looking forward to this.*

The door opened again and Superintendent Redpath came in. 'Don't get up. Matt wants us to keep this informal, and I'm fine with that, so,' he stared at the empty chair, 'who's missing?'

Matt swiftly brought them up to speed on the discovery of the telephone number on the photo.

'Sunderland?' Gemma queried. 'That's way up country, isn't it?'

'Certainly is. Surely it's got to be some kind of red herring? A wild goose chase to throw us off track,' added Jason.

'Well, we're letting the Northern bobbies check it out first,' said Matt. 'As much as I'd like to do it personally, there is a damn good chance he's just trying the old divide and conquer tack. Split the team up, then hit us with some other new disaster.'

'Then the number turns out to be just something he made up, or pulled out of an old telephone book.'

'Maybe, although frankly I doubt it. I think he's too clever to be bothered with anything that doesn't further his plan.' Matt was sure that the number would offer up something, he just wasn't sure what it would be. 'Right. Here's Bryn.' He turned around as the detective entered the room. 'Everything alright?'

'Yes, sir. They'll contact us as soon as they've spoken to the owner.'

'Thank you. Well,' he looked at each face in turn, knowing that he couldn't put it off any longer, 'I guess it's time to bare my soul.'

Matt talked for almost an hour. He told them about Laura, about Maggie, about the difficulties surrounding the original murder investigation, how badly the discovery of Jamie Matravers had affected him, and, in part, about his breakdown. He admitted that he had never been able to let the old case go, and that it had been his intention to continue working on it after he retired. Finally, he told them about the crucifixes. He hadn't planned to, but how could they conduct a thorough enquiry without knowing everything. By the time he finished he felt wrung out, mentally and physically.

'Liz has suggested that the answer to the killer's identity probably lies in my past, and although I have to agree with her, I cannot understand who would want to do this. I cannot pinpoint one individual that hates me enough to kill to get back at me.' He leaned back. 'Now you know the whole story, perhaps you'll be able to be more objective than I can.' He gave them all a weak smile, but his next words were directed at Jason. 'Some people believe that personal and professional lives should never overlap, especially in a job as intense as ours. I've always bought into that theory, one hundred per cent, so I hope that you don't think I've deceived you in any way by never talking about my past. That was never my intention. It has just been incredibly painful for me and I've preferred to be a full-time policeman, rather than a human being with home life and a history. If I've upset you, then I'm truly sorry.'

There was a long silence, then Gemma stood up and began to slowly clap. At first Matt didn't quite understand the gesture, believing that he had made a terrible mistake by being so candid. Then the others stood and joined in, all applauding him, smiles on their faces. Emotion grabbed him and he had to fight hard not to let it overpower him.

'Well done, Matt.' Liz gave him the softest of smiles. 'That couldn't have been easy for you.'

Oh, Liz. If you only knew.

When the team left, the super stayed behind. 'I was surprised that you mentioned the crucifixes.'

Matt sighed. 'I had to, didn't I? It was a member of the old team that was leaking information, and if it's who we suspected, he died of a coronary two years ago. My officers deserve to know the truth. And frankly they need every ounce of help they can get.'

'Then why am I left with the feeling that there's something you're not telling us?'

Matt stared at him open-mouthed. 'Sorry, sir? I've laid my life bare! Every damned detail.'

'Have you, Matt?'

'Yes, sir.'

The superintendent stood up, walked to the door, then turned and looked hard at him. 'Good. I'm only asking because I really believe that any more secrets could prove very dangerous, don't you think?'

'You've read my personal file, sir, and now I've admitted to concealing the crosses, there is nothing else. Nothing.'

As the door closed, and Matt was left alone, he had the overwhelming urge to cry.

He hated his life as it was right now, everything felt completely beyond his control. It seemed that every waking moment was given over to waiting for the killer's next move. The helplessness at being in the hands of someone else was exasperating. He'd had enough of that as a child. *Thank you, Mother dear.*

He walked to the small coffee maker that had been brought in for the meeting, poured himself a strong one then sat back down at the table. He must find a way to get some kind of advantage over his adversary, and to do that he needed to strengthen his own mind. He hated to admit it, even to himself, but the outpouring earlier seemed to have helped. He had no idea why, but he felt less weighed down by the past. He wondered if there was one more thing he should do before he threw himself, body and soul, back into the hunt for the killer.

He screwed up the polystyrene cup and threw it in the bin. Yes, one more cathartic action was required. If it worked, great. If it didn't, sod it, nothing lost.

Checking his pockets for his car keys, he left the room.

* * *

Fifteen minutes into his journey, Matt pulled over and rang Jason. 'Sorry, Jace, I know that I explicitly stated that no one go off alone, but there is something I have to do and it's personal.' He took a deep breath. He was going to the one place that he had never taken anyone else, and never would. 'As soon as I'm through, and that should not be long, I'll ring you, okay?'

'I seem to recall something about no secrets. Or was I imagining that bit?' Jason's gloomy voice had taken on that injured tone again.

'It's not a secret. In fact I'll give you the telephone number of where I'll be. If you haven't heard from me in forty-five minutes, you ring it.' He gave the number without needing to look it up. 'I'll explain when I get back.' He hung up, turned on the ignition and gunned the engine.

Hunter House was only a mile or so away. He had been lucky regarding his choice of specialist nursing home. He had never believed that they would deliver half of what they promised in the glossy brochure, but he had been surprised to find that they managed to be both very efficient and compassionate. Even the ever-present smell of urine was kept to the minimum.

He passed between the high red-brick pillars that stood either side of the heavy gates. Usually the place gave him the same depressing, miserable feeling that he got when he entered a cemetery. In his mind there was little difference anyway, Maggie was dead, and his mother might just as well be, considering the damned good imitation that she was doing. Today, for some reason, he saw the tree-lined walks, the neat lawns and the rows of wooden benches looking over huge beds of brave early spring flowers.

It cost him an arm and a leg to keep her here. It had eaten clean through the inheritance that his father had left him, and now chewed mercilessly into his salary.

He pulled into the car park. He wondered why he'd done it. It certainly wasn't guilt. If anyone should feel guilty, it was the bag of bones lying in that very expensive bed, not her only son.

He went through the double doors into the foyer. Maybe it was a sense of duty, or maybe it was just young Mattie, still trying to prove that he would never be like her, never allow himself to get his own back on the woman who had blighted his life. Because by doing what he was doing, it would hurt her far more. For him to rise above everything that had happened, would mean she had no power over him anymore, and never would have. Which was fine, but as she spent almost ninety-five per cent of the time away with the fairies, he was forced to wonder who he was proving anything to.

A woman's voice dragged him from his introspection. 'DCI Ballard?'

He turned and looked, not without some concealed amusement, at the nursing home manager. 'Mrs Taylor. How are you?' The woman had the oddest hair that Matt had ever seen. It was impossibly dark, almost raven black, with two pure white swathes at each temple. No matter how hard he tried, he always saw her as Fleur, the skunk from Disney's *Bambi*. His mother had been here for almost six years and he still wasn't sure whether the woman's hair was natural or a fashion choice.

'Very well, Chief Inspector.'

'Glad to hear it. I'm sorry I didn't ring ahead, but is it okay to see my mother?'

'Of course, but considering the circumstances that you mentioned on the telephone, we've seen fit to change her room. Actually, my secretary was going to call you this morning. When I saw you come in, I wondered if you were telepathic.' She smiled at him, but he saw badly disguised anxiety in her eyes.

'Is there a problem?'

'Not with the change of room, Chief Inspector. In fact, it's better for us to keep a closer watch on her. It's her condition that's giving concern, it's far from good, I'm afraid.'

It was Matt's turn to offer a wan smile. 'You've done wonders with her, Mrs Taylor. Probably extended her life by years. Whatever happens, you have my sincere admiration for what this home has achieved.'

Audrey Taylor nodded but said, 'I'm never quite sure if extending life, when it is the quality of your mother's, is a good thing or not. Whatever, it's not our call to make, is it?'

'Is she . . . ?' For once, he wasn't sure how to put the question.

'Dying? Yes, I'd say so, although . . .'

'I know. We've been here before, haven't we?'

'I really don't expect a recovery this time.' She shrugged, 'But as you say, she's surprised us before.' She gestured towards the lift. 'I'll take you to her. She's on the first floor, in the room next to the nurse's station.'

'Has she been lucid at all?'

'Hard to say. Ruth said she was rambling again last evening. Seemed quite distressed by something.' The lift doors opened. 'I'll get Ruth herself to tell you about it. It may make sense to you, or . . .' she gave a little shrug.

'Or be the usual mixture of mangled memories from her childhood or some soap she watched ten years ago. At least she's past the self-harming stage.' Matt remembered the claw-like fingers, picking and tearing at the paper thin flesh on the scrawny arms. Even for him, that had been the worst part.

'Yes. Small blessings, Chief Inspector.'

They stepped out onto patterned carpet and moved swiftly down the bright corridor. The long casement windows, although secured for safety, at least let in a lot of light.

The woman held open a door. 'Ruth? Katherine's son is here to see her.'

Matt held back for a moment. He took in the new room. Light, airy, spotless, a good size, not poky or claustrophobic. Ruth, a chunky, smiley woman, his mother's dedicated nurse, looked up as she checked her patient's catheter. One large window allowed shafts of sunlight to fall on a vase full of red roses.

And there he stopped.

'We put the flowers where she could see them if she wakes,' the nurse said.

Matt turned to the manager. 'Where did *they* come from? Who sent them?'

It was Mrs Taylor's turn to look confused. 'Well, you did. They arrived first thing this morning.'

'And who brought them?'

'One of your officers. He said you'd asked him to deliver them.'

'You have security cameras in the foyer, don't you?'

'We have cameras everywhere, Chief Inspector. Half of our residents have Alzheimer's or some form of dementia. Cameras are essential.'

'I have to see who delivered the flowers. Can you show me the tapes?'

If Mrs Taylor was in any way flustered, she never showed it. 'We'll be back shortly, Ruth. Stay with Katherine, don't leave her under any circumstances.'

In her office, Matt paced up and down, dreading what the tape might reveal. He didn't have to wait long.

'This is the early-morning tape. The man arrived at eight forty-six, on foot.'

'No car?'

'No, he must have parked outside in the lane somewhere. He definitely walked in, and I was behind the desk checking the rosters at the time and I watched him walk out.' She fast forwarded, then stopped and jumped frame by frame. 'Here! That's him. He gave his name as Detective Constable Edward Dennis.'

In the freeze-frame, a familiar face stared at the CCTV camera. The grey hair, the close-cut beard, the arrogance of the sly smile. It was the same man who'd accosted Jason's daughter.

'Do you know him?'

'No, sadly I don't. But he knows me very well.' He pulled out his mobile. 'May I use your office for a moment or two, Mrs Taylor? I need to make a call, then I want to go and see my mother.'

She nodded and left the room, leaving him to speak to Jason.

'I've got some evidence bags in the car so I'll bring the roses and the CCTV tape back with me. I doubt the flowers will be of the slightest use, but I'm damned if I'm leaving them at my mother's bedside.'

'Can I get uniform to send someone to stay with her, sir? Just in case he goes back.'

'He won't come back, Jason. He's made his point. And if he did, and his intention was to harm her, he's too late. Nature is taking care of that, as we speak.'

'I'm very sorry, sir.' Jason's voice gave sombre a new dimension.

'Don't be. Just keep a close eye on the team until I get back.'

He hung up and left the office. Time to get a few things off his chest. *Even if you can't hear me, Mother. Things need to be said. Before it's too late.*

She was barely recognisable as the woman who had played such a big part in his life. He tried to superimpose the formidable matriarch with hard features and thick, dark brown hair, over this emaciated wisp of a woman, but he failed. It just wasn't possible.

'She talked a lot last evening. Even when the night staff arrived she was still unsettled.' Ruth handed him a cup of tea.

'Anything coherent?'

'Are you sometimes called Mattie, sir?'

'Sometimes. But usually only by people that care about me.'

Ruth moved across to the window. 'I'm sure it's not my place to comment, sir. But I think she does care.'

He stirred his tea but didn't look up. 'Whatever gives you that misconceived idea?'

'In between the gobbledygook, she kept saying that she needed to talk to you about Ben. She was sorry about Ben. Tell Mattie, she said, over and over.'

Matt flinched. 'Ben? She actually said she was sorry?'

'Repeatedly. And she kept saying the word *bad*, too.'

'In connection with Ben, or me?'

Ruth thought for a moment. 'I got the feeling she was referring to herself, not anyone else.'

Matt forced himself to sip the hot tea. *You are sorry about Ben?*

'Is he someone close to you? This Ben?'

'He was my dog. He'd been my father's before he died.' Matt felt a lump in his throat, felt again the rough brindle coat and saw the huge brown eyes. 'I was late home from school one day. I found that she'd accidentally shut Ben in my room, and he'd peed on the floor. I cleaned it up, but she went berserk. She threw Ben into the back of the car, drove off, and I never saw him again.'

'Oh my! What a horrible thing to do.'

'The pain was a physical thing. I thought I'd never get over it. Ben was my best friend, probably my only friend. But that, Ruth, was typical of my dear mother.'

'Then maybe, last night, she realised that there wouldn't be many more lucid moments and she was trying to apologise.'

'I sincerely doubt it.' He looked at the silent woman, so skinny that she barely made an indentation on the bed covers. 'It's a nice thought, but highly improbable.' He looked across at the nurse. 'I wonder if you'd leave us for a few minutes?'

'Of course, but I'll just be next door if you need me.'

As the door gently closed, he placed his cup on the bedside table, and took his mother's hand in his. It felt like dry leaves, and almost as fragile. 'I had this all worked out, Mum. The farewell speech. But even now you've managed to find a way to send it all to buggery, haven't you? One of the blokes at work, he's ex-military, he has a great bit of terminology for a time like this, he'd say "situation snafu." Know what that means, Mum? Situation normal, all fucked up.'

He gazed at the still form and squinted slightly, looking for some tiny response but there was none.

He talked to her for the next ten minutes. Said everything he needed to, then added, 'Are you really sorry about Ben, I wonder? If you are, you must be far more astute than I gave you credit for, because that was the exact moment when I realised that I was alone in the world, and how much I hated you.' He looked at the almost skeletal hand in his, at the wrinkled skin and the bulging darkness of the veins showing through. 'Even if you were trying to say that you'd been a bad mother, to say you are sorry, I can never forgive you, Mum, you do know that, don't you?' He squeezed her hand gently. 'But maybe I can stop hating you.'

Ten minutes later, he sat in his car, the roses and the tape carefully bagged in the boot, and wondered if he had imagined that slightest hint of pressure on his fingers.

CHAPTER NINETEEN

Matt entered the murder room. There was a distinct difference in the atmosphere. Everyone was working with renewed vigour. Maybe his talk had kick-started them. They all wanted his attention, everyone had something to say.

'Report in on Gabriel. Definitely a city boy. The forensic checks have pinpointed his place of origin as Sheffield. From the particular kinds of detritus and pollen found on the body, they suspect he was a street kid.' Liz closed the report and threw it on her desk in disgust. 'And most likely untraceable.'

Jason walked over to him. 'How is she, boss? Your mum?'

'Not likely to regain consciousness, but before you tell me to go back, Jason, they have my mobile number, and she could remain like that for a very long while, okay?' He touched Jason's arm. 'But thanks for asking. I appreciate it.'

The detective gave him a small smile. 'I worry about you, sir.'

'You worry about everything, Jason. Now what else is happening?'

'Right, well, I've requested those crucifixes be released from the evidence store, sir. Shall I get uniform to pick them up?'

Matt thought about it, then said, 'No. Just get them photographed if you would. They are probably safest left where they are right now.'

'No problem. I'll get that done right away. Oh, can I see the new CCTV footage that you've brought back?'

'It's with the IT boys. They are isolating his face and making us some close-up prints. Oh, and there was nothing on the flowers, so I filed them in the waste bin.'

'Right, probably best place for them.'

As Jason turned away, Gemma approached Matt. She looked irritated. 'I've got the result back from the computer comparison. They used the CCTV likeness of the suspect and the old mugshot of Paul Underhill, sir.' She frowned, 'It's inconclusive. Some things are similar, height and probable age, but the techies are not happy with the particular CCTV camera used by the betting shop. They reckon it distorts the image.'

Relief washed over him, but he still felt for her. She'd been so certain about Underhill not being dead. He saw the determination on her face. She reminded him of himself as a rookie, all fired up and enthusiastic about his theories. He smiled and made two decisions. One, not to tell her about the new photo just yet, and two, to let her down gently. 'Well, at least it's not a definite no. We could well get a better shot, Gemma. Then you can run it again.'

'Yeah, maybe.' She hesitated. 'Sir? Would it be alright if I go round to the café for my break? Since we decided that Rob would be safe enough in his snobby gated estate, I haven't been able to see him.' She smiled. 'And as I'm under virtual house arrest at the DI's at present, it's a bit difficult.'

Matt told her he didn't like the idea.

'It's alright. I'll go with her,' Liz volunteered. 'I can pick us all up some bacon butties while Gemma has her cosy chat. I promise we'll stay within sight of each other, and the café is only a few hundred yards from the nick so the place will probably be heaving with wooden tops anyway.'

'Okay, but make it snappy.' He turned to Gemma. 'I'm not being difficult, but just see your bloke and get back here, understand?'

'Boss?' Bryn held out a phone to him. 'It's Sunderland for you.'

Matt took a deep breath, not sure what to expect. 'DCI Ballard here, thank you for getting back to me so quickly.'

The woman on the other end had a friendly Geordie accent and after a quick introduction explained what they'd found.

'Nothing much to help, I'm afraid. The tattoo place has only been there for a few months. The owner is from down south. Brighton, to be exact. He's not known to us. Never been in trouble of any kind. He did take a look at your design, but he said he's never been asked for anything like that before. He thinks it may be of Celtic origin, but definitely not a well-known standard or even an odd one from his book of designs. Sorry I can't be more helpful, but I've emailed you the full details of the owner.'

Matt bit on a jagged fingernail. He had hoped for more. 'We had already worked the Celtic bit out when the old case was running, Sergeant, but thank you for checking it out for us.'

'One other thing, sir. Maybe nothing. Before this chap bought the place, 16 Baltimore Street was owned by an adoption agency.'

Matt frowned, unsure if this was important or not.

The officer continued, 'I've put their details on the email too. You never know, it might be helpful.'

As he replaced the receiver, Matt felt a small shiver of excitement. This was it. Nothing to do with tattoos, everything to do with who owned the place earlier. He went swiftly to his office, logged in and opened his email. The memo was already waiting to be picked up. He scanned through the first part then saw what he wanted. The email read:

The Cadogan Fife Adoption Agency. No longer operative. Closed in 2005, although allowed the premises at 16 Baltimore Street to be used on a temporary basis as a charity shop supporting a local hospice. Manager when the agency ceased to operate was Mrs Alexis Peart, now retired. Home address: 82 Viaduct Street, Brownshill, nr Chester-Le-Street, Co. Durham.

According to our records, this was an approved Christian agency working closely with the local Diocesan Adoption Services. They had an excellent record and achieved a high success rate of linking children with suitable home environments.

Hope this helps. Sgt Helen Gaines. Sunderland. Northumbria Police.

Matt saw a telephone number beneath the address. His instinct was to pick up the phone, but thinking for a moment or two, he replaced the receiver. What exactly was he going to ask the woman? It would help to try and get a handle on why the killer had put them on this track in the first place. Maybe he'd talk it through with the team. Second thoughts, he'd throw it to the super first.

As he hurried up the stairs to the super's office, Matt began to feel uneasy. The killer had taken things to a new level by tossing in a clue. The problem was that whoever the murderer was, he was still pulling the strings, and Matt badly needed to change that situation, and fast, before someone else got hurt.

* * *

'Can I cadge a favour, Sarge?' Gemma looked hopefully at Liz as they entered the café and made their way between a crush of uniformed bodies.

'Depends. Does it involve large amounts of money?' Liz said.

'No,' she laughed. 'Nothing like that. The thing is, Roy doesn't know that this,' she pointed to the blue and yellow bruises on her cheek, 'came from a meeting with the killer. Don't tell him, will you? He'd be really upset if he knew, and I don't want him worrying about me any more than he does already.'

'What on earth did you tell him? You look like you've taken on the London Irish!'

'Riot training.'

'And he bought it? You're kidding! I know it can get a bit out of hand, but a few wooden bricks wouldn't do that!'

'Roy doesn't know that, does he? He's in advertising, remember? Different world.'

'Fair enough, but that doesn't make him a total plank,' she pulled a face, 'does it?'

'Of course not, but he really cares about me. Please, Sarge, if he thought I'd had a run in with a murderer, God knows what he'd do.'

'My lips are sealed. Even if your excuse was extremely crap.'

'There he is! Come and meet him.' Gemma grabbed her arm and dragged her through a small gaggle of customers. 'Roy!'

The couple hugged, then kissed. Not the sort of kiss that Liz suspected that they would have liked to enjoy, but considering a large percentage of the station was watching, it was intimate enough.

'Roy, this is Detective Sergeant Haynes.'

She held out her hand. Roy was not exactly what she had imagined. He was slim, quite good-looking, with longish dark brown hair, trendy black-rimmed glasses and a warm smile. He wore a dark T-shirt under an expensive suit, one that looked distinctly out of place in the greasy spoon. All in all, the only thing that she found mildly disappointing was the less than firm handshake. *And that, Elizabeth, is because you spend far too much time in the company of big, brainless macho blokes!*

'Pleased to meet you, Roy.'

'Hello, Sergeant Haynes. Nice to be able to put a face to the name at last. Can I get you a coffee?'

She smiled. The rumours that he was well-off were obviously true. The designer suit apart, his voice was soft, and the accent distinctly upper class. She wondered where on earth Gemma had found him. 'No, thanks. We're on a pretty tight schedule at present. The boss had got us both on a very short rein, so I'll leave you two alone while I sort out the butties. Good to meet you, Roy.' She looked across at Gemma. 'Sorry, but ten minutes max, okay?'

Gemma nodded and threw herself down next to her boyfriend, 'Skip the drinks, I just want to hold your hand and talk to you, and I don't want to waste a minute.'

Liz joined the queue. Even in this demanding job and in tough times, love seemed to find a way.

She glanced at her watch, then at the slow-moving queue. They shouldn't be too long or Matt would worry. The line snaked in front of her, and as she waited, a darkness began to cloud the idyllic scene. The young officer looked so happy with her man, but she'd already been badly knocked about, just for the sake of delivering a poxy photograph. Was she really safe now? The place was crawling with fellow coppers, but still Liz felt a chilly sort of disquiet surround her. Even the boyfriend Roy, well, she certainly couldn't imagine him wading in, if there were any rough stuff. Maybe he was a disposable target, too.

She glanced across, not wishing to intrude, but needing to be vigilant. From what she saw, it was pretty clear how they felt about each other. That could be a great hook for the killer. After all, he'd been damned accurate as to what would yank Jason's chain. Just involve his kids.

Liz shivered. Jason's daughter had had one hell of a close call. Who was next on the hit list?

She took a few steps forward and shuffled her feet impatiently. *What, or who, was her Achilles heel?* She had no kids. There was not even a dog or a pet budgie to worry about. Caring about Gary went without saying, but he was a highly trained soldier with years of service under his belt. She was forced to smile. And that was apart from being built like one of his own tanks. She would never worry about someone trying to jump Gary, in fact, God help anyone who did. Her only sister lived in New Zealand, and Gary's twin brothers were also serving in Iraq. Both their parents lived miles away and visited rarely, so they were more or less out of the equation. Which left just one person. And that was someone who really shouldn't be as important to her as he was.

Liz watched Gemma and Roy as they talked earnestly together, heads almost touching. Matt had never meant to become anything more than a sexual outlet, but right now, she was forced to admit that her feelings for Matt had changed. She felt a slight confusion when she was with him, and there was a comfortable, easy feeling when they were alone, one that, considering the circumstances, just shouldn't be there. Before all this, the sneaking around had evoked only a strong sense of danger and excitement. Now, although the sex was still electric, there was something else as well. *And that could be truly dangerous!*

As she approached the counter, she offered a small prayer of thanks that Matt didn't feel the same, because if he had become her weak point, then she could be his, which was a nasty and frightening thought. Thank God he'd made it clear that she was just a useful and pleasant distraction.

She finally placed her order, feeling a little better. No way, after everything that Matt had suffered in the past, was he going to go all soft on another woman, especially one in her complicated situation.

She took the bag of sandwiches and gave herself a swift dressing down. *And you can just forget all that sentimental garbage about feelings, too. It's just a very convenient and satisfying interlude, and that's exactly how it's going to stay.*

* * *

The super stared at the telephone number. 'Could it actually have anything to do with the woman in the photograph? Your old sweetheart, Laura, isn't it?'

Matt had already considered that. 'I can't think how, sir. Laura wasn't adopted, and to my knowledge no one in her family was either. They were from Cambridgeshire, and I can't ever recall them having any ties with Sunderland.'

'What if the killer tracked Laura down after she'd done her runner? Maybe she worked at the agency, or knew someone who did?'

'After all these years? I suppose it's possible, but I hunted for her using every technique at our disposal, and I never even had a sniff of finding her.' Matt shook his head. 'More likely that photo is just something else to wind me up, another pop at me, saying how much he knows about my past, and the telephone number is really a clue to either the killer or maybe one of his victims.'

'Gabriel? Maybe he was adopted, and Sunderland would definitely be classed as big town/city with regards to the forensic findings.'

'Would the killer really care about the kid he murdered?' Matt asked.

'That would depend on whether the child was known to him, or to one of us. An integral part of the plan or just a random choice.' He paused. 'Frankly, my money is on random.'

'Me, too. Which brings us back to the killer himself. Perhaps he's trying to lead us to his own identity.'

The super nodded. 'That's plausible. Serial killers can crave notoriety, and they can also love to play with the authorities.'

'It can't be much fun when you have all the cards stacked in your favour, can it? He's got to give us a break soon, or it's pointless playing.'

'Well, check out the woman who ran the agency, and let me know what you come up with, okay?'

Matt stood up to leave. 'I thought you'd like to know that I've decided to stay with a friend until all this calms down, sir.'

'At bloody last! I was beginning to think I'd have to evict you by force.' The super smiled and reached for a pen. 'You'd better give me the address and contact number.'

'I'm moving in to Adie Clarkson's hotel, sir. The Waggoner's Rest. You know it, I'm sure.'

The super leaned back in his chair and threw Matt a shrewd look. 'Oh yes, I know it. And I know Clarkson too. Sadly, in a professional capacity.'

'He's straight now, sir. Has been for donkey's years.'

'Forgive my cynicism, Matt, but that's one man I never thought would stay out of prison for long.'

'There's an exception to every rule, sir. Adie's a good bloke, honestly.'

'You trust him?'

'He turned out to be an unlikely ally, and a bloody good friend when I really needed one, sir. I have no reason not to trust him.'

'Well, if that's the case, you've probably picked a pretty good place to lie low. I can't see Adie Clarkson backing off from a fight if one presented itself, can you?'

Before Matt could answer, there was a loud knock on the door and a young PC stuck his head around the door.

'DCI Ballard, sir. The desk sergeant sent me. Said to say that there's been a report of a youngster gone missing from the Carson's Marsh area. A boy. He thought you'd want to know.'

'Too bloody right! Okay, Constable, tell him I'll be right down. Oh, and by the way, do we know the age of the child?' He'd asked the question, but he sure as hell didn't want to hear the answer.

'Eleven, I think, sir.'

Matt's heart sank.

CHAPTER TWENTY

'Jason! Where are the others? We've got a shout!' Matt said.

'Bryn's in the locker room, and the girls haven't got back yet. Shall I give them a bell?'

Fear slammed into Matt's gut. They had been gone for twenty-five minutes. Far too long. 'Yes, do it! Right now.'

'Boss?' Liz swallowed back a bite of her sandwich and said, 'You look a whiter shade of pale, what's happened?'

Matt choked back his relief on seeing the two women enter the room, then cloaked his concern with irritation. 'Where the hell have you two been? I said be quick, didn't I? We've got another child reported missing, so if you've quite finished stuffing your faces, we need to get out to Carson's Marsh.'

'All of us?'

'No, no. Liz, you come with me. Gemma and Bryn crack on here with Jason. We'll let you know what we find.'

Liz threw the bag of sandwiches to Gemma and hurried after him.

'Share those out, Gem. I've got the boss's here. He can eat it in the car, if he's calmed down enough not to get galloping indigestion, that is,' Liz called to her colleagues.

Outside, he checked the address that they had been given. 'I shouldn't have shouted at you. You scared me,' he said to Liz.

'The café was really busy. I'm sorry.' She got into the car, 'Maybe I should have rung you.'

'No.' He backed the car out of his parking space. 'It's me. It's hard to relax when you know that some psycho's got people you care about in his sights.'

'Tell me about it! I was watching Gemma with her bloke earlier. It almost freaked me out realising how vulnerable everybody is.'

'What's he like, the boyfriend?'

'Apart from a handshake like wet lettuce, he's seems to be a pretty cool guy. Oozes money. And he's obviously got a severe case of the hots for our Gemma, which gave me the creeps, knowing how our killer works. I just hope, for his sake, that his posh des res is as security conscious as we think.'

Matt sucked in air between his teeth. 'Maybe we should organise something safer for him. You wonder how far to go with the protection. You can't wrap everyone in cotton wool, but . . .'

'Yeah, I know, but if anything happened to them, you'd feel responsible.' She leaned across and gently touched his leg. 'But you shouldn't, Matt. None of this is your fault. It's entirely down to that psycho.' She squeezed his leg then reluctantly released it. 'Now, as the smell of bacon is overpowering your air freshener, why not eat your buttie and tell me about this missing kid. Is it likely to be connected to our case?'

Matt tried to suppress the excitement that her touch had caused. 'Hopefully not, although his age has got me pretty wired.'

'Who reported him missing?'

'Who indeed? Certainly not his family. Uniform are having trouble finding anyone closely related. Some old lady who lives on the farthest part of Carson's Marsh was worried about him. His name is Ryan Fisher, by the way. The old girl, uh, Mrs Stokes, said she rings him if she needs anything and he delivers it for her. She reckons his mobile is out of service.'

'He's probably run out of airtime and got no spare cash.'

'Or done a runner. He's a chronic truant from his school, and apparently his family aren't exactly supportive of the boy.'

'So, we're going to see the old lady?'

'Yes. Uniform reckon she's really agitated about the kid.' Matt settled into fifth and with one hand carefully folded back the bag that held his sandwich. He ate some, then said, 'The further we get out onto the marsh, the more I'm worrying about him. In fact, I'm beginning to get a really bad feeling about this youngster.'

Liz sighed. 'Lives in a remote spot, eleven years old, unwanted or uncared for. I hate to agree, but he fits the bill, doesn't he?' She stared out the window across the vast flat fields that edged the marsh. 'How far out does the Stokes woman live?'

'Back of beyond. Past the mere, on that narrow stretch of drove that leads to the pumping station.' Matt finished the sandwich, screwed up the paper bag and pushed it into the door pocket. 'How's Gary?'

Liz laughed at his abrupt change of conversation. 'Goodness me! The chief is missing me already!'

'I asked how Gary was. That's all.'

'He's very well, thank you. Although not too happy about what's happening right now. The timing couldn't be worse. He wants me to take some leave.' She turned and looked at him seriously. 'Although he knows that I wouldn't do that, any more than he would, if the boot were on the other foot.'

'When's he going back?'

'Day after tomorrow. Then I can go join Jason's Home for Displaced Policewomen.'

Matt grinned, 'After another ear-bashing by the super, I'm going to relocate as well.'

'You're kidding! Matt Ballard moving out of the Adams Family house? I don't believe it.'

'Just temporarily. Adie's putting me up.'

'I should have known. What a shame I'm stuck playing My Little Pony with Gemma, when there are so many other games I would prefer to be playing, Mattie.'

'Please! Don't!' he groaned.

'Well, we'd better hurry up and catch this bloody killer, then maybe we can get back to normal, whatever that is!'

This time it was Matt's turn to place his hand on Liz's leg. He felt it move beneath the smooth fabric of her skirt, then her own hand covered his and drew it slowly up her thigh.

'What time is Mrs Stokes expecting us?' Her voice was husky.

He swallowed noisily, his breathing almost laboured. With a great effort, he squeezed the hand and pushed it slowly away. 'She's expecting us ten minutes ago. And we need to focus.'

'Pity.'

* * *

Mrs Stokes was a true Fenlander, born and bred on that watery part of the landscape called Carson's Marsh.

'It just ain't like him. Young Ryan's a good boy at heart. He just has a rotten family, that's the crux of the matter.' She placed two mugs of tea in front of them and sat down herself.

'You say he calls every Wednesday? So he was here yesterday. Why do you believe he's gone missing?'

'I rings him when I thinks of something. He makes a list, then fetches it for me every week, regular as clockwork.'

Matt wanted to ask why she didn't make the list herself, but as he looked around the neat little room, he realised that there were no books, no papers and no magazines.

Poor old duck can't read or write. 'We wondered if his phone needed a top-up, Mrs Stokes? Perhaps he can't afford it, especially if his parents aren't providing for him.'

'No.' She shook her head defiantly. 'It's not that.'

'How can you be so sure, Mrs Stokes?' asked Liz.

'Because I've known Ryan since he was a little scrap. He's been in trouble, certainly, but it wasn't of his doing. A drunken mother and a waster for a dad, what chance does he have?'

'But what does that have to do with the phone?' Matt felt confused.

'This is what.' She reached down the side of her chair and produced a plastic document case. She carefully selected one section and withdrew an invoice.

Matt looked at the folder with interest. On the top of each section was a small roughly drawn picture. One had a light bulb, one a tap with water pouring from it, and the one she held had a tiny telephone drawn on it.

'Clever system, Mrs Stokes,' he said with sincerity.

'That's Ryan, he done it for me. Helps no end.' With a leathery, weather-worn hand she passed him the telephone bill. 'It's not much, and he never takes advantage.'

'You pay for a cell phone for him?'

'I thought it might help keep him safe. If he had an accident or something. This place don't get too many visitors, if you landed in one of the dykes you could lay there for a month before someone found you.'

Matt felt a shiver slip down his spine and he thought about Paul Underhill.

'And I gives him a bit o' pocket money when I can.'

Matt took out his notebook and scribbled down the number for the boy's phone, then he pulled out his own mobile and rang the number. He got the usual mechanical voice telling him that it wasn't possible to connect him at that time. 'Have you seen anyone strange around here recently, Mrs Stokes, anyone you didn't recognise?'

She sipped her tea thoughtfully, then shook her head. 'No, can't say I have.' She looked across the coffee table at them. 'I listens to the wireless a lot, especially the news. I puts it on for company. Has that murderer got my Ryan, do you think?'

Liz leaned forward. 'We hope not. Really we do, and we'll do everything we can to find him, I promise.'

Mrs Stokes nodded, accepting what she was told as gospel. 'That's good.'

Matt reached into his pocket and produced one of the printed pictures of the man who had accosted Jason's girl. 'I suppose you haven't seen this man at all, have you?'

The old lady pulled on a smeared pair of glasses and peered at the photo. 'When you were talking about strangers, I didn't realise you were including your own policemen, dear! Yes, of course, that's that nice Detective Dennis. He called last week, said his inspector wanted him to make sure all us far-flung residents were alright and not having any problems. Lovely man, isn't he?'

Matt tried not to look at Liz, or to outwardly give the old lady any cause for concern.

'Uh, yes. Excellent officer. What exactly did he say to you?'

Mrs Stokes drew in a long breath. 'Oh, well, he asked if I lived alone, was I worried by anything? How did I manage now I couldn't drive anymore? How did I get my shopping? Were the nearest neighbours friendly? You know the sort of thing.'

Oh, yes. I know exactly the sort of thing. Matt rubbed his forehead. 'Do you have any relatives close by, Mrs Stokes?'

'Not close by, not anywhere, dear. I'm afraid I'm the last in our family.'

This time he turned to Liz. 'Sergeant, we need to make some arrangements here.'

'Yes, sir. Shall I make a call?'

'Signal's best outside, I think. I'll help Mrs Stokes clear these cups away.' He raised his eyebrow.

'Understood, sir.'

As Liz went to ring the station, Matt gently explained that it wasn't safe to remain out on the fen alone. At first she protested, there were the cats and the chickens to think of, and where would she go.

'Our people will find you somewhere warm and comfortable, just until we know that it's safe for you to come home. And I'll go and see your nearest neighbours and get them to feed your animals and your birds, okay?' He put an arm around her shoulders. 'I can't leave you out here, honestly I can't.'

Something about her seemed to deflate. 'I knew it. That madman's got young Ryan, hasn't he?'

Matt didn't want to lie to her. 'He may have. But we can't give up hope, can we? With your help, we'll do all we can to find him. Now, why don't you go and get some things together. Pretend it's like going on a holiday.'

'I've never had a holiday, dear. Never slept one night out of my old bed.'

Matt's heart ached as she turned and went slowly upstairs.

Liz appeared at the door and whispered. 'Sorted. A car's on its way to pick her up. Everything alright here?'

'Hardly, poor old duck.' He gritted his teeth. 'This bastard's got such a lot to answer for. It's not just the main victims who are suffering here, it's good people like her.'

'He's certainly a clever little shite, getting her to tell him all that stuff. "How do you get your shopping, dear sweet old lady?" and "Oh, my Ryan gets it for me, officer.

Such a nice boy!" I can almost hear him salivating into his beard. Makes you want to puke!'

'Oh no! Was it me?' Mrs Stokes stood at the top of the stairs, hands clasped to her mouth and her voice shaking with emotion. 'Did *I* say something to put that poor child in danger?'

Matt threw a dark look at Liz, then ran up the stairs to the old woman.

'Absolutely not! You are not to blame in any way. I believe the man who came here impersonating a police officer knew every detail about Ryan before he ever set foot inside your door. He was just checking on what he already knew. Now, let me help you get your things ready, then I'll go sort out the cats, etc. Our colleagues will be here to collect you very soon.'

When they finally left, they took with them an old school photo of Ryan Fisher, courtesy of the woman who had paid for it, and a very concise list of his favourite places, football teams, foods, clothes and pop songs. Matt thought that it was just a shame that it wasn't the kid's own family who had supplied that very personal information.

CHAPTER TWENTY-ONE

'Hope they've found somewhere suitable for her.' Liz looked up from her desk at Matt. 'And I'm really sorry about earlier, me and my big gob. I thought she was in the bedroom packing. I was just so bloody angry at the way he manipulates everybody.'

'I know. But she's okay now. And they got her a temporary furnished room at the Elmdale warden-controlled flats in Barley Street. The officer who went with her said she was well impressed, and her new 'neighbour' was talking her into joining them for bingo tonight.'

'She could use some friendly faces around her right now, take her mind off that lad.'

'Any luck with his family?'

'Yes. The father is working on some building site in Nottingham. He's been notified and is apparently on his way home, and the mother was found out cold at a friend's house earlier. As soon as someone has managed to sober her up, they'll bring her in.'

'I would have thought the news that your only son might have been abducted would sober anyone up.'

'You haven't seen Mrs Fisher, boss. Perfect *Jeremy Kyle Show* material.'

'Lovely. I can hardly wait to meet her.' Matt sat on the edge of the desk. 'Uniform are doing a house to house out on the marsh, but,' he shrugged, 'what a godforsaken area to have to cover. Any leads yet?'

'Nothing, but we've got every available officer out there asking questions and showing the photographs of Ryan and the bogus Detective Dennis. Maybe we'll get lucky.' He stood up. 'While we wait, I'm going to try to follow up this Adoption Society place. I know the boy is missing, but as most of our complement is working on that, I can't ignore the only clue that the killer has given us.'

'Of course not, sir. By the way, what was the name of that officer from the old case who you reckoned was leaking info to the press?'

'Detective Constable Colin Bristol. Retired out, ten years back, and it was reported he collapsed and died while on holiday in Tenerife in 2009. Why?'

'Just making sure he really is brown bread. Don't want something nasty popping up out of the woodwork at a later date.'

'Good thinking, Liz. Although I'm pretty sure I read his obituary in the *Daily Telegraph*.'

'I'll check it anyway. And I thought I'd try to chase up the other holidaymakers who accompanied you on that voyage of personal discovery to that Greek island, see if any familiar names or faces show up.'

Matt puffed out his cheeks and exhaled loudly. 'And how the hell do you propose to do that? It was so long ago.'

'The kind of holiday that you described wasn't your average bucket-seat cheapie to Ayia Napa, now was it? That sort of alternative vacation usually occurs after a major life upheaval, and it stays with you, sometimes forever. People come back from that kind of break to find themselves changed, their lives altered. You don't forget it. Or the people who were around you.'

'But I never mixed with them. I kept to myself, other than hours spent with my mentor, Dimitri. I walked the olive groves and the beaches alone.'

'Then they'd remember you as the loner. You probably made more of an impact on them than the ones who threw their miserable lives down for all to see and accompanied it with constant verbal diarrhoea. They probably thought of you as polite but aloof, a man who needed to find answers outside of the personal development classes. I'd think that a good few of the women spent their nights fantasizing over the tall, brooding and handsome stranger in their midst.' She smiled at him and her eyes twinkled mischievously. 'There's nothing more attractive than a silent mystery man, believe me.'

'Yeah, right! Well, I'll take your word for that, but that line of enquiry could turn out to be a big waste of time.'

'And I *could* find out who took those photos, couldn't I? Now hand over the name of the tour company and a girl can get some work done around here.'

Matt threw up his hands. 'Okay, it was called the Angelos Healing Centre at Karissa. They were based in London, the Fulham Road, I think. Do whatever you need to, just don't do it alone, okay?'

* * *

Back in his office Matt dialled the number of Alexis Peart. There was no use procrastinating any longer. He had no idea why the killer had sent him this particular clue, and certainly couldn't afford to wait until he did.

She answered on the second ring. She had a strong, no-nonsense kind of voice, which promoted Matt to cut the bullshit and after introducing himself, tell her quite bluntly exactly why he was ringing.

There was a short silence, then Alexis Peart said, 'Naturally, I will help you all I can, but I'm at something of a loss as to where to start.'

You and me both, lady. 'How far back would your records go?'

'Since the day we started, Chief Inspector. We are required to keep them indefinitely, and as I have the facilities available here, I decided to store them all.'

'Excellent. Well, my initial enquiry would probably start with the name of the young woman whose photograph he wrote your number on. It is more to eliminate her than anything. She was a close friend of mine, Mrs Peart, but she disappeared back in the early eighties. Her name was Laura Schofield. I suppose that doesn't mean anything to you?'

'Schofield? No, not off the top of my head, but give me some time and I'll search for you.'

'Time is not something we have too much of, I'm afraid. Maybe you'd allow me to send a couple of officers to help?'

Mrs Peart gave a small laugh. 'I didn't mean that I'd take days, Chief Inspector. My system is very easy to access. I can cross-check that name before your officers have unlocked their cars, let alone driven up here.'

Matt's visions of something similar to the police evidence store, with its long lines of shelving and cardboard boxes, vanished. 'It's all on computer?'

'Naturally. Although when I said storage, I meant it. I do have all the paper records if required. Now *they* may take an hour or two longer to sort through!' She paused for a moment. 'You said the number was written on a photograph?'

'Yes, it's an enlargement taken from an old snapshot.'

'Could you send it to me? You never know, I might just recognise her.'

She gave Matt her email address. He brought the picture up on his computer screen. 'Are you ready?'

'I'll go to my office and pick it up. Are there any other names to check?'

Matt thought hard as he selected the photo file and clicked Send. 'I'm sure there are a lot, if I just knew where to start.'

The line crackled as the woman carried the cordless phone into another room.. 'Okay, well one at a time is fine by me. Let me just get this up and running.'

'Tell me about your organisation, Mrs Peart. You say you founded it?'

'With my husband, John. We managed to help a lot of children in our time, I'm pleased to say.'

'Were there many agencies like yours operating in the area?'

'One or two smaller ones. It was mainly the larger Christian charitable agencies really.' She paused. 'Got it. Ah, what a beautiful girl, but so miserable-looking!'

Matt laughed. 'That was what her mother used to call her —mardy face. The one she wore when she didn't get her own way.'

'Were you in love?'

The question took him by surprise and he didn't answer immediately.

'So you were. I thought so, but I'm afraid I don't recognise her, Chief Inspector. I'm sorry.'

'I didn't expect you to, Mrs Peart. And I don't expect her name to turn up in your files either. As I said, it's more to eliminate her involvement.'

'Okay, well, leave it with me. I'll ring you back shortly.'

* * *

Jason put the phone down and jumped up. 'The uniform search has finally thrown up a suspected sighting of the boy.'

'Recent?' Matt said.

'Yesterday.'

Matt rubbed a hand through his hair. 'Damn! Where was this?'

'Out on the fen, on the lane to the seabank, near Giles Farm.'

'Doing what?'

'Just walking. From the direction he came, it seems liked he'd taken a shortcut across the fields from Mrs Stokes place at Carson's Fen.'

'And has anyone else been spotted out there?'

'Migrant workers were in the fields at the back of the Giles place. Most of them are Polish so we aren't one hundred per cent sure on this, but I think they saw a jogger out there.'

'Okay, find out whoever interviewed them, then take Bryn and go and see them for yourself. The jogger could be the killer. We know he's fit. Gemma can certainly testify to that fact. And he knew Ryan's schedule from Mrs S. He was probably waiting for the boy.'

'So how did he get the child away?'

'He probably had a vehicle somewhere close by. Check with uniform, see if they've spoken to the workers at Giles Farm, then ring me. And Jason, this is our best lead yet, but don't get carried away, stick with Bryn, watch your backs, and be careful.'

'Roger, sir. On our way.'

A civilian messenger came in as Jason and Bryn left. 'From forensics for you, sir.' She handed him a report.

Inside he found a typed note with a case number and a reference attached. For a moment he didn't want to look at it, then with a slightly shaking hand he unfolded the paper and read:

For the Att of. DCI Ballard.
Findings re: one gold-coloured ring.
The ring is established to be of 18-carat gold. It is a plain wedding band with a rope design edging. At some point it has been altered (made smaller). Tool markings and quality of workmanship particularly regarding the rope edging suggest this was not carried out by a craftsman. From the wear on the surface of the metal, it is

believed that the repair was carried out many years after its original manufacture.

The hallmark indicates the assay office as London, and has the date letter for 1951. Inner band has maker's mark BV. Tests show that the ring has not been worn for many years. Its present condition suggests that it has been kept clean and boxed. There were no traces of fingerprints, fibres or other deposits present.

Matt read it and re-read it. Irritation coursed through him. This told him nothing that he didn't know already. Maggie's ring had been second-hand, so 1951 could have been correct, but he hadn't a clue. And yes, she'd had the ring made smaller, in a local high street jeweller who had done a less than brilliant job. But he really didn't know its origins, and he had no way of checking them. He was not the sort of man to keep old receipts, no matter how significant.

He walked slowly across to the coffee machine and stabbed viciously at the buttons. He had been so certain that it was Maggie's ring. Now he was sure of nothing. The super had insisted that it was a clever ploy to get him running to her grave, to see if it had been tampered with, and to find the flowers and the next photograph, which was exactly what he'd done. Maybe that was all there was to it. *Roll up! Roll up! Light the blue touch paper and watch the detective run around like a crazy man!* Well, maybe, but the seed of suspicion that a madman had somehow got hold of his dead wife's ring, was still lying dormant beneath the surface of his mind, and he could do nothing to shift it.

As he removed the polystyrene beaker from the machine, and picked up the report from the table, he saw a small note still in the envelope. Placing the hot coffee down, he stared at the handwritten message.

Chief Inspector — Do you have a clear photograph of your wife's ring? The wedding photo showing you cutting the cake, for example. I may be able to do a high-magnification comparison with the ring itself. After all, I can work wonders!

And it's certainly worth a try, I think.

Rory Wilkinson

Matt closed his eyes for a moment. There certainly had been pictures, but where were they? In the attic? No, they were in an old leather attaché case in the cupboard under the stairs. When he went home to get his things, he would fish it out and get it down to the pathologist. He wondered how he'd found out about the ring in the first place, Matt certainly hadn't told him it was his wife's. *Thanks, our Jason. On one of your jolly visits to the mortuary, was it?*

Matt sipped his coffee, and had the sudden urge to go home, go to bed and not set the alarm clock. Everything was going at breakneck speed, he needed to get off the merry-go-round and regroup, but the killer was not giving him time to breathe. Which was probably exactly what the bastard intended.

Back in his office, he had barely sat down when his phone rang. 'Mrs Peart. Already! Your filing system really must be good. Got time to come down here and give some of our admin kids a few lessons?'

'Love to, Chief Inspector. But sadly this time I've nothing to offer you. That name doesn't show up anywhere, and I've tried variations on the spelling, although that wasn't the kind of mistake we could afford to make when it came to legal documents.'

'Thank you for looking. If it's alright with you, as soon as I get a moment, I'll compile a list of other possible names, if you'd be kind enough to check them out for me?'

'No problem. I'm both retired and widowed, so I have plenty of time on my hands.' She hesitated. 'You are sure it has nothing to do with the new owners of our old premises? What's it called now? Oh, yes, the Inksmith Tattoo Studio?'

'We've checked them out already and can't make a connection. Our man is devious, and I'm sure the answer lies with you somehow.'

'How intriguing! Although perhaps on reflection, maybe a little disturbing.'

'Please don't worry yourself, Mrs Peart. He is not in your neck of the woods, I promise you. He's making himself very busy down here at present. In fact, he's managing to make our lives very uncomfortable indeed.'

'How frustrating. Even I feel some sort of indignation that he should dare use my phone number to taunt you. I can't begin to imagine how you feel.' She gave a snort of disgust. 'If there is anything I can do, just ask, Chief Inspector. And in the meantime, I'll do a little sleuthing of my own. We had to do a lot of evaluations and some pretty deep digging into people's history when finding a safe home in which to place a child. Luckily I had a keen sense of intuition when it came to the rum ones! Sixth sense, my husband would say. While I'm waiting for your list of names, I'll run a few outside-the-box checks to see if there were ever any placements or old prospective adopters from your area. See if anyone sets off my alarm bells.'

Matt liked her initiative. 'That would be great, if you can spare the time, it would be much appreciated. I'll give you my mobile number, phone me directly if you find anything interesting.'

He finished the call, swallowed back the coffee and wondered if Jason would come up with anything. Frankly, he doubted it. If the jogger was the killer, and he'd been seen, then he'd wanted to be seen. He was far too careful to leave clumsy clues behind.

He checked his watch. Maybe he'd go home, find that old photo, and pack up a few clothes and toiletries. Yeah, he'd do that while he waited for Jason to return. But, after everything he'd said to the others, he didn't dare go alone.

He glanced through the glass panel into the outer office. Gemma and Liz were deep in conversation on their respective phones. Better let them get on. He could beg a uniformed officer from the desk sergeant, but he didn't feel like making polite conversation as they drove.

With a sudden smile, he picked up his car keys and took out his phone. Thinking about it, he knew the very man for the job. He dialled Adie Clarkson.

* * *

Adie drew up outside the front door to the nick, threw open the passenger door and called out, 'Get in, my friend. I need to keep moving, this place gives me the screamers!'

'No wonder. You've spent enough time in it.'

'And not one single visit is a pleasant memory. Thanks for reminding me.' He grinned at Matt. 'So what's going down? Why am I the chauffeur as well as the landlord?'

Matt sank back in the comfy seat. 'I needed a friend, not another copper, for company.'

'What about your foxy little woman? I'm sure she's very friendly.'

'Too right. But with all this heavy stuff happening, I'm happier with her and the rest of the team in safe places.'

'And I'm expendable?'

'You, mate, are big enough and most definitely ugly enough to look after yourself, and me, for that matter.'

'So this lunatic is for real?'

'He's in deadly earnest.'

'What's he after?'

'Now that's a question that I would dearly love to know the answer to.' Matt sighed. 'Listen, I never told you this, okay? He may have taken another child.'

Adie's scarred knuckles turned white as he gripped the steering wheel. 'The sick shit! I know exactly what I'd do to him if I got the chance.'

They drove out of the town in silence. Fifteen minutes later, they arrived at the farmhouse. Matt got out, stood on the path and stared up at the windows. *This is my home. And he's been in here.* It felt like everything was contaminated.

'Want me to go first? Or are you just working out an estimate for an external paint job?'

Matt hurriedly fished in his pocket for his keys. He'd been right to bring Adie.

They stepped into the hall.

'Blimey! Your lot have been in here, haven't they? Right load of messy buggers! Hey! This all looks so familiar. It takes forever to get rid of this poxy carbon black powder.'

'And you should know.'

'Tell you something, if ever I screwed a drum, I didn't leave it in a shit state like this. I took pride in my work, I did.'

'So I recall.'

'Ah yes, well, moving on, what are we doing here exactly? A swift clean up?'

Matt looked around. It wasn't too bad. 'That can wait. I just need some things. Clothes mainly. Look, while I sort out some stuff, would you do me a favour and see if you can find a leather attaché case for me? I think it's in that cupboard there.' He pointed towards the door beneath the staircase.

'Sure.' He opened the door. 'Got a torch?'

'There's one of those touch-activated lights on the back wall. Single candle powered I think, but it should do.' He ran up the stairs. 'Won't be long.'

He found a gym bag in the bottom of his wardrobe and went to the bathroom where he gathered up his shaving gear and toiletries.

He had a gut feeling that he was going to be at Adie's for some time, so he pulled out an old suitcase, put it on the bed and began scouring his cupboards for suitable clothes. He was just grabbing a pair of boat shoes from the rack, when he heard a heavy tread on the stairs.

Adie stopped in the doorway. His usual expression, one of mild amusement at everything, was missing. 'Think you'd better come and take a look at something, mate.' He turned and retreated back along the hallway.

'What's the problem?' Matt didn't like to see Adie this serious. It made him nervous.

'You've had visitors.'

Matt saw the old leather case sitting beside the open cupboard door, and Adie, crouching down and easing himself back inside the crawl space. His voice sounded muffled as he said, 'A bug. To be accurate, a well-hidden covert listening device, but I don't expect matey-boy was thinking that you'd send an old pro like me creeping around in your junk hole. I spotted it immediately.' He backed out and brushed dust from his shoulders. 'Sorry, mate, but someone has wired you up.'

Matt said nothing for a moment, then he was overcome by pure white-hot rage. 'How long do you think it's been here, and what's its range?' he asked through gritted teeth.

'Been here quite a while. It's a sophisticated piece of kit, but not cutting edge. Six months maybe. I'd guess it's got a range of about fifty metres.' Adie raised an eyebrow. 'It'd certainly reach your bedroom, if that's what you're worried about. I've temporarily disabled it, but do you want me to strip it out?'

'No, don't touch it. I'll get forensics to remove it and hopefully even get a trace on it. Jesus!' He slammed a fist into the wooden banister rail. 'Six fucking months!' *Oh my God, what has he heard?*

'I guess you don't go poking around in here too often?'

Matt felt sick. 'I *never* go in there. Mrs Cable keeps the Hoover and the dusters there. Other than that, as you say, it's just old junk.'

'Well, unless your Mrs Cable is a spook in another life, she certainly wouldn't have noticed it. Even your SOCOs missed it.' Adie reached forward and gripped his shoulder. 'Sorry, mate, this arsehole really does have it in for you, doesn't he?' His face was still serious. 'Good move coming to my place for a while. If he shows up and I'm around, he'll be picking his teeth out of his arse while he waits for the judge to pass sentence.' He gave Matt a rueful smile. 'I found your case.'

They stared at it. 'If you hadn't come looking for that . . . ' Matt said.

Adie tilted his head to one side. 'So, what's so important about it?'

Matt knelt down on the carpet and opened it. It was packed full of photographs. As he sorted through them, memories flooded back. Like waves crashing onto the shore, each picture evoked a new and stronger recollection than the one before.

Adie squatted down beside him, lifting photographs, staring at them, then putting them back. 'Were you ever that young?'

'Apparently.'

'I assume you are looking for something particular, and this is not just a rehearsal for a new run of *This is Your Life*."

Matt didn't answer. He'd found it.

'Ah, the lovely Maggie, with her handsome groom.' Adie's smile faded and his brow crinkled up into furrows. 'Why the hell do you have the overwhelming need to find a photograph of a bloody cake?'

Matt stared at Maggie's hand, alongside his own, grasping the ornate cake knife. 'It's not a cake, it's a wedding ring.'

Adie threw him a helpless look. 'Whatever you say. This has obviously all got too much for you. Can we go now?'

'Yeah. I just need to ring my boss and tell him about all this, he can organise another SOCO to come out.' He sat on the hall floor and stared around. 'I can't believe it. My home's a crime scene again, that's twice in as many days!'

'Who has keys for here?'

'Just me and Mrs Cable. And there's a spare in the key cabinet in the kitchen.'

'Is it still there?' Adie asked.

'Dunno.' Matt gathered up some of the photographs and stood up. 'I'll check.'

'Still here.' He called back from the kitchen. 'I'd better take it. Forensics will need it to get in.' He pocketed the key. 'I'd better get my stuff down from upstairs.'

'You ring your gaffer. I'll sort that, then I'll reactivate the device again. If your stalker notices, he'll just think it's a glitch.'

Adie brought everything down, then loaded the car while Matt locked up. 'I'll run you back to Stalag 19, then I'll take this stuff back to my place. I've given you your usual room, is that okay?'

'Fine. And I really appreciate this. I owe you one.'

'Only one?' Adie turned the ignition and smiled grimly. 'You're welcome. You've done enough for me, one way and another.'

Matt slammed the car door. 'As you say, you're welcome too, but no matter what I did, I'll never be able to repay you for holding me together when I hit rock bottom.'

'Oh, lovely! Here we go again! Get out the bleeding violin. Shut your trap, it's what friends do. Now forget it.'

As they drove back to Fenfleet, Matt tried to think of all the things that his eavesdropper might have heard. Most of it would be harmless chitchat, but some things didn't bear thinking about. And apart from delicate police issues, spoken about over the phone and definitely not meant for others' ears, they were all connected to Liz.

He remembered their intimate conversations, their lovemaking. He closed his eyes and felt like someone was standing on his chest. Up until now, he had had the stupid belief that the killer only knew Liz as his work colleague, but that obviously was not the case.

He groaned. 'Thank God that Liz is safely back at the station. We really do have to talk, and soon.'

CHAPTER TWENTY-TWO

After dropping off his spare key for the SOCO with the desk sergeant, Matt went to the murder room. He was met by a slightly flustered Jason. 'I was just going to ring you, sir.' He ran his hand through his hair. 'Another development while you were out. We've found a bundle of clothes that could belong to Gabriel.'

Matt glanced around the room, still anxious to talk to Liz, and mildly concerned that her desk was empty.

'Where did they turn up?'

'A farmer found them. Out over Holland Fen way, they'd been pushed in between a pile of old pallets that were ready to be burnt.'

'Why the hell did he ring us about some old clothes? People dump everything from sofas and washing machines to bags of dirty nappies, rather than go to the bloody tip.'

'They were carefully folded and wrapped in brown paper, boss, not screwed up in an old black bin bag. And when he opened it, he saw a complete set of kid's stuff, from shoes to underwear. He'd heard about the missing boy and put two and two together.'

'Smart man.' Matt's eyes still searched the outer office for signs of Liz. 'Have they been brought in?'

'Straight to the lab for examination, sir.'

'Good. Eh, where's Liz?'

'She was here a few minutes back.' Jason looked around. 'Gemma, where's Sergeant Haynes?'

Gemma put her phone down and quickly ticked a name on a long sheet of paper before saying, 'Got a call from her husband, sir. She's just popped downstairs to see him for a moment. Do you need her?'

'Yes. I don't want to drag her away from Gary, but it's important. Could you find her and tell her to come to my office as soon as she's finished with her husband?'

Gemma stood up and groaned. 'No problem, sir. I could do with stretching my legs, I've been on that phone for hours.'

Jason moved a step closer and whispered, 'The super said you've had more problems at home.'

'The bastard's bloody well bugged the farmhouse.'

'Shit!' He puffed out his cheeks. 'But that may explain how he knows so much about you.'

'It's sure helped him. I just want to know how long I've had a silent fucking house guest for. He could have been waltzing in and out when the fancy took him, for bloody months.'

'How the hell did he get hold of your key?' Jason looked at him hard. 'That is how he's got in, isn't it? A spare key?'

'Can't think of any other way,' said Matt. 'I haven't tackled her on it yet, but I'm guessing that Mrs Cable may have had a visit from our lovely, and oh so convincing, Detective Edward Dennis sometime in the recent past.'

Jason raised his eyes to the ceiling. 'Of course. His specialty is duping old ladies, isn't it? Which reminds me . . .' He went to his desk and picked up a large folder. 'I've got the enlargements from the CCTV at your mother's nursing home. I thought you'd want to see them first.'

Matt took them, relieved to know that so far Gemma had not been able to grab one to run another comparison check on Paul Underhill.

The face that had stared deliberately at the camera made his flesh crawl. The half-smile was insidious, purposely meant to taunt. It said, "I know everything there is to know about you, and guess what? You still know fuck all about me. Loser!"

Jason stared at it with him. 'What a slimeball. I'd like to slap that cocky grin right off his face.'

Matt thought about Adie's slightly more graphic comments. 'You aren't alone there, Jace.' He slid them back into the folder. 'Can I ask you not to show these to Gemma just yet. She'll immediately go off on her 'Underhill is alive' crusade and we've got more than enough to contend with right now.'

Jason shrugged. 'No sweat, guv. But I do rather wonder if she has a point.'

Matt sighed. He was too tired to fight this battle yet again. 'You guys weren't here back then, Jason. I promise you, that was one identification they would not have cocked up, no way! Now can we let it rest?'

Before he could answer, Gemma came back in. 'Can't pass on the message just yet, sir. Desk sergeant said Sergeant Haynes had another call to meet her husband in the car park. She said she's quite safe with him and she'll be back in ten.'

A shard of icy fear slipped down Matt's backbone. 'Gemma! Did you check the car park? Did you confirm she was there?'

'Uh, no, sir. When the sergeant said she was okay I . . .'

Without giving her time to finish, Matt raced from the room. He took the steps downstairs three at a time and after fumbling frantically with the security numbers, burst through the back doors to the parking bay. With a sick feeling welling up in his throat, he looked this way and that. He dashed outside and ran up and down the rows of parked staff vehicles. After a moment or two, he stopped, leaned heavily on a 4x4, and carefully gazed down the rows once more. Bay 15, where Liz parked her red MG sports car was empty.

When Jason and Gemma caught up with him, they found him staring at his mobile. 'Her phone's switched off.'

'Try her radio! I'll get uniform after her!' Jason turned back and ran for the door. 'She's only got a few moments head start on us.' He paused and yelled. 'Gemma! Check our cameras, see which way she went!'

'And if she was alone!' added Matt, his voice cracking with emotion.

'Boss! Hold up!' Gemma was pointing to the far end of the car park. 'Look, in the visitor's bay.'

Both front doors of a silver Lexus had swung open and two figures were scrambling out.

'Sir? Whatever's wrong?' Liz's voice rang out.

Gemma was also struck dumb. With difficulty, Matt swallowed hard, took a deep ragged breath and said, 'We lost contact with you.' He indicated vaguely towards her parking spot and tried to pull himself together. 'And your car's not there? We thought . . .'

'Gary brought me in this morning.' She frowned. 'And I told the desk sergeant exactly where I'd be.'

'Sweetheart! Don't knock their concern about you!' Gary Haynes chided his wife. 'I actually find it very reassuring.' He advanced towards Matt, his hand outstretched. 'Hello. I think we met once before, didn't we? I'm sorry if we've inadvertently caused you a minor heart attack, but Liz really thought she'd covered all the bases.'

Matt shook Gary's big hand, and then fought off the urge to gently massage some feeling back into his own after the vice-like grip finally released him. 'Not her fault,' he mumbled. 'We're all pretty strung out at present.' He rubbed his hand across his forehead. It felt more than weird to be chatting amicably to his lover's husband. 'Look, uh, why not come inside, finish your talk over a coffee?'

'It's okay, we're through. But thanks anyway.' The soldier climbed back into the car, then looked back at Matt shrewdly. 'I appreciate you looking out for Liz like you did. It makes me feel a whole lot better about her safety.' He turned to his wife. 'Ring me when you're ready to come home, babe, and I'll come and collect you, okay?'

Liz reached into the car and squeezed his shoulder affectionately. 'I'll do that. See you later.'

As the car moved off she turned and looked at Matt with sad eyes. 'I'm sorry. I really frightened you, didn't I?'

Matt glanced around and waited until he saw Gemma and Jason go into the station.

'Could be said.' He gave her a small smile. 'Jesus, Liz! I was terrified! I thought he'd got you. I really *believed* he'd got you.'

They held each other's gaze. He wanted to reach out to her, to touch her, to hold her, but he didn't need her swift glance towards the CCTV camera to tell him that he shouldn't. Neither spoke, but Matt realised that there had been another subtle change in their relationship, one that he suspected Liz was feeling as acutely as he was. He shivered. Under the present circumstances, that was not good. Not good at all. 'Let's get inside. I need a very strong coffee.'

'You and me both.' He felt the lightest of touches on his shoulder as they passed through the doorway, and he knew that he was right to worry.

* * *

Twenty minutes later, Matt gathered his team in the murder room. 'I've just seen the super. As you will probably know, because of the missing child, all leave is cancelled. We are getting officers drafted in from neighbouring forces to help with the search, and after talking to the parents, the superintendent has decided not to let them do an appeal, he's going to do it himself.'

'Mother still too juiced up to be coherent?' asked Liz.

'Probably, but the official position is that they just aren't considered suitable to go in front of the media at present.'

'Right. Definitely still slaughtered.'

Matt continued. 'Now, the search is headed up by uniform, plus they have a large contingent of community officers and volunteers, so we are better deployed here. I know, considering the situation that you'll all want to burn the midnight oil, but we do have to keep sharp, so we'll work on until it's sensible to grab some sleep. Our job will intensify when we know a bit more about what has happened to the lad. So, does anyone have any problem with staying on tonight?'

'With a boy missing and a fruit loop out there watching us? What do you think, boss?' Jason raised his eyebrows in amazement that Matt would even ask the question. The others all chipped in their agreement.

'Right then, let's get updated, shall we? First thing, all check your emails and messages, see if anything occurred while we were racing around the car park like total prats.'

Matt pulled Liz to one side and, as they made their way to his office, told her about the listening device that Adie had found.

'Oh great!' Liz pulled a face. 'But that explains a lot, doesn't it? Overheard phone calls, personal conversations, our psycho could have built up a wealth of information about you that way.'

'You don't seem worried about,' he paused, 'well, about some of the other sort of things he may have heard? At night, maybe?'

Her voice dropped to a whisper. 'I'm not. I just hope we gave that sicko a bit more entertainment than he was expecting. Fucking wanker.'

'But it makes your situation even more dangerous now, doesn't it?' He bit on his bottom lip nervously.

'I don't think it changes anything, Matt. It's just that we now realise that he knows a hell of a lot more than we thought. We're all in danger, and have been since the moment that he came on the scene.'

'I suppose.' He sat down heavily.

'Look, I'm going to see if I've had anything back from either the holiday company or any news about ex-DC Colin Bristol, deceased, or not, as the case may be.' She smiled at him. 'Come on, it's the whole force against one nutter, we'll get the bastard.'

Matt nodded, and wished he felt as confident as Liz sounded "We'll get the bastard" sounded just like the empty promise that his old sergeant had made.

'Sir!' The urgency in Gemma's voice whipped his thoughts back to the present. 'Jason says can you come to the murder room, sir.'

When Matt got there, Jason was just hanging up his desk phone. 'Forensics rang a few minutes ago, boss, there was something in the list of Gabriel's clothing that they wanted you to know about.'

'Before you tell me anything, do we know for sure that the clothes do belong to Gabriel?'

'Well, the DNA tests aren't back yet, but what they do have is pretty conclusive. They have matched his shoe and clothes size, his hair colouring from a few stray strands, and there are some blood stains on his clothes that match exactly to the location of injuries on the dead boy's body.'

'Same blood group as Gabriel?'

'The same, sir.'

'Okay, so what did they ring about?'

'In the pocket of his jeans, they found a cheap market-stall neck chain, sir, with a relatively expensive gold cross on it.'

Matt felt his mouth go dry.

'I've already asked uniform to pick it up from the lab. I hope that's alright?'

Matt nodded mutely and tried to absorb the new information. A crucifix? Somehow he really hadn't expected that little twist. His thoughts flew to Paul Underhill. What if Gemma had been right all along? What if the dead man that they pulled out of the ditch had not been Underhill, but someone dressed in his clothes to mislead them? His head flooded with thoughts. And where had that damned post-mortem report gone? What if the identification had been screwed up in some way? Maybe his recollections were clouded, he had been pretty screwed up himself. Maybe . . . ?

'Sir? Are you alright?' Gemma's voice rescued him from the past again.

He rubbed his temple. 'Yeah, stonker of a headache, that's all.'

'No wonder. You looked stressed out. Can I get you a coffee, guv? I'm getting some for the others.'

'Please, and can you rake up a couple of Paracetamol from somewhere?'

'No problem. Be back in a mo.'

Liz came over, clutching a large sheaf of papers.

'They've found a crucifix in Gabriel's clothes,' he told her.

She looked up from sorting through the paperwork. 'I heard.' She shrugged her shoulders. 'Frankly, I'm not reading too much into that. If our psycho can bug your home and know just about every damned thing there is to know about you, then why shouldn't he know about the crosses, too?'

'Because I never told a soul about them.'

'Then he found out about them from someone else.'

'Like who, for instance?'

'I have absolutely no idea, but I do know that there are very few true secrets in this world. What if someone who works in the evidence depository was having a sort out and questioned their history? Or maybe he knew our old pathologist and got to him before he died. I really don't know.' She put the papers on the desk and crossed her arms. 'This guy is clever, and he's clearly been planning this for bloody ages. Don't get too hung up on this new find, Matt. You, more than anyone, know that he's a mindbender, so just remember that, okay?'

'I should know that by now, shouldn't I? My mind's in overdrive.'

'Which is exactly what he wants. His timing is impeccable, isn't it? Sorry, Mattie, but he's really stuck you on a rollercoaster and left you there for the full ride.'

'With no time to draw breath before he drops his next bombshell.' He shook his head, as if trying to clear the confusion that was threatening to swamp him. With difficulty, he turned his attention to the pile of papers on the desk. 'So what's all this?'

'Right, well, it seems that your old and very dodgy colleague, DC Bristol, has definitely cashed in his chips, unless his wife has had him locked in the attic for years. Life insurance was paid out and there's a plaque on the crematorium wall in Greenborough.' She turned over a few pages. 'One copy of the death certificate and, as you rightly said, there was an obit notice in the *Daily Telegraph*. Which brings me on to your holiday of a lifetime.' Liz perched on the edge of his desk. 'Believe it or not, Angelos Holistic Healing is still operating, in fact, it's practically gone global. They still have the original centre in Greece, but have opened centres in Tuscany, Provence, Thailand, and the Caribbean.' She threw him a grin. 'And now we get to the interesting part. I had IT blow up that photo of you and your guru in the olive grove? I sent it to head office and they relayed it out to Karissa. Now, guess what? That old guy who used to counsel you is still there.'

'Dimitri? My God, he must be ancient!'

'Yup, he's in his eighties, but apparently he still spends time helping the confused and the bewildered.'

'Thank you for that description, Sergeant.' He smiled. 'Fancy that! I can't believe he's still there. But, frankly, does it matter? He'd never remember a specific group, yet alone an individual, from all that time ago.'

'Don't be so negative, Mr Glass Half-Empty! As it happens, I spoke to the head honcho who runs the Greek side of the outfit. Apparently she's been with the company for donkey's years, started with them even before you made your epic voyage of discovery. I gave her the dates of your holiday, and she says she may be able to put me in touch with someone who was definitely on Karissa at the same time as you!'

'And how the hell can she be sure of that?'

'Because one particular woman loved the place so much that after her first trip in 1985, she went back regularly at the same time every year, right up until five years ago.'

Matt screwed his face up as he tried to recall something he'd heard. 'Yes, I have a vague memory of the staff talking about someone who made Karissa into an annual pilgrimage. As far as I can recall, she used to stay for a month at a go. God knows where she got the money from, those holidays cost an arm and a leg.'

'Whatever. Hopefully we'll have a number for her shortly and I can continue ferreting.' She gathered the papers together. 'Shall I go and see if Jason's had any more news from uniform about those sightings of young Ryan before he disappeared?'

'Yes, we should have heard something from those migrant workers who saw the jogger by now. It's really not looking too good for that poor kid.'

'If the killer took him, not good at all.'

* * *

Ted carefully cut the crusts off the sandwiches and placed them in the centre of a piece of kitchen roll. He went to the fridge and poured a small amount of orange juice into a polystyrene cup. He certainly couldn't allow his guest access to anything sharp or breakable. Placing both items on a tray, he picked up his keys and made his way down the corridor from the kitchen to the annexe.

With one hand he balanced the tray, turned the key with the other, and kicked the door open, calling out. 'Room service! Hope you're decent.'

The boy was awake, but gagged and still securely strapped to the bed. When he saw his captor, fear shot across the dirty face. Then Ted saw something else, an emotion that he certainly hadn't expected to see.

'Well, well, little man! I do believe you're angry at me!'

The boy blinked furiously and gurgled something into the gag, but there was no doubt in Ted's mind. Sure, the boy was terrified, but he still had the capacity to be angry at the man who had abducted him. Ted liked that. That was something he could respect.

'Scream, and I promise you it will be the last noise you ever make.' He placed the tray on the floor next to the bed and stared directly at the child. 'Stay calm and silent, and you can eat and drink. It's your choice, but listen carefully because this may influence your decision somewhat. One single word, and I will place my hands around your throat and choke you until the blood vessels in your eyes rupture, your eyeballs bulge and then burst from their sockets. You decide.'

For a short time the boy defiantly held his gaze, then slowly dropped his head forward and remained looking downwards.

'A good choice.' Ted loosened the tape and allowed the gag to slip down over the boy's chin. 'Now, don't speak unless I ask you a specific question.' From underneath the bed he pulled out a wide leather strap and before releasing any of his prisoner's other restraints, he slipped the strap around the upper part of the boy's body and secured it tightly. It allowed the child to use just his hands, and his arms from the elbows down, while his upper arms were still secured fast to his ribcage. Without taking his steely gaze from the pale face, Ted undid the restraints that were attached to the iron bedstead, then placed the food close to the boy's hand. 'Eat.'

The boy hesitated and a pained look crossed his face. He shifted uncomfortably on the bed and bit his bottom lip.

'Eat first, then I'll let you take a piss, okay?'

The boy understood and reached silently for the sandwich.

Ted moved to the other side of the room, squatted down on his haunches and leaned back against the wall. He had expected this kid to be like the last one, a squirming mess of snot and dribble and wild eyes. Ted's nose wrinkled slightly. A most unpleasant sight! It had been something of a relief to find that he'd accidentally choked him.

'I get the feeling that being used and abused by adults is not new to you, my friend. Not at this extreme, I'm sure, but nevertheless, I suspect you've taken your fair share of bad shit in your short life.'

The boy shoved half the sandwich into his mouth, chomped hungrily on the bread, but said nothing.

'Let me guess. I suspect an uncaring family. Maybe drink, maybe drugs, maybe just pig-ignorant slobs who know no better, being themselves products of dysfunction.'

The boy concentrated on the food and seemed to be ignoring his words.

'No one in the world to care,' Ted paused for effect, 'except perhaps for that batty old duck who lives all alone out on the marsh.'

The boy's head snapped up and he threw Ted a look of undisguised hatred.

'Ooh, I do believe I've touched a raw nerve!' Ted was amused. He could insult the kid's family with impunity, but mention the old woman and the boy was ready to take him on! 'Look out for her, do you? Or maybe she looks out for you, as best she can. You can answer me, if you wish.'

'You leave her alone!' he said through gritted teeth.

'Don't worry, young Ryan. Oh yes, she told me your name. You see, I've seen her already.'

The implications of his softly spoken words sank in. The boy's jaw sagged imperceptibly and his shoulders slumped down.

Ted stared at him. This was one feisty kid. Just for a short moment he even wondered if he might feel sorry about killing him. 'It's alright. We just chatted. She even made me a cup of tea, you know. A little strong for my taste, but nice of her anyway.' He smiled. 'I understand the police have taken her to a very comfortable old people's home, where she'll be looked after until I'm caught. Sadly however, if the police continue to bumble along at their present rate, she could be there for quite a long time.' He abruptly stood up. 'Right. Now, I have better things to do than talk to you. And you need to pee, don't you?'

He crossed the room to the wooden chest, unlocked it and withdrew a plastic urine bottle. 'Use it, then take your hands away and keep them away, understood?'

He placed it on the bed between the boy's legs, then took a few steps back and pulled a pair of disposable gloves from his pocket. 'Privacy isn't an option, I'm afraid, but if you don't play up, I'm prepared to let you sort yourself out. Just hurry up about it, I've got things to do.'

After the boy had relieved himself, Ted carefully removed the bottle, handling it as if it were nitro-glycerine, and placed it on the floor outside the door.

'Right, now listen to me. I have another decision for you to make. This house is situated in a remote spot, with no neighbours and no passing traffic. The only reason you were drugged, then gagged, is because your constant shouting irritated me, and I wasn't sure if I could be trusted not to kill you just to shut you up, *comprende*?'

The boy swallowed, then nodded.

'Excellent. So, as you're a sensible kid, I will either truss you up and silence you exactly as I did before, or leave you without the gag and with only minimum restraint if you promise to keep quiet and do absolutely nothing stupid. Oh yes, and the original rules about throttling you still apply. What's it to be?'

Ryan swallowed again and muttered. 'I'll be quiet.'

Ted slowly nodded his head. 'Right.' He moved forward and picked up the tray, then placed the beaker of juice on the floor within the boy's reach. 'Know this. The bed is bolted to the floor. There are no removable parts to help you to escape. If somehow you managed to free yourself, the door is reinforced, and is locked and bolted on the outside. The only window has steel bars and shutters. There is no natural light, so if you tried to touch the only light fitting,' he pointed at the ceiling, 'you would find yourself not only a prisoner, but a prisoner in a pitch black cell. Now, have I forgotten anything?' He chewed for a moment on the inside of his cheek.

'Ah yes, of course, you may need to crap. You will find a plastic bucket under the bed.' He frowned. 'However, if you can refrain from using it and hold on until I say, I will escort you to the bathroom once a day, as a reward.' He took a deep breath. 'On the other hand, if you mess the bed, I will burn the soiled linen, with you still in it. Now, lie still.'

Ted worked for several minutes, hobbling the boy's ankles together, then placing one thick leather belt around the child's waist and padlocking it to a chain attached to the bed leg. When the job was completed, he took out the tray, and finally dragged the wooden chest from the room and left it in the hall. No use leaving any temptation.

'Okay, Ryan. You have a small amount of freedom. If you want to stay alive, don't abuse it.'

The boy glowered at him.

'Okay, let me put it another way. *If* you try anything silly, just remember, I know where your dear old friend has been housed, and I'm sure she'd love another visit from me, but this time, we'll skip the tea, gottit?'

He didn't wait for an answer, he'd seen the angry, rebellious look turn into one of stark terror.

* * *

Just before eleven that night, Matt stood on the front step of the police station and watched out for Adie's car. He had already seen Liz drive off with her husband, and Jason escort Gemma to his old Vauxhall Astra. Bryn had left a little earlier with one of his flatmates; a muscly six footer with a German shepherd dog glued firmly to his ankle.

He sighed and pulled his jacket closer around him. He could do no more. The incident in the car park had really shaken him and now he felt weary. Not just tired, but mentally exhausted. The killer was wearing him down, down to an all-time low. He stared up into the clear night sky and wondered just how many more shocks his wired brain could take. He knew it was someone's idea of a way to pay him back for something, but if kids were going to suffer, he really didn't want to do this anymore.

'Come on, Galileo! If you are trying to find the answer to your fate in the fucking stars, I'd give up right now if I were you!' Adie leaned across the passenger seat and pushed the door open. 'Better to look for it at the bottom of a bottle of Bell's.' He grinned broadly, 'And I'll give you a hand with the search. Now bloody get in, cos I've got a large portion of Spaghetti Bolognese heating up as we speak, and it's got your name on it, Chief Inspector.'

'And that bottle of Bell's?'

'Ready and waiting.'

The tension of a few moments ago began to fade. 'So what are you hanging around for? A parking ticket? It can be arranged, you know.'

'Typical bloody rozzer!' Adie raised his eyes to heaven, threw the big car into gear and pulled away. 'Why I stick my neck out for you, I have no idea!'

Matt sat back and sighed. 'Neither have I, but right now, I'm pretty glad you do.'

CHAPTER TWENTY-THREE

Matt had passed out for a few hours, rather than slept. He woke up to find a watery dawn filtering pale light through the small window of his room. For a moment he wondered where he was, then reality crept back and he moaned softly to himself. Before, whenever he woke up in this particular bed, he could reach over and touch the warm, smooth flesh of Liz cuddled close beside him. Today the bed felt cold, the perfect match for his mood. He swung his legs over the side of the bed and slowly stood up. A crushing, pulsating headache thundered across from temple to temple. *Jesus Christ! Just how much Scotch did we down last night?* He sat back down on the bed and fought off the rising nausea. Maybe staying with Adie had not been such a bright idea after all. Adie's home-poured shots were about as lethal as a monkey with a loaded Uzi.

He staggered to the bathroom, cursing the fact that he had tried to drown his sorrows. It might have helped last night, although even that was little more than a dim memory, but it sure wasn't going to help him today. Swearing softly, he turned on the shower, and while it warmed up he searched through his washbag for some Paracetamol.

By the time he had showered and dressed it was just after six thirty. Adie had promised to run him to work, but Matt had the feeling his friend would probably not surface much before ten, all things and half a litre of Scotch considered.

Matt made his way down the back stairs and was just about to slip out, when he realised he wasn't alone. Adie was sitting on a small window seat close to the back entrance and was deeply engrossed in the morning paper.

'Blimey! Your paperboy gets up early! So do you for that matter.'

'Ah, Matt. At last. I thought you wanted to get on the road before the crack of dawn? I've already been down to the store and collected the morning rag, *and* cooked you a heart-warming breakfast.' He stood up, folded up the newspaper and stretched. 'Come on. You can't start the day on an empty stomach. A Lincolnshire fry-up is what you need to catch the bad guys.'

Matt clutched at his belly. 'Oh please! After last night's skinful! You have to be joking.'

'All the more reason to eat. You'll feel better in no time, I promise.' Without allowing argument, he propelled Matt into the tiny restaurant and sat him down at a table set for two. 'Give me two minutes.'

Strangely, it worked. By the time Adie had delivered him to the nick, Matt felt close to normal, well close enough to fool his colleagues and avoid the usual teasing, not that he thought anyone would even notice his condition considering the missing child.

In his office, he logged onto his computer and brought up the latest reports from uniform. The search had so far proved negative, but the terrain they were searching was just about as bad as it gets, acres of marsh, fen and bog. The only new development was the report of a white van with some kind of writing and a telephone number on the side, parked close to where the boy was last seen. Officers had isolated a set of tyre tracks where the vehicle had been parked, and had identified them as not being a British make. Although they had not actually been pinpointed to a particular brand, they were definitely foreign in origin and, according to the investigator, a really obscure pattern, possibly Eastern European.

Matt skimmed through the rest quickly. Surely no one in their right mind would go out and snatch a child in a sign-written van? One with a bloody great telephone number on it? And Lincolnshire's population was full of Eastern Europeans working the fields and in the food processing factories, most likely the van belonged to one of the pack-house gangs and had nothing at all to do with the taking of Ryan Fisher.

He closed the file and began checking his emails, deleting most, making notes regarding others, and printing off a few important ones.

'Ah, now, I wonder what you have got for me?' A message with the subject *Re: Cadogan Fife Adoption Agency* was listed. He double-clicked it open.

Dear Chief Inspector Ballard,

Forgive the early hour in sending this, but your problem has been on my mind ever since we spoke. Last night I trawled through pages of listings from the 80s and 90s. To my surprise I have found something that may be of interest to you, something I would prefer not to simply write down in an email. I know you are busy but I wondered if you may be able to come up to County Durham and see me. Please call me when you can, I have a hospital appointment this morning but hopefully will be home by midday.

I look forward to hearing from you.
Alexis Peart

Matt printed off the message and re-read it. It was still early, maybe he could catch her before she left. He flipped open his pocketbook and found her telephone number. Halfway through dialling he stopped and hung up the phone. He had no idea what sort of hospital appointment she was attending or where it was. Maybe his call would upset her or make her late. Sure he was intrigued by what she had said, but even so, she had requested that he ring in the afternoon, so he'd better go along with that. Just to make sure he didn't get embroiled in something else at that time, he set his phone alarm for noon, then tried not to second guess what it was that she'd uncovered in the archives of Cadogan Fife Adoption.

* * *

'So who is this Adie Clarkson, sir?' Gemma buttoned one of her epaulettes and took a quick look at herself in the passenger vanity mirror.

Jason turned down the car radio and shrugged, 'He's someone that the boss trusts. They go back a long way, I believe.'

'Mm, I heard he's an ex-con, too. Funny kind of mate for a DCI.'

'With the hours we work, it's a wonder we have any mates at all, other than the ones we meet in the line of duty,' Jason said glumly.

'Yeah, but an old lag? I thought that was frowned upon, and he's not that hard up for friends, surely?'

'PC Goddard, I don't believe the DCI needs you to vet his friends for suitability. An inquisitive mind is fine, young lady, but being downright nosey is unacceptable.' Jason dropped down to third gear and overtook a tractor. 'And you should know by now that the boss keeps his cards close to his chest regarding his private life. I know no more than what you've picked up on the grapevine.'

Gemma smiled apologetically. 'Sorry, sir. It's just that I really worry about him. He's under such a phenomenal amount of strain right now, anyone from his past makes me feel twitchy. Especially if they're a bit dodgy.'

'I know how you feel, but Clarkson has been straight for years, that I do know.'

'Funny how it was him that found that listening device, though? I mean, it seems like he knew exactly where to look for it.'

'You've got it wrong, Gemma,' Jason gave a deep sigh. 'It was the boss who asked Adie to search in that cupboard, to find some old photos.'

Gemma narrowed her eyes. 'Still seems a bit fishy to me.' She stared out of the window. 'Can I ask you something, sir?'

Jason immediately noticed the serious tone. 'Sure. Fire away.'

'Why won't the DCI entertain the notion that Paul Underhill may still be alive and possibly still killing people?'

'I really don't know. They must have been damn sure about it at the time though. Or maybe he knew exactly what was going on back then when it all happened, and well, perhaps he just can't admit that maybe they got it wrong.'

'But why? Everyone cocks up. Even with all our modern technology, we still balls things up. Surely all those years ago it must have been far easier to make mistakes. You know, I've been awake half the night thinking about those crucifixes. If it was such a well-guarded secret, who else but the killer knew about them?' She turned and stared at Jason. 'What do you think? Honestly?'

'Honestly? I really don't know, Gemma.' He gripped the steering wheel tighter. 'Ninety per cent of me believes that the DCI is right, after all, he should know, he was there in the thick of it. It's okay for us to judge in hindsight, but he *was* there.' He paused for a moment, 'Then I think about the same things that bother you, and well, even I'm forced to admit that sometimes I wonder if that body in the ditch was really Underhill.'

'Bryn thinks exactly the same.' She touched his arm gently, 'We really should dig him up, sir, then we'd know for sure, settle it one way or the other. Will you speak to the boss? Perhaps he'd listen to you, rather than a know-nothing rookie.'

'He doesn't think of you like that, Gemma, and you know it. You wouldn't be on his team if he didn't think you had the makings of a damn good detective.'

'Maybe, but because I don't have the years of experience that you guys have, I'm still considered something of a muppet, aren't I?'

'Believe me, in ten years' time, when you are talking to the youngsters in *your* team, you'll be saying exactly the same thing, "There is no substitute for experience."'

'Yeah, yeah. But will you talk to him, guv?'

'Actually I've already said as much, but I will bring it up again, okay? No promises, though?'

'Thanks. We appreciate it.' Gemma sat back and relaxed, 'Hey! Changing the subject, what about that hunk of a husband that the sarge has! He's well fit!'

'Am I the right person to comment on that?' Jason gave a puzzled smile. 'He's big, I'll give him that. And a nice bloke to boot. I've met him before.'

'What rank is he?'

'Lieutenant Colonel.'

'Impressive! How come the sarge doesn't talk about him more? I'd spend all day showing my mates his photo and dribbling over that gorgeous body!'

'Same reason you don't go round telling everyone that your boyfriend is loaded, I guess.' He glanced at her reprovingly. 'Because it's private, isn't it? And Gary Haynes has a very dangerous job. I'm sure half the time, Liz is expecting to hear that he's coming home in a body bag. She just gets on with her job, it's the best she can do.'

'Ouch! Touché, Inspector.'

'Well, it's true isn't it? When you really care about someone, you don't want the whole mess room dissecting your relationship, do you?'

'No, you're quite right, that's the last thing you want,' Gemma grinned. 'And I wouldn't say Roy's actually loaded.'

'His address says otherwise.'

Gemma's smile faded. 'That's his family, flashing their cash. Roy would be happy living with me anywhere, but they don't want their precious boy living on the wrong side of the tracks.'

'Can't he tell them where to go?'

'Not just yet.' The grin returned. 'Although they may get a bit of a surprise, when the trust fund that Roy's grandfather set up for him is released.'

'Ah, worth the wait, then?'

'Absolutely. He'd be a fool to upset the applecart right now. But apart from that, there's a lot of other stuff to weigh up. I've got my career to consider, and that's very important to me.'

'So he's asked you to marry him, has he?' Jason asked.

Gemma stared into her lap and rubbed absentmindedly at a small mark on her jacket. 'He may have hinted at it, in a roundabout way, but he knows that I'm not ready. And I'd be throwing away all the chances that my Mum and Dad have given me, that's apart from all the hard work I've put in to get here.'

Jason slowed the car and pulled up to the electronic gate to the police station. As he slid his card through the machine and waited for the barrier to lift, he said, 'I married young and kept my career. It can be done, if you really love each other.'

'But it isn't easy, is it? Not in an environment like this? I know, I've seen the statistics.'

'Bugger the statistics! Be one of the anomalies, be the exception that proves the rule. If that's what you want, of course?' Jason pulled into his parking space and looked at the young woman with interest.

She smiled back at him and tilted her head backwards and forwards, as if weighing up his words. 'Food for thought, sir. Something to consider.'

As she climbed out, Jason was left wondering what she really wanted. She wasn't easy to read, but somehow he didn't think that rich Roy and his fancy pad were her main ambition in life.

* * *

'Nothing nasty in this morning's post, sir?' Bryn flopped down at his desk.

'Not so far. But who knows what the day may yet bring?' Matt stood at the window and watched as he saw the big silver Lexus swing into the car park. As Liz stepped out, he felt a rush of relief that she was back safe, then the feeling was overtaken by a surge of jealousy, as she leaned into the driver's window and kissed her husband. He turned sharply back and looked around the room. 'Anything else in from uniform, Jason?'

''Fraid not. They are extending the search area, and they've been joined by some of the Air Cadets from RAF Casterfen. It's a wicked spot to try to cover.'

'The tides are dangerous too, particularly along that stretch of the coastline.' *For God's sake! What right do I have to feel envious of Gary Haynes?* Matt took a deep breath and tried to channel his concentration on the present. 'And as every hour passes, I can't help thinking that when they do find something, it will be a body. Any news on those tyres and the white van?'

Gemma flipped through a small pile of papers. 'Yes, sir. Confirmed as a Romanian make. At least when we find the van, they'll be a doddle to match up.'

'Even if we do, I sincerely doubt it will help us one iota,' said Matt gravely. He knew he sounded as miserable as Jason on a bad day, but dejection was slowly filling him. Even the sight of Liz entering the room didn't lift his spirits, in fact her untouchable presence, so close to him, made him feel even worse.

As the others caught up and shared the latest information, Matt went across to the whiteboard that nearly covered one wall, and stared at the photographs that had been placed on it. It was like a potted history of his life. The three dead boys had become an integral part of him from the moment that he had seen the pale face of Jamie Matravers beneath the moonlit water. Gabriel had now joined them, years later, but he was still another lost soul in the ghostly band of brothers that haunted his dreams. Then there was Laura, then Maggie's wedding photo, and looking at the pictures of them, he felt again the agony that had sent him scurrying off to Greece. To that intensely private place where he had sorted through the wreckage of his life, to see if there was anything left that was worth saving.

He stared at them one at a time. All that pain and anguish reduced to a picture show for the world to scrutinise, maybe to scorn. Maybe even something worse than that, if a photograph of Ryan Fisher's corpse was added to this ghoulish collection.

He smelt Liz's perfume close behind him even before she spoke. Her voice was soft. 'Sorry to interrupt those deep thoughts, Matt. But could I have a word?'

'My thoughts are far from happy right now, Liz. Your distraction is actually very welcome. In my office?'

She nodded and fell in behind him.

He held the door open for her, then closed it carefully. 'Don't worry, I saw Gary bring you in this morning. I won't be doing several laps of the car park in a screaming frenzy, like last time.'

She raised her eyebrows, then sat down. 'Best not. I can't think what the security video looks like.'

'A modern take on the Keystone Cops, probably.' Matt sat on the edge of his desk and looked down at her. 'So, what's the problem?'

'Gary is leaving later today, back to Iraq.'

'Ah, I'm sorry to hear that.'

'Don't lie, Matt Ballard, you're not sorry, you're delighted.'

'Well, I'm sorry he's going back to a war zone. Really I am.'

Liz leaned on the arm of the chair and rested her head in her hand. 'He wants to come in and speak to you before he goes. Is that alright with you?'

Matt blinked. *I'm not sure 'alright' is quite how I feel about that scenario.* 'I guess so. Oh, yes, of course he can. But do you know what he wants?'

'What do you think? The poor guy is terrified, leaving me here with a killer running round loose. He wants to talk to you about my staying with Jason, and what kind of protection he can expect for me. That's all.'

Matt nodded, not sure of what he had actually expected her to say, 'Any idea what time? I'll make sure I'm around.'

'He'll ring first, but probably about noon.' She sat back and threw him a long, apprehensive look. 'Matt, I've been thinking.'

He frowned, not liking the intensity in her tone, 'This doesn't bode well.'

She ignored his comment and continued, 'To be honest, I was wondering how you'd feel about me telling Gary about us?'

The sentence hung in the air, then Matt gave a low whistle. 'Well! I didn't see that coming!'

'Matt, we both know things are . . . well, things have changed, haven't they?'

His mind raced. She was right, but he had no idea what to say to her.

She continued, 'Okay, maybe it's this godawful situation that we're in, or maybe it would have happened anyway, whatever, everything is different now, and I'm pretty sure it's not just me. Or is it?'

He swallowed loudly. 'No, Liz, it's not just you, but . . .' He rubbed his forehead hard. 'Hell! With everything else that's going on, I don't know if I can cope with that, too. What if he really kicks off? The poor sod is off to a war zone tomorrow, it's hardly fair, is it?' He hated what he was saying. He knew it must sound like a lame excuse. 'Liz, we promised we'd never let it become common knowledge. Can you *imagine* what the station gossips would do to us? And we couldn't work together, we—'

'Hold it, right there!' She looked aghast. 'I don't mean take out a sodding ad in the police magazine! I just meant to tell Gary, no one else. I've told you that our marriage is not conventional. I thought it may actually help him to know that I've got someone here, to look out for me, to care for me.'

Matt's head still spun. 'Do you really think, I mean, *really* believe it would help?'

Liz groaned. 'This is no flippant little notion! I've been awake all night thinking about it. Gary was on the phone for hours yesterday trying to get some kind of special leave to stay on, but there is some really serious shit going down where he's stationed, and he's right in the thick of it. Without him there to finish the job, the bad guys are pretty certain to get the upper hand. It's all classified, of course, but it really is bad, believe me. He'd never go otherwise.'

Matt chewed his thumbnail. 'I don't know what to say to you. What if it didn't have the effect you hoped for? Wouldn't that make things worse for him?'

'We had a pact. We made it before we got married.' Liz looked at him earnestly. 'He asked me to tell him if I ever met someone special, someone who really meant something to me. He didn't care about the casual stuff, didn't want to know any details about what I got up to outside our marriage, as long as it was very, very discreet.' Her eyes were fixed on Matt's. 'Thing is, in all the years we've been married, I've never had call to tell him anything, until now.'

'So do you think you should rock the boat at such a traumatic time?' Matt wanted to reach out to her, to hold her hand as they talked. But this was not the place.

'Gary and I are still best friends, always have been. I really want him to know. I honestly believe he won't be able to operate at hundred per cent if he's worrying about my safety. And that could get him killed.'

Matt threw up his hands in surrender. 'Then I'll go with whatever you think best. I have a good idea why you married him, and I know that the deception has worked perfectly. I just don't want you doing something you'll regret later.'

'Then listen to what he has to say to you when he comes in, and if you still think I'm making a big mistake, then I'll forget it, okay?' Her voice dropped to almost a whisper. 'Now, this may be very bad timing, Detective Chief Inspector, but I really need to tell you that I love you.'

His heart thundered in his chest. 'Quite correct, the timing stinks, but you'd better know that I totally endorse that statement.' He looked at her, unable to keep the warmth from his eyes, and shook his head slowly, 'And this is a conversation to be continued at a more suitable moment, and in much nicer surroundings.'

'Yes, sir. Absolutely.' She gave him a comical salute and slipped from the office.

* * *

Two hours later, Matt had a call from the pathologist.

'Just to put your mind at rest in one area of this investigation, dear Chief Inspector.'

He could hear Rory Wilkinson tapping on his computer keyboard as he spoke. 'I think you'll be very relieved to hear that the wedding ring was not your wife's. Computer enhancement of the photograph showed a pronounced bevel. The ring we have here is considerably flatter and although it seems to be of a similar age and it has been altered at some point, as was your wife's, it is not the quality or weight of the one in your wedding photo. So, dear heart, you can forget your notions about Burke and Hare being alive and well and living in Lincolnshire.'

Matt blew out a sigh of relief. 'Thank you for that, Professor Wilkinson, and thank you for suggesting that particular line of enquiry. I appreciate it.'

'I hear that your search for the old picture resulted in the finding of a nasty little bug in your home.'

'It certainly did. I think your technicians are looking at it now.'

'Oh, they are. I've been cracking the whip all day. So are you any closer to finding out who it is that dislikes you so much?'

'Sadly no.' Matt glanced down to the open folder on his desk, and the blow-up from his mother's nursing home of the man who had delivered the flowers. 'It's creepy. I even have pictures of him, but they mean nothing. I've never seen the bastard before.'

'And you've got nothing on file?'

'Nothing at all. I'm sure that's why he's so happy to smile for the cameras. He knows he's bloody squeaky clean.'

'And has his photograph been released to the press?'

'No, not at this stage, although it's been posted to all forces on the Police National Computer.'

'And no one recognises him? Mm, could I be really cheeky and ask to see one of the photos?'

'Sure. I'll send a copy over to you. I suppose the more people who see it the better. If he's local, I could get lucky and find someone who recognises him.'

The pathologist gave a small snort. 'I was thinking more along the lines of a professional appraisal on his physical appearance. You may or may not know, that one of my many particular areas of expertise in this vast and varied field, is forensic anthropology. The study of humans and their cultures. Now I know that usually means the study of human remains, in particular human osteology, but I can deduce an awful lot about someone from their bone structure and physiognomy.'

'Right, well, in that case, I'll send you copies of everything I have. They are all taken from various CCTV cameras so some of them are a bit grainy, But, I'd be grateful for anything you can give me.' Matt silently cursed himself for talking too fast. He sounded like a third year student not a detective.

'It's alright, the lecture's over. Class dismissed.' He could hear the amusement in the pathologist's tone. 'So, as soon as I have a spare moment between cadavers, I'll take a look for you.'

* * *

Jason looked uncomfortable. 'I realise that this might not be the best time to bring this up, but . . .'

'Don't tell me. It's Underhill again, isn't it?' Matt placed his hands over his ears. 'Can't we talk about something else? Like have you heard from your wife and kids? How are they doing?'

'Yes, I've spoken to them. My wife's at her wits' end, and the kids are being a total pain and want to go home, and I really do think that we should look closer at the theory that Underhill may still be alive.'

Matt shook his head. 'Gemma stuck the thumbscrews on you again?'

'No, well, yes, but I really do wonder, when you consider points like those crucifixes, if she's right.'

'Okay.'

Jason stared wide-eyed at Matt. 'Okay? You mean we are going to request an exhumation?'

'No. I mean, okay give Gemma the new picture, the blow-up from my mother's nursing home. She can get IT to run their ageing comparison on it. It's a far superior photo and it should give her a definitive answer, which will prove that it's not Underhill reborn.'

'You really are dead certain about that, sir, aren't you?'

'Yup, but give her the picture and let her run with it.' Matt leaned forward and picked up the photo. 'The more I look at this, the more I know it's not Underhill. I know that I never really spent time with him, but the memories that I do have, throw up a very different kind of man.'

'Time distorts memory, and he might have taken pains to alter his appearance.'

'Possibly.' He tossed the picture across the desk to his inspector. 'Take it and make Gemma's day for her.'

Jason picked it up and looked at the bearded, insidiously smiling face and growled. 'I think digging him up would give her more of a kick, but I suppose this is a start.'

'It's as good as it gets right now.' He grinned, 'And knowing how much you enjoy going to the mortuary, perhaps you'd like to take copies of all the CCTV shots of the killer over to Rory, and check on the status of that last crucifix, while you're there, okay?'

Jason stood up. 'My pleasure, sir.'

'And no more gossip, right? Rory seems to know an awful lot about me.'

'As if, sir.'

CHAPTER TWENTY-FOUR

At eleven thirty, Liz let out a muffled whoop of excitement. 'Excellent!'

'Want to share it?' asked Bryn. 'So far this morning I've hit more bloody brick walls than I care to mention.'

'In the fullness of time, my boy! One more call, and if that doesn't go pear-shaped, I'll be ready to tell all.' She picked up the phone and began punching in numbers.

'Oh well, at least one of us is getting results,' Bryn grumbled. 'My line of enquiry is about as easy as kicking a dead whale down the beach.'

'Chin up, cherub.' Liz placed her hand over the receiver. 'If this pans out, I'm going to need your help to chase someone up, and fast. Oh bugger!' Liz's mobile was ringing from inside her bag.

Bryn looked at her hopefully. 'Can I make the call for you?'

'It's okay.' With one hand, she emptied her bag on the desk and grabbed her phone. 'It's a text from my husband. No problem. Oh shit! And now I've got an answer phone on this line.' She ran off a brief message asking the recipient of the call to ring her back, then slammed down the receiver and pushed back her chair. 'What did I say about things going pear-shaped?' She glanced at the clock and picked up her security pass. 'I've got to go and let Gary through the gate, then call into IT to get a techie to check out my computer. Bloody thing's got a life of its own, and right now I really need it to behave! Will you listen out for my phone? I really need to talk to this woman ASAP. Oh, and don't let the boss freak out again, remind him he is expecting Gary to drop in, okay?'

'Calm down and leave it with me, Sarge. Anything's better than what I'm trying to do at the moment.'

* * *

Matt's direct line rang as Liz left the murder room.

'Mrs Peart! I got your email. Thank you.'

Alexis Peart's greeting was subdued. Matt hoped it wasn't because of her hospital visit.

'I'm sorry to pester you, Chief Inspector, but I got back a bit earlier than I was expecting to, and I really do need to talk to you. Is there any chance you can get up here?'

Matt wanted to say yes, but knew the logistics of the trip were impossible. 'Any other time, I'd already be heading for the motorway, but considering the nature of the serious crime investigation going on at present, I'm afraid it's out of the question. I could send another officer, if the matter can't be spoken about on the phone?'

'Oh dear, no, that wouldn't do at all.' She sounded as though she were trying to come to some sort of decision.

'Alternatively, I could get a car up to you and bring you down here?'

Matt heard a sigh, then she said, 'As with you, under normal circumstances I wouldn't hesitate, and I wouldn't need your kind offer of a car either, but right now I'm afraid I have other things to consider.' Again he sensed the indecision, before she went on, 'Well, I suppose I have no choice. There is no easy way to say this.'

'Have you found something that can help us?'

'I'm not sure about your case. What I've uncovered is, I believe, deeply personal,' she broke off for a second, then added, 'to you.'

Matt tensed, then the mild sense of uneasiness burst into full-blown fear. Whatever Alexis Peart was going to say next, if it was connected him, was going to be the reason that the killer had added the telephone number to the photo of Laura.

The woman obviously took his silence as her cue to continue. 'Last night I ran a check through my computer files for any of our cases that had a link with Fenfleet or the immediate surroundings. There were very few. Certainly no mothers or babies from your area. Then I widened the search to take in relocated families, and I discovered an old case, one that had caused my husband and I a great deal of distress at the time.'

Matt wanted to scream at her to get on with it. He didn't need her life story right now, he just wanted to know the facts.

Alexis Peart seemed to pick up on his impatience. 'Please bear with me. I know this all sounds irrelevant, but you really do need to know the background of this particular case. Some seem doomed from the outset, and this one was a tragedy. On at least three occasions, one child managed to slip through the net that was supposed to be there to support her. She had been removed from what was considered a dangerous environment and put into care at the age of five. Her stepfather, a man who became violent when he drank, was arrested after badly beating her mother. At first the mother refused to bring charges against him, but after a second beating, one that hospitalised her for some time, and in an attempt to get her child back, she agreed to go to court. Before this could happen, he got to her again. Apparently she recovered, but as soon as she was able to walk, she ran away. Some clothes, later confirmed to be hers, were found neatly folded and left on the rocks at a lonely spot on the coast about five miles from where she had lived in Northumberland. Sadly, her body was never recovered, but given the circumstances, it was thought that she had taken her own life. The child was taken back into care, then fostered. Because of the legalities surrounding the mother, adoption was not considered appropriate until after a reasonable amount of time had passed. The first foster home didn't work out, and at that point, a catalogue of errors began and she dropped off the system. When she finally surfaced again and came onto our register, she was seven, and she had just been removed from another suspected abusive situation. Thank God, we were finally able to find a suitable family for her with a local couple here in Brownshill. At last the child was given stability, love and a safe home environment.'

Matt felt exasperated. 'I don't understand. What does this have to do with me? And surely your story had a happy ending anyway?'

'Oh, it did. But even when she was rehomed, we were still uncovering horror stories about the kind of places that she had been sent to. Poor little mite.'

Matt gritted his teeth. 'And the connection with Fenfleet? With me?'

'Her new family moved to your area twelve years ago, and that's how her case file showed up. As soon as I saw it, I recognised it.' Alexis Peart took a deep breath. 'So I dug deeper. I went to the basement and pulled out all the old paperwork connected to it, then with the help of the Internet, I managed to access some information from local papers at the time, and also some reports that couldn't be traced all those years ago. The thing is, DCI Ballard, I now know that the child belonged to the woman in the photograph, your Laura Schofield.'

'Laura? She had a baby? But when?' Matt felt as though he had been sucker punched.

'The child was born in 1990. A date which ties in with when Laura disappeared,' replied Mrs Peart. 'She married very quietly in a registry office a couple of years later. She became Laura Findlay, and at about three this morning, I discovered that her maiden name was Schofield.'

'Laura married? And to a brute who knocked her about?' Matt gritted his teeth. 'Are you certain about this?'

When she spoke, Alexis Peart sounded close to tears, she was obviously far from happy having to pass on such delicate information in such a blunt and hurtful manner. 'Now can you understand why I wanted to see you, Chief Inspector? I've accessed everything that's available to me, and double-checked everything as best I can, but unless I've made a terrible mistake, I really believe that you might have a daughter.'

Matt's mouth had gone dry and his heart hammered in his chest. 'I don't believe it! Why would Laura run away from me in the first place? Why didn't she tell me?'

The voice on the other end of the line was full of compassion. 'Oh, if only you knew what goes through a girl's mind when she finds out she's pregnant. Not all cope well. Some don't cope at all.'

'But . . .' Matt felt tears well up in his eyes. After all these years, his gut feeling told him that Laura really was dead. The policeman in him reminded him that this was totally unsubstantiated evidence, and all of it would all have to be thoroughly checked, a full investigation, in fact. He forced back the tears. Deep down though, he just knew that they would find Alexis Peart's findings to be correct. She was an intelligent woman, and she would never have dumped that on him if, in her heart of hearts, she hadn't been ninety-nine per cent sure.

Her last words suddenly hit him like physical blow. For God's sake! If it were true, he had a daughter. And not just that, but one here in Fenfleet.

'Mrs Peart.' He struggled to speak, 'What's the name of the family who adopted the child?'

'James and Linda Goddard. The child was called Gemma.'

For a full ten minutes from ending the call, Matt paced the floor of his office. His mind was exploding with ridiculous suppositions and insane ideas.

Gemma? Was it possible that she was his daughter? And how old was Gemma? Could she be twenty-seven? She looked so much younger. And could he see anything of Laura in her? Anything of himself? She certainly had Laura's colouring. And his enthusiasm for their chosen career. Yes, she was a dedicated police officer, like him. She never mentioned being adopted, but how many people did? According to Mrs Peart, she'd had a very bad start in life, maybe she'd been traumatised and wanted to forget her early years. For a moment he was filled with anger at Laura for running away, for taking his unborn daughter and leaving her to some awful fate. He rubbed at his eyes until he made them sore. More than anything, he was bitterly angry at her for never telling him he was going to be a father. He'd wanted to marry her, for God's sake. What did she think he was going to say? He'd have been in seventh heaven! He halted the flow of thoughts. Or would he? He suddenly remembered those early years in the force. So full of fire and ambition. And had he really ever told Laura how much he wanted to marry her? Maybe all he'd conveyed to her was the fire and ambition, not for her, but for his career. Perhaps it wasn't her fault at all.

He desperately wanted to call Gemma in, sit her down and talk to her, then reality kicked in hard. *Like hell! What kind of insensitive arsehole, are you?*

Matt leaned back in his chair, and was suddenly overtaken by gut-clenching nausea and a really sickening thought. What if this was just some kind of devious and sadistic joke, dreamed up in the sick mind of the killer? Not one shred of it real. He remembered Liz saying, "Remember, he's a mindbender, Matt, and he's stuck you on the roller coaster."

Yeah, thinking about it, what did he know about this Peart woman? What if she was part of it? What a great line to spin him.

He badly needed to talk to someone, but he had to try to clear his head or, not for the first time recently, he'd probably come over as some kind of raving basket case. Somewhere he had heard that your brain can only cope with ten things at a time, then, to prevent overload, it would throw one out. Right now he was pretty sure that his sanity was going to be the first to go! If it hadn't gone already.

As he stood up and pushed his chair under the desk, he heard a knock on the door.

Now this is going to be interesting. How the hell do I act normal after the news that I've just received?

Bryn stuck his head around the door. 'Sorry to bother you, boss, but Sergeant Haynes' husband is on his way up to see you. Shall I bring him to your office?'

Matt fought back the urge to laugh out loud. *Oh great! This just gets better and better! It's good old Gary!*

When he answered, his voice was calm and controlled, something he later marvelled at, considering that inside he was silently screaming for a syringe full of something powerful and mind-numbing. 'Yes, that's fine, Bryn, and a couple of coffees, if you would. Make mine strong as hell, and check how he likes his when he arrives.'

He had a fleeting glimpse through the closing door of the back of a PC, walking hurriedly along the corridor. Was it Gemma? For a moment his heart jumped, then he roughly pushed aside all the emotional garbage that was threatening to envelope him. The more he thought about it, the more he doubted his earlier ideas. This was a sick joke. Another nasty, insidious twist in this dark game that he was unwillingly embroiled in.

He went back to his desk and sat down. He had to get on top of this. Keep his cool. One thing at a time. He'd see Gary first, then talk to Liz, and finally go see the super.

By that time he should be able to rationalise. *Well, that's the plan. Unless you've got anything better, Sherlock?*

* * *

'My God! This place is heaving! I could hardly get through all the uniforms out there! It looks like a siege!' Gary said.

'I know. We've drafted men in from all over to help with this search.' He held out his hand and prepared for another crush injury. 'Lieutenant Colonel, come on in, have a seat.' Matt pulled out a chair for his visitor, and took delivery of two cups of coffee from Bryn.

'Oh please, skip the formalities. It's Gary.' The big man eased himself into the chair and smiled. 'And can I call you Matt? We've already met before and Liz has told me so much about you, I feel as if I've known you for years.'

Matt placed the drinks on the table and tried to avoid eye contact until he'd managed to quash the surge of guilt that he was feeling. 'Absolutely, me too.' He went around his desk, flopped into his chair and braved looking at the soldier. He was good-looking in anyone's book. A tough guy on the surface, tall and well-built, but when you looked closer, his face held a fine sensitivity, and his eyes, although now full of concern, were obviously capable of real warmth and humour.

'Liz says that you have to return to Iraq. I know you're going to be worried sick about her. If there is anything I can do to make things easier, just say.'

'*Worried* is not quite adequate. Scared shitless is more accurate. And funnily enough, that's not a position I ever recall being in before.' He leaned forward and wrapped his hands around the hot mug, as if seeking reassurance from it. 'She says you've made arrangements for her and another officer, to stay with Detective Inspector Jason Hammond?'

'That's right. We all felt it's probably the safest option at present. I certainly don't want her home alone.'

'You and me both, no question of that. But I really need to know if you can vouch for your inspector?'

'Jason? Too right! He's a top man, I promise. I've known him for years and I trust him implicitly.' He raised his eyebrows. 'Mind you, he's no barrel of laughs.'

'I don't care if he's Mr Grumpy, just as long as he's sound. It's difficult to trust someone when you don't actually know them.'

Oh dear, how very true, Gary. How very true. 'Jason is solid, I promise you, a real family man, and by billeting the three of them together, there will be safety in numbers.'

'Well, I guess I feel better on that score.' Gary leaned back and sipped his drink. 'I'm not a fool, Matt, I know you can't watch her every move, and I know you've all got a job to do, but I really don't like this situation one bit. It's like when we are out on patrol and you sense a sniper. It's weird, after a few tours of duty, you get to kind of smell them. You know the bastard's there, but you can't see him. Then you wait for the bullet to tear half your face off.'

'I'll be frank, Gary. I've never come across a criminal like this one.' A shiver went down his back. 'And I pray that I never do again.'

The soldier looked across the top of his mug. His eyes bored into Matt's. 'He's after *you*, isn't he?'

Matt drew in a long breath. 'Yes. But I don't know why. He's hurting and murdering innocent victims, and that is very hard to live with. In fact, it's killing me.'

'Maybe that's the idea?'

Matt lifted his hands in exasperation. 'But he could have taken me out at any point, if he'd wanted to. Jesus! He's been creeping around my home and watching my every move for fucking years.'

'Then he obviously needs to make you suffer. Torture comes in many different guises, Matt.'

'I'm beginning to realise that. I'm just not certain how much more I can take.' *A daughter? I may have a daughter?*

'Something's happened, hasn't it?' Gary narrowed his eyes. 'Something recent.'

Matt wasn't sure he wanted to answer.

'Come on, man! Your body language doesn't lie. You may appear cool, but I see serious sweat on the top line.'

Although it was not planned, Matt suddenly found himself telling Liz's husband the bare bones about Alexis Peart and what she had apparently uncovered. The one thing he omitted was that she had named PC Gemma Goddard as his newly acquired offspring.

Gary sat back in his chair, still cradling the coffee mug, and looked at Matt. 'No wonder you're freaked! This guy is the real deal psycho, isn't he?'

'I've always though the best liars are the ones that use a few grains of truth to confuse you, but this bastard is taking deception to a new level. I haven't a clue what to believe anymore.'

'Is there a chance this woman's right about the child?'

'Who knows? My girlfriend vanished, and that's all I ever knew. Our man could have uncovered that juicy little fact and created this bogus scenario, or maybe he stumbled on something that I never knew. As with everything else he's thrown at me, without further investigation, I have no way of knowing.'

'What does Liz think?'

'She doesn't know the latest news, but generally she believes he's an ace mindbender, and thinks I shouldn't trust anything he says or does.'

Gary nodded. 'Yup, that sounds like Liz.'

'She thinks he sows evil seeds, then sits back and watches while my fertile mind enables them to grow like bloody giant beanstalks.'

'She's probably right.'

'I'm sure she is, but he hits on such raw and painful emotions, that it's hard to act rationally, especially when you have no idea who he is going to target next.' Matt regretted his choice of words. 'But this isn't helping you, is it? In fact, I'm probably making things worse.'

'You're being honest, which brings me to my main reason for coming.' Gary placed his mug on the desk and gazed steadily at Matt. 'I'll say this, and get out of your hair. If anyone is not helping, it's me. You have a killer running around the county and I'm bleating on about my wife.' He lowered his voice. 'Matt, as I said before, I'm not a fool. I have the ability to read people, if you know what I mean? And I'm reading that something pretty intense is going on in Liz's life right now. Something other than this manhunt.'

Matt held his breath, dreading what Gary was going to say next.

'I've come to ask you to look out for her, Matt. I mean really take care of her. She's been the most important woman in my life since the day we met, and I don't want to lose her.' He threw Matt an apologetic smile, 'I'll be honest, I asked her to get transferred out of here, get the hell away from you and the madman who's threatening you and yours. As you will probably guess, she point-blank refused. So, I just wanted you to be completely aware of how she feels about you, about her loyalty to you. Don't let her down, Matt.' He slowly stood up and held out his hand. 'Good luck.'

Matt stood up and solemnly accepted the handshake. He was unsure of exactly how to take what he'd just been told, but thought he might have just been let off very lightly. 'And to you, stay safe from the snipers. And I'll be there for her, I promise.'

They walked out into the corridor. Matt felt a strange and unexpected camaraderie with the soldier. 'I'll escort you down to the murder room, Gary. I'm sure you and Liz will want some time together before you leave.'

'I'd appreciate that, thanks. And, Matt, I really hope you get this lunatic before he turns your brain to mush.'

He pushed open the door, 'You and me both.'

The murder room was surprisingly quiet. Only Bryn and a couple of other detectives were at their desks. 'Where's Sergeant Haynes?'

Bryn looked up. 'IT, I think, sir. She said that she needed them to sort out a glitch on her computer and she'd call in on them as soon as she'd let the lieutenant colonel here through the security barrier.'

Gary stiffened. 'What? But I never came in that way. I parked out on the street.'

'I thought . . .' Bryn looked confused.

Gary's face had hardened and he turned to Matt. 'I had a text from her telling me that the car park was full, park outside and go straight to your office, she'd see me after our meeting.'

'But she said that she'd had a text from you, sir,' interrupted Bryn, 'asking her to let you through the barriers. She dropped everything and ran.'

Matt looked at her desk, and to the open handbag, its contents including her radio and her mobile phone, still scattered across her surface.

Professionalism overpowered the rising panic in Matt's mind. 'Where's Inspector Hammond?'

'He's not back from seeing the pathologist, sir.'

'Gemma? Where's she?'

Bryn fought to think. 'She had a call to go down to the front office to collect something.'

Matt raced across to Liz's desk and grabbed the mobile. He flicked it on and brought up the last text message. 'Did you send this?' He thrust the phone in front of Gary's face.

'No. No way.' He grabbed it and viewed the details. 'Oh Lord! It's Caller ID withheld. I rarely disable mine on my iPhone, because of the kind of work I do. She would have thought it was me.'

'And she was fielding several other calls at the same time,' Bryn threw in. 'If she was distracted she would have thought nothing of it and just read the message.'

Matt took the mobile back and pocketed it, then shouted, 'Quickly! Come with me, both of you!'

Taking the stairs three at a time, they raced down to the basement where the CCTV control room was housed.

'Bryn!' barked Matt. 'What time did Liz leave her desk?'

'About twenty-five minutes ago, maybe a bit longer, more like half an hour, I suppose.'

His heart began to thud against his rib cage. *Too long. Far too long.* He burst through the door and called out to the officer in charge. 'Locate Detective Sergeant Haynes for me. She was last seen on the second floor, leaving the murder room, approximately thirty minutes ago.' He lowered his voice. 'Priority! Understand?' Turning back to a white-faced Bryn, he said, 'Go find Gemma. And ring Jason and get him back, I want the team assembled.'

He said to Gary, 'I might be overreacting again. I pray that I am, but I can't afford not to.' Still staring at the flashing video footage that was dancing across the screens, he picked up the phone and asked switchboard to request that the superintendent join them immediately in the control room.

'I've got her, sir!' One of the civilians who manned the surveillance equipment pointed to her screen. 'On the back staircase. Timed at eleven forty-one. Then we have her leaving by the back door, eleven forty-three.' The woman switched to a different screen. 'And yes, here she is, seen from the car park camera, same time.'

In the dimly lit room, Matt stared at the figure of Liz, as she walked one way, then hesitated, before walking in the opposite direction. 'What on earth is she doing?'

'Looking for me, I guess,' Gary said gravely.

'She can't be. You didn't have a security card to get in. She was heading towards the gate to start with, that makes sense, but why did she turn around?'

The superintendent touched his shoulder lightly. 'I think she heard something! Run it back.'

They all stared as the tape re-ran, then they saw as Liz abruptly stopped and looked behind her.

'You're right, sir. Do we have a camera pointed in that direction?'

'Yes, sir,' said the civilian, 'But I suggest we stick with the sergeant for a moment, see the exact direction she takes.'

With exasperating slowness, the video continued. They watched as Liz hesitated, waited, then suddenly almost ran from the camera's sight.

'Where did she go?' asked Gary tensely.

'Don't worry. I'll pick her up on the next angle, hold on.' The screen blanked and the operative swiftly brought up a different section of the car park. 'Got her! There! Damn!'

To their dismay, a minibus, full to the gunnels with uniformed officers returning from their stint on the marshes, blocked their view of Liz.

'Different angle! Quickly!' the super demanded.

'Sorry, sir, but I haven't got another to cover that area. I'll fast forward.'

Speeded up, the officers raced from the vehicle and disappeared into the station like drones into the hive. Then the yard was once again visible, and empty.

'There must be another camera.' Matt felt physically sick as he stared at the deserted area.

'There's one at the gate. It may just take in a small chunk of this area, but it's only intended to log vehicles entering and leaving the car park.'

'Then find it! And fast.'

Footage flashed across the monitor, vehicles flew in and out, the barrier lifted up and down, making them blink and rub their eyes.

'That's it! Stop!' Matt squinted, trying to understand what they were looking at.

In the farthest field of vision, and partially obscured by a wall and the side of the big police personnel carrier, a dark coloured 4x4 was parked. The driver's door and the boot were wide open. As they looked, they saw a tall figure bundle something into the back of the vehicle. Then, before they could try to identify who or what it was, another figure burst into the scene. A PC, her ASP already drawn and raised, threw herself at the driver.

'Jesus Christ! That's Gemma! What the fuck is she doing?' Matt hardly recognised his own voice. 'Can't we get a better view, for God's sake?'

'Not with that bloody minibus there buggering everything up. Oh no, look!'

For a moment, the struggling figures moved out of sight behind the 4x4, then they saw the back door slam down, and a man run to the driver's door and jump inside.

'We'll get a better shot as he approaches the barrier! But how the hell will he get out?' asked the super, talking to himself in concern.

'Like that,' said Matt flatly.

They watched an arm extend from the open window, and a hand carefully swipe an official card through the machine. As the barrier dutifully went up, they saw the hand give one defiant wave to the camera, and the vehicle accelerated away.

For a moment no one spoke, then the door to the control room flew open, and Bryn rushed in, his usually bright face contorted with anxiety. 'I'm sorry, sir, but I'm really worried. I can't find Gemma anywhere.'

CHAPTER TWENTY-FIVE

'I'm afraid it's as we suspected, Superintendent.' The uniformed inspector's hand trembled slightly holding the typed report. 'The four-wheel drive was stolen, probably sometime last night. The thief picked a vehicle that was not regularly used. That's why the theft wasn't noticed immediately. And after he abducted our colleagues,' she paused to gather herself, 'he apparently left the main roads and took off across country. Our last sighting was at the Holderedge roundabout on the eastern edge of town. Unfortunately the helicopter was delayed with a technical glitch, so we lost some valuable time there. With a thirty minute start, he could be anywhere in a radius of fifty miles of fenland.' She looked at the superintendent miserably. 'We've got every officer and every vehicle available on high alert, but so far there have been no sightings.'

David Redpath tried to maintain a calm exterior while he fought his growing fear. 'I've reported it to the highest level. News bulletins are being released nationally, including the previously withheld photographs of the killer. We can only pray that this stirs the bulldog spirit.

Then we'll have most of the country behind us, hunting this monster.'

'Who's doing the public appeal?'

'The chief constable of the county.'

The inspector nodded. 'Good. With top brass covering the media, the severity of this should at least sink in straightaway.' She drew in a long, ragged breath, 'I'd better go and get on, although with every minute that goes by without hearing anything . . .' She left the sentence unfinished and turned to open the door. 'Still, I guess we can't do any more than we're doing, can we?'

David shook his head. 'Exactly, and one thing's for sure, every single officer will be giving one hundred per cent to get our people back.'

After the inspector had left, he picked up the phone and rang the murder room. 'Matt, come to my office. Bring Jason and Bryn with you.'

* * *

'Where is Lieutenant Colonel Haynes?' Superintendent Redpath asked Matt.

'A military car came for him, sir. He's been taken to a top level meeting with his commanding officers. Given the present circumstances, he's being debriefed and relieved of whatever duty he was returning to. He said he'll be back as soon as he's able. He's desperate to help us find his wife.' Matt felt the heavy weight of guilt dragging every word from his mouth.

'Poor devil! Still, we have to remain focused, Matt. If we are going to find them, we have to go over every scrap of evidence that we have, to try and discover who the abductor really is. If we can do that, then we have a chance of finding where he's taken them. Agreed?'

The three other men nodded. 'We have no other direction to take, do we?' said Jason grimly.

'Frankly no, so let's get to work.' The superintendent pulled a pile of folders across his desk towards him. 'I've asked DI Lawrence to free up his whole team to act as gofers for you. Don't spend time searching old files or making calls, if it's something they can do for you, okay? Prioritise. For once, you can be sure that there's going to be no rivalry and no gamesmanship. To a man, they've all volunteered to do whatever it takes to make a difference. So, as you guys have the edge and the history here, use them as and when you need to.'

'They're a pretty awesome team actually,' added Bryn, 'their DS is a techno-wizard, which could really help.' He turned to Matt. 'Hey, why not give him the sarge's cell phone? He may just be able to trace the withheld number that the killer used to lure her out.'

Matt gently put his hand in his trouser pocket and felt the reassuring form of Liz's mobile. For one irrational moment, he didn't want to let it go. It felt like it was all he had left of her. Then a shiver coursed through him, as he thought about some whizz-kid detective nosing through her private texts. Jesus! Had *he* left anything damning in her inbox? He bit his lip. He didn't think so, but he wasn't totally sure. Being careful was second nature to them, but after a year of well-kept secrets, had they got sloppy? They saw each other so regularly in the course of their work that he rarely called her mobile number. But he might have. He desperately tried to think, then he felt a sick, sinking feeling as he realised that he had no choice. If tracing the bogus call were possible, it had to be done, no matter what amount of shit he found himself in. He passed the phone to Bryn and said, 'Good idea. Do it as soon as we're through here.'

David stared at them all, 'Okay, I've got one more thing to say, then we'll move back down to the murder room, gather the other team, and go over the basics together. Anything that we feel needs further investigation, or something we may have missed, we tackle immediately.' He looked at all of them with his gaze finally resting on Matt.

'So, crunch time, and I'm sorry, Matt, but I have to ask. Are you up to being a part of this? I want an honest answer, and not one based on loyalty, because that is not in question. I want to know if you believe that you are mentally strong enough to be a help, and not a liability. Officers' lives could depend on you holding your nerve, in what most would consider an intolerable situation.'

Matt didn't hesitate. This was his case, from start to finish. Deep down, he knew that only he could solve it. 'I'm in, all the way, sir.' As he said the words, a strange calmness flooded through him. This piece of scum had taken or destroyed everything that was precious to him. The only thing left was his life, and right now he didn't hang too much value on that, unless he could trade it for Liz and Gemma's. So what the hell did he have to lose? *Oh yes. I'm in, to the bitter end.*

'Good man.' The super gathered up his files and stood up. 'Right, let's go.'

'There's something I really need to tell you, sir.' In the furore surrounding the abduction, Matt had completely forgotten to tell his senior officer about the call from Alexis Peart.

'Does it concern the case?'

'Yes, definitely, but I think you should be aware befo—'

'Then save your breath, and tell us all together. Now, come on, man.'

* * *

The first thing Matt saw when he entered the room was the addition of two large portrait-style photographs on the whiteboards. Both police pictures. One of Liz and one of Gemma.

He stared at them, allowed them to fill his whole field of vision, then he closed his eyes for a moment. Behind the lowered lids, he still saw the two beautiful faces. Surprisingly, his calmness from earlier still remained, and that strengthened him, because he knew it was not a serene, peaceful calm, but a cold, hard determination. Everything else seemed to have been stripped away, and all he was left with, was a ruthless, flint-edged resolution to get the man who had caused all this pain and suffering. And when he got him? Matt slowly opened his eyes, took in the room full of officers, and gave a small smile. *Well, we'll see, won't we?*

'DCI Ballard? If you're ready?' The super indicated to the seat next to him. 'Let's take it from the top, as they say.'

'Actually, there has been a development. One that occurred moments before the incident in the car park.' He couldn't quite bring himself to say the word 'abduction' out loud. 'I had a telephone call from the woman at the telephone number written on the photograph of Laura Schofield. A Mrs Alexis Peart from a village called Brownshill, in County Durham.' He pointed towards the black-and-white picture on the wall. Laura pouted disdainfully back at him, and he looked away. *Go on! Tell them! The time for secrets has long gone.*

Matt paused, aware that all eyes were on him and that the room had gone quiet. Maybe it was his own heightened sensitivity, but he felt that they'd picked up on his discomfort.

In a voice that was nothing short of clinical, he told them everything that Alexis Peart had allegedly discovered. At the point of telling them about his girlfriend having her baby, he could almost hear a dozen minds doing the maths. A few murmurs and lifted eyebrows confirmed that they had all reached the same conclusion.

He waited for the soft ripple of whispers to subside, then quietly said, 'And if you think that is the worst of it, believe me, it isn't. It doesn't end there.' He stared pointedly at David Redpath. 'Fifteen years ago, the child and her adoptive family moved to Fenfleet. The name that Mrs Peart gave me for the girl, was Gemma Goddard.'

Somehow, saying it had the effect of making it real. Although his heart told him otherwise, it was fifty-fifty odds, that Gemma *might* be his daughter.

The room erupted into uproar. Questions fired back and forth, and finally he held up his hand. 'For God's sake! Shut up, all of you! Just for one moment, think how I feel, after all those years, to find this out! And courtesy of a man who is a manipulative, head-fucking, child-killing son of a bitch.'

'And,' the super's deep voice cut through like a knife, 'as police officers, you all know that this is totally unsubstantiated hearsay, until it's proven otherwise.'

No matter how shocked his senior officer might have been, Matt was thankful that he'd got a grip on it so quickly. The noise had abated to a low murmur and the super quickly brought them back into line.

'Focus! We have a job to do. We have a missing child, plus two of our colleagues, and it's going to be down to your expertise as bloody good coppers to find them, so,' his glower passed over each of them, 'damn well stop speculating, and concentrate on the investigation.'

He turned to Matt. 'DCI Ballard, and you, DI Hammond. If you would be kind enough to give us the basic details of this case for the benefit of the officers who are new to this inquiry, then we'll allocate jobs.' Still glaring, he added, 'And damn well listen carefully, we don't have time to go over things, in fact, time is something that's ticking away as we speak, so zero in on what you're told, then get out there and find them!'

* * *

It took almost an hour to fill their colleagues in on what was already known, then to agree on the best way forward. They were just about to leave the room when Bryn jumped up.

'Sir! I've just remembered! The sarge believed that she was onto something. Just before she dashed off, she was waiting for an important call. She was quite animated about it, reckoned if it panned out, she'd need my help to chase someone up, "and fast" were her actual words.'

Matt frowned. 'Do you know who she was contacting?'

'No, sir, but she left a message on someone's answer phone. I can soon check it out.'

'Do it right now. And let me know what she was chasing, okay?'

Jason pitched a concerned look at Matt. 'You don't think she was getting too close to something, do you?'

'The thought had crossed my mind, but how would he have known what avenue of enquiry she was working on?'

'He could have found out from whoever it was that Liz was trying to contact. Whoever that was.'

'Hopefully Bryn will soon answer that question. The last time we spoke, Liz was working on whoever may have taken those old photographs of me in Greece. I can't see that that poses any sort of threat, can you?'

'Not really,' Jason made a face signifying total bemusement. 'This guy really shuffles my grey cells, every time I try to be logical.'

'Yes, he has quite a talent for that,' said Matt bitterly.

Bryn looked up from Liz's desk and called them over. 'There was an answer back on the sarge's phone. It was from a Mrs Cohen. She's left a contact number. It's concerning something called Angelos Holistic Holidays. Shall I ring her, or would you prefer to do it, boss?'

'Give it to me, I'll call her. You continue checking that CCTV footage, see if you can pick up anything more about that driver of the four-by-four.' He gripped the young detective's shoulder. 'And good work on remembering this, Bryn. We are so strung out right now, it would have been easy to forget.'

As Jason went off to organise some of the detectives from the other team, Matt rang the number and introduced himself. From her voice, Mrs Cohen sounded pretty old, but if that were the case, her mind was certainly not suffering the effects of her years.

'Your sergeant explained everything to the administrator of the holiday company, Chief Inspector. I told them they were perfectly at liberty to give her my number. I'm just sorry that I missed her call.'

Matt decided to gloss over the recent happenings, he didn't want to have to explain and then listen to the commiserations that were sure to follow. Going directly to the point, and expecting nothing, he told her about the photographs.

'Oh, I can help you there. You see, they were my pictures.'

'What!'

'Karissa has been my life for the past thirty years. And as I was a professional photographer in my younger days, I have taken hundreds, probably thousands of shots on the island.'

'Sorry. Let me get this straight,' Matt tried to unscramble his head. 'You took photographs of me? And you can still remember them!'

'Certainly, I took photos of everyone, but the ones of you were good, very moody.' She gave a little laugh, 'I have them all catalogued on my computer, Chief Inspector. All in date order, right back to my very first visit, my epiphany, as I like to call it.' She laughed again, 'It quite impressed the other officer who came to visit me last year. Such a nice man, he called me a silver surfer, but I told him, I've been using computers since Bill Gates was in short trousers.'

Matt felt his jaw tighten. 'Other officer?'

'Yes. He was from something called a cold case unit? Trying to track someone involved in a murder back in the early eighties, apparently.'

'And he asked to see your photographs?'

'Yes, he said he'd interviewed several other people who had visited Karissa at the same time, but no one could help him. He was very pleased when he saw my collection.'

I bet he fucking was! 'Mrs Cohen, if I email you a photograph, would you be kind enough to tell me if you recognise the man it shows?'

'Of course.' She gave him her email address, then her voice betrayed concern. 'I haven't done anything wrong, have I? I mean. he didn't use those photographs inappropriately, did he?'

As Matt typed her name into his computer and clicked Send, he said, 'I'm afraid he did, Mrs Cohen, but you certainly were not to blame.'

'Well, he had no right! No right at all, and him a policeman!'

'He wasn't actually, Mrs Cohen, although I'm sure he presented you with some very convincing identification.'

'Not a policeman, you say?' For a moment the woman was silent, then she said, 'Can you tell me how he used my photographs?'

'I suppose you would call it a form of blackmail. Have you received the emailed picture yet, Mrs Cohen.'

Again there was a pause, the he heard a slight intake of breath. 'Oh yes! That's him alright. Now I see his face, I can even recall his name. Detective Constable Edward Dennis from the Metropolitan Police Cold Case Unit.'

* * *

'So, at least no one actually dogged your footsteps to Greece. That's something of a relief.' The super rubbed his temples. 'But we're still left with not knowing who the hell this bogus Edward Dennis really is.' His face was craggy and grey with worry and tiredness, but his voice was still strong, 'And, Matt, you do know that you have to be prepared for some kind of demand, don't you? If it's you he's gunning for, and he already has two of your officers, then the next thing will undoubtedly be contact of some sort.'

'Bring it on! Anything has to be better than grasping at straws and playing sodding guessing games.'

The super nodded. 'And thinking about games, I can't help but wonder if Gemma's undoubtedly brave, but possibly foolhardy attack, may have thrown a spanner into the killer's well-oiled machine.' He stared around his office at the myriad of old photographs, seemingly searching for assistance from the officers who had gone before them. 'There's no doubt that he had a meticulous plan in place to take Sergeant Haynes. The timing was immaculate, and although I suspect that the arrival of a busload of wooden tops was a heaven sent bonus to him, he had chosen the most inconspicuous spot in the whole yard, and one that is only poorly covered by our cameras.'

'I thought that too. It's only usually used as a turning area, and unlike most of the rest of the car park, none of the main offices look out onto it. Which indicates an intimate knowledge of the layout of the police station.'

'Worryingly enough, yes. Although it would be simple enough to get in as an official visitor. But as I was saying, all that was planned, but coping with another, and completely unexpected, woman hostage could severely bugger up the fine tuning on his timetable.'

'Quite possibly, so let's pray he doesn't just top her as quickly as possible in order to get back on track.' Matt felt the awful weight of responsibility on his shoulders. He shook it off and forced himself to concentrate. 'The thing that really bothers me,' he paused as Jason slipped into the office and took the chair next to his. 'I was just telling the superintendent that I'm concerned about why Liz went across to the driver of the four-by-four in the first place.'

'Yes, but we saw her look up, as if she had heard something.'

'So did she recognise him? I would have thought that she would only have approached him if she knew him, wouldn't you?'

'Maybe.' said Jason. 'Unless he called to her by name. She'd go then.'

'But she would have recognised him if she'd got close enough. She's had his ugly mug plastered on the wall in front of her desk for days! She would have raised the alarm.'

'Perhaps she didn't have time, or he may have been disguised. By the time she realised something was wrong, it was too late.'

'Maybe,' said Matt. But something rankled. Something wasn't right with the whole scenario.

'Sorry to change the subject, but the reason I came in was to find out if anyone has contacted Gemma's parents yet?' Jason asked.

'Yes. HR sorted it, before we went public with the appeal. A car is bringing them back from Yorkshire. They want to be on hand in case of developments,' replied the super. 'As you can imagine, they are pretty devastated.'

'And her boyfriend?' Jason lowered his voice to a conspiratorial whisper. 'They are pretty serious about each other, you know. She told me he had been talking about marriage, although she seemed to be more concerned about her career.'

'Ah, that would be Roy Latimer, wouldn't it? Yes, they contacted him at the same time. He was at work, but he said he'd come straight down, see if he could help. Not that there's anything he can do right now, poor chap.'

'What time is the appeal going out, sir?' asked Matt. 'Maybe we'll get lucky with sightings by members of the public. *Someone* has to recognise that face.'

'Already gone. It was considered serious enough to warrant a 'Breaking news' status.' The super sighed. 'Of course that brings with it its own problems.'

'Bogus callers, sensationalists, timewasters and the plain barking mad?'

'All of those, and more. I'm glad I'm not manning the switchboard. Which reminds me, I have outside personnel to organise.' He stood up. 'Keep me posted on absolutely everything, okay?'

* * *

The murder room was littered with polystyrene coffee cups and chocolate wrappers. The waste bins were overflowing with fast food cartons and sandwich packets. When they got a moment, the officers grabbed some food and dined, *al desko,* and they'd be doing that until they found their missing colleagues.

Matt approached Bryn, who was hunched over a series of photographs, but before he could speak, he saw that the young detective's shoulders were rising and falling in a jerky fashion.

'Hey, come on,' Matt said softly, squeezing the man's arm. 'We'll find them, Bryn. We will.'

'I should have gone down to the car park with the sergeant. I shouldn't have just let her rush off like that. I should have thought.'

'Don't beat yourself up, son. No way could you have known that the call wasn't from her husband.'

'Gemma had the brains to know that the sarge shouldn't have been out there alone, didn't she, sir? Or she wouldn't have been there, would she?'

Matt felt that same misgiving again. 'Where did you say Gemma had gone? Prior to the incident.'

'Front desk, sir. She had a call asking her to collect something.'

'Then why use the back stairs? The main staircase leads directly to the desk.'

'Perhaps she saw the sergeant go off alone, and went after her.' Bryn wiped roughly at his cheek with the back of his hand. 'I'm sorry, sir. I don't normally let myself down like that.'

'Between you and me, you aren't the only one out of the two of us who has shed tears since this whole shitty business kicked off.'

'The killer's had us by the balls since day one, hasn't he?'

The question didn't need an answer. 'Anything useful on those CCTV pictures?' Matt glanced at the photos.

'I'm still checking them. I'll get on with them right away.'

'Good. I'm going down to have a word with Sergeant Jones, see if Gemma ever picked up whatever it was that she was collecting. Call me if you spot anything useful. And Bryn, they *are* your friends, it's okay to show emotion, even if you are a big Welsh wuss.'

* * *

The reception area was packed, and Matt had to push his way through to where the desk sergeant was barking out instructions to the officers around him.

'I can see you're rushed off your feet, Jonesy, but I need to ask you something.'

'Come through to the back, sir. It's like the fucking parrot house at the zoo here.' He shouldered a bull-necked PC out of the way, and held the office door open. 'Mind your back, you great lummock. Let the DCI through.'

The sergeant closed the door, muffling the havoc outside to a dull rumble. 'That's better. So, what can I do for you, sir?'

'Before she was snatched, Gemma Goddard was apparently on her way here to collect something. Do you know if she did? Or what it was for that matter?'

Jonesy shook his head. 'Sorry, but that's the first I've heard of it.'

'One of my detectives said that she had a call asking her come here to collect a package or something. That would have been somewhere around eleven or eleven thirty a.m.' Matt felt uneasy.

'I can easily check for you, but no one ran it past me.' He stuck out his bottom lip. 'And knowing the state of everything right now, Matt, I'd have got one of the civi-messengers to bring anything important up to you.' He moved back to the door. 'Hold on a mo, and I'll get it checked out.' He stuck his head out of the door and bellowed out, 'Robyn! Come here!', then sent his clerk hurrying off in the direction of the computer.

A few moments later she returned. 'Nothing either delivered or left for anyone in the CID office at or around that time, Sarge.'

He thanked her then closed the door again 'I thought not. So, do you think this has something to do with Gemma's abduction?'

Matt nodded grimly. 'It's a possibility. Sergeant Haynes was lured outside by a bogus call, I guess the same thing could have happened to Gemma, although I'm damned if I know why she used the back stairs to get here.'

The sergeant smiled. 'That's an easy one. The drinks machine is that end of the corridor. Most of the youngsters grab one of those latte things or a diet cola while they're out of the office.'

'Good point. Thanks, Jonesy. I'll let you get back to work.'

Matt left the chaos of the reception and made his way to the back doors and the entrance to the car park. On the far side, the whole turning bay was cordoned off, and several white-suited technicians were carefully checking the whole area for any evidence, but Matt wasn't interested in that. He was more concerned by the discarded polystyrene cup that lay on its side just outside the double doors.

He knelt down and carefully checked the large wet stain that had spread around the beaker. A plastic lid lay a couple of feet from the cup, and splashes of drying frothy milk coated the lid. Cappuccino. Gemma's favourite. Dropped, or hastily thrown down.

This really doesn't make any sense. Gemma surprised the man while he was snatching Liz. Fact, we have it on camera. Matt swallowed. What if things weren't quite as they appeared? He leaned back against the brick wall and thought hard. Maybe Gemma was an intended victim all along! He sprung upright. *Yes! He wanted both of them! And with his love for split-second timing, that's just what he got! Oh shit, I've got to see the super!*

* * *

'So that's what I think, sir. He wanted both Liz *and* Gemma, and he even knew her movements well enough to know which direction she'd take to get to the front desk,' Matt concluded.

'Mattie! You're jumping the gun here. There are far too many variables. No one other than James Bond could have pulled off such a feat. What if she'd gone the other way? What if she didn't fancy a coffee? What if she didn't bother to look out across the yard? If she'd been a minute or two either earlier or later, she'd have got caught up with twenty or thirty flatfoots piling out of that van. No, we have to go by what we saw on that video footage. She surprised him, no question.'

Matt rubbed his eyes. 'But what about the call from reception? They never rang her, so who did?'

'Maybe it was just a mix-up? For God's sake, everyone's operating on jangling nerves right now. Maybe someone simply rang the wrong extension. And there's another issue to consider, if we believe your hypothesis.' The superintendent looked at him thoughtfully. 'To know all the staff *that* well, the killer would have to be an insider. Someone we work with? A colleague? Someone we number as a friend?'

A long sigh escaped Matt's lips. 'I hadn't thought about that. But I suppose it just could be true.'

'No, it couldn't. Think, Matt! We have pictures of him. No one in this station, or any other that we've sent his likeness to, knows him. He's a stranger, Matt.'

'Excuse me, sir?' A white-faced Bryn appeared in the doorway. 'The boss here told me to find him if I found anything.' He approached the desk and placed two photographs on the polished surface. 'Look, sir, I've zoomed in on the driver of the four-by-four, just as it left the barrier. The shot is poor, but it is definitely the same man from the other CCTV footage.'

Matt and his senior officer both leaned over the pictures. The driver was partly hidden and wore a stretchy beanie, but the close-cut beard and cruelly smiling mouth were by now horribly familiar.

'No doubt there, I'm afraid,' said the super. 'We have to admit that he's got them. Both of them.'

As Bryn left the room, Matt sank back into his chair and tried to fight the urge to run away. In his head, he saw his farmhouse kitchen, with Liz pouring wine into crystal glasses, and him chopping tomatoes and peppers and laughing together as he prepared supper. More than anything in the world, he wanted those days back, but without the bug under the stairs and a madman killing the neighbourhood children.

'Matt?'

The super's voice quickly dispelled his fruitless and painful daydream. 'Sorry, sir.'

'I said, who is following up the validity of the information from the adoption agency?'

'Lenny and Tina from the other team are onto that.'

'Ask them to come to my office when you go back out, will you? I've decided to speak to Gemma's parents personally, as soon as they are back. It's the least I can do, and we'll be able to verify much of what your Mrs Peart told you at source, so to speak.'

'Has no one asked Gemma's parents that all important question yet?'

The super shook his head. 'The doctor considered they were too upset and shocked by her abduction to talk at that time. I'll see them in their own home, it will be less stressful for them.'

'One hell of a lot hangs on their answer, doesn't it, sir?'

'For the case, certainly, but for you, well, I can't imagine what's going on in your head right now, Matt.'

'You wouldn't want to know. It's a pretty bad place at present. One moment I'm full of determination and ice-cold resolution, the next, well, it's like I've tripped my panic button, and the reality of this godawful mess blasts in on me.'

'Hardly surprising, is it?' Before he could continue, his desk phone blared out.

'Okay, right, I'll be there in two.' He replaced the handset and stood up. 'That was Jason. Gemma's boyfriend is downstairs. He's dusting the ceiling over what's happened, and I can't say I blame him, poor sod. This is one glorious cock-up, if ever I saw one.'

'Shall I come with you, sir?'

'Not this time, Matt. You'll only finish up blaming yourself, and in front of someone who is just about to take us to the cleaners, that may not be a very sensible move.'

Matt returned to the murder room, and as always the row of photographs attracted him like a magnet. *Laura? Did you really have a child? Our child? And did you reject her and kill yourself?* Matt looked at the killer's face. *Or did it all come out of his sick head?* The supercilious smile oozed cocky confidence. *Who are you? And why do you hate me so much?* No answer came, but his mobile rang and made him jump.

'I've just seen the news! Is it true?'

'Yeah, Adie. All of it.'

'Jesus, mate! How are you holding up?'

'With difficulty.'

'Well, look I'm sorry, but I'm about to make things a whole lot worse. I need to see you, and pretty smartish.'

Matt groaned. 'I'm well stuck here. No way I can get out. What's wrong?' He asked but wasn't sure he actually wanted an answer.

'Can't tell you on the phone.'

'Well, I know you have a pathological dislike for the place, but can't you come here?'

There was a loud exhaling of breath from the other end, then Adie said, 'Yeah, yeah. For once, I'll make an exception to my rule, but you better find us somewhere really private to talk, because you are not going to want to share this with your mess-room buddies.'

The phone went dead. Matt was left staring at the words, "Call Ended."

CHAPTER TWENTY-SIX

'This should never have happened!' Roy Latimer smashed a fist on the table. 'How *did* it happen? How could you let a monster like that into this goddamned place? Jesus! It's a fucking police station!'

Before Jason or the super could formulate a reply, Roy slumped forward, head in hands. 'It's a police station,' he whimpered, 'she should have been safe here, shouldn't she?'

'Yes, she should have. And everything you've said is perfectly correct. He should *never* have got in, but, if you'll just give me a moment?' The super looked at Roy. 'I don't want to waste precious time on recriminations, I want to spend every waking moment working out how to get her back safely, not trying to calculate how things went so badly wrong. I will do that later, I promise. Do you understand me?'

Roy looked up, then slowly nodded his head. He had tears in his eyes. 'Of course. I'm sorry, I'm just so scared. And I don't understand. Why Gemma?'

'We don't know for sure, Roy,' said Jason. 'We have some ideas, but—'

'When she got beaten up? She said it was riot training. She lied to me, didn't she? It was him, wasn't it? He's tried this before.' Roy swallowed noisily. Panic was once again building up in his voice.

'He did meet her, but he wasn't trying to abduct her. He was delivering a message.' The super's voice was low and calming. 'Gemma very bravely tried to apprehend him, that's how she got so badly bruised.'

'But was he after her all along?'

'We think he's after someone else.'

'Then why take *her*?' He bit angrily on a carefully manicured nail. 'And that other woman, Sergeant Haynes? Why her?'

Jason sat back and shook his head. 'As I said, we really don't know, Roy.'

Roy removed his black-rimmed glasses and wiped his eyes with the back of his hand. He stared accusingly at the two police officers. 'It's him, isn't it? Her detective boss-man, the chief inspector. That's who he's after.'

The super held his gaze. 'It may be. We think it's connected to an old case, many years ago, one that the DCI was working on as a younger man. He's the last remaining detective from back then, and we believe the killer is punishing him for something that happened. Sadly, we have no idea why he's tormenting him like this.'

'Tormenting *him*! What about my Gemma? She's the one he's taken. God knows what he's done to her. She could even be dead by now!'

'Calm down, Roy. I'm sure she's alive. If the man who snatched her had wanted to do that, he could have done it there and then. I think he's holding her with the intention of using her as a hostage, someone to barter with. Which means we have a little time, so . . .' He reached across and touched Roy's arm. 'Will you help us?'

'I'll do all I can to help. Just please find her.'

'Good man! And I know how much you care about her,' Jason gave him a weak smile, 'because Gemma told me herself. And we'll do everything we can to get her back to you, alright?' Roy nodded slowly and Jason continued, 'Now, there are a few things about Gemma that you may be able to help us with, but first, I'll get us some drinks.'

The super stood up. 'You continue here, Inspector, I have to go and inform the team that I'm going to see Gemma's parents. They should have returned home by now.'

'Oh my God! James and Linda. I'd almost forgotten about them.' Roy cried. 'I haven't spoken to them yet. That poor couple, they'll be beside themselves. Superintendent, will you tell them that I'll call them later, and tell them, oh what can I say? Oh, just tell them if there is anything I can do, anything at all, to ring me.'

'They will have a family-liaison officer with them, Mr Latimer, and be assured, we'll offer every kind of support possible. But I will definitely give them your message. Now if you'll excuse me?'

Outside the interview room, the superintendent looked gravely at Jason. 'You'd better organise a liaison officer for him, too. Apart from being at risk himself, I'd say he's pretty wobbly right now.'

'Will do, sir, and good luck with the parents.'

* * *

'Are you sure this is the best that you can do? These places give me the screamers!' Adie said.

'You've been in enough of them, I thought it would be home from home! And it was you that said *private*, so as my office is about as private as Fenfleet community centre, this is it, I'm afraid. With the In Use sign alight, no one would enter an interview room, I promise,' Matt replied.

Adie threw him a contemptuous look, then removed a large brown envelope from his jacket and placed it carefully on the table. 'This came to the hotel earlier. Bloke on a motorbike delivered it and as it was addressed to me,

I opened it. It didn't take long to realise that you were the intended mark, not me.'

'Oh please, not another one.' Matt felt as though he had taken a well-aimed medicine ball to the scrotum.

'Sorry, but I'm afraid it's not *just* another one, mate. Take a look.'

Matt picked up the envelope. It was thick and heavy. No simple picture this time. 'Did you recognise the delivery man? Is he on your CCTV?'

Adie rolled his eyes upwards and sighed. 'CCTV! Don't be naïve! That's a dirty word when you operate an establishment as discreet as mine. My special clientele would run a mile if they saw a camera, now wouldn't they, Detective?'

Matt thought of Liz tiptoeing up the back staircase to their room. 'Point taken.' He stared at the envelope. *Got to do this.* Matt tipped the contents onto the desk.

Dozens of black-and-white photos slid across the table's smooth surface, and he immediately understood why Adie had been so cagey.

'They are *hot*, man! I had no idea you were so athletic!'

Matt was speechless. He picked up one picture after another, and shook his head in disbelief.

'I've already fathomed out how, if that was going to be your first question?'

Matt mutely nodded.

'Well, you know the derelict old school on the site opposite the side entrance to the hotel? I took a sneaky look around it, and someone has been in one of the attic rooms on a regular basis. Whoever was watching had an interesting view straight into the dressing area of your room, and with the use of the full-length mirror that I kindly provided, and a very high spec camera . . . Voila! Naughty bedroom pictures!'

'They are not naughty, Adie, they are . . . oh!'

'My thoughts exactly, chum! The things that go on under my own roof. Quite shocking!'

Matt knew that Adie was trying to help by making light of the situation, but anger was beginning to burn through him like the onset of fever. 'The bastard! The evil bastard!'

He flipped through the pictures. Even he was shocked at the intensity, the passion — the ingenuity, even — of their lovemaking. The pictures had frozen moments of such sexual pleasure, that perversely, they made it hard not to stare at them.

'In case you're wondering, I didn't actually look, mate. Well, maybe just a glance or two when I opened the packet, but frankly, they knocked me sideways! I shoved them back in the envelope and rang you straightaway.' Adie was not laughing any more.

Matt gathered them up. The son of a bitch had soiled something incredibly beautiful. He bunched them together and pushed them roughly back into the envelope,

One suddenly stood out. His hand shook as he picked it up. It was of Liz. He was out of the frame, but Liz was naked on the bed, on her knees and astride him, leaning backwards. The picture wasn't crystal clear, but the pure delight in her face shone out. Mat looked closer. Delight, and something else, something less obvious. She wanted him. She really wanted him. And not sexually, that more subtle expression revealed love, not just desire.

All this knowledge washed over him in a second, but the real reason that he had been drawn to the picture in the first place, was the three letters, PTO, written in red pen along the bottom of the photo. He flipped over the photograph.

You know by now that I have them. Both of them. They are still alive. It is up to you as to how long they stay that way. It is your turn to join us, and I know you will understand that

you have to come alone. No
wires, no cameras, no
policemen. As soon as I contact
you, you will come directly to
the location that I give you. Try
to be clever and you will find
only corpses. This I promise
you.

PS I have copies of the
enclosed. Maybe the foxy lady's
soldier boy would like to see
what a generous woman his
wife is. Like I said, come alone.

The air seemed to have been sucked out of the room.
Matt's chest heaved as he strained to breathe. What did the
super call it? Crunch time.

Adie leaned across and took the photograph. To
Matt's relief, he looked only at the back of it. 'Friggin'
heavy stuff, Mattie. I wonder how long he'll give you
before he makes contact?'

'Not long, I should think.' Matt re-read the carefully
written note, then folded the photo in half and pushed it
into his pocket.

'Then I hate to tell you your job, but shouldn't you be
getting things in place? Little things, like rallying the
troops, getting someone lined up to get a trace on the call,
putting in a request for the heavy artillery, notifying your
senior officers, maybe?'

'No, I don't think so.'

'Matt, you're a copper, and I hate to say it, but a
bloody good one. You go by the book. Surely you're not
thinking about doing what this weirdo says?'

'You'd show the superintendent these pictures, would
you? Can I just remind you that this is Detective Sergeant
Elizabeth Haynes, wife of Gary Haynes? Can you imagine

what this,' he gestured towards the thick envelope, 'would do to her, and him, for that matter?'

'I see your point about the dirty postcard stuff, but right now I'm more concerned with what your psycho could do to her *and* your other girl.'

'Sorry, Adie, but I believe every word on this note. Unless I go alone, there is going to be nothing and no one to save. If I go to him, I may just be able to convince him to let the women go. It's me he wants. It sounds like a pretty good deal to me.'

'Well, I think it sounds like a truly crap idea. You'll have no leverage at all if you walk in there unarmed and with no backup. He'll have all of you then, and topping a couple of women may just be a bit of added fun on the side to a fruit loop like that.' Adie folded his arms and stared at Matt belligerently, then gave a loud sigh. 'Okay, let's look at it another way. I note that he never mentioned ex-cons in his list of the unwelcome.'

'Alone means just that, Adie. Old lags included.'

'Damn, and I was *so* looking forward to meeting him.' Adie leaned back, arms still folded. 'I'm trying to work out what has shunted you off the righteous rails, and sent you into this Lone Ranger suicide mission.' His eyes suddenly narrowed to little more than slits. 'Correct me if I'm wrong, but I seem to recall your illicit nights with your paramour being something of a casual affair to begin with? Needs must and all that. Has something changed? And if it has, please tell me that you haven't fallen for her?'

The ensuing silence said it all.

'Holy Mary! You have, haven't you?'

'I have to find her, Adie, and Gemma, too.' Matt gave a short barking staccato laugh. 'Oh yeah, I forgot to mention, his nibs reckons Gemma's my daughter! And here's the punchline, she just might be! What do you think of that?'

'Frankly I think you've spent too much time in the evidence storage room sampling the confiscated wacky baccy.'

'I wish.'

'So let's get this straight? He's got the love of your life, and let's be generous here and allow him the benefit of the doubt, your daughter, both captive. Oh deary, deary me, it would appear he has you by the short and curlies.'

'Nicely put, Adie, but not exactly comforting.'

Matt felt Adie's eyes bore into him. 'If you do go banzai and take off alone, you do know that I can't promise not to follow you to your rendezvous, don't you?'

'If you do, you could get us all killed. You have to let me go alone.'

'I would put up very good odds that he would not spot me. He may be a top-class psycho, but I'm a better thief than he'll ever be. You should see the mess he left in that old schoolroom, appalling lack of finesse. No pride in his work.'

'For God's sake, don't underestimate him, Adie. He's far cleverer than you think. He's been planning this for years, and he's got the whole station running round like headless chickens. Worse than that, we still have no idea who he is or what he wants.'

'What he wants is simple. He wants the three of you, and for you to suffer beyond understanding. Think about it. He has the woman you love, and the ability to take her away from you, permanently, and possibly very violently. He has also found your long lost daughter, and like Liz, he can give her to you, then take her away, forever. It's all about power, mate.' Adie's voice was low and uncharacteristically serious. 'Somewhere along the way, Matthew Ballard, you have upset this man enough for him to do absolutely *anything* to get back at you. And there's one last thing you should consider. What if he doesn't want to kill you at all, just wants you to witness the death of the two women closest to you, then let you live with the memory.' He puffed out his cheeks at the horrible thought. 'And that would mean they are safe, until the moment you get there, then they are in grave danger.'

The thought made Matt feel physically sick, but for some reason he didn't believe that was what the killer's goal. 'I know what you're saying is logical, possible even, but, but I think I have to take that chance. I have to—'

Matt's phone ringing in the small room made him jerk upright. The two men stared at each other, their faces stony.

The number meant nothing to him. He pressed answer, but before he could speak, a weird mechanical-sounding voice rattled off one sentence, then the phone went dead.

'Where?' asked Adie.

'Don't know. He must have been just checking up on me. He said to wait for his next call.'

'Fuck!'

'Double fuck! He used a voice distorter, and ten-to-one, the phone is pay-as-you-go, and probably already at the bottom of the nearest ditch.'

'So what now?'

Right at that moment, he hadn't a clue. 'To tell you the truth, I'm not sure. The copper inside is still screaming at me to get a grip and do it by the book. But my gut instinct says it's my shit, so it's down to me to clean it up.' He rubbed his hands together. 'Listen, Adie, you've been a good mate, the best—'

'Shut the fuck up about all that crap. Let's concentrate on now, shall we?'

'I'm just saying, if you'll get real for a minute, that we both know there's a damn good chance that, whatever way I choose to play it, this could go seriously tits-up.' Matt held up his hand. 'Hear me out. We may have spent half our lives on different sides of the fence, but since we called a truce, you've been the only one who always had time for me, time to listen, when I was up to my neck in mental shit, and I want you to know that I truly appreciate it.' He drew in a deep breath and passed the envelope across the table. 'Take these and destroy them for me, as soon as possible. And finally,' he gave Adie a half-hearted grin, 'I'm afraid I have to ask you one last favour.'

'Surprise! Surprise!' Adie pocketed the envelope. 'Are you certain you want them destroyed? They may turn out to be evidence, or we could sell them to a Dutch magazine and make a fortune.' He stopped when he saw Matt's face. 'Joke! Bad taste and bad timing, I know, but anything is better than you going all maudlin on me. Oh, and I prefer to think of us as playing the same game, just on different sides of the net actually, which allows me to respect a player almost as good as myself. And that said, this one last favour had better be bloody good, Matt Ballard, or I break all my hallowed rules, and go straight to your super and grass you up.' Adie glared at him. 'So. What is it you want this time?'

* * *

Other than a slight tremor of the hand as she turned the pages of the photo album, Linda Goddard, neat and petite, was giving little away as to how she felt inside.

'Yes, Gemma was adopted. James and I lost our only child in childbirth, and after that I had miscarriage after miscarriage. After the last one, I awoke to hear that a hysterectomy had saved my life.' She raised her eyebrows. 'When the reality of that statement dawned, I wasn't sure if I had a life left anyway.' She gave David a weak smile. 'We had both wanted children, lots of them.'

James, a tall, rangy stick of a man, joined in. 'Adoption seemed to be a natural next step, but we had no idea how complicated a procedure it was. We nearly gave up, then we had a call from a local agency that we had signed up with.'

'They were so kind,' went on Linda. 'Mr Peart himself dealt with Gemma's case, and he bent over backwards to get her placed with us, poor little thing.'

'You knew that she had been maltreated as a baby?'

'Oh, we knew the full, horrific history, Superintendent,' replied James. 'You have to, as there may be severe repercussions in later life.'

'But luckily she was fine, wasn't she, darling? From the moment we brought her home, she flourished.' Linda Goddard passed a picture across to David Redpath. 'This was Gemma not long after we adopted her. Do you know, the first time we saw her, she looked at us and smiled, as though she had been waiting for us to come for her.'

He looked at the picture. A normal, happy child. Bright-eyed and smiling. After the terrible start she'd had, he wondered how she had managed to bounce back so easily. 'How did she cope at school?'

'A1 student. Smart, intelligent, sporty. Even exams didn't faze her.'

'Friends?'

Neither parent replied immediately. Then James Goddard said, 'She is very loyal to those close to her, although as a kid she was always something of a loner. She was happier with her head in a book, on the computer or out walking the dog. She's never been what you'd call a party animal, and frankly, with all that dreadful binge drinking and drugs these days, we were grateful for that.'

'We were told she could find socialising difficult, considering her past,' added Linda. 'But all in all, apart from having a bit of a temper on her, we think she has done brilliantly. She even coped with three years at uni before she joined the force.'

'When did she decide that she wanted to be a police officer?' The superintendent accepted a cup of tea from the family-liaison worker, and looked back to James.

'Right from a little kid. It was always her goal. She wanted to right all the wrongs in the world. Fight the bad guys and lock up the villains.'

'We never doubted for one moment that that was what she'd do, Superintendent.' Linda hesitated as the thin veneer began to crack. She swallowed back a sob. 'Even if it was such a dangerous job. Now look at what's happened!'

'Shh, sweetheart. They'll find her. She's a brave girl.' James slipped an arm around his wife and hugged her tightly.

A brave girl? thought David. If she *was* Matt Ballard's daughter, he could believe that. 'I'm sorry to upset you at such a difficult time, but I only have a few more questions.' He placed his cup on the coffee table and sat back. 'Does Gemma know that she's adopted?'

James let go of his wife but still gripping her hand, said, 'Yes, of course. I mean she didn't come to us until she was seven. She's been aware of that fact all her life.'

'And has she asked about her biological parents?'

Linda shook her head slowly. 'When she was eleven, we offered to answer any questions that she had about her earlier life. Bless her heart, she said that she didn't have a life before she came to us, and now she had a family who loved her, so that was all that mattered.' She wiped her eyes with a tissue. 'Every year until she was twenty, we asked her again, and every year she said the same thing, so then we stopped asking.' The tears suddenly turned into a worried frown. 'But I don't understand, what's this got to do with her being kidnapped?'

'We have to build up a wider picture, Mrs Goddard. We need to know everything we can about her. Things that aren't on her police file. Someone from her past may be involved somewhere, so I'm afraid I have to ask you these difficult and personal questions.' David gave them a compassionate smile. 'I know it's hard for you, and I'm truly sorry, but can you tell me about her relationship with Roy Latimer?'

Both parents perked up at the mention of the young man's name. 'Best thing that ever happened to our Gemma, apart from when she came to us, of course. He's a lovely young man, and he adores her. We rather hoped . . .' Linda stopped, mouth slightly open, apparently realising for the first time that all plans for the future had been put on hold.

'He asked for me to tell you that he'll be ringing you, and if you need anything to call him.'

'Poor Roy! He'll be beside himself with worry.' The tears started again and she looked towards the window, fear stripping away all of her earlier composure. 'It will be dark soon, and my baby's out there somewhere, with a madman!'

* * *

Superintendent Redpath left, feeling a great sadness for the two people who had taken a broken child and lovingly put her back together again, only for some evil bastard to steal her away from them.

As he sat back in the car and looked out of the window into the gathering twilight, he wondered how Matt would take the news. It was confirmed that Gemma was adopted, and from the very place that the killer had led them to, so why should the rest of the information be incorrect? Gemma Goddard could well be Matt's girl, and now she was missing.

He stared at the back of his driver's head and decided it was time to take Matt off the case. It was getting far too personal and far too dangerous. Matt's already battered mind would not take much more, and that would get people hurt, killed even. He would speak to him as soon as he got back to the station. No polite requests, just an order, and he'd have him removed to a place of safety. He knew it would be hell for the poor guy, waiting out the investigation and unable to physically help, but it was better than having an avenging angel, a loose and loaded cannon, running wild around the Lincolnshire countryside.

Once again he looked out into the gloom, this time he offered up a prayer for his two missing officers and the little boy.

CHAPTER TWENTY-SEVEN

A thin watery mist descended over the marsh, its cloying dampness drenching everything it touched. As the twilight deepened, and the barren lonely landscape became only a memory, Liz slowly dragged herself back to consciousness.

The side of her head felt as though it had been caved in, and a throbbing, nauseating pain coursed through her when she tried to move. Not that there was much point to her exertions, she soon realised that she was tightly bound by some kind of harsh and unforgiving gaffer tape. The ground beneath her was solid, rock hard, and there was a strange smell to the place.

She resisted the initial urge to fight with her bonds, then lay back and tried to remember what had happened. All she could recall was someone desperately calling her by name. Saying something about someone being hurt. She had the vague recollection of running to help, then nothing. But what had happened to her? And where the hell was she?

Panic threatened to engulf her, but over and over she reminded herself that she was a senior detective, a police officer, and she must get a handle on her situation as quickly as possible. Her life might depend on it. She took a few deep breaths and slowed her racing heart to something half acceptable. She knew she was injured, but hopefully not too badly, and frankly, worrying about herself would have to wait until she got free.

She moved her head, more slowly this time. The pain was bad, but not as crushing as before. The room she was in seemed to be windowless, although there was the tiniest amount of dim light filtering from somewhere on the far side. It had to be a cellar, or maybe a storeroom. The smell was unpleasant but vaguely familiar. She stopped trying to make things out in the gloom, closed her eyes and allowed her sense of smell to help identify where she was. There was an overriding mustiness, a dank staleness that indicated that fresh air was rarely allowed in. Then there was that other stink. She sniffed. That was it! Fertilizer. Phosphates. Yes, the place smelt like her uncle's barn, although it lacked the nice scent of sweet hay brought in for winter feed.

So, with the concrete floor and the storage of agrochemicals, she was clearly in an outbuilding. Not in a cellar. Which, if you were a real optimist, was a good thing. At least her captor probably wasn't in the same building.

She tried to move her legs, but like her arms, they were firmly bound, at the ankles and around the calves. For some reason, she wasn't gagged. Now that wasn't good. More comfortable certainly, but it meant that whoever had left her there, knew that she could yell her head off and no one would hear. Help was definitely not at hand.

Water dripped and trickled incessantly somewhere, and there was another sound, a creaking sort of noise, coming from nearby. As she listened, she realised that a wind had got up, and from its mournful wailing and long whispering sighs, she had the feeling that she was somewhere very remote.

Somewhere like the marshes or a far-flung part of the fen.

A shiver passed through her, and her earlier optimism faded. She could be miles from the next inhabited building, and if she were close to the seabank, she could be in a very dangerous area as well. A place surrounded by boggy salt marsh, made inaccessible by treacherous tides, and completely isolated.

No! Just get a grip, woman! No point in throwing in the towel when you don't even know where you are. You could be in someone's back garden on the outskirts of town, for all you know, so, concentrate and . . . Liz froze. A rustling noise interrupted the bollocking she was giving herself. *Oh please, not rats.* If she had a phobia, twitchy-whiskered, long tailed vermin would be it. She swallowed hard and tried not to move or make a sound.

'Oohh!' A low moan echoed round the small room.

That was no rat. 'Hello? Who's there?'

'Liz? Is that you?'

Liz let out a cry of relief. 'Gemma! But what on earth . . .?'

'Oh Liz, I'm so sorry. I really cocked up. Oh God, I think he's broken my ribs.'

'What happened back at the station, I don't understand.' Liz's head thundered as she tried to fathom out why Gemma was in the stinking room with her.

'I saw him attack you. I was so incensed that I just ran at him. I know I should have radioed for help, but I forgot all my training, I forgot everything. All I could see was him making off with you, so I had to do something.' She gasped with pain. 'But I should have remembered the bastard from last time.'

'It's not your fault, Gem. I shouldn't have gone to him in the first place. He took me in completely. Shit! If anyone's a fool, it's me. Are you badly hurt?'

'A bang on the head, but it's mainly my ribs. He caught me in exactly the same place as before. It really hurts to breathe. How about you?'

'Just my head, I think. It's hard to tell when you're trussed up like an oven-ready turkey.' Liz joked, but inside, she was scared for the young policewoman. Broken ribs could puncture lungs. Which, when added to her fears of their possible location, had just turned their situation from bad, to deep, deep shit. 'Are you tied up with this sodding duct tape stuff?'

Gemma coughed, then screamed with pain. After a moment of two, she wheezed out, 'Yes. Just my wrists.'

Liz thought quickly. 'Can you get over here to me? Without hurting yourself any more?'

'I'll try.'

It took several minutes of agonised moans, but finally Gemma sank down beside her. 'What's the plan, Sarge?'

'First, has he taken your radio or your phone? Your torch?'

'My whole equipment belt has gone, and I can't reach my pocket where my phone was, but I think he's taken it.'

'That would have been too much to ask for, I guess. So, do you think you can lie down here and position your hands close to mine? Perhaps I can peel off the tape. Then, when you're free, you can do the same for me,' said Liz. 'And although I hate to hurry you, the quicker the better. We have to get away from here before he comes to check on us.'

Even finding the end of the tape was difficult in the darkness of the storeroom, but pulling it off, while bound herself, was damned near impossible. Soon Liz found herself almost crying with frustration.

'Damn it! Damn it! The bloody, fucking awful stuff! Am I hurting you?'

'Bugger that! Just keep trying. I've got no wish to meet that sadistic shit again if I can possibly help it.'

Liz felt her nails tear, and the powerful adhesive soon covered her hands, making her task even more difficult. 'I've got to stop for a moment, Gem. I'm sorry, but if only I could see what I was doing it would be . . .'

'Liz, shh! Did you hear something?'

Somewhere not too far away, a child was crying. Not just crying, but wailing and howling like a wounded animal.

'Oh Jesus! That gives me the willies! Do you think it's Ryan?' whispered Gemma.

'Who else? Unless he's taken another one.'

'Please God, let it be Ryan. That means he's still alive. But we have to get free to help him.'

Before Liz could answer, there was another sound — of a padlock being unlocked and a bolt released. Fear ripped through her as the door creaked and opened. A dark shape loomed in the opening.

'Good evening, ladies. I'm so pleased to meet you. My name is Ted.'

* * *

Liz wasn't sure how much time had passed. There was no longer any light seeping into her stinking prison. The concrete floor was freezing cold. Her teeth chattered uncontrollably and her head throbbed with pain. Bad enough, but it was physical at least, something to fight, something to find a way to overcome. Her mind, on the other hand, was suffering much deeper trauma right now.

Earlier that day, she had believed that her life was difficult because she was confused about the two men in her life. An almost manic laugh escaped from her dry throat. If she'd only known what the rest of the day had in store.

She needed to get free, and although she was exhausted from trying, she refused to give up. The alternative was too awful to contemplate. If she could just get herself into an upright position, she might be able to find something in the old building that was sharp enough to slice through the tape.

In desperation, she rocked back and forth, then with all the energy that she could muster, she threw herself over onto her side. The pain that seared through her head made her retch, and she was forced to lie still until it began to pass. Her idea was to try to bring her tightly bound legs up to reach her hands. If she could release one set of the restraints, she might be able to find a way to stand.

After what seemed an eternity, she fell back and sobbed. It was useless. All she wanted right now was for Matt to find them, but she had no way of giving him the slightest clue of where to look. And time was running out.

As if on cue, she heard a long and agonising scream. Even from the confines of her makeshift prison, it made her blood run cold. It echoed in Liz's ears, then faded, only to be replaced by another, and another.

This was no child's cry. Liz knew exactly who was being hurt this time.

'Oh Gemma! Why did you have to be a fucking hero? You stupid, stupid girl!' Liz shouted angrily, then her voice dropped to little more than a whisper. 'I'm so sorry! It's all my fault. What have I done to you?'

Unable to shut out the cries, Liz lay helpless and alone in the old store, and wept.

* * *

David Redpath entered the station. Jason was waiting in the reception area for him.

'Sorry to jump on you before you've even taken your coat off, sir, but there's something I really need to run past you,' Jason said.

Irritation flooded through him. Before he did anything, he had to talk to Matt.

'Give me ten, Inspector, and I'm all yours. I have to speak to the DCI first.'

'He's busy in one of the interview rooms, sir.'

'Who with?'

'His friend Adie Clarkson. He was here earlier, then he went away and came back again. The DCI asked if I could give them a while in private. He said he wanted Mr Clarkson to take care of some personal stuff for him.'

'Okay, okay. Come to my office, but as soon as the chief inspector's free, I want to see him.'

'Right, sir. I'll make sure he knows.' Jason loped along behind him, 'Forensics have found something out in the car park, sir. I want your permission to get it followed up.'

He held the door open and Jason followed him in. 'Of course you can, why ask?'

'Budget, sir. The test is a costly one. We have to get them okayed, remember?'

Bloody fucking protocol, thought David. Two, maybe three lives are hanging in the balance, and he had to consult his sodding budget. 'Do it, whatever it is, and continue to do it, until I have my officers back safely.'

'Sorry, but I need a signature,' Jason said glumly.

David wanted to throttle him. 'Whatever you need, order it. I'll gladly sign my life away afterwards.' He threw himself down in his chair. 'So what did they find?'

'Apparently, when the 4x4 sped off, some mud was dislodged from under the wheel arches. We know that because the sweeper truck cleaned the car park only thirty minutes before the incident. Initial soil analysis showed up an unusual mineral content, but it also had some plant material in it. Professor Wilkinson wants a friend of his, a forensic botanist, to carry out some more specialised microscopic identification of the samples. It could tell us something of where the vehicle has been since it was stolen.'

'Tell Professor Wilkinson, yes, go for it, and as quickly as he can. The stolen vehicle was nicked some time before it was used for the snatch, so there's a good chance the killer took it back to his base overnight.' David was used to seeing his inspector looking mildly anxious, but today the eyes were tired and bloodshot. Jason's whole being cried out distress, and David felt a rush of guilt for being so short with the man. His family had been removed from him, his sergeant and a young police woman had been grabbed from under their very noses, and a child killer was smiling and sticking two fingers up at them from CCTV film, and still the man worked on. David shook his head. He had no right, no right at all, to be irked by any of this extraordinary team.

'Hang on in there, Jason. We'll get them back. If I have to spend ten years' budget in one night, we'll get them back.'

Jason smiled weakly. 'I'll go along with that.' He went to the door. 'I'll ring the lab straightaway, then go and dig the DCI out for you.'

'Thank you. I think he's had long enough now, and what I have to say may alter the plans he's making anyway.'

Jason paused in the doorway, 'You're not thinking of taking him off the case, are you, sir? That'd just about finish him off.'

'I can't help that, Jason. I've let him stay with this far too long already. He's too close, too involved and, if I were him, I'd be running on empty by now. Apart from a missing child, which on its own is a devastating and terrible thing to have to cope with, I have all the other officers involved in this to think about. They are my responsibility, Jason, and so far I have let two of them down very badly, so Matt has to stand down, before he, or someone else, gets hurt.'

'I guess you're right, sir. I'll go and get him.'

David watched the inspector's back as he left the office. He moved swiftly, but his shoulders were hunched and despondent.

David looked out the window. It was after six, and darkness had fallen. It would be pitch black in the fenland countryside or on the bleak marshes. He knew that the search would go on. You didn't leave a child and two officers to the mercy of the night. A deep sense of camaraderie motivated all the men and women involved in the search. If they had been told to go home, they would have refused point-blank. There were certain places that they had to avoid at night. He couldn't risk accidents, and some of the dangerous stretches of marsh were treacherous in daylight. But that still left addresses to check out, people to question, garages, barns and abandoned farm buildings to search.

David drew his finger slowly across the glass pane, and prayed silently for the cloud to clear and the moon to shed its welcome light on the officers and volunteers who were doggedly combing the fenland around Fenfleet. He felt so helpless, so inadequate, even though he was doing everything possible. He had ordered Halogen lights to be shipped out to rendezvous points along the marsh, and several village community centres had been converted into temporary bases for the search parties. Add to this the massive media coverage that had swung into action.

Oh, it all sounded fine, in fact, one could be forgiven for thinking that if the killer even stuck his nose outside his lair, there would be a police marksman there to take him down. But David knew that the watery and lonely landscape that had been his home for over twenty-five years, was fully capable of concealing whatever it wanted, for a very long time. There were places that even he got lost in, places that he'd never heard of, and places even the oldest of yellowbellies, the true Lincolnshire born, would not set foot in. *And no doubt, it is one of those that you've chosen for your lair, isn't it?* David drew in a deep breath. He didn't want to do this, but he couldn't put it off any longer. And if the mountain showed no sign of imminent arrival, Mohammed would have to make the first move. It was time to talk to Matt, one way or another. David flipped open his mobile and pressed 'M.'

'Matt?'

'Yes, sir.'

'Where the hell are you?'

'Interview room 2, Super.'

'Has Jason given you my message yet?'

'Yes, sir. Sorry, I've just finished tying up some loose ends with Adie.'

'Well, get yourself up here, right now, Matt. We need to talk.'

'Adie's just left. I'm on my way.'

David shook his head. *Thicker than thieves, that pair.* The strangest alliance he'd ever come across. He thought about Adie Clarkson, well, more about his criminal record, and hoped that Matt knew what he was doing by entrusting him with private matters.

The desk phone rang loudly and pulled him from his thoughts.

'Superintendent Redpath? Rory Wilkinson here. May I come over and talk to you? I've found something rather disturbing and I can't reach DCI Ballard.'

'Please do, Professor. Matt is on his way up here right now, so you can tell both of us.' He hung up the phone and felt a deep bone chilling shiver course through his body. He really hadn't like the sound of that word "disturbing."

The next person through the door, was Jason, not Matt or the pathologist. 'I'm sorry, I'm not having much luck. The professor is out of his lab, and I haven't been able to deliver your message, either. I can't find the DCI anywhere.'

Eyes narrowing as he spoke, David said, 'But I spoke to him ten minutes ago, he said he was in interview room 2, and that he'd already seen you.'

Jason looked nonplussed. 'No, I never saw him. I went down there, and although the light was on, I went in, but it was empty. I thought maybe he was already on his way up to see you.'

'This isn't right!' David jumped up, pulling out his mobile and pressing last number redial. 'Switched off. Shit! Get word around the station. I want Matt found. And, Jason, get hold of that bloody ex-con of a friend of his. I want to know what the hell their cosy little chat was all about.'

'I'm onto it, sir.'

'Let me know the minute you hear something. I'll be here with Rory Wilkinson.'

David turned angrily back to his desk, picked up a ceramic pot full of pens and hurled it against the wall. Shards of pottery flew across the office. 'Damn you, Matt Ballard!' The words were little more than a hiss of air between his gritted teeth.

'Oh my! Quite an effective method of anger management you have there, Superintendent.' Rory Wilkinson stood in the open doorway.

'It was a souvenir from Crete, given to me by my youngest daughter,' replied David ruefully.

'Ah, not the best thing to hurl at the wall. What's happened here?' The pathologist stooped down and began to retrieve pens and pencils from the carpet.

David told him, and as he did, it became clear that he wasn't so much furious with Matt, as livid with himself for not acting sooner. 'He believes that he's entirely to blame for all this, and in his present state of mind, who can blame him.'

Rory laid the pens carefully on his desk. 'Poor chap! He's been hounded, his life laid bare in front of his colleagues and peers. God! I'd have died a thousand deaths. It's a wicked thing this person has done. May I?' He indicated to a chair, then sat down without waiting for a reply. 'Which brings me to my reason for coming. DCI Ballard sent me copies of all the pictures that you have of your suspect.'

David brushed a few small shards of pottery from his own chair, then sank down and stared at the pathologist, 'Yes, he told me. And?'

'I believe I know why he was so happy to sweetly smile for the birdie on so many occasions.' He produced a series of diagrams and prints from a folder. 'The man you see here.' He placed one of the original CCTV photos of the bearded man on the desk in front of him. 'Doesn't exist.'

David's overworked mind refused to compute. 'Sorry?'

'Your confusion is totally understandable, so let me explain.' Laying another picture down, he pointed to the man's face. 'After close comparison of all the shots, I realised that his bone structure varies slightly from one picture to the other, and in the last one, his face is slightly contorted, asymmetrical in a different way from the earlier pictures.'

'But surely they are distorted because of the picture quality.'

'No, that's not it. This man has used padding, pushed into his upper jaw and the back of his mouth, in the last shot, it had moved. And the beard is not real either. I've zoomed in on a spot just by the left ear, and you will see a feint line where make-up has not quite covered the join. Even the skin around the neck may be synthetic. It's a good disguise, a very good one, but when enlarged to this degree, there are minor flaws.'

David studied the image of the man's face. He saw what Rory meant. 'Can you give me some kind of idea of what he looks like without the false bits?'

'I've got one of my students working on that right now, although to be honest, I don't hold out too much hope. It's not like doing an ageing process because we've got no basic structure to work with, but we'll give it a try.'

'Thank you. And that reminds me, I asked my inspector to tell you to go ahead with any tests you think necessary and sod the budget.'

'I rather thought that would be the case, considering what's at stake. I've already ordered the advanced soil sample analysis.' Rory gave him a tired smile. 'Where do you think the DCI has gone?'

'I truly have no idea, but to take off like that means only one thing, the killer made contact.' David felt a sick emptiness inside. 'I think Matt believes that he has caused all this, so he should be the one to end it, but I have the distinct feeling that he will make everything an awful lot worse.'

CHAPTER TWENTY-EIGHT

The fact that he had spent the last few hours lying to everyone, from his best friend to the superintendent, didn't bother him one iota. Matt had only one thing on his mind right now — finding Liz and Gemma. And he didn't give a flying fuck how he did it.

From the second he had seen the message on the back of the photograph, he had known what he would do, and it didn't involve another living soul. He had suffered no pangs of guilt about not following procedure, in fact he hadn't even considered it, despite what he had said to Adie. When the phone had first rung in the interview room, he had been told to get out of the police station, get his car, and ditch his friend.

He hadn't wasted time worrying about how the killer knew that he was with Adie at that exact moment. His nemesis seemed to know absolutely everything, so why bother racking your brains wondering how.

Adie had, as instructed, collected Matt's car for him, parked it in a side street close to the station, then returned to the interview room with the keys. Then they'd slipped out of the building through an old and rarely used fire door. Matt had felt bad about speeding away and leaving

Adie stranded, but he had no choice. Adie could do what he liked now, tell the super or not, it was all the same, and quite irrelevant.

His car splashed mud and water onto the verges, as he sped along the back road to the meeting place. He wasn't nervous. He didn't feel anything really. He had no plan, no ingenious surprise to spring on his enemy. There was no point. The killer was too clever to be deceived by tricks. The best he could do was pray that somehow he would get a lucky break. Not for his own sake, but for Liz and Gemma, and maybe little Ryan.

On one side of the road, he saw a team of searchers in the distance, their lights sweeping over the deep muddy furrows of the farmland. *Sorry to tell you this, lads, but you won't find them there.*

The second call had given him the location. The voice, garbled by the scrambler, had snapped out the address. Matt had panicked that he wouldn't understand in time, that the killer would hang up leaving him unsure of where to go. It only took a few seconds of intense concentration though, and he had it clear in his head. An inspired choice, if you had murder on your mind. For anything else it was a miserable lonely spot, certainly one to avoid at night, which meant that the search teams would not go there tonight. It was remote, unfriendly and very dangerous. Perfect.

As he accelerated onto a straight stretch of fenland drove, he felt a tiny thrill of excitement. At last he would have some answers. He would meet the man who had screwed up his entire life in the space of a few days. A man, who right at this moment, had control over everyone that he loved. Matt's lips twisted into a grim smile. A man who, given the chance, he would gladly kill without hesitation or remorse.

* * *

The murder room was packed with officers. David stood, ramrod straight, beside the picture boards. To his right, was the pathologist, and next to him, the thin shadow of a man that was Jason Hammond.

David had already explained that Matt had gone. He had put forward his theory about why a detective chief inspector would do such a hare-brained and irresponsible thing. He hoped that what he had said would somehow keep Matt's reputation in one piece. Matt, it seemed, had left the building via a route rookie officers took when playing a game that required you to get from A to B without getting caught on camera. Matt had accomplished his escape perfectly, and they only knew how he'd done it, because of Adie Clarkson, who was right now, back in his favourite interview room for the third time that day.

'From the spot in Anchor Street, where he asked Clarkson to park his car, we can only assume that he planned on leaving town in a similar manner to the way he got out of the station. That is, a route with no, or at least very few, cameras. And, as Fenfleet is classed by most as a backwater, a sleepy little country town, not warranting a large budget for security systems, it is more than possible.' He paused, his voice heavy with concern. 'Something that is backed up by the fact that we have had no sightings of him at all.'

The room remained silent, and David was acutely aware that the usual jokes or comments weren't being bandied about. Everyone was simply waiting for instructions. They wanted to get out there and find their colleagues, not sit here and listen to some old fogey bleating on. He sighed. He felt like they did.

'I know how frustrating this is, but we have to throw all our energies into discovering the identity of the killer. This is imperative, and unless we get lucky and someone spots the chief's car, it's the only way we will know where to look for him.'

He gestured to Rory Wilkinson. 'Now, I'm going to hand over to the professor here, he will fill you in on a discovery he made earlier regarding the appearance of the killer.'

Rory rose to speak. David pulled Jason to one side, and whispered, 'I know this is somewhat unorthodox, but I've just been speaking to Liz Haynes' husband. Considering his high rank in the British army, I've decided to allow him access to the investigation as a consultant.'

'Is that wise, sir? The poor bloke can hardly be said to be rational with his wife missing.'

'He's a trained and very experienced professional soldier, Inspector. And what is not common knowledge, is that his specialist field is tracking and interrogating terror suspects. Believe me, we can use his expertise — and right now. He's going to shadow you, okay?'

Jason pulled a face.

'I wouldn't do this if I didn't believe he could be of use, Jason. And he's no thick squaddie either. He's a clever man, with a degree in psychology, and frankly, if it ever came to something physical, I'd pick him for my team, wouldn't you?'

'Yes, sir. No doubt there.'

David looked at his inspector shrewdly. 'But you still have a problem with it, don't you?'

'No, not as such, sir, but something just occurred to me.' He screwed up his forehead in concentration. 'Can I ask, sir, is the lieutenant colonel something pretty important in the army?'

'Why?'

'Is there any chance that all this stuff about the old Gibbet Fen case and Matthew Ballard's past could be an elaborate smokescreen? What if Liz was the intended target all along? As the wife of an important army officer.' He rubbed his temple. 'Or what if they are after the soldier himself? What better time to take him than when his head's screwed, because a psycho's got his wife?'

David blinked a few times as he tried to get his own head around Jason's theory. Maybe he was getting old, but thinking outside-the-box sapped his energies. 'Okay, let's put it to the others.'

Rory was winding up his presentation.

'Go on, Jason, share your thoughts,' David said.

When Jason had finished, some of the officers nodded their agreement, others were more inclined to stick with the more obvious explanation that Matt was, and always had been, the target.

Debate filled the room:

'It's far too complicated a plan, just to take a woman who spends most of her spare time home alone anyway. They could have snatched her any time they wanted.'

'Perhaps that's what they want you to think.'

'Why do you think the killer needed to disguise himself?'

'Because we'd recognise him?'

'Probably, which means he's either known to us as a criminal, or he's a familiar face around here.'

There was a sudden silence, then one young detective said, 'What, like a colleague?'

The room went silent. David stepped in. 'There are a lot of people affiliated with us, not just fellow officers. There are civilians by the dozen, specialists of all kinds, relatives, witnesses, just don't start suspecting each other, okay?' He looked around the room and was relieved to see a hand go up. 'Yes, Detective?'

A young woman stood up. She was from the team that had been brought in to help. 'While we are kind of brainstorming, sir, what if Gemma Goddard was the real target? If what you told us about the DCI possibly being her father, then that might explain why all the pressure's been on him, wouldn't it? She may have been deliberately lured outside to the car park after all.'

'You said that she had a really bad start in life, sir. What if someone resents the fact that she fell on her feet?'

'Someone who maybe didn't fare so well themselves? Someone from one of those abusive foster homes, maybe?'

David held up his palm. 'These are all valid points that we must investigate. DCI Ballard himself thought that it was the killer's intention to take both women. I didn't buy it at the time, now I'm forced to consider it as a possibility.'

'Sir?' Bryn stood up. He looked tired, his clothes were creased and untidy, but his eyes burned with desire to find his friends. 'This whole thing has been so meticulously planned, there has to be a really serious motive behind it. I find it hard to believe that one man has devised and carried this out alone.' He pushed his hands deep into his pockets and stared at David. 'How could one man find out so much classified information about the guv'nor and about the workings of the police station, and still dash around the countryside abducting and killing at will?'

'Are you suggesting that he might have had help, Detective Constable?'

'I am. And I think we should have an in-depth chat with the boss's "loyal friend." The one who goes "way back," and hence knows more than anyone about the DCI and his past history. The one who found the bug in his home, and knows the police station pretty well, from first-hand experience. The one in the interview room, sir. Adie Clarkson.'

* * *

As the lanes became narrower and the more difficult to negotiate in the darkness, Matt was forced to kill his speed somewhat, but he was still taking risks in his desperation to get there, to get it over with.

Rounding a bend at forty, he almost hit a badger. As he swerved to avoid the animal, he overcooked the corner and skimmed a hedge on the other side of the road. This was madness. No way could he afford to end up dead in the wreckage of his car because of his own haste.

He dropped his speed to a slightly safer pace. Up until now he had known exactly where he was going, but now it was getting difficult. This was not a place he knew well, and at night, on the unlit roads, it was hard to get a feel for distance.

He scanned the bleak fen to one side of the drove, and the scrubby windswept hedges to the other. He was looking for a signpost and he prayed that he hadn't missed it already, although he was still pretty sure that it was on this stretch of the road.

After a few minutes, he saw it, half covered in ivy and leaning drunkenly into the hedge, a rusted and almost illegible sign. Just visible in his torchlight, he saw the weather-worn, painted words: "To the Quay."

His heart suddenly lurched in his chest. This was it.

He eased the car into the single-track lane, and drove very slowly. Even at a snail's pace, he bounced uncomfortably over the rutted track, and had trouble keeping a hold on the steering wheel. His vision was limited as there were hedges either side now, and the lane seemed to go on forever.

Then he saw it. Ahead of him, was a faint light. He peered through the filthy windshield. The road was widening and the hedgerows had become uneven thickets of tangled undergrowth. He accelerated slightly.

The lane led through a gateless opening and onto a large open area of concrete. On the far side he could see dark oily-looking water. It wasn't the main Westland River, he knew that for sure, but he thought that it was probably a tributary that fed into the big tidal waterway that flowed right through the fens and out to the Wash and the North Sea. An area flanked by treacherous salt marsh, ditches, dykes and inhospitable wetlands.

His hands gripped the wheel tightly, and his heart rate rose, as he pulled the car to a halt.

The light that he had seen came from a storm lantern balanced on the top of a concrete bollard. He looked from one side to the other, but the only other thing in sight was a small corrugated structure close to a steep slipway that ran down to the water's edge. A hut of some kind, and as it was the only place to hide, he guessed that was where his host would be waiting.

He sat within the comparative safety of the car. He could hear his own heart beating. No way back now. What next? He decided that he really didn't want to know that yet. Swallowing hard, he flung open the door, and stepped out.

It had stopped raining, but a surprisingly cold wind hit him hard, and he shivered as he looked towards the hut. For a second or two he closed his eyes, trying to get them adjusted to the black night that surrounded him. Then he stared back at the hut again, looking for the slightest shadow, the smallest movement.

'Step right away from the car! Hands where I can see them, and keep facing the river.'

The voice came from immediately behind him, and Matt felt a shock surge through his body. The bastard must have been waiting in the hedgerow. He took a deep breath. *Crunch time!* He raised his hands, and moved very slowly away from his car.

'Further! Further! Now stop.'

The voice was no longer disguised, and he longed to get a look at the face, but this was clearly not the right moment.

'Okay. Now strip.'

Matt froze.

'You heard. Strip. Now! And don't touch your pockets.'

No way! 'Hey, look! I've done everything you asked. I've come alone. I've told no one. I'm hardly likely to secrete something lethal on my body, am I?'

'How do I know that, unless I check?'

'Are the women safe?'

'They are, as I told you, alive. Now do what I say.'

'To use your words, how do I know that?' Matt fought to keep his tone level and his questions reasonable.

'You don't. And you, policeman, are not in any position to risk a gamble. So strip.'

The words hit home, and although Matt could barely believe what he was doing, he began to unzip his jacket. The thought of a psycho conducting a full body search on a concrete pier, on a cold March night, was inconceivable. But thinking of Liz and Gemma in danger, Matt took off his jacket and placed it on the ground. He loosened his tie, removed it and flung it down with the jacket. The biting cold made his shirt feel as it were made of tissue paper, and when he slipped it off and felt the wind tear across his bare chest, he began to feel the first frisson of fear.

'Everything. Shoes and socks as well.'

He undid his belt and unzipped his trousers. He had not, in his wildest dreams expected this. He let the chinos fall, then kicked his feet free of them. But he should have, shouldn't he? This man was not some pea-brained thug who would have wrestled him bodily from the car and given him a good kicking for a welcome. No, this man was clever, highly motivated, and held all the cards.

He eased his feet from his shoes, then stood on one leg and removed a sock. As he placed the bare foot on the ground, both cold and slivers of wet gravel bit into him. With difficulty, he pulled off the remaining sock, threw it down, then stood still and waited.

'What don't you understand about the word, "everything," policeman?'

With shaking hands, Matt grasped the elastic waistband of his boxers, and eased them down. As he stepped out of them and straightened up, he realised that he'd never before felt so vulnerable.

'Move away from your clothes.'

With grit cutting into his feet, Matt knew that he had no option but to do as he was told.

'Okay, stop there.' He heard soft footsteps moving closer to him. 'Now lay down, flat on your face, arms and legs spread-eagled.'

'Oh please! For fuck's sake, you can see I've got nothing on me!'

'You are beginning to annoy me. Now, the sooner you do it, the sooner you can get your clothes back on. Or would you like my other guests to see you like this?' He gave an unnerving giggle. 'Although one of them has seen that body plenty of times before, hasn't she?'

Matt gritted his teeth, then eased himself down to the ground. A second later, he shuddered as his naked body pressed against the cold, damp concrete. He moved his legs apart, drawing a sharp breath as the rough ground scratched delicate skin, then he finally stretched his arms out to the sides. The frisson of fear was becoming something akin to full-blown dread. Earlier he had prayed for luck, but now he realised that he would be looking for a fucking miracle to outwit this evil shit.

For one moment he considered his chances of leaping up and rushing him. But his captor would have thought that through already. He'd either be armed, or ready for him. Whatever, his present condition was not exactly conducive to combat. And of course, if he died right there, in the night, naked and alone, he would have died without getting one single answer, and more importantly, without having even attempted to save Liz and Gemma.

As he lay prostrate on the freezing cold ground, like a strange version of Leonardo Da Vinci's Universal Man, he tried to find his courage. No way could he let the killer know how terrified he really was. 'Happy now?'

'Perfectly, thank you.' Behind him, he heard the man carefully going through his clothes, and he knew that he would be checking pockets, seams, linings.

Then Matt heard the footsteps approach him again. Something jabbed against the back of his neck. It felt as cold as the ground and hard as iron. A gun.

'One move, and you'll never make another.'

Matt believed him.

Hands swiftly and expertly flew over his body. Matt shut his eyes tight and tried to think only of the two women, held hostage and maybe injured and in pain. He'd endure anything, if he just had one good chance to save them.

'Move your legs together.'

Again he winced as the shards of gravel bit into his flesh.

'Okay, now, very slowly, get up. And put on just your trousers, jacket and shoes, got it?'

The full beam of the man's powerful torch fell on him. His skin looked pale, almost white in the bright light. 'Clear as crystal.' He stood up and moved towards his clothes. As he bent to retrieve his trousers, he chanced a look towards his captor, but all he saw was a dark shadow behind the blazing circle of light.

'Look away, policeman. You'll see me in all good time. Now, walk back towards the lane, the same way you came in.'

With slow steps, his bare feet feeling odd in his shoes, Matt made his way to the back of the quay. After just a few moments, and in a rare shaft of moonlight, he saw another vehicle tucked away close to the hedgerow. It was a 4x4.

'Go to the back of the vehicle and place your hands on the rear windscreen.' The muzzle of the gun touched lightly into the short-cropped hair at the back of his neck. 'Just a tiny reminder, in case you were thinking of being silly.'

As fucking if! Then, as he half-expected, a pair of bar cuffs snapped onto his wrists. He was now pretty much defenceless.

He started to shiver. The cold wind from off the river, seemed to have eaten into every centimetre of his exposed skin, and added to the shock that was starting to set in, the jacket alone was doing little to warm him.

Hands grasped his shoulders and pulled him round, bringing him face to face with his captor. In the light of the man's torch, Matt saw the familiar face from the photographs. The sly eyes, the beard, the greying hair. The killer.

'Who are you?' he whispered, his teeth chattering uncontrollably.

'As if I'm going to tell you that!' He gave a sharp laugh. 'And so early in our relationship.' He moved to one side and opened up the back of the vehicle. 'We have got a lot of talking to do, policeman. Now, I'm sorry about this, but I have things to do before we sit down for that promised chat, and I can't be worrying about you, so . . .'

Matt felt a sharp sting in the top part of his thigh, then he looked down, saw the syringe, and the man withdrawing the needle.

The weakness hit him almost immediately, and by the time the man had rolled him into the back of the vehicle, a rushing sound was filling his head. His last thought, before the black roaring darkness enveloped him, was that he really should have had a plan.

CHAPTER TWENTY-NINE

Having split his teams to pursue what felt like appropriate lines of enquiry, David went with Bryn to interview Adie Clarkson. Although he wanted to go along with what the young detective had suggested, a big part of him didn't believe that Matt could be so wrong about a friend. They formed a weird pair, and David was no fan of the ex-con, but deep down he just couldn't see Matt being hoodwinked for so many years. And after only ten minutes of questioning, Adie Clarkson had said nothing to make him think differently, and he was horribly aware that the clock was ticking. He didn't want to spend even one second more than he had to on a false lead.

'I don't know about you,' he said to Bryn, as the door closed on the interview room. 'But I really think he's telling the truth. In fact, I think he's as worried about Matt's safety as we are.'

Bryn ran a hand through his hair and sighed. 'Yeah, I hate to say it but I think the concern is real too. He's either levelling with us, or giving Johnny Depp a run for his money as a bloody good actor,' he indicated to the door. 'Shall I send him on his way?'

'He said he wanted to help, didn't he?' David leaned back against the wall and inhaled deeply. 'Take him and get him a coffee, or something. Make him prove that he wants to help us. Let him hang around here. Unless I'm very wrong, that man knows more about Matt the person, as opposed to Matt the DCI, than anyone. We may just need him.'

Bryn smiled, 'And if you're wrong, at least we've kept him close, haven't we?'

'Best we can do, right now.' David pulled himself up straight. 'I'm going to have another talk to the Goddards. I want to know more about Gemma's past.'

* * *

'The doctor's given my wife a sedative, Superintendent. The shock of all this, on top of her original illness . . .' James Goddard shrugged his narrow shoulders. 'I'm really worried about her.'

'What illness does she have? If you don't mind me asking?' David accepted the offer of a seat.

'She has a nasty form of arthritis that flares up from time to time. Causes her a great deal of pain. She'd had a spell of it just before all this happened. I'd rather not try to disturb her, if it's all the same.'

'I'm sure that you'll be able to help me, Mr Goddard.' David felt the soft armchair beneath him and felt guilty for sitting down while others trudged the marsh in the dark. 'Can you tell me everything you know about Gemma's life before she came to you?'

The man raised his eyebrows and gave David a feeble smile. 'I told Linda that I wasn't wasting my time. I knew this would be the next thing.' He stood up, went over to a desk in the corner of the room and retrieved a faded folder. 'I wanted something to do, needed to keep occupied, you know?' He passed the folder to David. 'It was in the attic. Take it. Although believe me, it doesn't make pleasant reading, unless you're into horror stories.'

David opened it and looked through the sheaf of official typewritten and handwritten reports. Even the briefest glance caused a knot to form in his gut. James Goddard was right about the horror story. He knew it happened, sadly all too often, but how one little kid could be exposed to such a catalogue of errors was beyond him.

'You can take them, Superintendent. I really don't ever want to look at them again.'

'They'll be returned, Mr Goddard.'

'Then I'll burn them when this is all over.' He looked drained. 'I suppose there's no good news, is there?'

'Not yet, although every man and woman involved in this search is giving their all, I promise you. Your Gemma is very highly thought of. Her friends and colleagues are totally distraught about what's happened.' He closed the file. 'Do you ever recall Gemma talking about any of the other children in those foster homes?'

James shook his head. 'Not really. She never talked about her past. The doctors originally wondered if she had some sort of amnesia, that she had repressed the earlier years and pushed them out of consciousness as a defence mechanism. They found it hard to understand how, after everything that had happened to her, she could be such a kind and thoughtful child.' He glanced across at the file in David's hand. 'Most of her psychiatric evaluations and follow-up reports are in there. Although, now you mention it, one thing isn't. When she first arrived with us, she used to have nightmares, and she would always call out for the same person to help her, a boy called Richard. Strangely, she never seemed to remember him when she woke up. It was only in her nightmares that she would call out his name.'

'Do you think this Richard was a real person?'

James shrugged. 'We never knew. When the nightmares stopped, we sort of forgot about him, I suppose.'

David felt a quiver of unrest in his mind. Something he'd felt before on many occasions, and something he never ignored. He stood up, grasping the folder carefully in one hand, and stuck out the other to James. 'Thank you for this, it could be a great help. And be assured we are doing everything we can to get her back.'

'I know. I just hope it's enough.'

* * *

'Mrs Peart? My name is Superintendent David Redpath. I'm sorry to call so late, but I really need your help. It's about a child, a friend of Gemma Goddard.'

It took fifteen minutes for Alexis Peart to search her records and ring back.

'There is mention of another boy, but he wasn't one of our children, Superintendent. Richard and Gemma were placed by different adoption agencies, I'm afraid.'

'Were they fostered by the same family, prior to you becoming involved in her case?'

'Yes, it seems so, and not just the one abusive family by the looks of it, Gemma spoke of a boy called Richard at another home prior to that. One where we later discovered that most of the children, especially young boys, were badly treated in one way or another.'

'Do you know where he went? What his surname is? Where Richard's new adoptive parents lived?'

'I'm sorry. I have no idea, but I can give you the adoption agency's number. It's still operating. It's the largest in the county.'

David scribbled down the name and number. 'You've been most helpful, Mrs Peart. Just one more thing though, would you say that Richard was abused as well?'

'I don't have the full details here, Superintendent, only comments made in Gemma's file about a boy called Richard, but I'd say, yes, most certainly. Reading between the lines, he was damaged, too. Possibly far more so than little Gemma.'

David threw the phone back in its cradle and practically ran from the office.

'Jason! I think I've got something! Get hold of Rory Wilkinson and see how he's doing with that restructured photograph of the killer. We need it, fast!'

Jason hurried from the murder room. David grabbed a chair at the nearest desk and picked up the phone. The chances of getting anyone working this late were slim, but there might be an answerphone with an out-of-hours number. He punched in the first number and waited.

'Good evening, can I help you?'

'Is that the Diocesan Adoption Service?'

'Yes, it is, although I'm afraid I'll have to ask you to ring back in the morning. I'm only here because we had something of an emergency earlier.'

David briefly explained the situation, crossing his fingers that he hadn't got through to a jobsworth employee.

There was a silence, then the man said, 'I can't help you myself, I've only been here for five years, but I can give you the name of the man who dealt with that particular case.' There was an edge to the man's voice.

'But you do know about Richard?'

'Everyone here knows about Richard, Superintendent Redpath.'

'How so?'

'It would be better if my superior, Leonard Johnson, told you. He knows the whole case. If you give me your number, I'll contact him immediately and then he can ring you directly.'

David put down the phone, every nerve in his body jangled. He knew this might be the break they needed.

'Are you alright, sir?' Bryn placed a steaming mug of tea in front of him.

'Other than shitting hot bricks while I wait for a call that may turn this case around, Detective, I'm just dandy, thank you.'

Bryn's eyes opened wider. 'Really?'

'Cross everything you physically can, and stand by to move, DC Owen.'

Bryn grabbed his jacket. They both stared at the phone, willing it to ring. 'By the way, Clarkson's sticking it out, sir. Although he clearly doesn't like his surroundings. And he told me that the DCI had asked him to buy him some time, something he chose not to do. He came straight to us as soon as Matt had driven away.'

'Even more reason to trust him, I guess.' David fidgeted uncomfortably in his chair and took a sip of the hot tea. 'Has anyone heard from Gary Haynes?'

'Not to my knowledge. His meeting with the top brass will probably take some time, won't it?'

The phone finally shrilled out. He grabbed it and took a deep breath. 'Yes, Superintendent Redpath here.'

After a brief explanation of the seriousness of their situation, David listened carefully, making scribbled notes. 'So, Richard was definitely a friend of Gemma Goddard, and he was successfully placed in a good home, like her?'

'Well, yes, but his problems didn't quite end there, Superintendent. Richard was a highly intelligent child. His biological parents were well-off, his father an academic and his mother was some sort of scientist. They both died in a light aircraft crash in Surrey when Richard was three years old.'

'So why didn't relatives take the child?'

'There was no one at the time, well no one suitable to take on a toddler.' Johnson continued, 'and there was precious little money left either. Just debts. Richard was let down by the system that should have protected him, Superintendent.'

'Like Gemma.'

'Exactly like Gemma. Although she fell on her feet, and Richard initially didn't.'

'Explain, please.'

'After the same dreadful early years as Gemma, Richard was finally homed with a couple in Cambridge. They had excellent references and had lost a child of their own in an accident. It seemed perfect, but sadly, when Richard joined the family, the mother came to resent him. Eventually she took to the drink, and when Richard was ten, she tried to burn the house down, with him in it.'

'Jesus! Poor kid!'

'Well, it does have something of a happy ending. Although both parents died, and Richard did suffer burns, he survived and was formally adopted by his adoptive maternal grandfather. A man who had adored the child from the start, and who felt a great burden of guilt about what his daughter had done to her family. Richard was taken in by him.'

'And Richard's surname?'

'Cotton.'

'And a date of birth?'

'We never knew that fact, Superintendent. I can tell you that he is 28 years old, but we never had a birth certificate.'

'What was the grandfather's name, Mr Johnson? And is he still alive?'

'Oh, he's alive alright. His name is Harry Cotton, and if you could hold on for a moment, I'll check his address for you.'

David heard the familiar tap of fingers on a keyboard.

'Well, that's a bit of luck! He lives in Alford. That's not far from you, is it?'

This is it! David felt his blood pumping though his veins. 'Not far at all. If I could have the full address and a telephone number, sir.' He wrote it down and ripped the paper from the pad. 'Thank you, Mr Johnson. Thank you very much.' He slammed the phone down and jumped up. 'Bryn! Tell Jason Hammond where we are going, then get us a car! Quickly! I'll ring this man en route and tell him to expect us.'

CHAPTER THIRTY

Matt's return to consciousness was sudden. He snapped back to life, eyes wide, and heart juddering in his rib cage.

'A damned effective antidote to the sedative, I'd say.' The killer stood next to him, staring admiringly at the syringe. 'As long as you get the dosage right, and as I'm not exactly an expert, I have been known to throw the odd heart into a fatally abnormal rhythm. Still, the uncertainty of outcome all adds to the fun, I suppose.' He laughed softly. 'Which reminds me, I've got a few things to do, so I'll leave you to get yourself together, then we will have that chat that I promised you.' He looked around critically, like a functions' organiser checking his venue for his client. 'I've taken great pains to get this right, so I hope you'll appreciate the effort I've gone to, to make you feel at home.'

Matt barely heard him. He was far too busy fighting for breath and trying to calm his racing heart. With his eyes closed tightly, he concentrated entirely on controlling his breathing. *You can do this! In, relax, out. In, relax, slowly out. And again.*

When he finally believed that he would survive the effects of the drug, he opened his eyes. Initially his heart rate leapt up again, but after another few moments of monitoring his breath, he was capable of comprehending where he was. It wasn't easy. And he needed to come to terms with the fact that he wasn't alone in that strange place either.

Three other figures were also held captive with him. They were slumped in their chairs, unmoving and silent.

He looked through the gloom, then gasped in shock. It was hard to make out details, but he knew he had found Liz and Gemma. The other smaller figure was probably Ryan Fisher. He called their names, but got no reply. He had to get to them, to reassure himself that they were still alive!

He looked down, and saw that he was seated on an old metal-framed chair, the type you found in a church hall or a community centre. Tubular metal framework formed a box-like chair, with unyielding padded armrests, a low back and flat hard seat. Just the right sort of design for strapping someone to. And Matt was certainly strapped. He heaved himself up, and wrenched his stomach muscles. Groaning with pain, he realised that he had missed that it was bolted to the floor.

His arms were taped to the arm rests, his ankles bound to the chair legs, and his torso strapped to the back of the chair with a series of thick leather belts. He strained against them. Even Harry Houdini would have had problems here.

Matt looked around. He knew what kind of building he was in. He'd seen enough of them in his time. Old ruined windmills were scattered all across the fens. A few had been lovingly restored, with working sails and millstones to grind the corn. Some had been converted into upmarket homes, but most were like this, decrepit, ruined and dangerous. No sails, no upper floors left intact, just a tall hollow tower with pigeons roosting on the loose brick ledges of the unstable walls.

He shivered as he tried to take in their shadowy stone prison. Suddenly a barrage of powerful spotlights almost blinded him. He screwed up his eyes, squeezed them tightly shut, then tried to peer from narrow slits, until they adjusted.

Someone had rigged up some seriously clever lighting. Which, his police brain noted, meant that though it was a ruin, there was power here. Five spotlights shone down, each one illuminating one of the five chairs that had been carefully placed in a large circle in the centre of the floor.

Matt looked in horror at his silent companions. The bright spots had thrown the tableau in front of him into sharp, knife edged relief. Ice-white light, and deep dark shadow imprinted on his mind a sight that he had never contemplated even in his nightmares.

He whimpered softly in the darkness.

He was too late. Tears welled up in his eyes. And what the hell had he been thinking of anyway? How in heaven's name could he have helped them, bound hand and foot and totally helpless?

He needed to look at them, but couldn't find the courage to even lift his head.

This was all his fault. He swallowed back salty tears. It was almost a relief to know that he wasn't going to come out of this alive. At least he wouldn't have to live with the guilt for too long.

Coward. He slowly lifted his head and looked around the circle of seats.

Next to him on his right, was the boy. At least, he thought it was Ryan, although it was hard to tell. The lad was slumped forward. His head at a peculiar angle, turned away from Matt. Some of his hair seemed to be missing, burnt maybe? The light made it hard to know exactly what you were looking at. He moved his gaze down. The hands were certainly blackened, and the one nearest to him, seemed to be twisted and contorted. He felt bile rising in his throat and didn't want to see any more.

He dragged his gaze from the child, and although his brain screamed for him to look away, he unwilling forced himself to look at the next victim.

Liz! Oh Liz! Not you, not you. Not when he'd finally realised he loved her.

She was also slumped forward. Her hair matted with caked and drying blood from a large gash in her scalp. Blood had left a dark stain on the floor beside her.

Matt stared at the woman who had so recently declared that she loved him too. He felt a rush of burning, white-hot anger. Somehow, somehow, he would get the monster who'd done this. Get him, and with his bare hands, tear him limb from limb. The old feeling, of cold, hard determination, slid back into place. He'd do whatever it took, and it may require guile and cunning that he wasn't sure he possessed, but he'd find it from somewhere. Then he'd drain the very life from this sadistic animal, and send him back to the hell from which he'd come.

He moved his head sharply towards the next chair, and saw Gemma. Gemma, his young, bright and enthusiastic policewoman, and perhaps the daughter he had never known existed. For a moment, his resilience faltered. It was hard to make out her actual injuries, but it seemed that the girl had suffered more than the others. Her face, already bruised from the last beating, looked raw, as if she had been dragged over sharp gravel. With mounting dismay, Matt saw that her clothes were ripped and bloody. One sleeve was missing from her uniform shirt, and a deep laceration, one cutting through skin and muscle, almost down to the bone, had seeped dark fluid over the arm of the chair. He looked closer and saw that her trousers hung in shreds, and beneath them, just visible, both legs were criss-crossed with cuts and scratches. Either she had put up one hell of a fight or her assailant had paid considerably more attention to her.

Unable to look any longer, Matt focused on the last chair. The empty chair.

Was it ready for another guest? Or was it for that bearded son of a bitch who had done this? As Matt thought about the man, he saw the words on the back of the photograph. "They are alive, but it's up to you how long they stay that way." He forced himself to look at his motionless companions, to search for the slightest hint of a rise and fall of their chests, but he could see nothing in the glaring light.

He remembered Liz's words: *He's a mindbender.*

Were they dead, or alive? He really didn't know, but rather than feel again that terrible hopelessness that he had earlier, when he'd first seen them, he had to believe they were alive.

Matt stopped fighting the bonds that held him and tried to think. The killer had said they would talk. So, the only way he might get a reprieve for the others, if they were still alive, would be with words. Somehow he had to drag this out for as long as possible, to give his police colleagues, the ones he had treated so badly, a chance to find him. He gulped back air. Somehow he was going to have to find out what the killer wanted to hear from him, and then talk for his life, for all their lives.

* * *

Adie Clarkson paced the long hallway and tried to keep his cool. This place was making him stir-crazy, which was quite understandable, given his history.

The only reason that he was still there, was for the chance to tag along when they finally worked out where Mattie had gone. And he knew they would. He'd never been the type of villain to underestimate the fuzz. That would have made him some kind of a prat, and he was no mug. Even if, as a young man, he had spent more years inside than he cared to mention. That had just increased his grudging respect for people like Matt, for the ones who had been smart enough to catch him and put him away.

Like it or not, he guessed he was old school, when it came down to it.

He turned at the end of the hallway and shoved his hands deeper into his pockets. It had been fun when it had been 'them and us.' Years ago, you didn't shoot the copper who nabbed you. You may have had a fucking good punch-up, but a bloody nose and a few lost teeth would have been about it.

Two young coppers passed him, their heavy equipment belts and stabproof vests bulking them out. That kind of said it all, thought Adie. When Mattie was a young bobby he would have had a nightstick and a torch, if he was lucky. He smiled when he thought of the old police cars, with their full-sized telephones, no smart hands-free units and satnav back then, and yet they still caught the villains.

He watched the door closing behind the young officers. Shit! He had to get out, do something positive. He followed them, caught the door before it locked and slipped through. His car wasn't far away.

Adie got to the foyer and stopped. If he left now, he'd have no chance of finding Matt. With a sigh, he sank down on one of the seats in reception. Better to stick it out here. When the balloon finally went up, he'd be there. Another pair of hands, or fists for that matter, might be just what Matt needed.

He tried to think of who hated Matt enough to do this to him. The baby-tec, Bryn, had explained why they thought Adie himself might be involved, and he could see exactly where the lad was coming from. And the idea that more than one person was involved made sense. One as the brains, and one as the muscle. Which would mean that Mr Brains was free to be anywhere he liked, with a perfect alibi, while Handy Andy did the dirty work.

Adie slid down in the chair and considered who, in Mattie's circle, fit the bill. *Oh dear, now here we have a possibility, don't we?* Adie straightened up. The one thing that

303

he and Matt didn't talk about in detail was his relationship with Liz Haynes. "She has an unorthodox marriage," was one of the things he said. Well, there were a dozen different ways of looking at that. "It's a no-strings arrangement, it's convenient for us both." For you two, maybe, but convenient for her husband? The more Adie thought about it the more he wondered about Liz's soldier husband. Had he spent a little too long dodging bullets and watching his friends die? Had he found out about the supposedly discreet affair, and was he channelling all his hate and frustration into torturing the man who was shagging his wife? It was just a hypothesis, but maybe it was one that no one had thought of yet, considering they didn't know about the shagging bit. Adie sank back again and sighed. If he told the fuzz about his idea, it would drop both Matt and Liz fair and square in the doo-doo, something Matt had been desperate to avoid. Sod it, better that than Matt dead.

He stood up and walked over to the desk. 'I need to speak to the superintendent, urgently.'

* * *

Matt sat in the cold and quiet mill, trying to work out where they were. His captor might have stayed local to the meeting place at the quay or driven miles away. Matt had no idea how long he had been unconscious. It was still dark. He was sure of that. Before the spotlights had come on, he had seen a small window, way up in the wall of the windmill. There was no glass and no shutter, but beyond it had been only blackness. So perhaps they were still near the quay and his car. He had purposely left his keys in the ignition, not to use for an escape route, but to let the man think this was the case. He had taped the spare key under the flap of the rear passenger door handle. If they could make it to the car, they had a way out.

Rather than torment himself by staring at the still figures of Liz, Gemma and Ryan, Matt tried to recall the layout of the countryside around the quay and the river. He knew there was no village close by, and no other homes within a mile or so. The nearest that he knew of, was a small farm, further downstream and close to the seabank and the marsh. He racked his brain for the name, but nothing came to him. Not that it would be much use, but the mental exercise kept him from looking at the blood in Liz's hair, Gemma's cheek or Ryan's mangled hand.

He threw his head back and tried to stretch his cramping body. The killer was clever. No doubt about that. Leaving him here, alone with his loved ones, not knowing if they were dead or alive, that was clever. Evil, wicked and shattering, but clever.

Without even thinking, he let out a loud cry of agony. It echoed up into the black roof of the mill.

He looked at the others, but no eyelid flickered, and no head moved.

'They won't hear you, policeman. Not until I say so. And maybe not even then.'

Matt jerked upright. He had been so engrossed in staring at those still forms, that he hadn't heard the door open behind him. 'You sick bastard! What have you done to them?'

'Temper, temper! And we'll get to that a little later.' The man sniggered, then swaggered around looking at each of his victims in turn. 'Now, do you like the Circle? I know it must bring back memories for you. What did you call it? The Ring of Damaged Minds, wasn't it? That's very apt. Only this one has damaged bodies, too.' The man stooped down and placed two small trays on the floor in the centre of the circle. Each contained three full syringes, their needles carefully capped.

'How did you know about that?'

'The same way I know everything else about you, Matthew. Years of painstaking and thorough study.'

'Who the hell *are* you?' Matt screamed the question.

The man eased himself into the last remaining chair and stared hard at him. Even under the weird lighting, Matt could see that his eyes were unusually bright. A quality generally reserved for addicts or the insane.

'At last!' He sighed. 'I can hardly believe it! After all this time, it's finally come together. We are ready for the last chapter of a very long saga.' He stared at Matt for what seemed an eternity, then he smiled and said, 'I am Ted, Detective Chief Inspector. And you have no idea how pleased I am to have you here like this.'

CHAPTER THIRTY-ONE

'I know it's late, sir, but thank you for seeing us,' David said.

They were led into a book-lined library. 'Drink, Officers?' Henry Cotton looked well into his seventies, but fit and ramrod straight.

David could have torn his arm off to get at the Scotch, but heard himself decline. 'Got to keep sharp, sir. This is a bad business.'

'So what has my grandson got to do with it?'

David chose his words carefully. 'We are trying to build up a picture of the early life of the young constable who was abducted today. We think your grandson Richard may have known her as a child.'

'I'm not sure that I'll be able to confirm that, Superintendent. I suppose you know that he was adopted? The boy had a very bad start in life, more traumatic than any child deserves. He never speaks of his past.'

'This girl was another child who was also abused, Mr Cotton. We think they were sent to the same home when they were quite young. Her name is now Gemma Goddard.'

'Yes, I heard it on the news earlier, but it means nothing to me.'

'Could we speak to Richard, sir? I would be very diplomatic, of course, but we do have officers missing and we need help from absolutely everyone.'

'Well, you could, but he doesn't live with me anymore, Superintendent. He moved out over two years ago.' The old man looked a little sad. 'And he's not at his flat right now either. He takes himself off every so often. He's a bit of a loner, really, and when he works on projects for our company, he likes to be independent and fly solo, so to speak.'

'He works for you?'

'He used to, now he's a freelance. Very clever, too. As my adopted boy, I wanted to make him a director, but he wasn't interested. He loves the practical work, but he hates the business side of things. You know, the budgets and the finances. Not his thing at all.'

'What is your business, sir?'

'I own a small film studio.' The man gave a short laugh. 'Although don't start thinking along the lines of MGM, will you? We shoot adverts. Little ones, big ones. Very good ones, actually.'

'And Richard? What does he do, in his freelance capacity?'

'Oh, he knows the whole business inside out, and I'm very proud of him.' The man took an appreciative sip of his drink. 'Considering the dreadful things that happened to him as a youngster, he's studied, did his A-levels. In fact, he was a complete sponge when it came to learning. He came into the business when he left college, and insisted on doing the complete package, from making tea upward. Recently he has concentrated more on computer graphics and design.'

'And has he a mobile number? I really would like to speak to him.'

'He has, but I doubt he'll answer, Superintendent. If he's designing something, he shuts himself away. And,' he stared down at the thick expensive carpet, 'I'm afraid we had a bit of a disagreement a few months back, and although I still love him to pieces, we aren't exactly on speaking terms at present.'

David felt a distinct unease. 'Do you mind me asking what it was about, this row?'

'The usual thing with younger people. Money, of course.' Harry Cotton was suddenly beginning to look his age. 'He's always been headstrong, and when he finally received his inheritance two years back, he insisted in cashing in all his stocks and shares, all the investments I'd made for him over the years.' He threw up his hands in exasperation. 'His inheritance could be in a pillow case under his bed, for all I know, the little fool!'

'Do you have a recent photograph of him, Mr Cotton?'

'The last one that I have of him was taken a couple of years back, I think.' He walked over to a small desk and opened a drawer. After a moment or two he withdrew a photograph wallet. 'Here we are. I took some snaps of him while he was taking pictures at a local charity event.' He sifted through them and picked out three. He passed them to David. 'These are the clearest.'

Richard would not have stood out in a crowd. In the first print, he was dressed in casual clothes, an expensive camera held in front of him. He was smiling at a group of women in matching shorts, T-shirts and bandanas preparing for a race. He was nice-looking, although far from handsome. His hair was clipped short, and the best description David could find for the colour was mousey blond.

His build was slim, but not skinny. David looked at the next one, in which he was giving a half-smile to his grandfather. In the third he was more serious, casting a sidelong glance at the girls again. David suddenly found himself drawn to the familiar-looking logos on the women's navy T-shirts. He pulled the print closer and looked at the women themselves. Young policewomen! He looked back to the smiling man, and realised that it was one particular girl that his eyes were fixed on. He looked again. *Oh, my God! Gemma.* Concern threatened to choke him, but he was aware that Harry Cotton was speaking to him.

'Take them by all means, but I would like them back when you've finished with them. I'll write down his address and number for you, although as I say, I doubt you'll get hold of him.'

David's fingers shook slightly as he held the picture out for the man to look at. 'The girls in the photo, did Richard know them?'

'No, I don't think so. He was just taking shots for the *Standard.* He is a very talented photographer, so the local rag often bought from him.'

'Do you have any idea where he may have gone?'

'None at all, but I can make a few enquiries with some of my employees. One of them may know.'

'If you would, it's imperative we speak to him. Here's my card. And if you should hear from him, please phone the mobile number immediately.'

Harry Cotton took the card and nodded, 'I will, and I'm sure Richard will be more than happy to help you in any way he can.' He stopped. 'Oh, something that may help you find him, Superintendent. He doesn't use his real name, Richard Cotton, for his work. His professional name for his photographic work and his design work, is simply Ted.'

* * *

Outside in the car, David showed the picture to Bryn. 'That *is* our Gemma, isn't it?'

'Oh shit, yes, sir, and I really don't like the intense way that creep is looking at her, do you?'

'No, I don't.' David's face creased with distaste. 'I think we need to find this Richard Cotton pronto. If he's withdrawn a lot of money, he may be planning on taking a very long, one-way trip somewhere.'

'Maybe the theory that Gemma was the intended target was right. If this Richard/Ted bloke hates and resents her that much, he could be looking at killing her, and everyone close to her. Like the sergeant and the guv'nor.'

'Plus, it looks as though he's got enough dosh to magic himself away to somewhere hot and where the natives call him *amigo*.' David took out his phone and punched in the number that he had been given him for Richard, but as he expected, it was switched off. David swore then picked up the radio and asked for a unit to get to the address that Harry Cotton had given them, one that was both conveniently and worryingly, only three streets from the police station in Fenfleet.

* * *

'I know you don't like me, Inspector Hammond, but I do have Matt's best interests at heart.' Adie was wishing that the superintendent had not dashed off to interview someone. He was not comfortable with this muppet, and he didn't feel the inclination to be the one to tell him that his DCI had been bonking his sergeant for quite some time now. It was difficult, but he cut that bit out, and stuck to the shell shock theory, then added that the Lt. Colonel may have blamed Matt for his wife being so dedicated to such a dangerous job.

'So you think he's organised his own wife's abduction?' Jason's monotone declared that he was clearly unimpressed by the idea.

'I haven't a clue. I just think you should check him out, that's all. I've seen men who have spent too long at the front before. Military psychiatric units are full of them.' From Jason's expression he knew he was getting nowhere, so Adie stood up. 'Just mention it to your super, okay? As things are, it's worth a few moments of someone's time, surely?'

* * *

The name Ted meant absolutely nothing to Matt, other than the fact that he was undoubtedly looking at the bogus DC Edward Dennis. He stared over to the man and tried to place him from somewhere in his life. A villain who he'd sent down? A relative of someone who he had helped get convicted? The father or brother of some kid who'd died, and whose killer he'd failed to bring to justice?

That last supposition rang alarm bells. In the dark shadows, he imagined that he saw the ghosts of Danny Carter, Christopher Ray Fellowes, Jamie Matravers and Gabriel standing silently watching the circle. Was it connected to one of them?

'Oh dear, you're trying so hard to identify me!' The voice had an odd quality to it. 'But at this point, if I were you, and please take this from one who knows, you'd do better to think about other things right now.'

'Like what?' growled Matt.

'Like getting the answers to some questions right, for starters.'

'It's *me* who needs the fucking questions answered.'

'It's always about *you*, isn't it?' Ted snarled. 'Poor little Mattie! All the worries of the world on your shoulders! You know nothing about suffering! Nothing!'

The outburst silenced Matt. Those eyes glittered dangerously, and he knew that talking his way out of this was going to be far more difficult than he had ever imagined. Perhaps he'd try a different tack. 'I'm sorry,' he said softly.

'Yeah. And that makes it all better, doesn't it?' Ted stood up, and walked slowly over to Gemma. He paused in front of her. 'Now, this one,' he lifted the expressionless face up by the chin, 'she knows all about suffering.' He let the girl's head flop back to her chest, and moved on around the circle. 'And this one, this whore, she too knows about suffering. Well, she does now.' His fingers played aimlessly across her breasts.

Pure hate burned through Matt. 'Get away from her!'

'Or you'll do what exactly?'

Matt heaved his body against the leather straps, and cried out with frustration at his own impotence.

Ted ignored him. 'Mmm, and this one?' He ran a finger down the boy's grimy cheek. 'What do you think he knows about suffering?' He increased the pressure and the nail began to mark the flesh. 'Quite a bit, I reckon.'

There was nothing he could do to help them, to get the animal away from them. He could only talk. 'I thought you wanted "a chat," didn't you?'

Ted took a long deep breath, then slowly walked to the back of the mill.

Matt looked around as the spotlights dimmed down to little more than a soft glow. 'Yes, I want to talk.' He returned to his seat, sat down and leaned back, his hands folded in his lap. 'And as we're all sitting comfortably, I'll begin.' He half-turned to face Matt. 'I'm going to ask you some questions. During this time I will carefully monitor what you say, and if I'm satisfied, you may be allowed some privileges, do you understand?'

'Privileges?'

'You'll understand, as we progress. It's a bit like a TV quiz show, only your fellow contestants have a lot more to win or lose than usual.' Ted gave a small laugh. 'And the outcome is all down to you.'

A tiny shiver slipped across Matt's back.

'Right, policeman, if you're ready. First question. Would you break the rules for someone you loved?'

'I'm here, aren't I? No backup, no wires, just like you asked. I ran away like a criminal, and I told no one where I was going. So the answer is yes, I already have.'

'So who did you break the rules to protect?'

'Who the hell do you think? My fellow officers and a little boy, of course!'

'Ah, so leaving the boy out of the equation, it wasn't for your daughter, or the married woman that you are having a sordid little affair with? It was for your "fellow officers," was it?'

Matt hesitated, 'It was for Liz, Gemma and Ryan. They are all innocent victims here. That's who I broke the rules for.'

'Right. I see.' Ted rubbed thoughtfully at his beard. 'And do you believe that they are still alive? Was it worth not following procedure, if they are dead already?'

'I have to believe they are still alive, and you told me they were,' he added lamely.

'But I lie, policeman.'

'Really? What a surprise! Well, I hate to tell you this, but it was still worth the risk.'

Ted laughed, 'Good, good! Next question. If, and I only say if, one of the others were to be dead, which one would you prefer it to be?'

'How the hell can I answer that? I want them all to live!'

'Humour me, Matt. Hypothetically, who would you choose to be dead? Who would mean the least to you?'

'I won't answer that!' yelled Matt. 'I can't answer!'

'The clock is ticking, Matt. I need an answer.'

To his horror, Matt saw Ted slip out of his seat and walk towards the centre of the circle, to the two trays of syringes.

'Tick-tock. Tick-tock. Your answer, policeman?' He leaned forward and his hand reached out, hovering over first one tray, then the other.

'Please! That's an unreasonable question. Please, Ted.' Matt's eyes flew from one motionless figure to the next. Young Gemma? His lovely Liz? Or a little boy? He knew whatever he said was going to have a catastrophic outcome for one of them. His voice crackled with emotion when he spoke again. 'Please, Ted. How can I answer that?'

Ted seemed to consider what Matt was saying. He sat back on his haunches and pulled a face.

'Alright. I'll rephrase it. If you could save one of them, who would it be?'

'That's even worse. My answer would not just condemn one to death, but two.' He was almost screaming, and fought to control his temper. 'And it's equally as impossible to answer. I am a policeman, as you keep reminding me, and it's my duty to protect life. All life.'

'Shame.' Ted shifted his position and sat cross-legged in front of the possibly lethal syringes.

'Think about it, Ted.' Matt tried to make his shaking voice sound reasonable. 'You've already said you lie, so how can I decide? If I say save one, you'd probably kill that person, or then again, maybe you'd think I was trying to bluff you, and kill one of the others. And, of course, they may all be dead anyway. I can't trust you, so I can't answer. Simple as that.'

Ted rubbed his chin and nodded. 'Quite right. You've given me something to think about, haven't you?' With an athletic spring, he stood up, and marched across to Matt.

'Actually, I have something important to do.' He stared down, his dark shadow almost filling Matt's field of vision, those weird eyes still sparkling excitedly in the dim lights. 'And while I'm gone, I'll leave you with an important decision to make. No hypothesis. No suppositions. This time it's for real. You can save one of them. And I promise you that. When I return, I'll wake them up, if they are still alive, of course. Then you can choose, policeman.'

Before Matt could say a word, Ted strode away. A second later, the lights went out.

Matt howled his anguish into the darkness. It echoed around the abandoned mill, then there was just silence.

* * *

'We've checked the address in Hawley Street, Super. It's been cleaned out. There's a few pieces of furniture, other than that, it looks like the professionals have been through it.' The uniformed constable shrugged. 'Do you want the SOCOs to move in?'

David nodded, knowing it was probably a pointless exercise but one that he dare not ignore, then he looked hopefully to a long-faced Jason.

'Sorry, sir, but the phone number you were given registers no service, so what now?'

'Check out his workmates, I think. Harry Cotton was going to ask around for us, but I think we need to speak to them all personally. I'll ring the old man and get a list.' He checked his notebook for the man's number. 'And while I'm getting that, take the photo of Ted to Rory Wilkinson. If he thinks our killer uses disguises, then Ted may be the face beneath the beard and the tash.'

'Sir?' Bryn looked up suddenly from his computer screen. 'Can I go talk to the neighbours of Ted's flat in Hawley Street? If Ted disguised himself as the bearded man, perhaps someone saw him leave home in that particular persona.'

'Good man, go to it, and ring me immediately if your hunch pays off.'

* * *

There were three flats in 23 Hawley Street. The one closest to Richard/Ted's was empty. Bryn lifted the letter box and to his dismay, saw bare floorboards and little else. The one immediately beneath looked considerably more promising, as a wet umbrella leaned against the wall next to the door.

When the occupant finally slipped on the security chain and opened the door a crack, Bryn was surprised to see a toothless elderly man, wearing an even more elderly brown dressing gown.

'Funny goings on up there, young man, if you ask me,' he said.

After showing his ID, Bryn made it into the inner hall, but clearly wasn't going to be invited into the sitting room. From the glance he had already taken through the half-closed door, that was fine by him. And Jason had thought his flat was messy.

'How do you mean, Mr Coolidge?'

'I think they were cheating on paying the proper rent.' He puckered his lips in disgust. 'It's quite clear in the rent agreement. Single occupancy. One person per flat.'

'And you saw more than one go in and out, did you, sir?'

'Three, no less!'

Bryn gave a sharp intake of breath. 'Three?'

The old man nodded furiously. 'Three of them, coming and going at all hours of the day and night. If the fair one, the one who moved in first, hadn't packed up their stuff the other day, I would have reported them all. The rent is bad enough, but then there's the council tax that they're fiddling, too. It's not fair on honest, law-abiding pensioners like me, now is it? I've paid tax all my life, and young whippersnapper's like that get away with bloody murder, they do!'

'I quite agree, Mr Coolidge.' Bryn took a copy of the picture of Ted from his inside pocket. 'Is this the first man, Richard Cotton? Maybe you knew him as Ted?'

'I didn't know him as anything, he wasn't what you'd call neighbourly. But, yes, that's him alright.'

'And this man?' Bryn handed him a picture of the bearded man.

'Oh yes! That's one of the others.'

'And the other man? What did he look like, sir?'

A smug look came over the old man's face. 'I can show you, officer. Wait there.'

Bryn watched as the old man disappeared into the bedroom. There was a clicking sound, followed by a whirring, then Mr Coolidge reappeared.

'I said I was going to shop them to the landlord, didn't I? Well, I'm no fool, and I knew that I needed proof. Here it is.' In his leathery hand, was a printout from a computer. Two pages of prints of digital photos. Of three different men leaving and returning to the building. Each image had a date and time in the corner. Bryn scrutinised the third man, then gave a small gasp. It was someone he vaguely recognised. A man he'd seen earlier that day, and in the nick of all places. He looked again to make doubly sure. No doubt whatsoever.

'May I take these, sir? I'll be sure to return them.' Thanking the man, he ran down the steps to the street, pulling out his mobile as he went.

'Superintendent! This is really important! I've confirmed that Richard Cotton, AKA Ted, is also the bearded man, and sir, he uses another persona as well.' Bryn was running back towards the station as he spoke. In a breathy voice he said, 'I saw him earlier, with DI Hammond, sir. Going into an interview room!'

* * *

The lab was situated next to the mortuary in the basement of Fenfleet's busy hospital, just a few hundred yards from the police station. When he saw the pictures that Bryn had been given, David went straight to see Rory Wilkinson, who had based himself there for the duration of the case.

The corridor was sparsely lit with a series of low-voltage lights, and his footsteps echoed as he hurried towards the brighter lights at end of the hallway.

Despite the late hour, Rory and a handful of technicians were still working. He approached David, holding out his hand for the new pictures. 'I got the call, Superintendent. Let me have them, we'll run this straightaway.' He pushed through a door and into a room full of high-tech equipment and computers. 'I bet you've not seen this little beauty before, have you?' He pointed to a large flat screen. He slipped the photo under an attached scanner. 'If you are right about these, it will take only seconds to get a match. Simon! Over here please, and work your magic!'

A white-coated technician jumped up from his bench, ran over to them, and sat himself down in front of an oversized keyboard.

'Three photos this time, Simon, dear boy! Find me a connection.'

'Three, Prof! Most excellent.' The young man's hands flew over the keys, and the screen leapt into life.

David watched in amazement as the screen split into sections. The first contained a head and shoulders of Richard 'Ted' Cotton at the charity fun day. The second showed the bearded man, smiling directly at the camera in Matt's mother's nursing home. The third was a zoomed-in section of the third man, taken by his elderly neighbour. It showed the long dark hair and heavy-rimmed glasses of Gemma's supposedly 'distraught' boyfriend, Roy Latimer.

Before David could adjust his eyes, the screen began to flash repeatedly, each face changing and morphing into something slightly different. Bone structure shrank, then enlarged. Noses widened, and eyes changed colour. Finally, two of the faces, Bearded Man and Roy Latimer, moved across the screen and superimposed themselves over that of Ted. A coloured border ringed his face and flashed up the words, MATCH! MATCH! along the bottom at the screen.

'Bingo!' said Simon with smug satisfaction. 'Three in one! But deep respect for the seriously good disguises!'

'Does this small miracle help you?' asked Rory proudly.

'It helps, most certainly, but it also frightens the shit out of me.' He stared at the picture of Ted.

'Before you go.' Rory held the door open. 'Come to the office, I have one more report for you.' Together they hurried back to the path lab. 'Here.' He picked up a typed sheet and passed it over to David. 'It's that last crucifix. The one found with Gabriel's clothes. It's brand new. And very expensive.'

'So why would it have been found on a cheap, crap market-stall chain, in the clothes of a dead runaway?'

'I suggest that it wasn't Gabriel's at all. From the minimal handling since it was purchased, I'd guess it was secreted there by the killer, to make you believe there was a connection to the old cases. Sorry to have to break this to you, but he's just playing silly buggers again.'

David tried to make sense of it all. 'We all thought it one hell of a coincidence that those clothes turned up, complete with gold cross, just after Matt told us all about the crucifixes.'

'Oh deary me.' Rory pulled a face. 'That means inside information leaking back to the killer, doesn't it?'

'I'm afraid it does.' He patted Rory's shoulder. 'Rory, thank you for what you've done here. It's down to you that we know, without doubt, who he is. Now all we have to do is find him.'

'We aim to please.' His smile faded. 'You may have one thing in your favour. If I spent years planning something, I'd want to savour it, enjoy it. Not rush it.'

David turned to go. 'I know what you're saying, but I find that thought rather chilling. God knows what he's capable of, if he has the time.'

CHAPTER THIRTY-TWO

Matt really didn't need the added terror of sitting in the dark with three possibly dead people. His mind was a black enough place anyway.

The mill was bitterly cold, and the wind whistled eerily around the dilapidated old building. His jaw ached from trying to stop his teeth chattering, and whereas one part of him prayed for light, another dreaded the return of the madman who called himself Ted.

He forced himself to try to think about normal things, anything other than the terrible situation that he had walked into. He had once read that it was possible to transport yourself away from terrible circumstances by visualisation of something better.

Sadly it was more difficult than he had imagined, and his mind fixated on his missing underpants, which would have been comical in any other situation.

For a while he slipped back into the present, and tried to take stock of the mill. Ted had turned off his light system but there was still a dim light coming from somewhere behind him. There was workbench close to the wall. He strained to see what was on it and wished he hadn't. He could make out the dark shape of some welding equipment, a butane blow torch and a knife block with a selection of chef's knives. Matt looked away, praying they were just there for show, to frighten, part of the mind games. His mind turned to the question of what to do next.

Matt couldn't play the psychopath's games. He wouldn't condemn anyone to death. Matt wriggled uncomfortably. He heard a faint noise.

He sat still, straining to hear. Rats? Or was one of the others waking up? He peered into the gloom, aching to hear a familiar voice from one of the other chairs, then a blaze of light made him cry out in shock.

On the far wall of the mill, immediately opposite him, was Laura. Well, a huge coloured image of Laura.

'Welcome to the picture show, policeman.'

Matt wrenched his neck to his left. He hadn't heard his captor come back in or sit down.

'I thought you could use some help with your decision making. Remind you what is at stake.' Ted leaned back and crossed his legs. 'Your Laura. Lovely, wasn't she? Shame that thanks to you, her life became so intolerable, that she was able to abandon the child she loved, and walk into the sea.' The picture changed to a baby girl with white-blonde hair and deep soulful eyes. 'That was Gemma. But you wouldn't have known her then, of course.'

'Why are you doing this?' Matt whispered.

'Because I have to.'

'Why?'

'You'll see. Now watch the show. This was one of her homes, before she was adopted by the delightful Goddards.'

A black-and-white image, probably a press photo, showing a semi-detached house. Nothing special. Not rundown, but not immaculate. It quickly flashed to an image of the inside. A child's bedroom. Matt began to feel sick. He'd seen this kind of thing before. Too often. They weren't press photos. They were police photographs from a crime scene.

'They were taken a long while after Gemma was moved on to a children's home. The perverts who, and I use this term very loosely, *cared for her*, finally went too far, and another child in their care died.' Ted clicked the remote. And again. And again. 'Nice people, weren't they? Just the sort you'd want to look after your pretty little daughter.'

'I never knew! I swear I never knew.'

'But you should have, shouldn't you? I found her. So why didn't you?'

'I looked! I searched for Laura for years.'

'But not hard enough.'

Matt couldn't answer that.

'Oh, now this is familiar territory. The lovely Canvale Children's Home. Before it closed, there were twelve of us there, and every one of us was abused in one way or another. Some more than others.'

'So this is what it's all about, is it?'

'Most certainly. Do you know, eleven of those children found happy homes after Canvale? Marvellous statistic! Except for the last one. But hey-ho, that's life. Now, what's next? Oh yes.'

The image that then appeared was the school photo of Ryan Fisher. 'Great little kid this one. A real diamond. A fighter, too,' Ted said appreciatively. The school uniform disappeared, and was replaced by an image of a small room containing only a narrow bed and a wooden chest. *Click.* Ryan lay on the bed, strapped and tied down.

There were several like that, including one of Ted smiling broadly as he stuck a needle into the child's bare arm. *Click.* The last in the sequence showed the boy either asleep or unconscious, with a large metal petrol can strategically placed beside his bed. The image made bile rise in Matt's throat.

'And finally, we have contestant number three. The whore.'

Liz's beautiful face appeared. The back drop was his farmhouse, his home. He swallowed, knowing that he was not going to want to see what was coming next.

'I'm rather proud of the short film that you're about to watch. I've added some sound effects, and enhanced the location. I think you'll find it's much improved.'

Matt closed his eyes.

'Oh, do watch! It's one of my best! Pure techno-rapture!' Ted said. 'And if you keep your eyes shut for one minute more, I'll cut off your eyelids. And that's no lie.'

Matt opened his eyes, then grudgingly looked at the screen.

Soft music swirled and drifted up into the empty heart of the mill. Matt blinked as the bizarre film clip burst into life. In essence, it was what he had already seen in the photographs that had been instrumental in bringing him to this hell, but he now realised that they had been filmed as well. The pictures were stills lifted from the original footage. Not that he would have recognised it, after Ted had got to work on it.

Reluctantly Matt found himself drawn to the screen. Ted might be a psychotic killer, but his imagination and his digital skills were quite awesome. Straight photography blended seamlessly with computer-generated avatars of himself and Liz. It was like an acid trip.

Instead of the hotel room, the act took place in a jungle, on a bed of vivid flowers and plants that moved and rippled along with the two writhing bodies. The music was faster now, a pulsating rhythm that matched the movements of the two lovers, and erotic sound effects came from the speakers.

Matt stared helplessly as he watched their real skin and flesh, melt into the physically perfect, muscular, oiled bodies of their avatars. If it hadn't been such a flagrant invasion of their privacy, and if he hadn't felt so soiled, he might have said that as some kind of art form, it was no less than brilliant.

Just as the sounds and the music threatened to deafen him, there was one climatic scream of pleasure, and the picture returned to the shot of Liz outside his front door. He exhaled, then glanced at Ted, and to his horror, found the other man staring pointedly at Matt's crotch.

'Well done, policeman. Not a flicker. I personally find it hard not to be aroused by it.' He paused and licked his lips. 'No matter how many times I watch it.'

'You are one sick son of a bitch, aren't you?'

'Undoubtedly, but scarily talented too, wouldn't you say?'

The projected images were now of Ted's three captives.

'Time to choose.' He pointed with his finger to each face in turn. 'Your daughter.' Gemma smiled back, smart and confident in her police uniform. 'Your whore.' Liz looking at him soulfully, as she turned from locking her car. 'Or an innocent little boy.' Ryan Fisher smiling cheekily for the school cameraman.

Matt took a deep breath. 'I'm not playing.'

Ted grinned at him. 'Yes, you are.'

'No, I'm not. Because, for one thing, I have no proof that Gemma is really my daughter. You are a mindbender and a liar. This could be one glorious set-up.'

'True. It could be, but it's not.'

'I don't believe you. Nothing I do or say will stop you from killing us all anyway, so, I'm not playing.'

Ted's grin faltered momentarily, then he stood up, walked across to Matt, and hit him hard in the face.

Salty blood touched his tongue. 'I'm still not playing your fucking game. It's the final stage, you said, well, play it on your own.'

Again, a stinging, bone-jarring fist hit his cheek. The pain that flared through his jaw and into his skull, told him that his cheek bone had been fractured. 'Bastard,' he spat. 'For God's sake tell me! Why do you hate me so much?'

Ted stepped back. 'Me?' His face showed confusion, 'I don't hate you. I feel nothing for you. Why should I hate you?'

Matt rubbed his tongue across his aching teeth. He would have put money on the fact that Ted's startled expression was genuine.

Somewhere in Matt's addled brain, something began to fall into place. He swallowed blood, then began to laugh wearily. 'All this,' he looked around. 'All this drama, the eerie setting, the circle. It's a mind game, isn't it? And even though you are the clever one, you didn't think this up, did you? Sure, you're the whizz-kid, the techie, the magician, the one with the ability to make it happen, but you're still the puppet, aren't you? You've worked for years on this, but you're not the boss. You're not the one who pulls the strings. This isn't about you at all, is it?'

Ted stood looking at him, his head held slightly to one side, then he gave a dramatic, exaggerated bow. 'I take my hat off to you, policeman.'

Ted sighed with something like relief, then stepped towards the two trays and picked up three of the syringes. 'Okay, it's time to wake up your friends. Then, I suppose you'll want to meet the puppet master.'

CHAPTER THIRTY-THREE

Adie was on his third coffee and felt like he was about to climb the walls, when he saw a tall, sombre-faced man hurriedly enter the reception area. *Now, he looks almost as screwed up as me!* He drank back the last dregs of the coffee, pulled a face, and looked at the other man with interest. The eyes were sunken, and deep furrows rippled across what should have been a smooth forehead. Adie watched as he leaned his big frame across the desk to the civilian on duty and said, 'Superintendent Redpath, please. Tell him it's Gary Haynes to see him.'

Adie sat up. *Really? You're joking!* If things hadn't been so dire, he would have laughed at the thought of little Mattie stealing this Rambo of a man's wife. He looked closer, and noted the slump of the shoulders and the quick, unconscious snapping of finger and thumb together. This was bona fide concern. Maybe he should go find Jason Hammond and tell him to forget what he'd said. Adie might be wrong, but he was quite prepared to believe that he had probably screwed up royally in his judgement of the soldier.

'Gary Haynes?' Adie stood up and extended a hand, 'I believe we both have someone close to us caught up in bad situation right now. I'm Adie Clarkson, a friend of Matt Ballard.'

As the big man clasped his hand, Adie caught the eye of the receptionist. 'And you'd better tell the super that *I* want to see him, too.'

* * *

In the murder room, one large picture had replaced all the others on the board.

'This is Richard Cotton, also known as Ted.' The super spoke quickly and concisely to the gathered officers. 'We believe he is the man holding the boy Ryan Fisher, and our own Sergeant Haynes, PC Gemma Goddard and DCI Ballard. He has left his flat, is out of contact with his adopted grandfather, and has withdrawn an awful lot of money recently.'

'Ready to do a runner, no doubt,' said one of the officers.

'I believe so, Detective. Now, he works in the film industry as an animator and graphic designer. He is also a freelance photographer. He is described by people that he works with as highly intelligent, creative, charming, but very much a loner. He suffered severe abuse as a child, and at one point seems to have been in a care home at the same time as Gemma Goddard. A home, by the way, that was later closed down following reports of neglect and abuse of the children.' David stared at the picture. 'There are a lot of grey areas surrounding this man, things that really bother me, but the most important thing right now is to locate him. I have several officers pulling his work colleagues from their beds as we speak, in the hope that someone may have an idea of where he's gone. I have circulated this picture to all forces, and it has been released to the media.' David bit his lip. 'Although the chances of him being recognised at this time are slim. We already know that he has been using two other identities, the Bearded Man and Roy Latimer, Gemma Goddard's boyfriend, but I have just discovered after a phone call to his grandfather, that the multitalented Ted, is something of an expert at film make-up. Prosthetics being his specialty.'

'So he can reinvent himself when he feels like it. Oh great!' groaned Bryn.

Adie and Gary sat together at the back of the room and listened impatiently. 'Could things go any slower? Why don't they *do* something?' whispered Gary, shifting around in his seat.

'Sorry, mate, but this is the police. They can't go in with a tank and a squad tooled up with SA 80s, unless they are pretty sure they've got the right suspect in their sights.'

Gary grunted an unintelligible reply, then looked back towards the superintendent.

'Although nothing is set in stone,' David continued. 'I believe that we can rule out there being any connection to the old Gibbet Fen Murders. Even Gabriel's murder and the taking of Ryan Fisher may just be decoys, red herrings. Our man seems to have used both them and Matt's history as a very effective foil against the DCI. Something to confuse and distract us from what he was really after.'

'Which is?' someone asked.

'The abduction of three of our officers, for reasons as yet unknown, although there may be a connection to Gemma's childhood.'

Concerned murmurs echoed around the room.

'I have requested every psychiatric report and every file still available on both the boy Richard, and Gemma, to see if there is some kind of a motive hidden in the past. Until we have them, and we—' The desk phone next to him shrilled out.

'Superintendent Redpath,' he snapped.

Complete silence descended on the murder room, as David listened to the message. He thanked the caller and replaced the receiver. His eyes had regained some of their usual fervour.

'At last! We have a lead from someone who worked on a previous assignment with Ted.' He looked around. 'Right, will one of you check out these two addresses immediately. First, Jericho Farm, Lyntoft Creek. Apparently it's somewhere near the River Lynney, right out beyond the Roman Bank, in the area they call Waggoner's Marsh. The other one is Clay Corner, Old Keldyke. It's some sort of farm building, an old mud-and-stud house, with all sorts of outbuildings. Again it's remote, situated on the river bank and way out on the Golden Fen. Both nasty, dangerous and inhospitable places, which could be just up the killer's alley!' He looked up from his notepad. 'According to his colleague, they were both locations that Ted used for film shoots, and both fascinated him for one reason or another. He might be renting one of them. So move!'

* * *

'I think, in the interests of peace and quiet, we'll leave the boy until last.' Ted scratched his beard and stared at the three unmoving figures that made up the circle.

'And in case you're worried he's not alive . . .' Ted pulled a small folding knife from his pocket, opened it and slashed it across the boy's arm.

In the dim light, Matt saw a thin dark line appear, then tear-like droplets form and drizzle down towards the clenched hand.

'See! He's bleeding. Dead kids don't bleed like that.'

Matt gave a despondent nod. His tired mind sent him conflicting messages. He was naturally relieved to know that the child was alive, but to see the boy be cut . . .

'Now, eeny, meeny, miny, moe! Gemma can go first!' Ted looked at the syringe. 'Please God, I've got this right. If I inject the other one, she'll go immediately into a seizure, and bish, bash, bosh! All over.' He turned to Matt and threw him a hopeless sort of grin. 'I really should read up on this stuff one day. It's so hit and miss.' With a giggle, he turned back to Gemma and lifted her arm, patting theatrically for a vein. He positioned the needle against the pale skin, then stopped, so suddenly that Matt flinched.

'I'm sorry. This will have to wait for a moment or two. This is really bugging me.' He put the drug back on the tray, and strode over to Matt. 'No need for all this now, is there?'

Matt's eyes widened in horror, as the man began to tear his face apart.

Skin? Scalp, Hair? Matt wanted to turn away from the nightmarish vision. No, he took a deep breath and looked again. A wig, latex, fibre, padding and prosthetics lay on the floor at Matt's feet.

Ted walked back to his chair and picked up a towel that was draped over the back. He rubbed hard at his face with it, then ran his artistic fingers through his short mousey hair. 'Shit. That's better!'

The worse thing of all, as he stared long and hard at Ted's new face, was that he still meant nothing to him.

'Now, let's get these girls back with us, shall we?' He picked up the syringe, and in the semi-darkness Matt winced, as he saw Ted plunge it into Gemma's upper arm.

'May not be as spectacular as your own return to consciousness, policeman. I'm trying something new. Supposed to be more gradual. Got it on the Internet.'

He walked away from Gemma, and repeated the operation on Liz.

Neither woman moved, and Matt's mouth began to dry.

'And while we're waiting, maybe the time has come to let you meet the person who, as you rightly said, pulls the strings.' Placing the towel around his neck, Ted moved to the back of the mill. 'I won't be a moment.'

The lights were dimmed a fraction further, and a strange green glow seemed to suffuse the building.

Matt shook his head in exasperation. Drama, if you must, but a dry ice machine? Oh, please. This is hardly the Phantom of the Fucking Opera!

He looked around. He had been wrong. There was no mist. Just a subtle change in the lighting. He tried to concentrate on the women, watching for signs of life, but the weird light made it very difficult to see.

A door opened behind him, and he drew a deep, shaky breath in. This was it! Finally, he'd know.

Ted slipped back into his seat and sat quietly for once, casting darting looks to somewhere behind Matt.

'Who are you?' Matt's voice quavered, and terrible fear engulfed him. 'Please? Tell me who you are.'

There was a noise. Rustling. Then a creak. Matt's heart hammered in his chest as he strained to look behind him. But the sound wasn't coming from there.

It was coming from Gemma. She was finally regaining consciousness. Matt gave a tiny sigh of relief, then gasped.

Ted had not moved, not gone near her, yet somehow, Gemma's restraints were now lying on the floor beside her chair.

She slowly stood up, stretched, then smiled in the strange half-light. In a soft voice, he heard her mouth the words, 'Hello, Daddy.'

CHAPTER THIRTY-FOUR

'It's not likely to be Clay Corner, guv! The owner said he's been going out their every couple of days lately, overseeing some renovation work. He didn't see anything odd,' one of DI Packer's team called out.

'And I'm having trouble getting hold of anyone to do with Jericho Farm.' Bryn scratched his head with his pen. 'I've contacted the local bobby who covers that patch, and he reckons the owners live abroad, but they frequently let it out for film and television work.'

'That sounds right! But why? What makes it so special?'

'Apparently, it's so remote you can shoot historical stuff, with no chance of a hairy biker riding through your Victorian picnic, and it has a ruined mill attached to the property, which is great for moody, atmospheric stuff.'

David was already on his feet. 'How far out is it?'

'Twenty, twenty-five minutes, maybe half an hour in the dark.'

Adie and Gary both leapt up. 'We'll come with you!' The soldier's commanding voice left little room for debate.

'Okay, Gary, but Adie, I think you'd better leave this to us.'

Gary Haynes suddenly spoke out, 'Let him come. I'll vouch for him, Superintendent, and I'll keep him with me.'

David reluctantly agreed, frankly he needed every useful man he could get. 'Okay, although I'll probably get hung out to dry for this. It's hardly correct procedure. You two ride with me. Meet me downstairs in five minutes. I have to notify my senior officers, liaise with uniform and organise armed backup and paramedics. Jason! Get our team kitted out and ready. I'll brief the men in the car park in five. Go, go, go!'

* * *

As David's car raced out of town, Adie adjusted his borrowed Kevlar vest and said, 'You reckoned there were grey areas, superintendent. Things that worried you? Could they be a problem when we get there?'

'I can't answer that. But that's why I've insisted on a softly-softly approach. No two tones or blue lights. We will use a River Authority quay that's close by, as an RV point, and go in on foot. The situation may be very dangerous indeed.'

'You told the men to keep an open mind as to what they might find, to be ultra-wary, and trust no one.' Gary's voice was low. 'I'd only say that, if I suspected a trap.'

David looked out as they turned off the main road and began to leave the lights of the town behind them. 'I don't know what to expect. Apart from a few facts about Ted that I just can't get my head around, and some disturbing evidence that there is an inside source leaking information to him, I just know that Ted is some kind of super geek with computers. He could easily have set up some sort of warning device, or maybe . . .'

'Maybe he could have booby-trapped the place?' asked Gary.

'I wouldn't put it past him. If he can kill kids simply as a distraction, he would jump at the chance of wiping out a load of coppers.'

'In which case, this may help.' Gary pulled out a small device from his pocket. It looked like a cross between a wide-beamed torch and a Taser gun. 'If we suspect he's strung a series of laser beams around the property, you know, security beams, this light shows them up without triggering them. We can slide under, or go over them, if we know exactly where they are.'

'Very neat. I'm impressed,' said Adie. 'Hopefully you've also got a small arsenal and a mortar or two, in the other pocket.'

'Sorry, this a personal toy. The MOD would probably draw the line at heavy weapons.'

David noted their attempts at covering their apprehension, and grudgingly began to understand why Matt liked Adie Clarkson so much.

'Do we have any equipment with us that might help?' asked Gary.

'I've acquired a thermal-imaging camera from the fire service, and we have a microphone probe to listen in on the interior of the building, if we can find somewhere to get the probe through to the interior without attracting attention to ourselves.'

Gary nodded in the shadows of the back of the car. 'Better than nothing. How much further?'

'Fifteen miles, give or take.'

'How long will that take on those marsh lanes?'

'Too long.'

* * *

Gemma stared down at Matt. He felt like every neuron in his mind was ungluing, his mental building blocks were falling apart like a Lego wall hit by a Tonka truck.

He stared back at her, trying to hold her gaze, but it was difficult, because he didn't recognise the hard-faced woman in front of him. He felt like a specimen under a microscope. A specimen of something vile and disgusting.

Even the pain from his broken face had receded as he tried to work out what was going on.

He wanted to say something profound, but a garbled, 'I don't understand,' was all he could manage.

She didn't answer him, but instead reached down, and peeled off a series of synthetic "bloody cuts" and "scabs" from her legs. Without taking her eyes off him, she gently eased a fingernail under the skin below her right ear, and pulled away the sheet of pseudo-damaged flesh from the side of her face. She walked silently over to Ted, kissed him lightly, removed the towel from around his neck, and wiped the rest of her face free of fake blood.

She didn't touch the "horribly injured" arm, and Matt finally saw the wound for what it really was, just one more of their excellent special effects.

As he stared down at the floor, littered with prosthetic skin, a synapse somewhere fired and sent a signal of hope. Maybe Ryan's and Liz's injuries were also fake. The moment of delight faded quickly. *But she hasn't moved, not even once, has she?*

The new Gemma, this strange and frightening doppelganger, was also apparently clairvoyant. Leaving the towel around her own neck, she sauntered casually over to Liz, then stopped. She looked down at her, with an expression that was a mixture of repulsion and jealousy.

'Hey, Sarge! You're not looking too good. Did your gorgeous soldier boy find out you've been shagging your boss? Did he knock you around when he realised what "on the job" really meant?' She gently ran a finger down Liz's cheek, then cruelly slapped her face hard enough for the limp head to rock sideways. As it fell forwards again, Gemma grabbed her hair with one hand and wiped the other roughly over the wound in Liz's scalp, and held it, palm outwards towards Matt. 'Sorry, guv'nor. Look, real blood this time.'

'Leave her alone! For God's sake, Gemma, what on earth sort of game do you think you're playing?' The sight of Liz's defenceless body being treated so badly, fired some last vestige of anger. He yelled, in the hope that his voice would carry some kind of authority, and maybe reach the Gemma he had once known.

Apparently he failed. Gemma turned on him. She shrieked, 'So you think I'm playing games, do you? Well, maybe I am, and maybe I have been for a very long while, and guess what? This game is nearly over, and I'm winning!' Her eyes were as cold as ice. 'Strange how you jump to the aid of your whore, but you never spoke out for me, for your own daughter.' Her eyes narrowed. 'I've sat here for an hour and listened to you bleating, but not once did you plead with Teddy here to leave *me* alone, or to beg to be told what he'd done to me. He gave you the chance, Daddy. "Save one of them," he said. But you never chose me, did you?' Her voice swung from accusatory to bitter, then became an almost childish whine.

'I wanted you all to live. Would it have made any difference if I'd picked you?'

'I don't know. You betrayed my mother. You killed her, then you condemned me to the worst horrors imaginable. And now I've heard it for myself. You only care about yourself, and your precious career. Oh, yes, and the whore.'

'I never betrayed Laura. And yeah, I loved my job, but you would understand that. You loved being in the police, too.'

'You're stupider than I ever dreamed! You don't think I actually wanted to be a policewoman, do you? For God's sake! It was a means to an end, that's all. A way to get close to you.'

'And you really think you're my daughter?' It was agony to talk, but he had no choice. 'Because from here, I don't see too much family resemblance.'

'You'd better believe it, Pops. Maybe you'd like to take a DNA test?'

'Maybe I would! Laura ran away, Gemma. *She* left me. I looked for her for years. I really loved her.'

'Loved her? You only loved being a copper. She couldn't cope with playing second fiddle to a lousy job. And when she found she was pregnant with me, she was too scared to tell you! She thought you'd make her get rid of it, because a baby would have fucked up your fabulous career prospects! That, Father dearest, is why she went.'

'But I never knew, I swear!'

'And if you had known, would you have put your meteoric fast-track promotions on hold and spent time with your family? Been a loving husband and father?'

Matt didn't hesitate. Gemma's disturbed and dangerous mind was beyond reason. He'd say what she wanted to hear, regardless of the truth. 'Of course, I would! I loved Laura and I would have loved our baby. The thing is, Laura knew that. So I don't know why she really chose to leave me, but it was *her* decision, not mine.' His voice suddenly lost its power and he almost whispered, 'Oh Gemma, haven't you got what you wanted?' Tears formed in the corners of his swollen eyes 'You've tortured and hurt people close to me. You've deliberately spoiled everything that was special and precious in my life and humiliated me. You've turned love into a crazy porn film. You've ruined my last years in the force, and you've taken me close to madness. One child is already dead because of this vendetta,' he looked across at Ryan, 'maybe two, I don't know.' He searched her eyes for some small trace of compassion. 'Surely that's enough?'

There was a long silence, but Matt knew from the coldness that washed over him that compassion was not an emotion that resided in Gemma Goddard's icy heart.

'Not nearly enough.' She spat the words at him. 'And before we put an end to all this, there are some things you need to know.' She turned. 'Ted. It's story time.'

Matt watched as Ted brought two solid wooden crates from the back of the mill and placed them in front of his chair. On Gemma's signal, they sat down, side by side, shoulders touching.

Matt's skin crawled as he saw the strange couple staring up at him, two oversized and deeply disturbed children in the guise of ruthless killers. Even as helpless as he was, Matt strained against the leather straps to try to get further away from them.

'He thinks that *he's* suffered, Ted.' She gave a small humourless laugh.

'Shall we tell him what it's really like?'

'Why not? You start.'

Ted's voice dropped to something little more than a whisper. His voice changed to that of a frightened child.

Matt had a sudden flashback to the one thing he hated about police work. The delicate and carefully conducted interview of an abused child. He swallowed hard and decided that he really didn't want to hear what this man was going to say.

Matt saw Gemma's eyes half close. She reached over and gripped Ted's hand. Matt shivered. The ambiguity of seeing the slender, long fingers offering support, when earlier they had slammed into the face of his unconscious lover, was nauseating. Like the story he was being forced to listen to.

One began a sentence, the other finished it. It became like one unbroken narrative with two voices. It was deeply unnerving.

At first, he listened in horror. They were talking about their own childhood experiences. Things that should never, ever happen. He tried to switch off, to take his fragile mind to somewhere different, somewhere peaceful and happy, but filthy words and repugnant phrases still filtered through.

"They left me bleeding in a crawl space."

"I begged the man to take one of the other children, but he said he liked me best"

"I didn't like what they were doing, and when I cried, they tied me up and left me in a cold, dark cellar until morning."

After a while, Matt's brain began to take in what they were saying again. The policeman in him crept back to the surface, and he started to assimilate what he was hearing. He found himself staring at them. It was like trying not to look as you drove past a car crash. You just couldn't help yourself. Their experiences offered up some sort of twisted explanation for what they had done to him.

Only thoughts of revenge had kept them functioning and alive. Not sane, but alive.

He looked from one to the other. Somehow they had managed to survive a childhood that would have turned most victims into the hollow-eyed zombies that he'd seen so often in psychiatric wards. That, or the slack-mouthed, frightened wraiths that existed in darkened rooms with curtains pulled tight and security locks and chains on every door. Over the years he'd met plenty of those, as well.

He wondered what it took to teach yourself to smile. Somehow, Ted and Gemma had smiled their way through getting themselves rehomed, going to school, studying and working. They had excelled at pretending to be normal, when all there really was, was a shell filled with loathing and a desire for vengeance. And they had fooled everyone.

Matt stared at Gemma, half-listening to her, and trying to visualise the smart young copper arguing her corner with a load of other uniformed probationers. Jesus! He could not get his head around how good her deception had been. Other than a few outbursts of temper and a tendency to want her own way, he would never have suspected anything strange about her.

'And when the time was right,' Ted said, clutching Gemma's hand.

'We found each other again.' Gemma let out a sigh. 'Then our work could really begin.'

Matt shuddered when he considered how admirable their survival would have been if they had not been so terribly damaged.

Two pairs of eyes stared coldly at him, and he knew that the story was over. Their whole lives, since leaving the children's home, had been devoted to arriving at this moment. Just one question still remained.

'Why me?' Matt whispered. 'Why not the perverts that did those terrible things to you?'

'Because we wanted to get to the root cause of it all. We worked it back, and the buck stopped with you.'

'So you hunted me down.' Matt licked his blood-encrusted lips.

Gemma shrugged. 'Not difficult. With Ted's computer skills and my brain.'

'Why kill the boy? You didn't need to murder Gabriel.'

'Of course we did.' Ted grinned maliciously. 'That was where we really started the mind-fuck. The kid was just collateral damage.'

'And it helped that you were so screwed up anyway. Something we hadn't expected.' Gemma placed a hand on his knee and stroked it thoughtfully. 'Even if we hadn't come along, Daddy dearest, the Gibbet Fen case was already scrambling your brains, wasn't it?' She looked up at him. 'And I do wonder why? Because as soon as I really got to grips with it, I realised it was cut and dried.'

Matt shifted around on the hard chair and tried to escape her insidious touch. His whole body ached. He wanted to go home now. He wanted a hot shower, and he wanted to cut up vegetables and drink wine with Liz. He wanted to creep up the back stairs of Adie's hotel and be with the woman he loved.

An unexpected blow crashed into his injured cheek.

'I need your full attention right now.' Gemma glowered at him. 'I don't take kindly to wool-gathering while I'm speaking.'

He looked at Liz. For the first time since she had been snatched from the police station, he hoped that she was dead. If she was still alive, then he couldn't bear to think what was in store for her.

He coughed, spat blood and looked at his captors. He didn't want to go to the place where Gemma was leading him. He'd not been there since the 1980s. He was damned if he was going back. Somehow he had to sidetrack them. 'You don't much care about pain, do you? You can dish it out *and* you can take it. You *did* let Ted beat you up, didn't you? In the churchyard? Beat you up and put you in hospital?'

Gemma shrugged dismissively. 'It had to be realistic, and I've taken far worse than that in my life.'

'But how did you get the original photos that you sent me? The ones taken before the crimes?' He directed the question to Ted, hoping the man's ego would make him answer.

'They were Paul Underhill's.'

The pain made it hard to concentrate. 'We tore his house to shreds, there were no photos.'

Gemma joined in. 'Underhill's house, yes, but not his brother's, where he went when you lot got too close to him. The brother is dead now, but I found the address in the old files, and sent the charming and persuasive DC Edward Dennis to visit.'

Ted gave a nod of the head. 'Luckily the new owners were most accommodating, and hadn't quite got around to dismantling the old garden storage unit, where Underhill had carefully secreted one or two little mementos, before he took the starring role in that fatal hit-and-run.'

Matt's head throbbed. *Too close. Too close. I want to go home.* 'So all that stuff about "dig up Underhill" was just . . . ?'

'Diversionary tactics, to keep the team off-balance and confused' Gemma shrugged. 'I knew Underhill was the original kiddie killer, and Ted and I orchestrated the present chaos, so it was just a bit of fun distraction.' She threw him a shrewd look. 'And it really got *you* going, didn't it?'

'Gonna tell us why, policeman?'

'No.'

He never even saw the next blow coming. A fist hit him cleanly on the bridge of his nose. He heard the crack, and in seconds he was choking on blood. 'I said no.' His words bubbled as he tried to speak.

'Then perhaps this will help you to be a little more cooperative.' Ted drew back his clenched fist and aimed it directly at Liz.

'Stop!' His voice sounded odd, even to his own ears. 'Okay. Just stop . . . please.'

'Then tell us why you spent half your life pursuing that damned case?' Gemma's eyes glittered.

For a moment he hesitated. The fist slowly began to clench again.

'Leave her!' Matt gritted his teeth. What the hell did it matter now? The cavalry was not going to arrive. He and Liz were as good as dead. 'Don't hurt her anymore, and I'll tell you.' A staccato, barking laugh bubbled up into his throat. 'You see, no matter how fucking bright you two are, you got it all wrong!' The laugh increased. 'I was never trying to *solve* the damn case in the first place!' When he saw their confusion, his amusement threatened to become hysteria. 'What I was actually doing was . . .' The laughter suddenly constricted his breathing and a mouthful of blood threatened to choke him. He fought to clear his airway but felt a tightening in his chest and heaved out a cry for help.

'Get some water!' yelled Gemma. 'The bastard's not going to die before I know what the hell he was playing at!'

Ted ran outside. Matt was left fighting for breath. It was not the kind of death he had ever expected, but as a deep-seated fire burnt through his lungs, he was pretty sure that this was how he was going to leave this world.

Just as the world started to go black, cold water hit him in the face, then a glass was forced between his lips, and a small stream of liquid filtered down his parched gullet. He spat blood, and felt blessed air begin to seep back into his lungs again. Pain radiated through his whole skull. He gasped, and winced as the broken bones in his face radiated excruciating pain. He tried to talk but nothing happened.

'Give him a minute. Let him catch his breath.' Gemma smiled coldly at him. 'Even if it is one of his last. I just want to hear the end of his precious story.'

'Poor Mr Policeman. For once, he's stuck for words. Hey, while we wait, why don't I tell you what we have planned for you three, after you're all dead!' Ted taunted him.

Gemma grinned, but her eyes were steely cold. 'We thought about a fire. Teddy likes fires.'

Matt blinked and tried not to think about what that simple statement might mean.

'Maybe a little too much.' Gemma pulled Ted towards her and gently rolled up his sleeve. 'If you see what I mean.'

Ted stuck his arm under Matt's nose. 'Sadly, no prosthetics this time.' Ted pulled his sleeve back to reveal burnt skin. 'Anyway, we've settled for something less dramatic, but equally effective. This property only had mains water and power brought in last year. And the original well is right outside. Deep and dark and cold, with spring water aplenty at its bottom.' Ted sighed. 'Need I say more?'

Matt let his head fall forward. Even if he could talk, there would be no reasoning with either of them. The insane didn't respond to logic. There would be no appealing to their better side, because they didn't have one. He tried to tell them to just bloody well get it over with, but he immediately began to cough again.

'Shut up,' Gemma stepped closer, her arm raised, ready to strike, 'until I say you can speak.' She turned back to Ted. 'Get the drugs. Before he leaves us, I'm sure my daddy will want to know whether the child and the whore are still alive.'

Matt stiffened. It was the *only* thing he cared about right now, but he was terrified to show it. With an effort, he managed to shrug his aching, stiff shoulders.

Ted eyes widened and he stared up from the tray of syringes. 'Oh come! You arrived here, their gallant knight, well, not quite in shining armour, but near enough. Don't you want to know if they are even alive?'

'Of course he does.' Gemma snorted. 'Stick her, Ted. Put him out of his misery.'

Ted flicked off the cap from the needle, and plunged it into Liz's arm, pushing the plunger fully down. As he withdrew it, he looked suspiciously at the empty syringe. 'Oops.' He looked at Gemma. 'Sorry. Wrong one.'

For a second, the three of them stared at Liz, then Gemma's face contorted with anger. 'Sometimes you can be such a prat! And I'm fed up with all this. I don't give a fuck what stupid game Daddy was playing. Whatever it was, I'm going to finish it.' She darted towards the work bench, and grabbed a long-bladed cook's knife.

Matt's mouth went slack, he drew in a breath and held it. Gemma was out of control, there was nothing he could do anymore. He just wanted the last thing that he saw to be Liz.

Gemma strode towards him, the knife outstretched before her.

'Damn you to hell!' he croaked at her. 'You're no daughter of mine!' He swung his head disdainfully from her and looked at the woman he knew he loved.

'I love you, Liz,' he whispered.

As he did, the only door to the mill exploded inwards. Men in black with automatic weapons, like an avenging band of dark angels, stormed in.

'Police! We are armed. Down on the floor. Now.'

* * *

Shock distorts. David had believed that he had an open mind about what might be behind the door of the derelict windmill, but when he burst through it, his brain refused to take in what he saw.

The weird lighting confused everything. And the three victims, bound to chairs, bloodied and tortured, clouded his judgement. The frozen tableau made no sense. One of his own officers, her clothes in tatters, stood open-mouthed, a carving knife in her hand. Close to her was the man he knew to be Ted, or Richard Cotton. He held a syringe.

And then there was a man, his face swollen beyond recognition, but the only one in the room who seemed to have something resembling the power of speech. *Matt?* Through bloody lips, the man cried out, 'Take her down!'

No one moved. Then Gemma moved slowly towards him, and said, 'Super, thank God you're here! It's me, PC Goddard. You have to help me.'

David tried to work out what he was seeing. He heard men arriving behind him, but he couldn't give the order to shoot. For one thing, there were innocent victims in the line of fire, and no way could he decide who the threat was actually coming from.

'Don't listen to her. Take her down!' The voice was familiar but oddly distorted.

Then it was too late. With a howl of rage, Gemma lifted the knife and lunged towards the man in the chair.

David's order to shoot came a fraction of a second after another man leapt from the shadows. There was a reverberating volley of gun fire and a scream.

'No! Gemma, my Gemma.' Ted fell forwards, and clawed at the woman's body that lay bleeding on the stone floor. 'Oh no! Don't die, please don't leave me!'

'Adie!' Matt's cry was almost animal in its pain and ferocity.

David sprang into life. Shouting to the armed officers, he pointed to Ted. 'Get that man out of here! Now!' He then spun back to the man in the chair. 'My God! Matt! What have they . . . ?'

'Just help Adie! And Liz! He's injected her with something! God knows what, but if she's not dead already, it could be lethal!'

Gary's voice boomed out. 'Medical emergency! Call the medics down here, immediately!' He knelt down beside his wife, and stroked her face. 'Oh Jesus! Baby! What have they done to you?'

The soldier began to loosen her restraints, while David tried to staunch the flow of blood from Adie Clarkson's lower stomach.

'Fat lot of good your bloody stabproof vests are.' Adie's face was contorted with pain. 'Oh, you really owe me big time, Mattie Ballard.'

CHAPTER THIRTY-SIX

David sat on the edge of Matt's hospital bed. He looked from his friend's bruised and swollen face up to the TV.

The coiffed newsreader intoned: "The funeral was held earlier today for Adrian Clarkson. The former criminal, ironically, died saving the life of a police officer. The church where the service was held was packed to capacity. Loudspeakers relayed the service to two hundred mourners outside. It was attended by representatives of the Fenland Constabulary and many other local dignitaries. Lieutenant Colonel Gary Haynes said afterwards that he considered Mr Clarkson a hero, and that had he been a soldier, he would have been proud to have served with him, and he would have made sure that he received a posthumous medal for his outstanding bravery."

Matt turned off the TV with the remote control and stared silently at the blank screen. After a while, he said, 'I should have gone.'

'No, you shouldn't. Even I found it difficult. You, my friend, would have found it impossible. And that's just from an emotional point of view, let's not forget the recent surgery.' David gave him a weak smile. 'The boyish good looks really took a bit of a hammering, didn't they?'

'I'll live. Unlike Adie.'

'You were right all along, Matt. He was a good bloke.'

'The best.' His voice caught. 'I just wish *Superman* hadn't been his favourite film. It really should have been me, not him.' He gently touched a large dressing on his side. 'And I'm always going to have a reminder of what he did for me, aren't I?'

'How is it?'

'Bloody sore, but thanks to Adie grabbing her hand and deflecting the blade, it missed damaging anything vital.' He shifted in the bed. 'Have you been to see Liz today?'

'I called in earlier.'

'No change?'

'Not yet. But Gary said that the doctors are hopeful for a full recovery. At least young Ryan Fisher has been discharged.'

'He came to see me before he went.' Matt managed a smile. 'With his elderly guardian angel, Mrs Stokes. '

'Seems from what the boy tells us, that Ted must have had something of a sneaking respect for the kid. He could have seriously hurt him, not just a minor cut and a lot of stage make-up.'

'It had me fooled, the way he'd taped the boy's fingers and stained them, it was sickeningly realistic.' He shuddered. 'But even so, if you'd been a few minutes later, we'd have all been at the bottom of the well, Ryan too, respect or not.'

'Are you up to talking about things?' David still had some unanswered questions.

Matt nodded. 'Better close the door.'

David did, then pulled the chair closer to the bed, and sank down into it.

'Before we start, what's happened to Ted, or Richard, whoever he is? Secure psychiatric hospital, I suppose?' Matt asked.

'Yes. He's on suicide watch.' David pulled a face. 'Although I suspect he will succeed in topping himself, no matter how closely he's watched. He lived for Gemma and their weird games. Now she's dead, well . . . ? Some would say, best thing, I suppose. Personally, I'd like to see him suffer.'

Matt sighed, 'He already has. They both suffered.'

'You're being pretty generous, considering they spent years hunting you down in order to torment and kill you.'

'They weren't born with twisted minds, Super. It's horrific when you know what was allowed to happen to them.'

David pulled a face. 'Maybe, and you're entitled to your opinion, but I think there had to be evil in their hearts to do the things they did.'

'I suppose. But it's the innocent people they hurt along the way to their misguided revenge that tears me up. Not just Adie, people like Liz and young Gabriel.' He pulled anxiously at his sheets. 'And those poor families who adopted them. They must be devastated.'

'The Goddards certainly are. I don't suppose they'll ever come to terms with what has happened and how they were used by that child. Talk about a cuckoo in the nest.'

David exhaled. 'And Harry Cotton, well, could anyone have been more deceived? He blamed his own daughter for deliberately causing the house fire, for God's sake! He took the boy in, gave him everything and made him his adopted heir, when *he* was the murdering little bastard all along!' David shook his head in disbelief. 'Oh, I found out why he called himself Ted, by the way.'

Matt raised an eyebrow. 'Don't tell me, the inspiration is the charming and intelligent serial killer, Ted Bundy?'

'Spot on. Great sort of childhood hero, huh? A man who maybe killed and brutalised some thirty-six girls.'

'I don't think it would have been the killing that impressed our Ted, he would have been more stirred by the fact that everyone, including the judge who sentenced Bundy, liked the man.'

'You're probably right. Harry Cotton, the Goddards, and the people who worked with Ted at the studio, all said he was a really pleasant and friendly guy. Just shows how wrong you can be, or what a bloody good actor he was.' David sat back and looked at Matt. 'Now, I'm sorry to have to do this, but you said earlier that you wanted to talk to me about the Gibbet Fen killer? Is this a good time?'

'No time is good, but this is as good as any.' Matt moved uncomfortably and leaned back into his pillows, 'I should have told you this years ago. Do you remember PC Andy Lowe?'

'The officer who found the body of Danny Carter in his uncle's barn? Yes, he left the fens and went up country, didn't he?'

Matt nodded. 'My old sergeant didn't believe him, but he always thought that Paul Underhill was the killer. The final time that we had to let Underhill go through lack of evidence, Andy just freaked out. He told some of his mates that he was going to find him and knock the truth out of him. When I heard his plan, I went after him in my car.' Matt gently rubbed at his bruised temple. 'I didn't really care if Underhill took a thrashing, because at heart I agreed with Andy, but I didn't want my best friend getting thrown off the force.'

Matt's hands trembled, but he struggled on. 'At first I couldn't find them. Underhill wasn't at his home, then I remembered where his brother lived, and how the locals who lived out there often took a shortcut across the old Marsh Lane.' He swallowed, clearly finding it increasingly difficult to talk. 'It was pitch black, and I was driving far too fast for that single-track lane. Underhill just came out of nowhere,' Matt hung his head, 'and when I saw what I'd done, I panicked. I drove off and left him there.' He looked up, his eyes full of tears. 'Sorry, sir, but it was me that killed Underhill, and I never told a soul till now.'

David covered his shock with a question. 'So, was Andy Lowe ever accused of Underhill's death?'

Matt gave a short, humourless laugh. 'That's the really stupid part. Andy went off like a lunatic, then realised what a prat he was being, and went straight to the local pub and got rat-arsed in front of half of Fenfleet.' He shook his head, slowly and painfully. 'And my misguided loyalty cost a man his life.'

'And you never knew if you'd killed a murderer or an innocent suspect?'

'Not until Ted told me that he'd found the photos of the crime scenes in Underhill's brother's garden storage unit. Then I finally knew.'

David felt a rush of emotion. 'I always knew there was more to your breakdown than met the eye! Something that you just wouldn't, or couldn't, share with me.'

'I was so ashamed. Felt so mind-numbingly guilty that,' Matt gave a deep, shuddering sigh, 'I spent the rest of my career trying to make amends, trying to be a good detective and make a difference. And all the while watching that old enquiry, just in case . . .'

'If it helps, when we searched through Ted's stuff in the farmhouse by the mill, we found a tin box. It contained Underhill's original snapshots of *all* the dead boys, taken before and after their demise. There were also other mementos, things that prove beyond all doubt, that Underhill was the killer.'

'Well, I've told you this officially, sir. So, whatever action you decide to take is all I deserve. No matter how accidentally, I took a man's life, and never owned up to it. That's pretty much the lowest of the low in my book.'

David sighed. 'Frankly, I see no point, after all these years, in doing anything, Matt. Underhill was a child killer. He has no immediate family left alive. You are still hell-bent on retiring, and your admission will serve no purpose, no one will benefit from knowing, and no one will get hurt by not knowing.' He put a hand over Matt's, to stop it shaking. 'You've suffered enough. Let's put the past to rest, shall we?'

There were tears in Matt's sunken eyes. 'And Gemma? What about her?'

'Well, actually that's one of the reasons why I'm here. I have some news that may help you come to terms with things.' He kept his hand on Matt's. 'Using some of the information that Gemma and Ted uncovered in their search for her family, I did a bit of investigating of my own.' He paused. 'I did this *after* I had the results back on a DNA check that I ran on Gemma's body.' He gripped the hand tighter. 'Gemma was not your daughter, Matt. She got it all wrong.'

'Wrong?' Matt blinked in disbelief. 'So everything they did? All those devious plans and their wicked project? The deaths? Adie? All for nothing?'

David nodded. 'All for nothing. But for what it's worth, I believe that she got it right up to a point. Laura *did* run away because she was pregnant, but with another man's child. That's why she couldn't face you, Matt. That's why she left.'

Matt looked down at the bedcovers, took a deep shaky breath, then exhaled for a very long time.

David let go of his hand, lifted it and gently squeezed the man's shoulder. 'You've been the innocent victim in all this, right from when Laura packed her bag and disappeared. Now do you see why I believe that you've suffered enough?'

'I've suffered nothing compared with Adie Clarkson or Liz.'

'Don't underestimate what you've been through, Mattie,' David said sternly. 'I know of no other police officer who would have come out of all this with their sanity intact.'

'Let's wait and see on that score, shall we? I'm still getting flashbacks to that mill. Oh my God!' He gave David a horrified look, 'You found things belonging to

Ted! There was a film, Oh Jesus. He made a film of . . .' he stopped when he saw the shiny DVDs that David had just removed from his pocket and was holding out to him.

'I said there was more than one reason for my coming to see you. I believe that these are your property.' David gave him a shrewd smile. 'This is the one from the player in the mill, and the one with it was Ted's master copy.' The smile deepened. 'And, you'll be sorry to hear that there was a bit of a cock-up when we came to download information from the hard drive on Ted's computer. Certain files were accidentally deleted at source.' He pushed the disks into Matt's washbag. 'I suggest you destroy those as soon as you are discharged.'

'You didn't . . . ?' Matt's face was white.

'No, I didn't. I saw the picture of Liz at your home. I also saw that she was carrying a bottle of wine, and after finding some very expensive camera equipment in the house and already knowing what Ted did for a living, I had a very bad feeling about what was going to come next.' He grinned at Matt. 'I suppose I should be ashamed of myself. I have also used my authority to confiscate certain sensitive photographs that I deem may cause serious embarrassment to respected officers. They will remain with me until I decide what is best to do with them.' His face became harder. 'Naturally we have to suffer a long enquiry now, especially regarding why I allowed a civilian to be present during an armed raid, but whatever, those photographs have no bearing on the outcome of the enquiry. There is plenty of other evidence, without the world gawping at my detectives' private lives.'

David diplomatically chose to ignore the tears that were flooding down Matt's face, stood up and smoothed the creases out of his trousers. 'Finally, Jason and his family send their love, he wants to visit as soon as you're ready. And there's news from your mother's nursing home. She's still much the same, but the woman in charge told me to tell you that since your last visit, she's been a lot calmer. Something they don't quite understand as her medication hasn't been changed. She said perhaps you know something they don't? And now, Gary Haynes asked me to prise you from your sick bed, pop you in a wheelchair, and take you up to Lister Ward, to sit with Liz for a while. If that's okay with you?'

* * *

The two men sat either side of the bed. Liz appeared to be asleep. The tubes and pumps were quiet now that the respirator had been removed. The blood pressure monitor inflated regularly, and a catheter tube snaked from beneath the covers, but all the other life-sustaining equipment was no longer needed.

'She's breathing for herself, at last,' whispered Gary.

'Thank God. What did the consultant say?' Matt said.

'He more or less said, how long is a piece of string? The combination of drugs and the head injury should have killed her, but it didn't.' The soldier gave a small shrug, 'So we wait, and we hope.'

'I blame myself entirely for all this. If I'd waited for help, if I'd acted differently . . .'

'*I* don't blame you, Matt, and nor will this headstrong and stubborn woman in the bed here, when she finally gets round to waking up. And from what the super has told me, if you hadn't turned up so quickly to take the flack away from Liz, they would have tortured and killed her just to pass the time while they waited for you.' He puffed out his cheeks. 'Something that doesn't bear thinking about.'

Matt desperately wanted to hold her hand, but guessed it wasn't exactly the right moment.

'There's something I should tell you, if you're up to listening?' Gary ran his hand tenderly over Liz's hair.

'Sure. As long as it's not a sad story, because for some reason, I'm being a tad emotional about everything at the moment.'

'Nah, it's got a brilliant fairy-tale ending. Well, it could have.' He smiled at Matt. 'Liz and I have known each other since we were kids. Best mates, soulmates, really. She wanted to be a copper, and I wanted to be a soldier. No problem there, you'd think.' He grimaced, 'Wrong! Fine for Liz, but difficult for me.' He looked Matt full in the eyes. 'I was eighteen when I realised that I was gay, and the army environment was not what you'd call the perfect place for me. But I was *so* cut out for it, and I wanted to be a soldier more than anything.' He touched Liz's cheek. 'When I was twenty I was told that I had a brilliant future, and then things got really difficult for me personally. So, Liz jumped in and saved me. She reckoned that as she was dedicated to her own career, and had little time for anything else, we should marry. Incredibly, it worked. The heat went off immediately, and for years everyone has been happy.' He tilted his head to one side. 'Until now. You see, although she hasn't said as much, I'm pretty sure I know how Liz feels about you, and after everything she did to give me the life that I wanted, I'm hardly likely to stand in the way of her happiness. That's why I wanted you here now. I need to know if you feel the same about her.'

Matt smiled for the first time in a very long time, and quite irrationally his mind flew to colour charts and wallpaper books. He reached out for the slender fingers, and his voice was hoarse as he said the words that he never thought he'd hear himself say again. 'I love her, Gary. I really love her.'

Gary looked from Liz's pale face across to Matt's battered one and grinned.

'Well, that's a relief! I told you the story had a happy ending, although God knows what she'll say when she wakes up and sees her beloved detective looking like that!'

'As long as she wakes up and says s*omething*, I couldn't care less what it is!'

'Me neither.'

Matt looked up and saw a hand extended towards him over the bedcover.

'Take care of her, Matt.'

He took the hand, this time with a grip that equalled the soldier's. 'I will. I promise.'

THE END

Thank you for reading this book. If you enjoyed it please leave feedback on Amazon or Goodreads, and if there is anything we missed or you have a question about then please get in touch. The author and publishing team appreciate your feedback and time reading this book.

Our email is office@joffebooks.com

www.joffebooks.com

ALSO BY JOY ELLIS

CRIME ON THE FENS
SHADOW OVER THE FENS
HUNTED ON THE FENS
KILLER ON THE FENS
STALKER ON THE FENS
CAPTIVE ON THE FENS
BURIED ON THE FENS
THIEVES ON THE FENS

THE MURDERER'S SON
THEIR LOST DAUGHTERS
THE FOURTH FRIEND

GUIDE STAR

BEWARE THE PAST

Made in the USA
Middletown, DE
05 May 2018